THE PRAGASHINI - SMUTS

- CONSPIRACY -

AGNES SAM is a British author who was born in South Africa when it was a British colony. Her ancestors were from British India, French Pondicherry, and Europe. Her grandparents and parents, through religion, sport, and politics enjoyed friendships with immigrant Jews, Dutch farmers, English Catholics, Muslim and Chinese business people and African and 'Coloured' politicians. She had links with all ethnic groups at home, school and university, while apartheid began its intervention to halt this interchange.

After the Separate Universities Act she completed a degree in Zoology and Psychology at the Catholic university in Lesotho. Then under a United Nations recruitment programme, she qualified as a teacher in Zimbabwe, and taught Biology on the Copperbelt in Zambia.

In Zambia she wrote for young people under a pen name. She came to England and settled in York where she read English and wrote the short stories contained in the collection '*Jesus is Indian and other South African Stories*', and drama for BBC radio 4.

Dr Anna Rutherford in Denmark published an extract from 'What Passing Bells' in 'Kunapipi'. The BBC television script unit asked to meet the author after reading the television script of 'Dora' but did not produce the play. Gordon House at the World Service submitted the television script of 'Dora' to Penny Gold at BBC Radio 4 and the author adapted it for radio. Ros de Lanerolle who was at the Women's Press published 'Jesus is Indian' in London and Heinemann brought out the paperback in the African Writers Series. Without the intervention of these people the author might never have achieved publication or broadcast. The very restrictive nature of opportunities for publication, broadcast and teaching in the United Kingdom is not unlike South Africa under apartheid.

When Heinemann's African Writers' Series and the Women's Press ceased publishing the author set up the publishing company Paloma Books and published the novel, '*The Pragashini- Smuts Affair*' and the revised 3rd edition of '*Jesus is Indian*'. '*The Pragashini-Smuts Conspiracy*' is the sequel to the first novel.

* * *

By Agnes Sam

Fiction

The Pragashini- Smuts Affair
Paloma Books 2009

Jesus is Indian and other South African stories.
The Women's Press, London, 1989
Heinemann, African Writers' Series, Oxford, 1994
Paloma Books, York, 2011

***

Radio Drama

Dora
BBC Radio 4, London, 1990

The Tyranny of Karma
BBC Radio 4, London, 1994

* * *

AGNES SAM

THE PRAGASHINI - SMUTS - CONSPIRACY -

PALOMA BOOKS

Paloma Books,
12 Turners Croft,
Heslington,
York, YO10 5El.

British Library Cataloguing in Publication Data
Sam, Agnes
1. Title: The Pragashini – Smuts Conspiracy
ISBN 978-0-9562592-2-6

Cover illustration and design © Lance Chinnian.
Cover photo: 'Desert Girl' © Karthick Ramalingam
Author photograph © Lance Chinnian

Phototypeset by Paloma Books, York.
Printed and bound by CPI Group (UK) Ltd, Croydon, CR0 4YY

Printed on 100% recycled paper

***

For my sisters

And for

Yesterday's, Today's and Tomorrow's

Women

* * *

Acknowledgements

The author is grateful to Lance Chinnian for his work creating the cover, on obtaining permission from the photographer, and for his support and expert advice; to Jason Chinnian for advice on marketing this volume, and for his continued encouragement and support; to Rohan Chinnian for his commitment to the continuous maintenance of the technological elements of the author's computer and his advice keeping the author focussed on the writing of this volume; to the photographer Karthick Ramalingam for granting permission for the use of 'Desert Girls'.

* * *

Preface

Come Africa: Reclaim Your Past

Snake-like, 1994 uncoiled while the world's attention focussed on Africa. Happily for embarrassed Africans, this was not another appeal for millions of dollars or sterling that might or might never find its way into the bellies of their continent's starving people.

Everyman and his neighbour knew the synonym for Africa was no longer the heart of darkness but 'school of corruption': the money rained down on the dehydrated earth – and greedy earthlings below swallowed it up as if it were manna from heaven. While the people continued to starve.

If truth be told foreign governments were weary of promising money for disasters, promises they did not always keep. Yet, the people they were democratically elected to represent, to their credit, never failed to delve deep into their pockets. And children without the franchise broke into their piggy banks, to donate their pocket money with unstinted generosity.

On this occasion the focus on Africa was for a happy event. And this time one could assert with confidence – once again, because a happy event happened before, just once.

That first singularly happy event changed the world. Now that world included Africa – that poverty stricken source of gold and diamonds, - among other precious commodities – perhaps even untapped oil?

Leading up to 1994 the Berlin wall was scaled, chipped away, then bulldozed. Its impact was felt throughout Europe. But Africa was unscathed.

The political assassination of Chris Hani one of South Africa's charismatic leaders, had little impact on the rest of Africa, let alone the world. The word 'tsunami' had not yet entered the English language – so the future overspill of an eastern tsunami onto the East coast of Africa - was waiting to be ignored.

Nevertheless, by 1994 the northern, western, eastern, and even southern hemispheres, were willingly coerced into grappling with the phantasmagorical image of what they like to call the Third World - in reality being the original First World.

The possibility that the first human might have stood upright somewhere in Africa - was shrugged off as having little relevance to Africa's insignificant status.

The continent where Pro Magnum the first modern human may possibly have uttered the first sound that was neither grunt nor growl, but held meaning that others could understand - was unproven and irrelevant in a world ruled by Physics, Mathematics and Chemistry.

The idea that somewhere in India a little known individual used the zero as a number that opened the door to calculus, algebraic formulas, binary numbers and computers – left the Third World still clinging to the first rung of the ladder of recognition and acknowledgement.

But then a single historical event – that first happy event - shone a blinding light on the African continent. Amazingly the event was simply the release of a prisoner.

What is more the prisoner was neither citizen of Europe or America. He was a citizen of Africa. And the governments of Europe and America had not clamoured for his release. Ordinary people around the world did.

Many African prisoners had been released before, among them Kenneth Kaunda. Poor Kaunda spent unshaven years in prison. He was released without fanfare, waving his white handkerchief – certainly not a white flag of surrender, but rather a victorious symbol of a revolution unstained by blood.

For the release of this other prisoner, the world's media was despatched beyond the equator, to the south coast where hundreds of years before the first Europeans rounded the Cape of Storms that became the Cape of Good Hope that became Cape Town – the mother city of South Africa.

In South Africa there had been states of emergency; an American Senator visited an African woman; the United Democratic Front was formed, banned, and unbanned; a new State President was named; occasionally a political prisoner was released without publicity. Little else changed.

Then due to the efforts of a much maligned African woman, campaigns run by political parties, and women in political parties and organizations around the world, the African man became the centre of the world's attention.

What is more, for generations to come, children not yet born, who did not care to know where on earth Africa was, would know about this event and this one man.

People who could not utter a word in English – there are one or two - would whisper this word when they heard the word 'Africa' as if knowing this one word meant they knew everything there was to know about the continent.

The entire world watching their television screens, waited for this tall, elderly gentleman to dress up in a shirt, tie and suit, tailor-made for him. The self-obsessed modern world who knew little about Africa believing that lions roamed the streets of its cities wondered if this man had slain a lion with his bare hands. Had he discovered the largest diamond in the world? Was he presenting Africa with its own gold? Or was he a belated prophet? A messiah? A reincarnated spiritual leader?

He was none of these. Yet his name was the word on everyone's lips: 'Mandela' – not even an English word. But who was to know that?

He had been residing in questionable luxury after his forced removal from Robben Island to Victor Verster Prison.

It was his release that prodded the world into rethinking the status of Africa.

When the thin man emerged in 1989 his wife, the mother of the nation by his side firmly grasping his hand, a child iMbongi sang his praises.

No-one sang hers. She was the woman left to care for two little girls, who endured arrest, forcible removal from a city to a remote area, and harassment for as long as he remained in prison: twenty-seven years.

Observing her, women around the world may have reflected: finally he would protect her. She could sleep at night secure in the knowledge her protector was there to defend her. Now she would no longer have to watch her back, fear the South African police at the door, or be suspicious of those surrounding her.

Everyone around the world observing the couple may have believed that with him acting as a kraal for the dubious, the fearful, the sceptics, and with her standing for the underdog, the down trodden, those who carried the wounds and scars of the struggle, between them, they would unite the country.

But there were no African prophets on Kilimanjaro, Thabo Bosigo, or Table Mountain, preparing to descend with a tablet of prophesies about the future struggle that lay ahead. There were praise singers and traditional healers, but not one prophet.

Censorship, misinformation and selective colonial education meant that most Africans knew only their own history as told in the letters, diaries, and history books written by colonials who scrambled, conquered and carved up their continent.

They had little recourse to other sources except the unwritten oral histories handed down to them.

For one, they believed Christianity was brought to Africa by European missionaries from the fifteenth century onwards. How could they know otherwise?

How could they know that Africa's Carthage was a city before its destruction by Rome, and then became a Christian city long before the rest of Europe – except for Rome?

Which European missionary explained that the African Bishops of Carthage held Synods attended by seventy African Bishops in the second century after Christ?

Who told Africans that the first African Pope Victor of Carthage was described as the first Latin writer in the Christian Church?

Christianity was and still is associated with colonialism – 'the bible and the gun'. But Christianity is part of Africa's glorious past.

It is written that "Jewish colonies formed an unbroken chain across Africa from Mauritania to India", * perhaps belying the tales of Africa and Asia being Christianised by Europe.

There may be other aspects of Africa's past that are not recorded in the colonial histories but sourced elsewhere.

In 1989 while the world was relieved to see the aged African lovers holding hands, free at last, they could not call them Africa's Darby and Joan because they had not grown old together.

Interspersed among the observers were those enemies of South Africa's future, who were aghast at the image of the two – united at last.

But Africa had no prophets.

In 1994 if a famine loomed in Ethiopia, a drought in the savannah, a river threatened to flood – these did not divert the world's attention.

Rebels perpetrating genocide or massacring women, children

and aged civilian men might have done so without distracting the world's attention – as they often did. Perhaps even a terrorist about to perpetrate an atrocity somewhere might have waited awhile to see what was about to occur in South Africa.

Remarkably a celebrity - cyclist, footballer, film idol, green coated golfer, television chef, whistle blower, or other star was not on the front page.

Following this happy event, what more could South Africa expect in 1994? A momentous event that even those within the country doubted would take place: the first democratic elections. Every South African would cast a vote wherever they were in the world.

People searched for discarded identity documents of all shapes and sizes as if Special Branch were hammering at the door. The documents were needed to vote. Exiles rushed home while sceptics fled the country. Released prisoners freed caged birds. Colour bars were rainbow coloured.

The developments in South Africa were difficult to keep track of because change was rapid and sudden.

By the time 1994 uncoiled in the sun, the world knew what had never been imagined, nor had been prophesied: the African woman was no longer standing at the side of her husband.

Into this maelstrom of uncertainty, tension, division, joy and hope, stepped Pragashini Dev a political babe in the woods.

Not far away was the politically astute Smuts Matatiele. Each was a returning exile. Both were at a disadvantage. Waiting to greet them was John Matatiele, Smuts' father, who was also Pragashini's mentor, and their families.

***

Letter from the Custodians

Port Elizabeth

We lacked transparency.

Following the discovery of the cache of documents relating to the Affair, and our refusal to place them in the public domain, we negotiated and reached a settlement. We agreed that the people should choose one person to access the documents. That person was given time to peruse, examine, read and listen to every item in the collection. We locked it away. Then we waited for the person chosen to construct an account of the events contained in the documents.

Following prolonged deliberation on our part, and after agreement amongst ourselves that there should be no 'creativity' or 'creative licence' in the account of events, the word 'construct' and not 'create' was deliberately specified by us.

At last, the people's choice submitted the entire manuscript to us for our judgment of its fairness.

We agreed on only one matter: We judged it unfair. We could not allow it to go to the printers.

We disagreed on everything else. We could not reach agreement on matters crucial, critical, and trivial.

Firstly, we abhorred the title *The Pragashini - Smuts Affair.* For a variety of reasons, we ruled that Smuts' name had no place in the title. He did not deserve the honour of having his name appear alongside that of Pragashini Dev. The documents were about the girl and her relationship with John Matatiele, Smuts' father. He played a more significant part in Pragashini's life than did Smuts.

In our opinion, the format adopted by the chosen one was experimental. We preferred a single narrator, using a straightforward narrative.

Most of us experienced the journal entries as intrusive, both into our reading of the narrative, and into the life of the girl Pragashini.

And then we disapproved the commentary on the political situation in South Africa. The narrative should have been about the participants' lives. It should have been about events that could take place anywhere in the world. We felt South Africa played no part in the events. Not one of us approved the manuscript in its entirety.

Naturally, we rejected the manuscript as unsuitable for publication.

We accepted, however, that the people were waiting and expecting results from their chosen one's perusal of the cache. We therefore proceeded to censor the manuscript. This is ironic because together with the people we decried the former government's censorship of the media.

When satisfied we returned the censored manuscript to the chosen one whom the people now described as 'the writer' as if this was a fictional account of the lives of the participants.

Unfortunately, we had not anticipated the writer's reaction to censorship.

The writer on the other hand, had anticipated our reaction to the manuscript. An uncensored copy was smuggled out of the country before it was submitted to us for approval. Without our approval it would be published abroad.

We claimed rights of ownership of the documents on behalf of Pragashini Dev, and the other participants. The writer in turn, asserted rights over the manuscript.

Faced with dissensions within the custodial group and these unforeseen difficulties from the writer, we gave permission for part of the manuscript to be published under the much maligned title *The Pragashini-Smuts Affair*.

We should have made it clear in our letter preceding *The*

Pragashini-Smuts Affair, that the work was in contention, but we chose to withhold this information, because relations with the writer were tenuous and fraught.

While we studied the second half of the manuscript i.e. the part set in South Africa, the first part i.e. *The Pragashini-Smuts Affair* was published. We, however, gave it no publicity.

The sequel that you are about to read has been approved by only one individual, i.e. the writer, the people's chosen one.

We reached agreement on nothing.

We failed.

The Custodians.

* * *

PART ONE

The Wheel of Karma

1.

Coming home to karma. The phrase slithered into her mind with the soft fluidity of a snake. Serpent-like it coiled sinuously and settled there as if *it* had come home. It exuded a sense of belonging and gave no sign of how it would react if disturbed. It sent a cold shiver through Pragashini Dev's slight frame. The imagery, sexual in its nature evoked terrors from her past.

She was buckling into a seat on the night flight departing from Heathrow when the passenger beside her spoke. *He* triggered that phrase. She had not invited it.

Until that moment she hoped this journey was not the beginning of a flight into the realm of fantasy; that destiny had no further terrors in store for her or the plane; it would neither crash nor be diverted by crusading hijackers; and there would be no explosion in mid air over a shimmering expanse of sapphire blue water.

This beginning was to be simple and different from the beginning ten years ago when she was a vibrant girl, a female Narcissus preening herself before any available mirror, innocent of the journey destiny had already charted for her.

Now in the place of that vivacious girl who was sedated on that outward journey, there was a silent, serious young woman, returning with a purpose she was afraid to speak of. Then she was accompanied by a husband. Now she travelled alone. The only similarity between the two beginnings was the name in her passport: Pragashini Dev.

If the beginning had remained simple, the destination and time of her arrival hinted at complexities: Jan Smuts' airport prior to South Africa's historic elections. Change was buzzing in the air like an irritated bumble bee, but change was yet to be orchestrated. The complexities might unravel on landing.

She expected to sleep off a headache brought on by alcohol

she foolishly drank in the international lounge, when the unknown passenger disturbed her.

'You going home?' he asked. That was all.

She was never in the mood for conversation. And not at this early stage of the long haul. Simple enough, the question offered a dilemma she never considered. She had hedged around the welcome when she disembarked. Now this man added excess baggage to her problem. Was South Africa still home?

He leaned forward to peer into her face. She turned away. Let him think what he will. He had blue eyes.

'I am,' he said. 'Going home. Not visiting.'

Good for you, she thought. He did not appear to be one of the oppressed. But she could not be sure. One could never tell, South Africa having the strangest rules for deciding what one is or is not. Better to show no interest in him. His question was another matter. Was she going home or visiting?

She thought of herself as belonging to the African continent the way Smuts felt he belonged. Around her passengers and air hostesses were bustling in the aisle with overhead baggage. There were many Africans among them. Were they returning as South Africans? Or with United Nations papers? Had they also taken out citizenship of countries that harboured them? Had any country refused them entry? Were they like her going home as foreigners? She felt out of place and out of time now, more than when she received that piece of plastic with the turmeric stripe labelling her an Indian. Instead of feeling joy, she felt apprehensive.

The passenger also turned away, perhaps rightly interpreting her silence to mean she had no wish to speak to him. She felt no remorse. Just relief.

She rummaged in her bag for letters and post cards from friends she left behind in Port Elizabeth. Letters she never replied to fearing she might betray her whereabouts. She chose one.

"Well? The whole world's here. Are you coming in from the cold?" Roshni.'

She rubbed her hands together and put her palms to her eyes the way she concluded a yoga session.

'You alright?' the man asked.

Even such concern from a stranger did not elicit a response.

She edged the concept 'coming home to karma out of her mind supplanting it with one belonging to Smuts. With eyes closed she soaked up the warmth of the concept. Then she reached for her journal and made an entry.

Pragashini's Journal

Everyone begins in a place. That concept was one of the treasures I took with me on my journey out, expecting never to return. You treasure things you can take with you that will not occupy baggage space: abstractions; beliefs; ideas; mental photographs; narratives; personal histories; promises. That idea of beginning in a place was one of them. We love our beginnings.

***

She was returning to her beginning in Port Elizabeth. The hitch was returning with a British passport endorsed with a visa to enter her birth place. It introduced uncertainty, apprehension and contradiction.

Pragashini's Journal

Everyone develops an attachment to a source. That source may be as remote as the vigilant ovum, half key to our potential to exist; or the explosive blastula, unstoppable in its purpose to take us through to birth. The source that nourishes us, we love. We think of our mothers feeding us, forgetting the ovum and sperm, the uterus, the placenta, the cord binding us together.

***

Where we grow, - experiencing the placenta even after we emerge from the uterus and it continues throbbing our mother's blood into our vessels, - we love.

* * *

Our survival during gestation we may attribute to our mother. But our survival is also about the place where nothing harms us; the place that gives us a sense of belonging; the house, the street, the suburb, the town, the family, the religion, the community; the divinity or force we owe our existence to; the soil we are rooted in; the atmosphere we thrive in.

***

When we are in exile, we are part of the exiled continent, essential to its history. That belief was my personal satyagraha. I held it close throughout the exiled years.

***

Belonging. Recognising what moulded me: Africa; the care for humanity; the classless, casteless society; sharing the humblest food; welcoming strangers; the uninvited guest made welcome. uBuntu shaped me. I am indebted to Africa.

***

Another card: "*You're a half-baked, wet-behind-the-ears scientist. It's sad enough for a scientist to believe in Bhagvan. But karma? Forget karma. There's no such thing. Believe in yourself.*" *Roshni.*

Pragashini's Journal

This snake stirring. I am returning despite the past. Does it mean the wheel of karma is in motion?

***

The passenger distracted her. 'Your in-flight magazine. Can

I have a read?' he asked. She could not move away. The plane was packed. She handed the magazine to him without a word.

***

Pragashini's Journal

The karmic wheel for centuries on the move driven by a mysterious momentum that keeps it in motion; causing it to lumber across continents, from Asia, to Africa, to Europe, even to America. Its movement predestined and unrelenting.

Why did it begin, that exodus of peasants? Was it simply karma? Did the wheel have that power to take them where it chose to go? Or was it accompanying them where they were fated to go? Or following them? They tramped from the Indus River Valley, from the foothills of the Himalayas, the water margins of the sacred rivers, to the coast and the dysentery depots.

***

From there karma took them over the sea to virtual slavery in the European colonies of Africa. There karma thwarted their efforts to make new beginnings under foreign colonialisms. After all they had their own colonialism in India.

***

When those peasants initiated their revolt against the land; when they tasted money eked out from hawking vegetables and fruit; when they washed laundry although they were not dhobi-men and dhobi-women; when they progressed to one-door shops, to houses and cars, their undreamed of affluence, in their eyes, invited a backlash from indigenous people even the colonists.

***

Despicable karma. It caused their flight from Africa as refugees into the arms of Europe and America. Their second coming to renewed beginnings; their pain of exile repeated; their yearning to return, continuing towards the new millennium. They were still travelling, still sojourning, while the bloody karmic wheel was still on the move. Would it return to India in the millennium? Who would make that journey? What if they chose not to return to India?

***

How can I forget karma? Or its connection to women? Wherever the wheel performs its karmic repetitions a female is spread-eagled across its disk.

***

That female is the surplus infant girl left to die on the Indian mountain.

She is the child- bride.

The girl playing on the beach coaxed into a boat and rowed out to sea.

She is clutching her mothers hand when they are kidnapped at the riverside.

She is the virgin raped.

The woman men shared while they wait to be shipped.

She is the stillborn infant thrown into the sea off the shark coast.

She is the woman who jumps overboard and is not rescued.

She is the unaccompanied child married to an adult male.

She is the bright eyed girl in flimsy sari white men are astonished to see disembark at the Bluff.

She is the widow who becomes a prostitute.

She is the woman who dies in childbirth.

She is the woman imprisoned for refusing to pay the poll tax.

She is the baby killed by its mother and thrown into the sewer.

She is the child who watches men rape her mother.

She is the girl who bears a white man's child.

She is the girl who dies hanging from a sari tied to a mango tree.

She is raped and murdered in Africa.

She is the refugee from anti-Indian feeling.

She is the woman who protests day and night outside the embassy.

She is the woman who kills her abusive husband.
The wife of the dissident who breaks his marriage vows.
The woman killed by her husband.
The woman who dies with a letter bomb in her hand.
She is the woman forced into marriage throughout the ages.
Silenced by the colonizers language.
The woman who never learnt to read or write.
She is the woman who straps dynamite to herself and revenges all Indian women.
Hers is the reborn soul of every Indian woman since the creation.

***

Pragashini felt calmer. The headache eased. She covered her eyes again and when she uncovered them she discovered the man had been leaning forward and watching her. Perhaps reading her journal. She covered her face with her scarf.

'Sorry,' he said. 'I don't mean to pry.'

She could have said 'I'm not sure how to answer you,' but she let the opportunity pass. The movement of her lips in a smile that did not touch her eyes indicated she was not offended – she hoped. But the man was not looking at her. His face flushed with embarrassment he concentrated on the television screen.

Her beginning was a thousand miles away, its pavement sellers hawking pineapples, peanuts, and weird thorny pears. How would the salty air feel on her skin, and in her nostrils?

When the cabin crew began pushing their silver trolleys steaming with food down the aisles, she panicked. Travellers on either side blocked her in. She jumped up, extricated herself from the clutter around her, and climbed over them to reach the aisle before the trolley trapped her. In the aisle she loitered until the meal was over. The porter left several drinks on her table. There was nothing to do but drink.

The karmic wheel is in motion for all these returning exiles. Her return to Africa may be the signal she will visit India though she felt no connection with the place. If fate is kind her arrival in Port Elizabeth might be met by heart warming lights and fragrant incense.

Even then the concepts were incompatible. Her life was a catalogue of contradictions. She was a lukewarm Hindu who respected believers in one God. She professed to be a feminist yet succumbed to the idea men in the struggle might respect women, while being chauvinist in their personal lives. She used any excuse to escape marriage, yet she respected the role women play in the home. She constantly rejected the idea of motherhood, yet envied the rapport women like Heather have with their children. And here she was an exile yearning for home, returning home like an unwilling child to school.

She knew that contradictions, like opposites, have their place in the natural world. There was nothing wrong with opposites: electrons and protons; North and South; positive and negative magnetic fields; bilateral symmetries; one force necessary to balance the other. Except, opposites repulse each other. The one must exist far from its opposition. To maintain equilibrium they tend to position themselves as far apart as the poles.

Her opposites snuggled up close, drawing comfort from each other like symbiotic relationships. Prayer and doubt; feminism and respect for chauvinist men; womanhood and distance from oppressed women like herself; yearning for home and fear of return. Her own contradictions were contained. They were inside her. She was afraid she might not prove strong enough to maintain equilibrium.

She read other letters: *"You were an underage bride. Get over it. No one will bother about your age now. It's awful imagining karma waiting to greet you at home. Where does it leave your friends?" Roshni.*

She agreed. It is wilful imagining karma waiting to greet her. Where does that leave Matatiele? Roshni? Smuts? Jairaj, her father? Leela, her mother? She touched the blue green scarf.

Without fail, for every year in exile Jairaj telephoned her for three minutes, every Sunday before he sat down for lunch. He asked simply, 'You punishing me, Pragashini?' For years he listened to her silence until he offered the only excuse he could think of: 'When Mandela is released you'll return. I know that.' Perhaps he took her silence for acquiescence.

What a way to lie. A coward's deception. When did she ever consider Mandela would be released? Never. Not once in all the years did she even entertain the prospect of his release. Even through the Free Nelson Mandela years of campaign. Impossible. It would never happen. It was a law of physics. Nature abhors a vacuum. If Mandela was released someone else would take his place in prison. Winnie? Perhaps. The government needed Mandela to be locked away as far as possible from the people. To maintain the balance of power.

She was a pessimist. Smuts accused her of that. She never hoped. She believed Mandela would die in prison. She would never return. Jairaj's death would be a telephoned experience. That is what she expected. She was a coward. She hated Jairaj too much to say this to him. She never told him what was in her heart.

Sometimes he asked, 'Will you come home to bury me, Pragashini?' All parents of exiles ask that. Throughout her silences she never pitied him. Her heart was leaden. She told herself he would outlive her, knowing she had no wish to ever see him again, her own father. He wanted forgiveness. Her forgiveness. She had the power to forgive him just as he once had the power to free or imprison her. It was his need for her forgiveness keeping her in exile. Not Mandela's imprisonment.

Her happiness was entrusted to him. He gave it away. The way men barter their daughters' happiness for their own peace of mind.'

Mothers are a contradiction. Obedient to their fathers and husbands; hating their daughters' potential freedom. Leela? She was no different. She did not even figure in the equation. She hardly knew what to equate Leela with. Mothers are never a catalyst for change. Once again she touched her scarf.

Another card: "*Be prepared to forgive everyone. Mother. Father. Me too. If Mandela can forgive enemies, you can forgive friends." Roshni.*

She could never forgive. Life is too short to forgive people who ruined it. Even her search for another faith was aborted because Christians forgave.

Forgiveness. What a concept. When did forgiveness begin? Who was the first human to forgive? Adam pointed the finger of blame at Eve and did not forgive her. God certainly did not forgive them. Both Adam and Eve banished Cain without forgiveness. Why is the first forgiving person forgotten by history when all the war mongers are remembered and glorified? She could not forgive, so she could not abandon her religion and become a Christian.

Her return home had nothing to do with Jairaj. She would have stayed on, but for that failed meeting with the examiners. If she had submitted her thesis she might have remained in England. With her research sabotaged, she could return and rekindle the goal she had put aside.

The passenger said, 'thank you,' curtly, handing back the in-flight magazine. Without looking at him she reached out to accept it, wondering why he was intent on speaking to her.

The last card: "*Don't come. There's a conspiracy. Spiders are spinning webs to ensnare anyone who wasn't here during the struggle. Make no mistake. There'll be a web for you. Spun by spiders you trust and won't fear. And don't mention Smuts to me, ever. Roshni."*

***

2.

A praise poet vied with a Sangoma for a position to strut on the runway. The praise poet was naked except for a skirt of skins, a shield and a spear. Both men ignored the man in overalls directing the plane with his yellow table tennis paddles. While the plane approached she heard African tom toms beating out the rhythm of the sun. As the plane came to a standstill she heard African choirs harmonising in acappella style, competing with the high-pitched scream of the Boeing727's. Cameras flashed. Video cameras rolled. People cried, even the pilot and his cabin crew who were still all European. Those who were brass faced hugged and kissed everyone in sight; even the po faced immigration officers who were also still European. They all believed the brutal, violent story of South Africa had ended and everyone would live happily ever after. The old book could be shut, and a new one opened. Pragashini had landed at Jan Smuts airport.

* * *

3.

Fear. Located in the pit of the stomach. It felt tangible. Any one of apartheid's disenfranchised who has ever succeeded in leaving by plane, train, car, on horseback, on foot through the bush, on the underground, has experienced the emotion any border crossing arouses. Hands clammy. Mouth dry. Facial features rigid. Yet fear is in the stomach. There must be an evolutionary basis, Pragashini reflected. Rumour has it before flight man has to empty the alimentary canal to facilitate escape. At a border post, however, you must move towards the enemy, whether you are entering or leaving a country.

She anticipated walking straight from the plane through a tunnel into the airport building, and to be met by that sea of faces so familiar to long haul passengers at Heathrow. Instead she had to descend the steps of the plane into the cold; climb aboard a trolley bus; wait until it was full; maintain her equilibrium when it lurched into action and trundled to the airport building; eyeball and be eyeballed by European guards at the entrance; and find no one waiting to meet her or anyone else, the way people did at Heathrow's international arrivals.

Then she chastised herself. I should not be afraid. Returning – this is what the liberation movement has done for us – besides giving us the franchise. Whether or not the elections are held this year; whether or not we win the election; whether or not the election is declared free and fair; the atmosphere of oppression is already lifted, dissipated like hot air rising and blowing away. They have done this for us. Forget electricity. Forget housing. Roads, schools, jobs, crime. The atmosphere was changed. She felt it.

It seemed the whole world had the destination Jan Smuts' airport in mind. The hall teemed with arrivals. Having no one to meet her shocked her into a realisation of what she was returning to.

It overpowered her once she entered the area with officials standing at strategic places around the building. She breathed in the change. The air was fresh and light. The atmosphere of happiness and enthusiasm elevated her so that she floated through the place. Previously she was bowed down with the burden of oppression in the same place where the officials and the airline clerks were empowered to refuse her permission to board or to take her and lock her away somewhere. When she was with Nasaratt she wanted to be stopped and sent home, but she feared where they would take her. Now in her heart she thanked the liberation movement.

She queued with foreign passport holders in a hot sweat, and a hangover, clutching the old navy blue UK passport in her hand. Who could venture into exile and meet customs and immigration anywhere without trepidation? Worse to return from exile.

The Home Office advised her to renounce South African citizenship should she require British assistance while she was there. South Africa gave her such scant rights she had to renounce her birthright for her own safety. Could she do that? It would be like giving up the faith she was born into.

Around her people clutched United Nations papers and passports from the world that harboured them through the struggle years. The airport was tiny compared to Heathrow, yet she met no one she knew. She watched to see the reception they would receive from Customs and Immigration, and what manner she should adopt when meeting them. She was not confident the change had proceeded as far as the border because the officials were all European men and women.

How would they expect her to conduct herself? Had they changed? Would she appear insolent if she behaved naturally and looked the officer straight in the eye? Would she appear shifty, as if she had something to hide if she avoided his eyes? She held the documents in her hand with a holdall over her shoulders. The officer greeted her, extended his hand, and perused her papers. The liberation movement had assured her she could enter with just the plastic identity card, with a birth certificate, even with the old Dom pass. Yet she broke out into a sweat. The official took some time over her papers.

She fidgeted with the zipper on her shoulder bag. When she could contain herself no longer she presented her old out of date South African passport. It was her mistake. The officer told her since she was born in South Africa she needed permission to travel with foreign travel documents. Her brain did a quick calculation. She would be refused entry and sent back to London.

She breathed a sigh of relief. Here was her opt out clause. Fate was dealing her a good hand after all. She was not meant to be in South Africa. The officer, however, was returning her papers and wishing her well on her return to South Africa. He advised her to see immigration in Port Elizabeth to correct her status as a South African. She was dumbstruck.

Taking a deep breath, she pulled a trolley towards her, and manoeuvred her way through people and trolleys to the conveyor belt for her flight. An assortment of carpet bags, holdalls, suitcases, boxes, backpacks and checked carrier bags was already tumbling up out of the ground onto a black rubber belt that churned round the viewing passengers. People leapt forward to snatch their belongings unmindful of those standing around. She too extricated her suitcase from the pile, hauled it off the rubber belt, and heaved it onto the trolley, then wheeled her luggage towards the green gate having nothing to declare.

But when she approached a European official standing along the left corridor he gave a curt nod to an African official on the right. The African stepped forward and motioned her to the counter. She became wary. Would the white man's victory lie in transferring his fearful status to the African? However, instead of asking to examine her luggage, the official asked to see her passport. Having already shown her passport and put her papers away she rummaged in her handbag. The man who had sat next to her on the plane came up behind her. His passport was in his hand. He promptly submitted it to the official.

'Just one passport will do', the official said, as if they were travelling together. The official glanced at the man's passport and let both of them continue on their way to the exit.

Why was she expecting to be met in Johannesburg? Perhaps the trauma of absence from home and being back on South

African soil confused her. Even feeling estranged from South Africa and yet to touch down for the first time in a free country without a welcome was similar to walking like a ghost through this frightening arena of departure. Arriving in a place where no one meets you is the real world, distinct from her recurring dream. Or did she expect the international flight to go straight to Port Elizabeth?

Yet there was change. She stood staring at coffee shops, restaurants and bars on either side where people of all races lounged carelessly where they would never have entered before except as staff running around and waiting on European clientele, saying 'ja baas[1], nee baas[2], dankie baas'[3].

When at last she roused herself and approached the wide glass fronted exit that opened onto a covered road where taxis and cars were parked, a group of taxi drivers accosted her from all sides, offering to take her wherever they were going. 'Carlton! Holiday Inn! Protea!' they shouted at her. She wanted to throw her arms around them and hug them, these oppressed people the first to speak to her. She could not restrain the tears. There was too much emotion here. The drivers would have seen the same emotional reaction on hundreds of returning exiles. They may have wanted to hold her close, but they restrained themselves.

She did not require a hotel nor a taxi yet she walked towards the exit where there were huge glass doors wide open to the street. She stood outside merely to hear the voices, the accents, the music from the car radios. Observing the joy emanating from the faces of people despite being dispossessed, because they expected change, overwhelmed her. Through her tears

---

1 Ja baas means Yes boss.

2 Nee baas means No boss.

3 Dankie baas means Thank you boss.

she smiled and thanked her Goddess, the Durga.

***

4.

Decades frozen in a time warp. The domestic airport at Jan Smuts appeared the same desolate, uncarpeted place she had known. A modern round information desk faced the entrance. Telephone kiosks to the left, restaurants to the right. An impressive board with photographs of hotels lined the outside glass wall. A ramp connected the international and domestic airports. A flux of people moved up and down the ramp pushing luggage trolleys. Pragashini walked down the ramp. To the left was a series of doors marked 'showers'. There were orange plastic bucket chairs on metal legs around the walls, weighing in scales, and a small counter. There was no one at any of the counters. Everything was shut.

***

5.

A large poster on the wall showed a blue grey dove with outspread wings, hovering in the face of a policeman whose hands were outstretched below the dove as if he was making an offertory. It seemed an incongruous juxtaposition of images. Dissimilar to a girl offering her aarati[4] plate. Pragashini lifted her camera and snapped it. In the past she would have been arrested for doing that.

She did not expect to have a problem when she had been back on South African soil for ten minutes. From behind the weighing in desk a young lad appeared. Pragashini placed her bags on the scale. He ignored her. She produced her ticket.

4 The Aarati plate is the offertory plate used during the puja.

He shook his head then he accepted and read it.

'Full,' he said. 'All flights to PE,' he said. Then he went to a computer. 'Your name's not coming up on the screen. Maybe your tickets for the bioscope.' he added smiling. 'It's standby for you. Come back at twelve'.

She flung her left arm out as if she was going to salute him but then she tapped her watch. It was only eight now.

'All full up'.

There was a mess of holdalls, tog bags, and suitcases lying about at the side of the weighing in scale at the standby desk. She lifted her suitcase onto the counter.

The clerk pushed it back off. 'We don't hold luggage if you're on standby.'

She lifted her suitcase again and put it back on the counter. It was clear someone had accepted the luggage of standby passengers but this clerk refused to hold hers.

'Lady, you see that sign?' he asked. 'It says 'closed'. He began reading, 'Lady it says, open twelve. Come back at twelve. Someone will help you.' He opened his hands shirking responsibility.

There was no seating area in the domestic area. She could not tolerate the smell of food after drinking all night, so she pushed her luggage around the airport just looking about her, getting the feel of the place. From the ground floor she looked up and saw uniformed policemen in grey leaning over the railings watching the people below. Certainly, that had not changed. She passed into another area. She walked around the terminal and found the rest rooms. Here they were no signs designated 'Whites - Nie Blankes Nie.[5]' This was another change.

***

5 Nie Blankes Nie means Not for Non Whites.

6.

To be back on South African soil; to feel overpowered. Those were Smuts first thoughts. After seeing Pragashini from the first floor and elbowing his way to her he was reminded of the last time they were together. We were kids. I always accepted her Indianness and my Africanness. I could never build that bridge between the two of us. If I could have imagined what life was like away from here, maybe I could have built that bridge. Our differences must be strong if I could picture a new South Africa, but not the two of us together in it.

She eventually heard him calling to her, stopped then saw him above the heads of other travellers. She waited for him to reach her. For several moments they stood looking at each other.

'Leaving already?' he said.

She considered if she should speak to him. 'You wish,' she said. 'I've got waves to make!'

'Waves? You? Don't make me laugh. You can't even make ice cream ripple.'

'And you? Arriving or running away again?'

'Running home. Heather's chasing me.'

'Did you have a praise poet or a sangoma?'

'Not even a wolf whistle,' he said, 'never mind drums. But see, they're rolling out red carpets for tourists. iGoli's crawling with bums and bum bags. It's money they're after, Pragashini. They don't have time for exiles. Robben Islanders were enough for them! You expecting to be necklaced in iBhayi?'

She frowned at him.

'I mean that garland you people love.'

'After I cursed them at my wedding? No one's knows I'm coming. I'll take a taxi to a hotel. I'm overcome just being home. I can't believe this is South Africa.'

'I feel change,' he said. 'My bones feel revived. The air smells sweeter. Sekunjalo![6]' he shouted loudly, repeating the word, 'Sekunjalo' several times. 'This is our time, Prags.'

'No dude. There's no time for us. Not then. Not now. Not ever. Not as Indian and African. You indoctrinated me. Our races dislike each other. Like religions look down on each other. Christians on Jews. Jews on Muslims. Muslims on Hindus. Hindus on Christians. We'll have to come back as ... I don't know... Inuits[7]. '

'Still being clever! You're too pessimistic. You've got no faith in anything. We should've waited me and you. They say all things come to those who wait. Look at Madiba. Surviving prison. When so many died. Something must have kept him going. The will to live. Knowing it will change. If you give up you're dead.'

'Madiba was born under a lucky star. How many others waited? Where are they now? Six feet under. Feeding the worms. There was no sekunjalo for them.'

'Pessimistic Hindu! Typical Indian. So which family you going to throw yourself on for more punishment? The Nasaratts or the Devs?'

She shrugged. 'What's to choose between them? I don't want to see the Devs. Ever. They can come and throw rose petals on my grave. If they survive me. Is Nasaratt still underground?'

'One of the mysteries of the world I'll never understand. You get a chance to break free and what do you do? You come here. What you planning, Prags? Revenge? Heather's got some cock and bull story about Nasaratt and your viva. Is it true? Revenge won't get you anywhere. Come away with me.'

'With you? You'll warn him before you run away with me. You comrades', she said, making a loud clicking sound to

---

6 Sekunjalo means now is the time.

7 Inuits are indigenous people of northern Canada and Greenland formerly called Eskimos.

express her disapproval. 'You've got so much faith in each other's good intentions. Now here you're thinking it's a cock and bull story. Why? Because he's your comrade? I don't feel like arguing with you, dude. I wonder if I should even trust you. You're so loyal to him you probably won't believe anything I say. But it's the truth. I missed my session with the examiners because of him. You've got this notion he's a gentleman and you're a tsotsi. It's the other way round. If you hang around with him for long, you'll become like him.'

'Only because you're soft, woman. That's your problem. You let people stamp all over you. Then you come back for more. Like Gandhi – ji. You've got to be like Lauren Bacall. You're half way there, smoking like a chimney. Just light up when you meet the Nasaratts. Then watch some movies with Bogart and Bacall. And take notes. The Nasaratts will have heart failure if they catch you smoking. Then you'll have the place to yourself.'

'I was raised on Bollywood,' she said. 'Girl babies abandoned on mountain tops. Or sold to brothels.'

'Then why leave York? Why come back? My kids are wetting the bed! Crying their eyes out. They want to stay with their English Nana. They're petrified my elders will chop off their little finger.' He held up his little finger.

'They're babies, dude. Your fears become their fears.'

'Not any more. It's sekunjalo time. Those days are gone when you can disappear off the face of the earth, no questions asked. This is our country.'

'You have high hopes,' she said. 'I hope you're not betrayed.'

'To be honest with you, I was never hopeful, Prags,' he said. 'The hopeful waited for sekunjalo. I didn't wait. I never believed in it,' he said. 'Neither did you. We're the same. Pessimistic. Now here it is. Sekunjalo is laughing at us.'

He took her hand and saying 'Come, come,' he guided her through the crowds. She followed him pulling the trolley in the direction of the entrance. They left the terminal building and the covered taxi rank out into the open with the blue Johannesburg sky overhead. There he stopped in the middle of the road and looked at her without saying anything. She looked questioningly at him.

'This is our time, Pragashini,' he said.

'We must wait for another time,' she said. 'We still have other lives to live.'

'You know that movie where Bogart looks at Ingrid Bergman and says 'Here's looking at you kid?'

'You and your old black and white movies. I'm glad you admit it. She's beautiful to look at. He's ugly,' she said.

'With us it's the other way around. I'm the handsome devil – you're the ugly duckling with that shaved head and old scarf.'

'Handsome – in an ugly way. Like Bogart. There's this movie where Amitabh Bachchan sings 'Jumma Chumma.'

'Don't be clever.'

'It means, give me a kiss, silly.'

'I like that. Come here. We must kiss, Pragashini. Because it's sekunjalo even though it isn't our time. One kiss on South African soil for young love.'

They kissed in the middle of the crowds of people, luggage, talk, the sound-barrier-breaking noise of aeroplanes flying overhead, landing and taking off, and the people around stopping to stare, clapping their hands, then jiving in the street.

'Watch Bollywood, dude. You'll learn more about making movies and how not to do it, than from watching Hollywood. India is like Africa. Drumming. Music. Singing. Dancing. Beautiful faces. People with rhythm and – humility.'

He kissed her again. 'You know, I'll never ask you for an affair, comrade.'

'Sure? Why not?'

'I'm sure. We should've waited you and I. Got married.

Hindu way and traditional African way. Had kids. See who they'd resemble. Handsome like me. Or ugly like you.'

'You know what they did to an Asian friend of mine who married an Afro-Caribbean man?' she asked. 'The men in her family broke into their bedroom on their wedding night. They spent their honeymoon in hospital. Today you would be minus your family jewels. Your four children would be a pipe dream,' she said.

'You think I worry about kids? Kids make women happy, Prags. Not men.'

'Tell me what makes a man happy, dude?' She put her hand to his lips to silence him. 'Never mind. It won't be of any use to me,' she added, 'I'm not coming within a mile of another man. Your father isn't expecting you. I know. Nor me.'

'There's a bereavement at home. I'll call him from Shell House. Check my comrades. After that, I'll go to iBhayi. There's a traditional oration for whoever died. It may be my mother. I wanted to leave Heather in York. A funeral's no place for kids. She refused to stay behind,' he said moving away. Then he turned back quickly and held out his arms to her. She went into his arms and he held her close.

'You're too soft,' he whispered. 'That's your trouble. It's time you grew your hair. Like Samson. You'll get your strength back.'

'You don't know why it's shaved. It's a reminder. That's why I removed my niqab. We have other lives, dude. I'll grow it when we meet in another life,' she said.

They embraced for a few minutes, and then they separated. You see any 'Slegs vir Blankes[8]' signs?' he asked. She shook her head. 'They must've been removed during the negotiations.' He found a chair for her, balanced it on her luggage, and wheeled the trolley back to the weighing in area where she sat

8 Slegs vir Blankes means only for Whites.

down. Then he left her.

Now there were clerks behind the counters weighing passengers' baggage. She pushed her trolley along the row of scales, looking darkly at each clerk. Each was a European man or woman. Then an African man took his place behind a weighing in desk. She stopped. 'I've travelled all night,' she said. 'Not from Durban. Not from Cape Town. From London. I had to make a train journey to reach London. They won't put me on a flight and they won't hold my luggage.'

'I'm sorry, ma'am', he said, 'I just started working here Monday. Next time you come here all these places will be taken up by our people.'

When Smuts looked back at Pragashini she was writing feverishly in a notebook. He saw a clerk jump over one of the scales and run towards her then assist her through the various checks and carry her luggage onto the tarmac to a waiting plane.

***

7.

The plane, small, cramped and lightweight, easily buffeted by the wind, soared to a great height above sea level and Pragashini was holding the hand of an unknown European man sitting next to her.

Before it began to ride slowly on the tarmac from its stationary position towards the runway she was alerted to something amiss with the man sitting alongside her. Her first suspicion was that he might be drunk. Perhaps he had come in from a long haul flight as she had, having drunk free booze throughout the flight. She darted sidelong glances at him, to observe what he was up to. He fidgeted with his safety belt, manhandled the armrest on his seat, mopped his face, and just could not seem to relax.

She shifted her body slightly away from him, then turned to face the window. But his restless activity did not cease. She became apprehensive about sitting alongside him for the flight.

Her movement away from him may have triggered his speech: 'Excuse me,' he said.

She turned to face him, feeling hostile and unfriendly. He was a European in his late thirties. She saw the out dated Palm Beach summer suit with open necked white shirt before she focussed on his rigid body, his arms pressed against his sides, his hands gripping the armrest, and finally, his ashen face perspiring profusely. He was not drunk. He was terrified. He had spoken to her with his eyes tightly shut. She thought he was having a seizure or a heart attack.

'Yes?' she said, concerned, yet keeping her distance from him. 'Shall I call the air hostess?' Her impulse was to signal for assistance then leave her seat so that someone could attend to him. Then she realised he must have struggled to say those two words to her because he seemed unable to say anything more. His face was drained of colour. The knuckles of his clenched fingers were bloodless.

Then the plane stopped with the engine running, and the propellers moving, waiting to taxi down the runway, he said 'I... sur ... vived... a... plane ...crash. This ... is ...my ....first ....'

She did not know what to say or do, so she said, 'Breathe!' It was the first thing that came into her mind. It was a yoga thing. If he breathed he would relax. He appeared not to have heard her. 'Breathe!' she repeated. She had to bring her head close to his ear and repeat, 'Breathe deeply!' His breathing made no difference to his deathly appearance.

Then she said, 'Breathe and pray,' this time in a whisper. That too had no effect on him. He looked as if he was going to pass out. Despite her unwillingness to speak to him, she could not leave him like that. Something about his rigidity, his inability to make a sound, touched her. 'Think of a prayer if you can't say it,' she said.

His eyes opened and moved to her face. She could not interpret what might be going through his mind. He might have thought she was having him on.

'Any prayer,' she added.

He shut his eyes again, and shook his head.

'My friends pray about' ... But she stopped. It was the prayer about a valley of death. She added, 'When they're afraid.'

He made no response.

'I'm mixing it with a movie.'

'My head ...'

'Not valley of the dolls. Of the kings. It'll come to me.'

'Rubbish,' he said.

They were silent.

'You must know it. I don't know it or I'd say it with you. I've heard my friends say it.'

'Head's killing ... '

Slowly the plane began taxing down the runway. The expression on his face worsened with his eyes screwed up. So she began to mutter what she knew of the psalm, 'The Lord is the shepherd.' While he kept his eyes shut, she repeated the fragment of the psalm she knew. 'The Lord is your shepherd. You are not afraid. Say it with me.'

The plane had now taxied to the point where it was about to make the run into acceleration and then flight. She kept her eyes on his face, fearing he would have a heart attack.

Then she leaned closer to him and said, 'Take my hand.' But she had to prize his fingers from the armrest to take hold of his hand. She held his hand, whispering the line of the psalm until the plane was cruising along at high altitude.

When the voice over the intercom told them to unfasten their safety belts, she saw him relax, just slightly, and take a quick breath. He opened his eyes and smiled at her. The look she returned said, don't get friendly with me, dude. They did not speak to each other after that. He did not tell her his name, nor ask for hers. His smile was his gratitude.

Well, she told herself, another blow from bloody fate. Your first trip to check on apartheid and you end up holding the hand of a European man. She recalled all the men she had stubbornly refused to speak to over the years in exile, especially her father and Matatiele, and yet here she had spoken to this man.

But then she remembered a previous occasion. One night she was walking to the local supermarket in York. It was winter and the street was dark since it was not a main road. There was a pedestrian crossing nearby with large yellow flashing orbs balanced on black posts.

She was walking to the crossing when in the fog she saw a man in a wheelchair waiting to cross. In moments like that you never know if you cause offence when you offer help, she thought. But she did offer and he said 'please'. She left him on the opposite side of the road and walked on. But when she looked back he was coming along slowly and she was impelled to return to him. He was going to the supermarket. Again he said 'please'. When she left him at the supermarket he kissed her hand. One of the few times anyone had ever done that to her. Another blow from fate she thought.

The stewardess distributed little boxes containing a soft bap filled with ham, lettuce and cheese, a plastic tub of cheesecake, a box of cashew nuts and one of biltong. The service did not compare with that abroad. The stewardess did not ask if she were Muslim or vegetarian, if she could eat beef or pork, or if she was allergic to nuts or cheese. Pragashini made no protest. She kept the nuts and cheesecake for when they landed.

Matatiele who taunted her into returning did not know she was coming. She had no inclination to see him. The Devs' she no longer counted as family. The Nasaratts, if they knew about her having left their son, would avoid her.

8.

Approaching the airport, the pilot brought the plane lower and lower until it skimmed over roofs and tree tops. In her window seat Pragashini unconsciously tautened her back preparing for the plane to hit the ground at Verwoerd airport. She waited for the sequence of bumps on the tarmac. But the plane did not touch the ground. The pilot continued flying off the land mass until it was very near the southern edge of the continent and did not land.

It flew straight out to the sea heading for the South Pole. Beneath the plane stretched a limitless expanse of lapis blue sparkling water. The plane came down lower skimming the blue as if about to touch down in the water. Then the pilot took the plane into a wide sweeping curve. They were flying back towards the land, and Pragashini and the other passengers had a scenic view of the blue green sea, silver white foam, golden sand, harbour, ships, and green shrubs.

She was moved to tears. She could not gather and hold to herself the idea that this was her beginning. Her source: Port Elizabeth. Landing in Johannesburg did not have the same impact on her. From the window she saw bottle green shrubs, bisque cream beach, and blue coastline. The large coastal manufacturing city with a harbour where visiting aircraft carriers, submarines, and liners sat proudly like a laying in state, welcomed her.

Port Elizabeth is carved into the coast line on the southern tip of the African continent. When the plane left Johannesburg earlier Pragashini experienced it soaring up to a great height above sea level. When it swooped down to the coast, the change in altitude caused earache and temporary deafness. Passengers touched their ears. A child cried in distress while the plane made its steep descent.

On board, she held on to her seat remembering a plane that missed the landing strip at East London airport further up the east coast, landing in the sea. She wondered if her hand holding partner knew of that. Which plane crash was he involved in?

Unwillingly, she gave a furtive sidelong glance, at the man. He had not spoken to her since they left Johannesburg. She had no wish to embarrass him further by leaving him in terror until he felt coerced into pleading for her sympathy again. So, less reluctantly this time, and without turning her head to him, she put out her hand and he clutched hers. He had been waiting.

His hand was hot and clammy. They sat like that, two strangers, a young Indian girl, and a European man, holding hands on a South African aeroplane that had just flown from Johannesburg and was about to land in Port Elizabeth.

***

9.

Elizabeth Donkin is the English woman after whom Port Elizabeth was named. She contracted and died of tuberculosis and a hospital for the treatment of the disease was built in remembrance of her. The coastal city is where the first British settlers numbering 2,000, landed with their livestock bringing English into the colony previously ruled by the Portuguese and the Dutch. English was dominant as a language in the city until African children in Johannesburg's Soweto marched in protest against learning Afrikaans, a language similar to Flemish, containing elements of Dutch, French, German and English. The government responded by making Afrikaans the language of instruction in Coloured schools in Port Elizabeth.

This little history Pragashini was taught at school. It did not account for the history of Indians and others.

The Verwoerd Airport seemed the same as when she left: a landing strip; a large crowd of people on the balcony overlooking the tarmac; people up on the roof, others behind the brown glass pane on the first floor, still obedient to the ruling codes. Waiting where she had left them.

When she entered the arrivals room the races were clustered together: Europeans, Africans, Indians and Coloureds. How could she receive a homecoming when no one expected her?

There was the sound of laughter, chattering, shrieks of joy and the voice of a girl announcing the departure of another flight. The Nasaratts were there. Her friends were young adults. Adults had aged. There were newcomers in the family. A girl she did not know dressed like someone from the Punjab in a turquoise Punjabi and wearing her long black hair loose on her back stepped forward to place a garland of yellow and orange African marigolds around her neck. She bowed her head to receive the garland. The girl put her hands together and said, 'Pranaam[9], auntie.' This was astonishing. Apartheid had uprooted them from their multi-cultural suburbs and planted them in Indian soil.

The crowd most of whom she could not recognise, many born into the family after she left, milled around her, hugging and kissing her. All the girls wore their hair long. This was traditional and once considered unfashionable. She did not remark on it. The old women had their hair cut short. This was untraditional. The crowd parted making way for the Nasaratt brothers, Pravin, Saragan and Ravindra. She could not put names to faces. They wished to hold her close. She extended a hand for a handshake. They remarked on her shaved head. Someone asked if Maggie locked her up when de

---

9 Pranaam is a greeting.

Klerk was in town. They posed for photographs until a man raised his voice and said, 'There's no time for introductions – the chow's getting cold. For those domkops[10] who haven't guessed, this is Pragashini. Auntie to all you little snotkops[11].' They cheered. The same cheering was taking place in other groups. Another arrival was being videoed. A group of people were singing a welcome song.

She joined her hands, bowed her head, and thanked the Durga for bringing her safely home. Nasaratt was not there. No one asked about him. Roshni was not at the airport.

They drove in a convoy of cars, taking the route through the city centre for her benefit so that she could recognize the unchanged features of her hometown. They were busy pointing out landmarks to her. The Mayor's Garden, the City Hall, the Feather Market, St Augustine's, Main Street, Russell Road flyover, remained intact with some renovation or modernization. Other places were demolished. The churches and schools for the Coloureds, the Oliver Plunkett, the Dominican Convent, St Thomas and St Monica's School, bulldozed by the apartheid government, for no accountable reason. However, the Rudolf Street mosque stood in splendid isolation and victory over the apartheid bulldozers.

Passing these places, and receiving potted anecdotes about their resistance to the Group Areas Board, she experienced nostalgia, sentiment, anger, joy, as she travelled as it were, backwards in time. She had held close her beginnings in this city, even when her belonging to the African continent was negated by apartheid. Her parents were no longer here. Jairaj told her that during one of his Sunday phone calls. He did not know she was back in South Africa. Even now, overcome with emotion, she had no inclination to see him.

---

10 Domkops are fools.

11 Snotkops are snotty nosed children.

The convoy entered Muhalla Asha, the Indian suburb, with hooters blaring in the manner of a wedding procession. Someone in the car said the government derived great pleasure from naming the streets in the separate ghettos after places in India. They stopped first at the home of the oldest person in the Nasaratt family, an aunt who was born at the turn of the century and was in her nineties. Ramgopal Nasaratt, father of Anand, stood in the open doorway visibly shaking with emotion. Nalini his wife, stood alongside him.

Nasaratt was not there. It was a reprieve. It gave her time to prepare herself for his arrival. Throughout her time with them she would have to pretend she knew where he was and when he would return, and that he knew she was back in South Africa. She could do this if she maintained silence when they spoke. She listened to their conversation without comment and with minimalist answers to their questions.

They observed her silence and became uneasy. Later they might become anxious, then perturbed, and then alarmed and worried about her state of mind. She knew this would happen and remained unmoved by their potential dilemma. She listened and observed them; keenly aware it was essential for her to know beforehand of Nasaratt's impending return. It would not do for him to arrive on their doorstep and surprise her. It was payback time.

Throughout her exile she persuaded herself it was better done in South Africa, than in England. Had she remained in England, she may have let it pass, the desire for revenge. He forced her hand by frustrating her research. Her revenge would have a greater impact here, surrounded by his family, and her friends, than in England.

Could she perform her daily pujas in the Nasaratt's family prayer room, praying without the guilt that accompanies the need for revenge on Anand Nasaratt?

Then Nalini held up a round brass plate with both hands. It

was like Pragashini's aarati[12] plate, covered with mounds of red and yellow powders, a whole coconut, a block of white camphor floating in a tiny bowl of water, here a nutmeg, there a betel nut, in the centre a small brass bowl with a tiny yellow flame burning, and around these items were scattered red rose petals. Nalini oblated the plate making circles before her face. Her mother should have been doing this. She fingered the faded, blue green scarf now loose about her neck.

Nalini handed the plate to her husband. Then she took Pragashini's face between her two hands and peered into her eyes for recognition of the beautiful young bride who had left so many years ago. She thanked the goddess for bringing her safely home, then still touching her asked, - Why you shave your head, ma? It isn't auspicious'. They loved that word 'auspicious'. The good sign. Her African friends had the custom of shaving their heads when someone died. Her family shaved a baby's hair at the naming ceremony. She shaved her head for a reason she would never tell Nalini. She had too much respect for the kindly woman. She bowed her head with her eyes closed, 'Mourning,' she lied. When they asked if she had children, she deceived them again. She nodded.

Ramgopal returned the plate to his wife and then he held Pragashini's face in both his hands and kissed her on the forehead, and both cheeks. The family crowding behind him, those who had not come to the airport were reminded that she was Anand's wife. There were whispered questions about her shaved head. The elders ran their hands over her head, blessing her. The ancient aunt, small, thin, dark, and wizened, did not confuse her with anyone. When asked if she knew who this was, the old woman said her name and blessed her.

The elders led her to their prayer room. The room was on the ground floor, perhaps an extra dining room or family

---

12 Aarati plate is the offertory plate used in the Hindu devotion.

room. It was large enough to seat up to forty people on the floor. There was no silk curtain marking the prayer room off from the rest of the house, but there was a door matching the other doors. Their prayer room was carpeted in red and blue with velvet covered cushions stacked near the door, and a few on the floor near the altar. The altar was at the front, a long low table, stretching from wall to wall, and covered with white starched cotton. From end to end the altar was laid with icons of the Gods and Goddesses. Each icon had its own garland of tiny fresh flowers. Garlands of fresh orange and yellow African marigolds decorated the overhanging white cloth draped in soft curves. To one side of the room were grouped a tabla and other musical instruments, and a microphone. The room must be used for musical performances, she thought. The room was filled with incense. The family crowded into the room and performed a puja in thanksgiving for her safe return.

Sitting cross legged on a cushion alone in the room was Roshni. Her friend did not stand up to greet her. Pragashini sat alongside her and placed an arm around her shoulders. When she glanced at her face she saw that Roshni was crying.

***

10.

The Traditional Oration was about to take place. Smuts was perched like a hawk, on the edge of an orange plastic bucket seat in the small front room of his parents' home in the African township of New Brighton. His mother, diminutive and thin, huddled on a plastic chair on his left, swathed in a traditional brown blanket, patterned in cream, her head buried in its folds cloaking her grief. She was alive. His father sat regally on his right, tall, upright in a shabby grey suit, leather patches on the elbows, black armband around the right sleeve, his hat placed neatly on his knees, held in both hands.

There was no telling what his father thought or felt: the joy of receiving the son he thought had been killed after the uprising, infected by the horror of the son found dead, erased all emotion from his face. His father's face was hard, the skin tautly drawn across his cheekbones, his eyes red with tears privately shed.

Next to his mother sat Heather like a stranger to him in her humility and obedience. She was transformed. He loved her. He loved the transformation in her. There were scores of men in the room, sitting on wooden forms, bucket seats, Formica chairs, all solemn, dignified, wearing threadbare suits, heads uncovered, hats or woollen caps clasped on knees. Other men stood along the walls, hats and caps held in their hands. All the men wore a single black armband. The room was quiet and still. When anyone spoke, it was in whisper. A few women grouped around behind his mother, one sitting with head bowed forward an arm around his mother's shoulders, another also sitting behind stroking his mother's back.

To them he must seem no different from an American tourist inspecting the ghetto dressed as he was in Reebok trainers and tracksuit boasting the bright green, gold, and black colours of the African National Congress. Later, when he would begin to dish out the gifts he brought with him, it would compound his alienation from their past. Compared with them he was rich.

This was not the homecoming he dreamed of. He envisaged five generations of his family gathering together from all provinces; his father slaughtering a beast bought from Fort Jackson; the local Sangoma orating praises to his ancestors; women brewing Umqombothi[13]; naked breasted girls dressed in beaded aprons dancing for him; men beating drums; fires burning; women ululating. There would be an unimaginable

---

13 Umqombothi is African beer brewed at home by Xhosa people.

feast and celebration; and they would conclude the home coming with acappella singing. The premature death of his brother Mellikhaya did not feature in the dream.

His bitter disappointment gave way to the tragic emotion in the room. Heather and he had not been allowed to enter the rest of the house. They had no opportunity to wash or change into fresh clothing. Their suitcases were still in the boot of one of the cars that picked them up at the airport. Their four children had been bundled into the back of the house like stolen goods, hidden, waiting to be priced. He supposed they had been bathed, fed, and put to bed, although it was now about noon, local time. Barely able to keep himself from falling off his perch, he could not fight the sleep overpowering him. He habitually nodded off; jerked back up again, and then altered his position on the hard chair.

Heather was determined to understand isiXhosa and to adapt to Xhosa culture and traditions. She rejected the idea that Smuts did not know what was about to happen. She chastised him for being more English than the English. She had seen video footage of the townships. Yet she was overcome with dismay when the kombi taxi drove into the township. She never saw anything like this. It was a place of houses. The streets were sanded, encrusted with sharp stones that would make walking barefoot painful. Yet there were barefoot children playing. The streets were drawn higgledy-piggledy without one straight line or right angle. The houses were at uneven levels because the streets were not levelled.

When the kombi stopped, her dismay turned to humility at the prospect of the little house where Smuts parents lived. She felt even more humbled when even she who was of average English height, had to stoop to enter the front door set at the top of two red cement steps. The little space that served as a front room had a red cement floor, a low roof without ceiling and miniscule windows. She unconsciously assumed the guilt of her colonial ancestors. She received their warm kisses and embraces with tears and trembling and shame. She thrust her children into the eager arms of aunts and uncles. Not for the first time she feared rejection.

Smuts had no recollection of what this room looked like at the time of his escape from South Africa. It had seemed a big room to a child. Heather and he had come out of the car straight into this room, arranged with rows of orange bucket seats and wooden forms, borrowed from the neighbours and from the New Brighton community halls. Surely there must have been furniture in the room. Where could they have put it? He was content to sleep on the carpet, but the floor was bare red cement. Where would they sleep tonight? He had left South Africa too young to know of the custom of removing the furniture from the front room of a house to make seating room for mourners at a funeral.

He was exhausted from the journey. He was not a seasoned air traveller - once he reached England he refused to even make a trip across the channel, fearful that he would not be permitted back into the country. On the journey back he feared the enemy would strike at returning exiles. He hardly slept on the plane the night before. His feet had swollen and he had difficulty putting them back into his trainers. Now he had the urge to raise each foot, loosen the laces, and free his feet but the sombre atmosphere in the room stopped him. All he longed for was to rest his head in Heather's lap and sleep the blissful sleep of home coming.

Then a shadow in the doorway blocked the light from the passage. He looked up with mediocre interest. A tall thin man stood in the entrance to the room. He had short grey hair, and a sparse grey beard. Smuts had a vague memory of the old man. Once the old man was assured that everyone was looking at him, he stepped into the room with a thin black finger directed at Smuts.

'Who is this small boy?' he shouted, charging toward the hapless Smuts, who stiffened on the bucket seat. The elder spoke isiXhosa.

Smuts thought he had misheard, or misinterpreted the words. It was so many years since he heard the richness of his mother tongue he was forced to translate from isiXhosa to English. A slight nuance or inflection could mean something different.

When the elder was about to touch Smuts, and all eyes were upon him, the elder swung around making for the door, with the air of one who has been insulted. He stepped out of the room back into the passage.

Heather understood rudimentary isiXhosa. She was spared the embarrassment of understanding the question. Smuts was none the wiser. He did not understand what the elder meant. No one attempted to answer the question. No one introduced Smuts to the elder.

When the elder entered the passage he turned and advanced once more towards Smuts. This time he asked, 'who is this small nyana boy seated with his elders?' There was no mistaking it. The old man was using words for 'boy'. He repeated the question, substituting the words 'inkwenkwe' and, 'kwedini' each word meaning a boy.

The women of the family, weeping softly into their hands, wiped their eyes with already wet handkerchiefs. Heather's hands lay in her lap. She did not cry easily. The elder demanded again, 'Who is this 'Umtsha' (teenager) entering our bereaved home and sitting with the elders of the clan?'

Then the men turned from wherever they stood and sat in the room and looked shyly at Smuts. He was bewildered. He was too tired to come to grips with this line of procedure. He was half asleep, just waiting for the scraping of chairs and murmur of voices signalling the proceedings were over. Then his father stirred beside him. His father seemed to come out of a sort of trance and said, 'He is the first born of Siyabonga, who is the last son of the Balase clan who changed their name from isiXhosa when they settled in the platteland near the Karroo. But the clan have reclaimed their name Balase.'

His father deliberately omitted to say what name they had changed to. Smuts hoped the interrogator would not follow that line of questioning, although he was himself interested in the name change from African to Coloured. He just wanted the business over with. The muscles in his legs cramped because he could not stretch his legs with the elder marching back and forth in the room.

The memory of the ritual custom was gradually coming back to him. Although he now knew his mother was alive and it was his brother Mellikhaya who had died, he had to be informed in the customary manner. Someone had first to sing the praises of his brother. Only then should he be informed of his brother's death. Finally the circumstances that led to his brother's death would be narrated.

'Umzulkulwana,' (grandchild) the elder persisted, 'your brother was named Mellikhaya by the elders who are enriched with wisdom from the ancestors that visit us in our dreams.'

No arguing with that, thought Smuts. The elder may be his grandfather.

'One who takes care of the home,' he said. 'Mell-i-khay-a!' his voice boomed out the name. 'That's how the ancestors said our grandson should be named. Mellikhaya fulfilled his destiny. Mellikhaya took care of the home for his Tata and his Mmama.'

Someone said, 'Bless him Jesus,' and a woman began to sing. Everyone stood up and joined in the singing. Smuts stood up too. Then they sat down again.

The elder continued, 'Mellikhaya was a man.'

A woman responded, 'Bless him Lord Jesus.'

'Mellikhaya was a man to this family, a great man to the clan which bears the name Ba-la-se.'

The women responded, 'Bless him Lord Jesus.'

'Your young brother Mellikhaya loved his mama. He took care of uMama.'

Smuts arm stiffened along its entire length as his mother responded to this statement by rocking back and forth in her chair. Did they blame him, Smuts, for not sending money to his mother?

'Your young brother Mellikhaya honoured his Tata. He respected our customs and traditions.'

The entire family now chanted, 'Bless him Lord Jesus.'

'Your brother schooled his sisters and their children.'

The response was repeated, 'Bless him Lord.'

'Your brother Mellikhaya was born after you yet he is greater than you. He is a man and you are a boy.'

Now Smuts regretted the exile years. He regretted having brought an English wife to his parents in their humble home almost as if he was showing off how far he had advanced from them, as if he despised their customs and traditions. He began to weep for the first time since hearing of the death in his family.

'Your Mmama and your Tata waited ten anxious years for Mellikhaya's birth, yet Mellikhaya is older than Smuts. Mellikhaya has surpassed Smuts. Mellikhaya was a man when the Almighty recalled him and Smuts is still a boy.

Smuts heard the twins crying in another part of the house. He looked over his mother's head at Heather. She sat immobile in her chair as if the children crying belonged to someone in the street. Smuts made to leave his place, but his father restrained him with a light touch on his arm. The child's crying altered. Smuts sensed fear in the cry. The child may be frightened, tired, and among strangers in a new house, not seeing Heather nor him there. He began perspiring.

The elder now elaborated on the cause of Mellikhaya's death.

Mellikhaya was on his way to the Transkei. He was driving a bakkie at night. In swerving to avoid a beast crossing the road he crashed into the mountain. Had he turned in the opposite direction the bakkie would have gone over the krans. There was no other vehicle in sight. The beast was gone in the morning. A passing motorist saw the crash but did not stop to help fearing a hijacking trap. The motorist used his cellular phone to contact the emergency services.

Mellikhaya died between midnight and two o'clock that morning. The police arrived from Umtata at six in the morning. There were only two police vehicles at the station. They had not thought to phone the ambulance until they arrived at the scene of the accident. That was the story the police told them. It did not explain how Mellikhaya's dead body came to be on the Bisho March.

The cause of death having been given, the assembly began singing. Smuts could not participate. He had so much to relearn. The hymns were sombre. They stood up, clapped hands slowly in time to the music, and then sat down.

A man jumped up, clasping a Bible in his left hand and began preaching. Smuts closed his eyes, took a few deep breaths, and slept unashamedly. Each time he slumped sideways, his father propped him up. Finally, he crossed his arms, rested his head in his hand, and slept without losing his balance.

***

11.

A panegyric on love at first sight. That is what Shakespeare would have called it, thought Matatiele. My son is home. Now I have too much to worry about. One son dead. Another one walking into the trap. Why is he here? Why come without warning me? Is it because he is a man he comes and goes as if this is a school playground? Those were Matatiele's thoughts while he stood outside the unlocked security gate of his house watching the street.

Behind him the front door was wide open. He turned his head to look into the room where Smuts was asleep; his huge body huddled uncomfortably in a plastic chair. He locked the security gate leaving the front door open for fresh air to cool the house. He walked down the stone steps, around to the back of the house and into the kitchen, from the kitchen to the front room, checking once again on Smuts, waiting for him to wake, wanting to be there to greet him again. He was agitated and nervous.

How was he supposed to get to know this man who ran away when he was a youngster and grew not just into a man, but a foreigner? The language will come back to him when he hears it, but his ways? Is he African or European in his ways? Will he respect me, like I respected my Tata? Will he stay here with us, with this white woman, here in the ghetto? If he does not, at least if he wants to I will feel at ease. Will he go to some hotel on the beachfront? For sure I can't expect a white woman to stay in this house. There's no bathroom. She has to wash out of a bowl. The lavatory is outside.

He continued in this manner throughout the day, not wishing to disturb his son, and unable to get on with doing anything else. He went incessantly round the outside of the house, from the kitchen door to the front door, and inside to the front room.

He had just returned to the front room and was hovering in the doorway when Nolitando, a young African girl of about twenty, kneeling on her haunches at Smuts feet, gently shook him to wake him. Matatiele caught the look on Smuts face when he opened his eyes and looked at Nolitando's face. Smuts looked as if he was in the middle of a dream. He looked afraid to speak in case she disappeared. They were silent as they looked at each other, the wonder in Smuts eyes at the beauty of Nolitando's face, and the softness from a natural born shyness.

Shakespeare said it, thought Matatiele. 'All the world loves a lover'. It must be Shakespeare. He's the only one I can memorise, he thought, watching Smuts and Nolitando. I hope it was Shakespeare because that makes it even better. The same man who created Caliban included us in that statement. 'All the world loves a lover'. I can forgive Shakespeare for creating the animal Caliban because he condescended to include us. We Africans love. We love to be in love. We love people. We love children. We love family. We love our elders. We love our dead. We love our traditions. We love our culture. We love music. We love dance. We love our language. We love our continent. We love the earth. We love everything. We love to love. Even when iThixo hates us.

Even those of us who love-to-love, even we fear 'love at first sight'. That's for youngsters. We have a heart. We can forgive our kids their mistakes. We look with fear at our youngsters in love, knowing there are no qualities in young lovers for young love to last. We hope they will part before one of them has a broken young heart.

Love at first sight can happen to anyone. Married. Divorced. Single. Priest. Nun. Elderly. Enemies. What a problem for a man approaching middle age to fall in love at first sight. That is what happened to Nasaratt. He fell in love after taking one look at Pragashini. Who knew how he would behave? Would his friends laugh at him? For sure, they will laugh at him. They will call him an old fool just because the girl he loves is a youngster. That's what we all thought. Nasaratt will be embarrassed every time he is in the presence of Pragashini. That's all there was to his falling in love with a youngster. No one imagined he would ask her father's permission to marry her. He had the last laugh, Nasaratt. Her father agreed.

Pragashini is still a youngster. Did anyone think to ask if she was in love with Nasaratt? Ikona. Or if she was in love with someone else? Ikona. Smuts' young love was nipped in the bud. Pragashini served someone's purpose. It must be. Or her father is a fool. Even if they are both old, people who fall in love at first sight, they'll be fools to everyone else. To fall in love at first sight is a calamity. Shakespeare did that too. He made that woman fall in love with the one with the asses' head.

Now Smuts. With a whole wife and family. Falling in love at first sight. Like a youngster. It's no crime. His friends will pat him on the back and make light of this. But Nolitando? A struggling student. She is striving to be schooled. She wants to better herself, not to have a family. Can she fall in love with him? Even then, she's a youngster. She may just think she's in love with him. She may fall out of love with him quick-quick. While she thinks she is in love with him, what will happen to them?

Is it possible? Can both of them fall in love at first sight? My son Smuts, who is a man approaching his prime, and this young girl? Smuts is modern. Look at the woman he chose. Heather, all White, and all English. How will he react if Nolitando rejects him? Will he fear to express his love when he is faced with coldness from his lover? He is trapped with a wife. Will he think about the rights and the wrongs of it all? I know Shakespeare said all the worlds a stage, if he didn't say all the world loves a lover.

***

12.

He fell in love with her. He could not move. His eyes widened. He could not believe what he saw. A fresh-faced girl, with bright black eyes, flawless black skin, and shaved head in the custom of a family in mourning. She wore no lipstick. No make up. No jewellery. She lowered her eyes and smiled. Her teeth were white and shining. Her eyelashes curled. Her brows were thick and black. At that moment he fell in love with her. He felt a light hand on his shoulder gently shaking him. He inhaled the combined aroma of bacon, boerewors[14], hot fat, coffee, toast, tomatoes, and onions and imagined he was sleeping in a Wimpy bar when he sniffed paraffin from a primus stove, and remembered that he was home.

The girl raised the tray in her hands to his eyes because he could not look at anything but her beautiful face. He glanced down and there was a round blue tray offered to him, with a plate of crisp-fried bacon, sausages pricked and the juices oozing out, orange eggs, yellow Rama[15] melting into toasted brown bread, browned onion rings, a huge mug of coffee, and a side plate of vetkoek[16]. Smuts raised his eyes to look at the girl again.

He was like a boy, shy when face to face with the girl he loved from a distance. He tried with difficulty to smile his gratitude, but his lips remained parted, refusing to move. She placed the tray on his knees and bobbed a slight curtsy, before leaving the room. He was aware of Heather waiting to be served after him. He felt guilty at the pure love he had experienced in that moment; and satisfied that he was enjoying the status of the male in his home.

Throughout the afternoon, visitors called round to greet him and to pray in the bereaved home. Each group sang hymns. One person in every group always preached. Tea and biscuits were served. The sympathizers departed after passing around a saucer for a collection for the family.

Smuts and Heather with their four children were put into

---

14 Boerewors are spiced sausages originally made by the Afrikaner people.

15 Rama is a brand of halal margerine

16 Vetkoek is a fried savoury yeast pastry.

one room with a double bed and a bunk bed. Smuts stole catnaps throughout the day, through prayers, singing, chatting and preaching. That night he could not sleep that deep sleep he had wanted. His body ached. He lay awake in the dark, listening to his wife and children breathing deeply. He lay in bed without fear. He did not dread the knock on the door. He had no fear of the police kicking the front door in. He did not have to watch his parents scramble for their passbooks. There was nothing furtive about the White woman at his side in the Black township. But there was a new fear. Unimaginable.

'It wasn't me phoning you,' his father insisted. 'I'm not the one who called you home. You think I'm an old fool? How can I tell you to come home when we found Mellikhaya lying dead in the street? Ice cold from the mortuary, but in the street as if he just died that minute. You think we don't know what that means? Never mind about us, do you know what that means?'

He was tired. If it wasn't his father who called him home, who was it? What was this new threat to be feared in South Africa? When he eventually fell asleep the sun was rising. It was a sleep he had never before enjoyed in South Africa.

***

13.

John Matatiele met Pragashini several weeks after she had been with the Nasaratts. Their meeting in the Greenacres shopping complex was accidental and therefore strained.

'You disrespect me,' he said, but withheld the 'Why?'

She was silent.

'At least pay your respects to the Robben Islanders.'

She did. She visited the released leaders living around the city and gave them bouquets of red roses. Subsequent meetings with Matatiele were more relaxed but there were no roses.

'I'll bring you up to scratch about what's happening,' he said.

She did not express her lack of interest. Their meetings became regular and frequent. From him she learnt about a tripartite alliance between the ANC, the Communist Party, and the trade unions, the strengthening of the unions, and the situation in the homelands. The understanding about South Africa, limited and unwillingly received, she could never have arrived at from exile. She met up with radical activists, and formerly imprisoned and community leaders.

One of Matatiele's strategies was to accompany her on a bus ride through various segregated areas like Muhalla Asha and the Northern Areas. Sometimes they walked around an area such as Commercial Road, or went down towards Berry's Corner, or explored Sydenham, Sidwell, North End, and the extended Main Street while he narrated significant events.

On one extended bus trip under the flyover at Russell Road and through the grimy back streets, and up over Baakens Bridge towards the lower end of Walmer Road he expressed admiration for the Rudolf Street mosque and attempted to extract a response from her.

'Look at that mosque. Does it speak to you?' he asked.

Forever the teacher, she thought. The Rudolf Street mosque was small, and lacked the splendour of mosques in the Middle East and Asia. Yet, the houses surrounding magnificent mosques in those countries might be simply washed in bright blues and pinks. Here even the whitewashed Old Dutch styled houses that once stood there suited the Rudolf Street mosque. On that day the simple green mosque was isolated from its environment of rubble, a building incongruous in its bulldozed surroundings because the community it had served was gone. Still unwilling to speak to him, or to play guessing games, Pragashini shrugged. Her rights as a woman were of more interest to her.

'Look further than what you see standing here. Forget what's around it,' he urged.

The residents of South End were forced to move away to live in segregated areas. They left the mosque standing. Was that what he was getting at? You can move the people but you cannot move the building? You have to bulldoze it. Why did they not refuse to leave? Should they have taken the mosque with them? Dismantle it brick by brick? Was that possible?

Then Matatiele walked with her to where the Christian church now demolished, once stood. Her friends wrote to her that they were celebrating mass in garages. 'For years we fund raised for a new church. Imagine! We fund raised for churches they bulldozed!'

'We must learn from apartheid, by thinking like apartheid,' Matatiele said. 'Think like the Group Areas!'

Why? she wondered. Apartheid is in the past.

'You want to forget it?' he suggested, 'Like you wake up and forget a nightmare?'

She asked herself, isn't that what most people want? To move on? To put the bloody past behind them?

Matatiele assumed correctly that like most people she wanted to forget apartheid. 'A famous man said, if you forget your history, you'll repeat it,' he said.

She smiled. Matatiele knew it was because he could not remember the man's name.

'Agh! You're out of touch. Just like Smuts. You missed the excitement of being here during the struggle. Our minds became sharp, like razor blades.' Then he continued. 'This mosque is a lesson for all of us. Ask yourself how is it the mosque is standing and the church is rubble?' he said.

Did she have time to waste making sense of nonsense? Apartheid was nonsense. Its laws were nonsense. People say the law is an ass. The law under apartheid was an ass. She would never defend herself in court where the law is an ass.

'No one knows how many people towed the line with apartheid,' he said. 'The churches towed the line. Right up to apartheid's dying days. Your friends know what their churches did. I don't mean the people. I mean the clergy from the top right down. While we were struggling, our people took a step back and looked hard at their churches. Then they said, 'Agh! This church is preaching apartheid. That church is practising apartheid. That church is punishing us if we disobey apartheid. So it must be white. Like Hindus are Indian. Muslims are Indian. Back then, we had never met an African Muslim, not even an Arab. To us only Indians were Muslim.'

There was a lesson somewhere in his message. But it was beyond her understanding: 'Bo my vuurmaakplek,' as they say in Afrikaans. She anticipated he would make a direct attack on Indians because she was accustomed to it in school and in exile. People rejoiced when the economic boycotts intended for White businesses included Indian shops. She waited, but he stopped there.

'Everyone campaigned to save their buildings. Only the arguments to keep the mosque won the case. I don't know the arguments. Ask them. Christians lost their case. Not that one case was better than the other. Not even that the one was more prayerful than the other. Or that one God listened and the other didn't. It's because some churches sold out before apartheid was born. Ask your friends.'

There was no need to ask. She knew. Long before apartheid came along Christian schools were segregated on racial lines. Even the seating in churches was.

'So,' he continued, 'when the clergy cried crocodile tears for their buildings to be saved, apartheid scratched its head. Apartheid asked why they didn't tow the line like they did all those years?'

Pragashini did not know what happened to the temple. She

did not ask. The new temple was there in Muhalla Asha. She concluded South End's old temple had also been demolished.

Matatiele watched her. He led her down Rudolf Street to the bus stop going in the direction of Humewood and the beachfront. While they waited in the sun he said, 'Pragashini, you've also been towing the line for too long.'

She scowled at him. He sounded like Jairaj admonishing her. How could she tow the line from exile? In hiding there was no one to trust, let alone collaborate with. She was never a collaborator.

'Your struggle was against Nasaratt; against your parents; your brothers; your customs; your traditions. You lost that struggle. Then you freed yourself. You are free. You're free of Nasaratt; your parents; your brothers. So, why go to *that* house? Why put yourself in their power? You've got parents. Why don't you go to them? It's dangerous to be in Nasaratt's home.'

She turned her face away. But he moved to confront her seeing her furrowed eyebrows and firmly set lips. As with her father, Matatiele was also subjected to her obstinate silences when he called her from South Africa. Despite her silences, he talked to her. He continued telephoning and talking to her, knowing she would never put the phone down on him, and taking advantage of this as an opportunity to reach out to her.

He developed the habit of preparing what he would say to her before he phoned in the manner he prepared lessons each night for the classroom. Considering his theme, how to introduce a topic; catch and hold her interest; reinforce his theme. Always careful of what he was saying to her. Knowing she was isolated from family and friends. He returned repeatedly to the theme of working towards her goal, completing her thesis, what it would mean for her independence if she returned home with her doctorate.

As if matching his resolution never to give up on her, she

stoically maintained her obstinate silence for many years.

One day he sensed in her stillness something he was unable to identify even after he put the receiver down. Perhaps her breathing quickened, or became laboured? Was she holding her breath? What was it? He could not be sure what made him sense something had happened to her. It diverted him from what he had planned to say to her. He begged her to speak to him. She did not respond. It happened each time he phoned. There were times, however, when she seemed at peace. He did not understand how he could tell from her silences.

When he was gripped by the sense that she was once again in that strange realm where she was in pain, something prompted him to say he would kill Nasaratt. When he said that he heard a sharp intake of breath, and then she sobbed. It was as if she communicated her unspoken words to him. As if she asked silently, 'Will you?' He responded as if she had actually spoken to him. He promised her, ardently, with all his heart, on his ancestor's graves, that he would kill Nasaratt. He sensed a profound change in her from that distance. She believed him. She believed she had a protector. She believed she would be safe. He would protect her.

Now as they disembarked from the bus on the pavement along the beachfront returning in the shade of the cafes and restaurants, he kept this in mind.

'You're home now. Our struggle's over. It's time you put a full stop to this satyagraha thing. Not talking to me. It's obstinacy. A waste of time.'

She looked at him through narrowed eyes. She willed herself to say: 'Don't disrespect Gandhiji.'

Those were the first words she spoke to him. He reached out and held her close.

'I'm not practising satyagraha. I'm not stubborn. Not obstinate. Not disobedient. Not obedient. Not weak. I won't accept my life as it is. I'm in that house for a reason. If I fail, then I fail.'

He did not want to move until he was certain she had nothing further to say. He waited until he felt the tension in her relax. Then he said: 'I know. Whatever you plan, do it quick-quick. You're in danger in that house, Pragashini.'

After that she spoke openly to him. She told him how she broke her silence with the man on the plane from Johannesburg, and the man in the wheelchair. She was coming to terms with the loss of momentum following the sabotage of her exams. She had a purpose that she kept smouldering with the ritual incense she burned daily in her little prayer room. But her purpose had neither plan nor plot. All she had was an urge to defeat Nasaratt. To see him powerless. But she could not sit down and plot what to do. The idea of what she had to do in the Nasaratt's home might come as inspiration to her when he returned.

'Revenge is no good, Prags. Put it out of your mind.'

'It keeps me alive.'

'There's life before revenge and there's life after. Just don't kill him, Pragashini. I don't know what you can do to him, just let him live.'

'Have you killed anyone?'

He looked at his hands. 'You pray to your gods. I call on my ancestors to destroy my enemies. When my ancestors fail me, yes, I might kill. They hardly fail me.'

'Christians pray to their saints.'

'My saints are my ancestors. They've done no evil. If there's a god for Africans, then my gods are my ancestors.'

One day he reminded her of the last telephone call he made to her while she was still in England. 'You forgot?' he asked.

She had. The viva. Not having much money. Returning to South Africa. Adapting to the Nasaratts. The fear of Nasaratt's return. The elections – if they took place; the inauguration – if they won. All caused her to forget. When he phoned to ask how her session with the examiners went and if she was safe. He misread her silence. He assumed her doctorate had been rejected or she put her research aside for some reason. He asked but she refused to say what happened. He said, 'I've no right to ask you to come home, but if you come, you'll be useful to me. To all of us. Because I trust you.'

She never asked why he trusted her. She trusted no one. She did not warn him not to trust her.

Now he explained. 'We're far from safe. Everyone knows the worst is still to come.' He looked at her for a long time, thoughtfully, as if he was having second thoughts about her usefulness. She too appeared to be uncertain of her ability to help him. 'No one's threatening to attack us,' he added, 'Not openly.'

She was visibly relieved.

'Did Smuts tell you why Nasaratt was recalled?'

She shook her head.

He appeared gratified. He smiled and nodded his head. He seemed to admire Nasaratt for keeping his work confidential even from Smuts. It puzzled her. Why would Smuts tell her about Nasaratt's work? She felt uneasy. Was she imagining it or did she sense his admiration for Nasaratt? It discomfited her. While he spoke to her, she thought about the simple way she accepted his promise to kill Nasaratt. Now she doubted his loyalty to her.

He took her into his confidence. 'We heard about a sensitive document belonging to our enemies. A cell was sent to find it. When we heard the document went missing we celebrated thinking our cell had it. But it wasn't brought to us. Now we suspect the thief is one of us but is not with us.'

'Meaning?' she asked.

'You're innocent, Pragashini. You think there's two sides in a struggle?' He shook his head and smiled ruefully. 'Ikona! Politics is a box with a triangle on top of the box. We're the grassroots, jumping about in the box wanting to get out and be heard. In the triangle, the sides oppose each other. People at the base are keeping the rest of us in the box. At the tip of the triangle where the points meet the pressure is hardest. The leaders struggle. But the greatest struggle is at the base. The people at the base push the sides away. Even governments are triangles. People from the sides may work underground, and at the base, to undermine the opposing sides. At the base people move from one side to the other. There's the danger.'

'Nasaratt?' she asked.

'He was in the cell recalled to find the document. We suspect him too.'

'Smuts' comrade?'

'Comrades, collaborators, double agents.' He shrugged.

The idea of collaborators intrigued her. There were possibly many unanswered questions puzzling the majority in South Africa. She herself was plagued by the question 'who betrayed Steve Biko?' Biko was travelling in a car from a secret meeting in the western cape when the police put up a roadblock and stopped the car he was travelling in. How did they know he was travelling by car, on that day, at that time of night? How did they know he was on that road?

She remembered the incident of a man who was in hiding from the police. He was sleeping rough, moving around from house to house, taking refuge and food where it was offered. For months he was able to avoid his pursuers. Then his birthday approached. Someone arranged for his wife and children to meet him in a secret rendezvous to wish him and take gifts and a cake to him. The meeting took place. The children were overjoyed to see their father. They exchanged kisses and gifts. While they were together, however, Special Branch turned up and arrested him. How did they know he had made that arrangement? How did they know where he was meeting his family? In the area where he was hiding, only his own people could have informed on him. She supposed there were many such betrayals. Most South Africans would want to get their hands on a document that might reveal such secrets.

'One person can't go through the whole country nosing about for a stolen document,' he said. 'This document is hot. People are out there killing off anyone they suspect wants it.'

'You're asking me?'

'I feel ashamed. I never told Mellikhaya. I kept him out of it. I never wanted to place him at risk. I believed Smuts was already dead. Mellikhaya knew nothing. Still they killed him. For sure Mellikhaya's death was to do with that document. Only the devil knows how they came to suspect him. All I know is Mellikhaya worked in one of the departments. If they suspected Mellikhaya saw that document then that document is in one of the departments in Bisho.'

'And you're asking me?'

'No one will suspect you. You're a Biologist. You can pretend you don't know a word of Afrikaans or Xhosa. You'll get away with it. You're married to Nasaratt. You're staying with the Nasaratts. They're trusted. Only we suspect him.'

She was horrified. She considered him her friend and protector. She chastised herself. She would not stay on. Her thesis and theory were in the balance. Her department phoned to say she could meet her examiners in six months time. She would leave soon. She was not competent to do anything about collaborators or missing documents. Whoever suspects Nasaratt will suspect her. If they suspected Mellikhaya they would suspect her because of her contact with Matatiele. She was innocent of all this.

'Nasaratt was sent on a wild goose chase. A handful of others' – he clenched his fist to indicate the tight security of the cell – 'are searching for printed papers. They're breaking into people's houses and searching. There's talk the original document is on a computer. The new public services are in

Bisho. The old police buildings in Bisho may be used for the new Legislature. They're using computers left over from the old administration and the elections. Impimpis have already infiltrated public services and are searching for the document themselves. Someone's got to go there and find it before they do. We need trusted comrades who won't keep the document for themselves.'

'No!'

'No one will suspect you. You know about computers. We'll create a cover for you, so you can search every computer. We'll give you a job working on computers.'

'No!'

'Whoever gets their hands on this document can control the province. Even control our country. Cause instability. Weaken democracy. The province is split. Ciskei. Transkei. Old Eastern Cape. There's bad democracy, you know, baby.' He laughed at her again.

'You can draw up a list of your suspects!'

'Suspects? Without proof? Ikona. The document is proof.'

'How will I recognise this document?' she asked.

'Only the devil knows. Whatever you find, bring it out. There's one thing. For sure it will be marked Special Branch or Official Secrets or Top Secret. It will be hard to find.'

'Special Branch still operating here?' she asked.

He slapped his hand to his forehead and shook his head, smiling at her. "I give up! You're a baby, Pragashini!'

Throughout her time in exile Matatiele was one person who gave her the support a parent should have given her. She touched her faded scarf. She felt inclined to help him.

'Can't you look for work in Bisho? Apply for any post. Our people are on the interview panels. They'll accept you. If you pretend you don't understand Afrikaans and Xhosa they'll speak freely in your presence. Just don't trust anyone. You'll get your revenge against Nasaratt this way, without killing.'

She told him she would think about it and decide later. She visited Shell House to learn when Nasaratt would surface. She checked the tourist hotels without success. In Johannesburg, she was in conflict about visiting her parents. It was a short flight to Durban. She flew instead to Kimberley.

There she visited family who showed her a mulberry tree they said she played in as a child. They told her she became ill from eating its fruit. Its significance would be explained later. From Kimberley she flew to Cape Town then back to Port Elizabeth. She stopped over in four provinces, the Eastern, Northern and Western Cape, and Gauteng. Five remained for her to visit.

***

14.

Mellikhaya's memorial service was held before he was buried. Matatiele refused to allow the burial and would give no reason to the elders in the clan, saying he had appeased Mellikhaya's spirit and placated their ancestral spirits.

The memorial was a prelude to accommodate mourners afraid to enter New Brighton. The township was a no-go area. Non-African colleagues and friends would attend the service in the city centre; Africans would attend the funeral whenever it took place - in New Brighton.

The fearful mourners were bolstered by the news that they were not alone. Even florists in iBhayi joined their ranks. Telephoned orders for flowers and wreaths from the friends of Smuts and Heather in England to florists in the city refused to deliver to the Matatiele's home in New Brighton. The drivers dare not enter no-go areas.

Despite Smuts fury there was little he could do. Heather saw the bright side. It was a good thing she conceded, because it would cost fifty pounds in sterling that converted to five hundred Rand – at least. She had no idea how many flowers that would buy and imagined it would be a truck load. 'Our friends will be cheated, never mind drivers and no-go-areas.'

But the drivers employed by Mellikhaya's employer put the florists to shame. Undaunted they volunteered to drive half a dozen cars laid on by Mellikhaya's employer to transport the entire Matatiele clan from New Brighton to the city during the lunch hour on that Wednesday.

Having left the country as a young lad, Smuts was as confused as Heather by the events. Both had concepts of memorial services held on the anniversary of the death. But Pragashini told tales about Indian families in mourning abstaining from meat and alcohol for several weeks, even forbidding the radio and television from being switched on during the period of mourning. A religious service would only be held to declare the mourning period over.

Smuts was anxious for the funeral to go ahead. That was what he had come for. He did not want the elections to overshadow the funeral, as it was bound to do. When pressed, his father hedged about the date, and by way of throwing him off the track, hinted that Heather might have to adjust to tradition when the time for the funeral arrived. Smuts told her this and they speculated about what he meant. She prepared for the memorial service with a degree of trepidation.

The hall in the city was empty when Smuts arrived but the rows of chairs soon filled up. On entering he received a programme printed on pastel shades of copier paper. Smuts looked at the programme. This was new and strange. There was a photograph of Mellikhaya on the cover with the year of his birth and death and with computer generated images of doves and flowers decorating the page. Inside was Mellikhaya's life story, where he was born, his parents' names, the primary and secondary schools he attended. He fathered a child and died without marrying. The programme also contained the words of hymns, and the names of various speakers. Smuts' name was excluded.

On stage were three tables draped with black tablecloths on which stood vases of fresh yellow chrysanthemums and three microphones. A video camera balanced on a tripod stood to one side.

It was a working day. Many people were dressed for work in blue overalls or grey dust jackets. Other men wore black. Women wore colourful dresses and hats.

The speakers took their places behind the black draped table. A man operated the video. A master of ceremonies took centre stage. Each person on the stage was given the opportunity to speak. A mourner in the hall impulsively interrupted a speaker by standing up and singing a verse from a hymn or freedom song at which signal the assembly rose and sang together, then subsided onto their chairs when the speaker formed a 'T' with his hands.

Representatives of Mellikhaya's soccer team praised him and narrated anecdotes about him. Friends from his school days made speeches. His girl friends read out their poems of love to him. A shop steward spoke about the benefits of belonging to a trade union. There was a death benefit of a few thousand Rand to the family because Mellikhaya had been a member. A politician stood up and spoke about the forthcoming elections. The politician encouraged people to be disciplined and to vote. He urged those without the correct documents to apply for identity documents, to familiarise themselves with voting procedures, to find out where the polling stations would be to avoid frustration at future elections.

The assembly cheered, forgetting the purpose of the gathering. They jumped up from their seats, danced and clapped hands, singing political songs, chanting, 'Long Live! Long Live!' Then they became subdued once again, they settled down and the sombre mood took hold of them once more.

A man in his sixties, apparently a reverend minister of the church, dressed in a yellow suit, a black shirt, and white tie, without a dog collar, began to preach. The Reverend held the Bible in his left hand and made an impassioned speech. He repeated certain words, 'Dumisani! uThixo! Madoda! uYesu!' Some of the young people covered their mouths to hide their smiles. Others giggled.

Smuts turned to look at his mother, wrapped in the same brown blanket, her head still hidden somewhere in its folds. He put his arm around her. He would never know her heart, the heart of a mother burying her son. He disliked the proceedings. The Reverend cracked a joke. The assembly now laughed openly. Smuts sat in uncomfortable stillness surrounded by jocularity. The Reverend continued with his humour. Then the Reverend saw Heather sitting with the family.

The Reverend pointed a finger at her. 'Someone is not smiling,' he said. The gathering stretched and craned their heads this way and that to locate the miscreant. Heather blushed bright red. She was feeling the discomfit of being the only White person in the front row. The Reverend continued, 'Everyone is smiling. But one person is not smiling. She does not understand what I am saying. Perhaps the good gentleman sitting next to her will translate what I have said.' The Reverend resumed his jocular sermon and finally concluded with the words, 'Your son, your brother, your friend, your lover, will rise again.' Then he sat down

They stood and sang a joyous hymn. Someone gave a vote of thanks to those who arranged the memorial service. Everyone prepared to leave the hall. Heather rose with

Smuts. The Reverend rushed down from the stage to walk with her. 'I hope you weren't left behind by all that,' he said. Heather was embarrassed, pushing her hair from her eyes.

Smuts stepped forward and touched the Reverend's arm. 'Umfundisi',[17] Smuts whispered, 'This is truly a first time for me. To witness mourners laughing at a funeral service. You are at fault, sir, for making people misbehave at my brother's memorial and for making everyone turn to look at my wife. You embarrassed her in this gathering. I feel shame at your conduct, Mlekazi. All the young people here take their behaviour from you. You are an elder to us, sir, not a child.'

The Reverend was abashed. 'I apologise', he said, taking Smuts hands in his.

Smuts emerged into the sunlight with Heather. The family stood together. People shook his hand. He wondered what was so fearful that his father did not want him to return home; why his father would not bury Mellikhaya. How had Mellikhaya really died?

***

17 Umfundisi is the way a pastor or priest is addressed.

PART TWO

The Snake in the Sun

15.

Dusk. The morning of the first democratic election. Her morning meditation completed Pragashini was the first to emerge from the Nasaratts' home. She stood on the doorstep confounded by the stillness where noise and loudness were kings, searching for a heavenly sign that this day differed from every other day in their history. Then she looked up at the sky. She found nothing but eerie quiet, black sky, retreating stars, crisp air. No more. Nothing exceptional. Nothing to show that this time round there would be no qualified franchise as there had been in the early twentieth century under British rule. No separate voters roll for Coloureds and Indians. No total exclusion of African, Coloured, and Indian voters. No votes for Houses of Representatives and Delegates. No blood red sky.

Today they were presumed equal: Women with men, African with Coloured with Indian with White; and every other pencil defining category apartheid dreamed up. Today it would be 'One ID, one vote'. From then on every experience would be new, fresh, never before enjoyed. She sensed communion with every election officer standing under the same night sky in a kind of dream, making their way to their polling stations, on foot, on bicycles, in taxis, and cars, and buses. Rural voters were preparing to trek the distance to put their thumbprint on the ballot paper. Somewhere in Africa the man they married her to was also possibly considering the awesome power of this day about to dawn.

Since Nasaratt left England, she had no contact with him. To her his leaving her in England, even though she was in hiding, was the most powerful statement of her strength. Now she would no longer run away and hide from him. This time round she would not be dragged anywhere against her will. Whereas the majority of exiles returned home for the elections, and to be with family and friends, she returned for vengeance, nothing else. She had held everyone at bay with her personal satyagraha: silence, solitude, and shaved head.

Her religion did not encourage hatred for anyone, but neither did it give her lessons in loving her enemies. The words were there in the scriptures but there were no Vedic thumping missionaries along her way preaching to her. She heard secondary news reported from comrades of where Nasaratt was last sighted. He might know she was back in South Africa or be ignorant of the fact. She interpreted his leaving England without her was a signal of the end of their short life together, but suspected that was not the end. She was a young woman who had been a commodity item bartered over by her father and Nasaratt. She believed a woman should not leave a marriage while she is pregnant, depressed, ill in any way, or incapable of standing on her own two feet. She should walk out like a lion stands up over its kill.

But she had hidden in fear from Nasaratt while she lived in England. Now she wanted to confront him in his parents' home. She had no idea how she would do that, or how the Nasaratts would react. That was the reason she was home. The other, Matatiele's, was secondary, the killing questionable.

The front door opened behind her and Roshni, Nasaratt's sister, came out on to the steps and stood beside her without greeting or acknowledgement. Pragashini felt Roshni's thin arm around her shoulders. Together they stood in silence looking at the sky. There was little to be said. What could they talk about? What could anyone? How many people were standing like them under the sky in wonderment at the events that would unfold that day?

Pragashini's thoughts were with relatives and friends who had died missing this turnaround in their history. That was their karma. They were not meant to be here. Many exiles could not return. It required struggle and adaptation to survive exile and move on with their lives away from the despicable experience of apartheid. Even she was not meant to be here. Months ago, she was in York sitting in a laboratory intending to live there. This was her karma. She wished she could be like those who could forgive everyone, even those foreigners who had continued their relationship with her country as if it was just a misunderstood juvenile. She wished she could pardon the privileged Whites who retained their beach and braai lifestyle throughout the struggle years, who studied and holidayed abroad, and will remain here unaffected after today, and be welcomed overseas as sufferers of Black injustice should they choose to leave. She, on the other hand, was nowhere near to the road that led to becoming like the leadership: she could not forgive. Without wishing to, she cried. Roshni brought her close and held her.

Suddenly from out of the darkness and stillness, she heard the noise of crying kiewietjies[18], heralding the suns imminent rise. Without saying a word, Roshni separated from her and moved to unlock the car. She opened the boot, put some items in, banged it shut. Pragashini shook herself free of her thoughts and climbed into the passenger's seat. They buckled up and set off.

Roshni drove slowly out of the Indian suburb and towards the streets of the notorious northern suburbs. 'You don't want to know how we arrived at this', she said. 'Teachers, doctors, lawyers, dentists, business people – forced to live cheek by jowl with pimps, drug pushers, drunks, vagrants, prostitutes, murderers lumped together in areas designated Indian or Coloured. Drunken women and street urchins who never go to school but play in the street all day, are being raped somewhere here in the darkness.'

There was bitterness in Roshni's voice that gave Pragashini

---

18 Kiewietjie is a crowned plover.

the sense there might be sympathy for her if she confided in her about Nasaratt. 'To separate the rich from the poor is a form of apartheid,' Pragashini said. 'You're another one who needs reconciliation. It isn't just the architects of apartheid, the police, the officials of the Group Areas Board, the prison warders, and Special Branch, who need to ask forgiveness, to reconcile. Not just every White, man and woman. Even we need to ask forgiveness of the dead ancestors of the Africans, because we benefited from apartheid. Apartheid's officials acted on behalf of the white population, but there was a scale of differences, we others were not as badly treated.'

Now the rough streets of the northern areas were quiet and peaceful.

'That's what you think. After you left they began hounding us out of our homes', Roshni said. 'Frightening,' she added, 'when families began moving out. They despaired. They gave up resistance. Here only one family refused to move. An Indian lady still lives in her home. In Cape Town an elderly Indian lady refused to budge. Others were given a choice', said Roshni. 'To be Indian or Coloured,' she added. 'The Malays, the Chinese, the Indians, the Africans, I think. You'd have one man deciding his entire family should be Coloured, his brother remaining Indian with his family.'

'It's our racism we have to address. Between ourselves, Indians, Coloureds, and Africans', Pragashini said.

'When you left the separate areas weren't created.'

'That's why it's hard for me moving around the city.' Now she made a note of landmarks for the various turns Roshni made. Muhalla Asha was built on a hill next to a quarry. The quarry was believed to trigger asthma in Indian children. They drove down from the hill and passed the local Madressa where the Muslim children in her family rote learnt the Koran. They came towards playing fields where she and Smuts met that were just a plot of land grassed over, and saw one Christian church on the left, another just visible in the back street. Nearby was the Hindu temple where her nieces sang. They drove down pass the local video shop.

Roshni pointed to what she called 'designer house shops'. These were the lounge or dining rooms of a house or a garage adjoining a house converted into a shop. 'A desperate last resort for our frustrated Indian business class. They were beaten down into submission by the government on one side and a jealous underclass snapping at their ankles on the other side. One day the ruffians marched on Indian shops and set fire to them in the trading area. The Indians retreated to their homes with whatever goods they could salvage. They set up shop here.'

'Our history is ugly,' she said.

'Whose is beautiful? That isn't the issue. No one learns from history,' said Roshni. 'After the fires were doused, the drunks sobered, and the shopkeepers returned to salvage what they could, the perpetrators said someone put them up to it. Come tomorrow we'll all be puppets of some other puppet master.' She put out her hand to touch Roshni's.

'You're alright,' Roshni said. 'You can go to England. We have to stay here. Indians are vulnerable in Africa. I don't see a future for us in Africa, after Mandela and the Robben Islanders die. We'll be kicked out of Africa, like the Ugandan Asians. Just wait and see. I'm afraid, Pragashini.'

'What can I say to ease your fears? How can anyone create opportunities for the races to know each other and to feel they belong in Africa? Even before apartheid the races were separate with only some mixing. Apartheid widened the gulf. It's too late.'

They passed the BP filling station where they had to make a final turn, then up the hill to the school gates where they were confronted by uniformed white soldiers brandishing AK47's. Forewarned Pragashini and Roshni betrayed no sign of apprehension. To them the soldiers were mute shadows from the past. Their AK47's waved them in, as if the soldiers themselves were dumbfounded. Shell shocked. The boot of their car remained locked. The miracle was in motion.

Roshni moved the car into the pre-dawn playground. The headlamps lighted up uniformed soldiers in camouflage gear at every turn. When she parked the car, they alighted. She retrieved a picnic basket from the boot, - as if they were going picnicking in the woods, - and they walked through the darkness, conscious of soldiers all around them, a dimly lit building acting as their beacon in what was for them the twilight between apartheid and freedom. For Pragashini it was a phantasm.

They entered the building and made their way into a dimly lit classroom in a school. It was meanly furnished. One of the bulbs was fused giving the room the appearance of what people called a seedy joint. It was nothing like the laboratory where she spent her days. A dozen silent people in the room were seated at meagre tables ritually peeling Inkatha Freedom Party stickers from a sheet and pasting them into a book of ballot papers – with difficulty. The ballot books were thick. It required one person to hold the book open, another to do the pasting. Because they were under pressure of time to prepare and have ready sufficient ballot papers when the doors opened, each worked without the required help. Roshni and Pragashini found their tables and set to work. They had attended training sessions together.

Pragashini knew most of the people in the room. For those she did not know, Roshni gave a family history. She is so-and-so's sister. He was married to so-and-so's sister. A couple of retired schoolteachers. Old school friends. Housewives. Shopkeepers. Students. School secretary. Unemployed youth. Other returned exiles. She was touched by the feeling of a miracle happening with each one of them brought under its light. No one was excluded. They could not be excluded. It was there for them to be touched by, if they were open to it. They sat like ghost workers, silent, in the dimness, in a surreal landscape, working ritually. Later she would learn that a ghost worker was someone who came into work, took off his jacket, hung it over his chair, then went out to drink, shop, go to the beach, womanise, and return at five to pick up his coat, and still receive his salary each month.

She thought about the yellowing female Neanderthal skull waiting in its box for her to examine, draw and label; of her theory of evolution needing organisation and systematic argument. Years of effort put aside because Nasaratt had obstructed her goal.

At seven in the morning, an official bustled into the room reporting that voters were already queuing in the gloom. She closed her eyes unable to believe she was home, here in the room at the moment when her own family, her friends, her community, would come forward to cast their vote for the first time in their lives.

The struggle was over. The impetus, the passion, the motive that fired up their breath for life, was gone, put to rest like a tormented spirit that haunted each one of them these past centuries, since the moment the first European touched the Cape, oppressed the Africans, brought into being Coloureds and Afrikaners and imported Indian and Chinese labourers.

She turned her attention to the election proceedings. A few minutes before the polling station was to be opened the presiding officer called them to attention. The ballot boxes were sealed. They were called to stand together in a circle and to hold hands while someone prayed aloud for the elections to be conducted without incident. They prayed for the election to be a success; to end without a hitch; for everyone to cast a vote; for all the boxes to be safely sealed; to be delivered intact to the counting stations; all to be accounted for; all ballot papers to be counted; for the elections to be declared 'free and fair' by the international community.

She knew this scene was being enacted thousands of times in every polling station in the country. And in this city from Muhalla Asha, through Gelvandale, Lake View, Sidwell, Fair View, South End, Kwazakele, Schauder Township, Gelvan Park, New Brighton, North End, High Field Road, Noord Einde, Kragga Khamma, Humewood, Walmer, Newton Park, Motherwell, Forest Hill, and countless other separate areas created while she was in exile. At the conclusion of the prayer they hugged each other, with tears in their eyes.

They were the first to cast their votes using fat pencils tied with rough string. She stood aside trembling while the officials flung the doors wide open and the first voters stepped with trepidation into the room. She could not believe she was here. At other stations in the country there were White voters accustomed from the age of eighteen to vote. People coming to this polling station and to thousands across the country, had never voted before in their lives. Many were unconditionally illiterate. Others were literate in one of the eleven official languages.

The voting process was adapted to accommodate the illiterate. Each voter required an identity document which was a development of the Indian Pass[19] and later the Domboek[20]. There was a variety of identity documents in circulation. Each voter's document was checked, each hand was tested with a machine that revealed whether the voter had already voted, each hand was then marked with indelible ink. The voter was then given a ballot form, instructed how to fold the form,

19 Indian Pass under Act 28, 1897 under which Indians carried a pass to move from one colony to another in SA.

20 Domboek is another name for the Reference Book (an identity document) that Africans were obliged to carry.

before proceeding to the booth. The procedure was followed for every voter.

The voters wanted to appear serious and dignified, to be respected. They wanted to be sober on the day. They would most probably be babbelaas[21] tomorrow but today was the day thousands had died for. It was for the dead that everyone was sober that day.

The morning grew light. Then warm. A stream of people continued through the doors: the poor, the blind, the barefoot, the disabled, the elderly, the pregnant, women with toddlers, nursing mothers, people in wheelchairs, the youth, nurses in uniform, waiters, doormen, taxi drivers, amidst conflicting rumours that the Inkatha Freedom Party were, and then were not, participating in the elections. Roshni's aunt, called 'Hungie' meaning the fifth born, a dark small woman who could read without spectacles, was the oldest voter, aged ninety-four. She queued up like everyone else and cast her vote.

By mid-morning the school lavatories were blocked. Outside, voters fainted in the heat. Inside voters stopped constantly to embrace one or more returned exiles. People stopped at her table, smiling demurely, waiting for her to recognize them. Helicopters from the world hovered overhead for a bird's eye view of the snake in thc hot sun, making its way towards unity of the people.

Throughout the day, the polling officers added the stickers of the IFP to the ballot papers. A white policeman attempted to cross the line into the zoned area still wearing his gun and was unceremoniously evicted by the election officers to the cheers of the voting queue.

By teatime the ballot papers ran out. Hurried telephone calls were made to the other polling stations. The queue waited for

---

21 Babbelaas is to be drunk.

ballot papers.

***

16.

For this nation of singing, jiving, stomping, toyi-toyi-ing, chanting voters the day was quiet, calm, dignified. It was Smuts who came hurrying from somewhere with ballot books while the voters waited with dignity for the IFP stickers to be added. Even he was affected by karma, Pragashini concluded. It ruled that he should be here for the elections when he had reconciled himself to voting by proxy from London.

Other polling stations were also running out of ballot papers. By evening voters were bussed in from another polling station where the papers had run out.

She was seated at a table explaining to each voter how the ballot paper should be folded. The paper would be invalidated if the mark were shown. There was still an endless stream of people entering smiling at her, nodding their understanding, fumbling with the long ballot paper, shuffling away to the polling booth. Because of the high numbers of illiterate voters, there were no words on the ballot paper merely the symbols for each political party.

She hoped someone would come in and whisper they had seen Nasaratt somewhere, because she had been back for weeks now and the Nasaratts were oblivious of the fact that she had not seen their son for years. She was anxious to deal with his return then return to England.

Hotel staff dressed in short white jackets and maroon waistcoats, from the hotels and guesthouses around the city centre came in to vote when they came off duty. She looked around at the international observers, who could not experience the full impact of the day as South Africans did. They must feel the heat; but not the euphoria; not that sense of pride; that unsuppressed joy; that dignity as they waited patiently in the queue. They were observers. Not participants. They had nothing to compare this day with. Many Europeans did not exercise their right to vote in Europe.

Then at some indefinable moment in the heat, the contained emotion, the suppressed euphoria, the monotonous repetition of words and actions, Pragashini looked up and there he was in the middle of the room. Not Nasaratt. But another man. Her sprit surged. Another man possessing her the instant her eyes rested on him; looking a bit lost; directed towards table one, proffering his ID document; having his hand tested; finger-printed; striding towards her table; looming over her; listening to her garbled explanation of how to fold the paper; turning away with his ballot paper; walking to the polling booth; half hidden from her view; emerging; dropping the form into the ballot box; sidling between the officers standing lost in the room; making for the exit.

From the instant her eyes first lighted on him her spirit soared, out of control. She became like someone possessed. Exuberance filled her with every breath she took. She could not take her eyes from him. She stood up, propelled by a force she could not stop, moving in the direction he took, rushing after him, brushing past people, down the school corridors, through the doors, across the quadrangle, desperate to reach him, calling out to him to stop, stop, stop, until she caught up with him.

He glanced back at her. Stopped. Turned to face her. Then he smiled. His smile disarmed her. She slowed down. She stopped. The joy of recognition was unsurpassed by anything she had ever experienced. This unanticipated meeting in this tiny suburb, in this huge manufacturing city, was miraculous. She recognised him. She knew him. His name, she searched for his name. Yet her memory could not come up with his name. She could not move. His eyes opened wide as if he too recognized her. She stared at him. A tanned handsome face.

Green eyes. Pale brown hair. She gazed into his eyes. She could not speak. Her certainty about him diminishing the longer she looked into his face.

He raised his eyebrows. His face was close to her. His eyes looked into hers, searching. 'Do I know you?' he asked. There was temerity in his voice. She could not move, not even to nod or shake her head. Then his lips softened as they formed the words, 'I'm Mossel Klein,' he said. 'For just a moment there, I could've sworn I knew you from somewhere.'

And it was over. He did not know her. She did not know him. She doubted ever having seen him in her life. She did not know what had possessed her. Yet unbelievably her spirit continued to surge. Her spirit relished the thrill of recognition although she herself did not know him.

Then he was grinning at her, his green eyes sparkling. He was handsome. 'Foolish me,' he said. 'I could never forget a face like yours.'

She took a little step back. Her body went cold. The warmth of the miracle touching the people voting for the first time, the inner joy and warmth of recognising him, was offset by a coldness touching her body. Like a cold evil spirit had touched her body and cast a spell over her. Tears welled in her eyes. She could not explain why. Her people had the habit of becoming emotional over the powerful events taking place in their time. She was becoming like them. The years of exile scarcely changed her. But coming home did. Recognising this made her cry more. She turned and walked blindly back to the polling station, tears running down her cheeks. She did not observe how the voting ended.

That night friends and relatives came home to sit up through the night and watch videos until the results came in. They waited for breaking news of the election results. They related accounts of what transpired that day in the long winding queues. Each had vivid incidents to recount. All the political parties wanted to witness the voting of blind voters. The panic when the ballot boxes were full and they had no more. Voting with pencils amazed everyone who had never voted before. Caught up in the exhilaration of the day's events, they did not observe her mood.

Her world stopped from the moment she saw him. Seeing his face, recognising something when she looked into his eyes, but not recognising the man himself. The joy of recognition. That inner exuberance was still with her. The question of who he was did not take up space in her mind. The prospect of whether or not she would see him again was not a fear or desire for her. It was merely the recognition that was not of the physical man but of his spirit, that filled her with joy.

When she looked into the mirror that night her eyes glowed from an inner light. She performed the ritual of cleansing and meditating aware of the surging of her spirit within her, conscious for the first time of the existence of her spirit as a separate entity from her, whose experience of joy and bliss was independent of hers. If her body were to be in excruciating pain at that moment, her spirit would have maintained its exuberance. She had no doubt that her spirit knew something, had knowledge of something, which she did not know. This separation of her spirit and body, the experience of it was new to her. She could not predict what it would lead to. All she was certain of was that she knew this man, who called himself Mossel Klein.

Was this what her dream prepared her for? This strange meeting? Or was there something else to follow? In the past, each time something happened, she thought this must be it. This was what her strange dream was a premonition of. When nothing transpired she anticipated another event. With the next event, she said, this must be it. When the man who married her frustrated her research, she believed that was the dream's warning. Yet here was something else. Was it never ending? Will she ever know the meaning of her recurring dream?

***

The Recluse: Pragashini's Journal

17.

It was I who recognised him. I *knew him.* I *loved him. I found him without searching. I looked into his eyes and saw his soul. He is the man I love. I was unprepared for my recognition of him.*

For an instant it was there. I saw it in his eyes. His soul's recognition of me. Then it was snuffed out. Like the wind blowing and the flame dying. In that instant his soul died. He looked into my eyes and saw my soul for a second or two, then the light went out and he saw nothing. To me it was as if I looked at a stranger. He looked but could not see into my soul. Not seeing, he could not remember the love we shared. He and I are linked over a lifetime. He is the man I loved in another life.

It hurts, his failure to remember me. How was this possible? If I could recognise him why could he not recognise me? Oh my love. What has happened to you? Why are you asleep? What has happened to your soul? Why is your soul asleep?

Then I remembered his suffering. I recalled the pain they inflicted on him. The torment he endured. Is this the result? Am I permanently erased from his memory? Oh my love what have they done to you? Is this the death of your soul?

Today I know at last why I am here. This day of the South African elections. At last I know why I am here. Why I am with Pragashini. The question I asked myself for years. Why am I here? What am I doing here? What am I meant to do here? I have nothing in common with an Indian girl in South Africa. So I waited. I watched like a guardian angel, watching over a Hindu girl. I could not understand life or the soul. Throughout the years nothing happened.

Suddenly she went to Europe. How I feared being there. For that had been my home. There I relived all the memories of my past. Yet there was no one there that she loved. I sighed with relief, believing the danger was past. However, when she began praying, loving her prayer room, making a daily devotion, morning, and night, I trembled for her. When she shaved her head, I could not believe what I was seeing. It appalled me. When she took to the veil, I feared for her and for any man she was to fall in love with. She was repeating my actions.

However, when nothing happened in Europe I concluded my past life has nothing to do with this girl's present life. My presence with her will not impinge on her life. My being here is the next stage in the life of the soul. Perhaps it is to appease what I suffered in the past. So I watched. I learned, this time without waiting for anything eventful in her life.

When she returned to South Africa I was relieved. I relaxed. This is what life is. The passage of the soul from one life to the next I have experienced. I was learning about the soul. It has a life of its own. I am here to learn.

But this meeting is traumatic. Europe did not bring about this meeting. It was meant to happen in South Africa. Why?

For years I subdued my soul. I puzzled over my presence in this girl's life. I wondered if it was my fate to be passive and calm, to stop clamouring for the love of the man I adored. Was that why I was here? Never in all the years I have been here did I ever imagine I would meet him again. I never contemplated the possibility. I never looked for him in the eyes of anyone I ever met. I only knew who I was. I only knew what I had lived through. I knew only of my love for this one man. I knew how our love ended. I have been present here for years. I have remained dumb, accepting my destiny, unwilling to change it. Not knowing how to change it. Watching over Pragashini. Waiting. Uncertain of what role I am to play in the present. Not even seeking for answers, not interfering in the lives of the people around.

'Now today, on this historic day, this day that speaks of one word

– freedom – for millions of oppressed people that I have no connection with – on this day I come face to face with the soul of the man I have loved with my body and my soul. What am I supposed to do now? Oh my God help me.

***

PART THREE

New Day Dawning

18.

New day dawning. While the nation of first time voters were having a lie-in after the drunken street carousing and partying that lasted all night, Astrid Roebuck sat up in bed. While the sober were checking and counting the ballot papers she slipped her arms into a pink hand crocheted bed jacket hanging on her bedpost, reached for her spectacles, telephone, and phonebook, then systematically telephoned every one of her friends, African, Coloured, Indian and European, and invited them to a party at her home in the white suburb where she lived. The invitation was for Saturday late afternoon and into the night.

Her friends were slightly bemused and not too keen to plan the weekend. She was a refined, dignified lady and they anticipated a genteel celebration of tea and cake, when they had a collective desire to get blindly drunk again, carouse the streets of the northern suburbs, to the Mayor's Garden, knock on doors, sing the Cape Christmas songs, "January, February, March, April, May, June, July", rattle tin cans filled with pebbles, and lose themselves in the new South Africa. But who had the heart to tell Astrid this?

She was renowned for standing in silent protest outside City Hall in the rain with other Black Sash women; for raising money for the families of all categories of prisoners by baking biscuits and cakes; making dainty little items for the church bazaars; and keeping a loaf of sliced peanut buttered bread in her kitchen ready for any child who came begging at her door: 'Stukkie[22] brood[23] missus?' Who had the heart to refuse? Her friends accepted her invitation.

Except Nalini. 'You caught me napping,' Nalini said. 'I've

---

22 Stukkie means 'a piece of.'

23 brood is bread.

actually got a pain in my heart. I'm so heart sore. You're one jump ahead of me.'

The friendship between them went back half a century. When they first saw each other the one was like a thief caught in the place not belonging to her; the other like a fish trying to move on land. Nalini took to visiting the local Catholic Church after early morning mass on weekdays, never on a Sunday. She slipped into the church when mass was over and the handful of worshippers were walking home. Usually only a nun she later discovered was called Sister Sacristy was in the church, genuflecting each time she passed the tabernacle. Nalini went softly into the church. The nun may have glimpsed her. She always covered her head with the pallav[24] because she respected the holy place, but it also gave her anonymity. Like a shadow she floated to the statue of the mother of Christ draped in blue, and whispered Hindu prayers, begging the Mother for a child, a son, a miracle.

Astrid glimpsed the sari clad woman one morning while rushing back into church to retrieve her St Andrew's missal inadvertently left in the pew. She was interested and curious, but Nalini bowed her head, closed her eyes, and took protection under her pallav. After that first glimpse, Astrid lingered in church after mass, trying to see the face, creating opportunities for Nalini to look at her, willing the other woman to accept her friendship. She observed Nalini's daily devotion, then her pregnancy, and finally the baby Anand, brought into the church and placed at the feet of the statue of Our Lady.

Astrid bought a medal of Our Lady of Vellangani[25] and gave it to Nalini to pin to the baby's clothes. She showed her

---

24 Pallav is the loose end of the sari that can be draped over the head.

25 Vellangani is a place of pilgrimage on the southern coast of India.

a little holy picture. Nalini was touched. For the first time since stepping tentatively into the Church a year ago, seeing this Mother of Christ draped in a sari, Nalini stopped believing she was an intruder in the church. Astrid told her there were other shrines around the world besides Lourdes and Fatima. Even India had its shrine to the Mother of Christ.

Smiling Nalini accepted the gift, fumbled with the gold pin and pinned it to the baby's bib. Through the birth of Anand, the two women became friends. Their friendship developed. Astrid confided her deepest secrets to Nalini. They became inseparable.

But there was a secret at the heart of their friendship; they referred to in little asides only they understood.

When Pragashini met them she described their friendship as the intertwining of a vibrant climbing rose into the branches of a deciduous tree. Nalini was the Indian matriarch, and Astrid the English lady. The rose with its thorns, the tree with its seasons of vigour and rest.

However, as their friendship deepened, it appeared to friends and family in the Indian and English communities that each held the other in contempt. Astrid seemed perpetually trying to prove she was not prejudiced, while Nalini appeared to doubt her friend's sincerity in the game they played when in company. Both knew and alluded to the reasons in their chitchat, but they held it secret from the rest of the family and the community. Their friendship continued through the years of separate development, apartheid, Anand's two marriages, his departure from South Africa, and the return of the exiles in the period preceding and surrounding the elections.

Over the years the two friends vied with each other to gain one-up-man-ship. Nalini, because of the status she enjoyed at home, considered herself westernised. She was at pains to demonstrate she was a little more knowledgeable about the modern world than a peasant stepping down from a mountain village in India. Astrid was under pressure to show and convince her friend that her own manners and outlook were not superior. The skirmish to host the election party became such a tussle. Astrid was shrewd enough that early in the morning to place her closest friend's invitation at the end of her list, after everyone else had accepted with good grace.

Unfortunately the entire Nasaratt family were unwilling to accept the invitation. Nalini was therefore, despatched carrying a bribe: a dish of freshly prepared biriyani, cooked in ghee and sour milk, with cardamoms and cashew nuts - the only spicy dish Astrid professed to tolerate. Over the years the peace offering worked. It softened her. If she had taken offence at something said about her English habits, she pardoned the offender. If she complained that they excluded her from their conversation by speaking in the many languages married into the family they promised never to do it again. Yet it was this bribery so willingly accepted by Astrid that caused family and friends to doubt the true worth and integrity of Nalini's friend. In South Africa your right hand could betray your left they said.

The day after the elections the bribe failed. While Astrid spread a hand embroidered table cloth and set out two gold rimmed plates on the little table that stood in one corner of the living room, Nalini set to dissuading her from hosting the party. While they ate she was bold enough to suggest Astrid come home with her where everyone was busy preparing for a party.

'Young people know how to do these things. We two can lounge on the grass. You can drink sherry. I'll drink port. We'll just hang about checking how they're getting on,' she said, 'and there's champagne,' she added, bemoaning the fact that she wanted to give a decent celebration for her long lost son's return, hoping to alert her friend to the sensitive nature of the matter of the party. She was expecting Anand to return home now the elections were over.

Astrid would not hear of it. She stood up to fetch filtered water from the fridge. Returning with the jug she said, 'Everyone agreed to come. I can't back out now. What's more I was the first to invite them.'

Nalini said, 'Am I to blame? Are you holding it against me because I'm too old to arrange a party first thing in the morning? Is it my fault that son of mine is keeping his arrival a secret? You've got no idea how hard he is to pin down to a time and place. It's wrong for someone else to throw a party to welcome him home. I should be the first. It's my duty.'

'This isn't for Anand. It's for victory.'

'So you don't like the idea? A party for my son? He's not important enough? How's about a party when Mandela's in town?'

'What a question! The community will give a party when Mandela's in town. Let's compromise. You give a party when Anand comes home. I'll give the victory party.'

'People want a good time. They don't want to be sitting round the table sipping hot tea.'

'Then I'll have my party here. You have yours there. Our guests can move from my place to yours. How does that suit you?'

'Then you won't come to mine and I won't come to yours.'

'You should be happy I want to throw a party. I can't think of any of my neighbours celebrating the elections. They're probably listening to the World Service to get the feel for the new nation. They'll take their lead from London rather than what's happening in their own street. Think about it. Won't it generate a good feeling to know that at least one

White person is genuinely celebrating the election victory?'

'That's not how I see it.'

'It's all a game, Nalini. Play along. There's no harm in it.'

'It won't seem right, all of us traipsing over here to celebrate our victory in a White area. We'll have to hire a bus. It would be like ....' and she stopped, her mind going blank. 'Look at that. I can't even think of something to compare it with.'

'Too true! Too true!' said Astrid. 'Because it's never been done! I'll be a trend setter.'

'It's unnatural for an old woman to be a trend setter!'

'Unnatural? What a word! You disappoint me!' She stood up and took her plate to the kitchen sink. Nalini followed her into the kitchen bringing her plate. Astrid began washing her plate under the running tap. She took Nalini 's plate.

'My family will feel uneasy. They're not used to partying in White areas. It's okay for Jo'burg people. But this place has gone down since the seventies.'

'Remember what P.E. was like before Soweto?' But Nalini was unwilling to help her out.

'People were integrated in P.E. until the Nats despatched their hardliners to the Cape,' said Astrid. 'Don't pretend you can't remember. These days an English woman can't befriend an Indian.'

The two women hugged each other. Astrid walked into the lounge, went over to her polished piano, lifted the lid, took a clean yellow dust cloth that was folded in one corner and dusted the keys. Then she sat stiffly on the piano stool and began playing.

Nalini sat back in an armchair and listened and thought back to when they first met. 'You want to forget what you were doing back then,' Nalini warned. 'In the new South Africa you shouldn't talk about it,' she added.

Astrid continued playing. 'I could've ranked up there....' She said. 'I could've been as famous as you know who if only I'd stayed on in Jo'burg. This so-called friendly city, its the nation's stepchild. It used to be the heart of the Cape when the English settlers arrived. Now the nation behaves like a cruel step mother to this place.'

'I wouldn't sing that tune in the new South Africa.'

'I'm not talking about the English language or the British settlers. Just the ambience the place used to have.'

'I think the ambience of house arrest would have been the same in Jo'burg as in P.E. Would they have put you in the same house as someone under house arrest?'

'Don't be clever,' Astrid retorted, then added thoughtfully, 'Do you think Anand remembers me?'

'No-one remembers you, Astrid. Certainly not my children. They were too young,' said Nalini.

'I wonder will the TRC look for me?' asked Astrid.

'Will you come forward?'

'It's a matter to kill for,' said Astrid. 'Today more than ever.'

'Is it worth dying for? Now? There's no need. The struggle's over. You need to keep a low profile my friend. The last thing you want is to draw attention to yourself. You shouldn't be hosting any thing that highlights where you live.'

Astrid stopped playing. 'I'll be alright. I'm just a gentle old lady waiting for the grim reaper.'

'You inviting all your friends?'

'They don't have to come if they don't want to,' said Astrid adding, 'It's a gesture to bring everyone away from the separate areas, to begin integrating, socialising, the way it happens in Jo'burg and Cape Town. Someone's got to make a start here.' She resumed playing.

Nalini was beginning to relent. 'We wanted a braai[26], not a garden party.'

'A braai's fine with me.'

'Someone will want to make a potjie.[27]'

'Let them.'

'God Almighty! When did you ever have a braai?'

'I'll borrow a skottelbraai[28],' said Astrid. 'Is it settled then? You can welcome Anand and his wife whenever he turns up.' She relied on her friendship with Nalini to get her way. Nalini finally gave in to her because she too did not want to hurt her friend's feelings.

'You said you wanted a chance to observe Anand with his wife,' said Astrid.

'Yes, I need to set my mind at ease. I couldn't understand them running away like that. Her coming home without him. Him not meeting her at Jan Smuts. Something's not right,' said Nalini.

'She said she left her children in England.'

'She's lying. He would've told us,' said Nalini.

'Who are you concerned about? Him or her?' asked Astrid.

'How can you ask?'

'Well, I'm concerned about her,' said Astrid. 'I expected a self-assured young woman. She's angry. Quiet. Almost withdrawn.'

'What about her hair? I wonder what it means. She's not wearing a tali[29]. Not even the dot. Anyone looking at her will think she's single,' said Nalini.

---

26 Braai is a barbeque

27 Potjie is a three-legged pot that stands over an open fire in which a stew of meat, fish and seafood is cooked.

28 Skottelbraai is a dish used to braai meat.

29 Tali is a gold amulet worn around the neck by married women.

'He must allow her to do that. Is she wearing a ring?'

'Wouldn't that make her a Christian?' asked Nalini.

'She's a modern woman. She might prefer a ring.'

'I'll ask him when he gets here. You met the English girl? Heather, I think. She'll expect you to show an interest in her. You being English.'

'I put off meeting her. She keeps phoning. Chatting. She asked if I had friends somewhere over there,' said Astrid, adding 'It'll be the first time I meet her, if she comes.'

'She'll be friendly with you. English people coming over here make friends with each other, no matter how little they have in common. It must be sad, coming back to a funeral at such a happy time,' said Nalini.

'Was he an activist? That young man who's being buried?'

'No idea. They say he disappeared a long time ago. Then suddenly they find his body on the Bisho march. As if the police shot him that day. Strange,' said Nalini.

'Secrets that go to the grave with people,' said Astrid.

'That's what I don't like about Pragashini. She's too quiet. Secretive,' said Nalini.

'You expect everyone to be outgoing and friendly. Look at how we mistrust each other. How many years is it, Nalini?'

'Fifty.'

'What did you do with that medal I gave for Anand?'

'In a safe place. For his first born.'

'Poor girl must be afraid of you. After all, she's a career girl, and you're a homebody,' said Astrid.

'Perhaps that's it.'

'She was a child when she left here.'

'Don't start that again. Have that argument with Anand. I had nothing to do with it,' said Nalini.

'You washed your hands.'

Nalini ignored this remark. 'The way they rushed off like Special Branch was after them.'

'But they weren't, were they? I would've known,' said Astrid.

'I've no idea. Anand never talked about his work. Another secretive South African.'

'If he told you, would you have given a farewell party?' asked Astrid.

'Don't make jokes. I never thought I'd live to see him.'

'You're being morbid. When he gets back enjoy him. Before he runs off again.'

'Stop that! It might come true. I couldn't bear it.'

'Too superstitious, that's your problem. We've no idea what happened to them in exile. Chapters in their lives, even in ours, we've not shared. They never wrote, did they?'

'The Nats misread everything written. I must try and put her at ease. Astrid, don't say anything controversial. Please. People who don't know you will think you're prejudiced when you're just speaking your mind. They don't know you, so don't overact.'

'I'll behave, if you let me be the hostess.'

***

19.

Astrid's braai witnessed racially paired couples, African woman with African man. Coloured with Coloured; Indian with Indian, White with White, arriving at her home from five on Saturday afternoon. Except Pragashini who arrived with Roshni, and Heather with Smuts. Each couple, South African style, brought an entourage of children, parents, aunts, uncles, nephews, nieces and friends. Smuts party included his mother and father, Nolitando and her student friends. The guests also brought marinated lamb, beef, and chicken, sausages, boerewors – all halal - and whole fish, drinks, salads and bags of charcoal. Astrid's home was in a numbered street - Fifth Avenue, Sixth Avenue, Twelfth Avenue – with trees giving shade all along its length – that proved difficult to find.

The Nasaratt women experimented with a recipe for tandoori chicken, a dish unknown in South Africa, from Madhur Jaffrey's cookery book that Pragashini had given Nalini. Tandoori chicken became a topic of conversation, so too the success in England of Indian restaurants and their virtual absence in South Africa. They prepared green leaf salads in Astrid's kitchen. The men went out into the back garden to get the fires going for the braai. Many suffering hangovers from the night before began drinking again.

Conversation was strained or over friendly. They were unaccustomed to integrated socialising in people's homes. It happened occasionally at church functions, but rarely went beyond that. Apartheid was implemented with severity during the sixties and seventies. Racial groups grew away from each other, and became more aware of their racial identities than they had been until then. The exiles were discomfited to find that people from one segregated area had few friends or acquaintances in other areas.

Pragashini, Heather, Smuts and the Matatiele family were introduced. They spent time establishing if they knew siblings, parents and relatives of the guests. Astrid asked them for an account of their lives in exile.

Smuts exaggerated the importance of his fledging film company. He said he was looking for projects to video and send back to television companies abroad. Heather spoke about her work with microscopic life forms while Pragashini told them briefly about her research and the theory she was proposing. She said it was too complex to explain to the layperson, but the university insisted she make it simple enough for them to understand.

'It's a gender topic and I want to disclose my theory to

women before I reveal it to men', she said. There was good humoured uproar while they attempted to eject her from the party.

Heather, confident that being from England was sufficient connection with Astrid, warmed to the woman who was teased because her dress was a subdued shade of pink while they were in flamboyant colours. Astrid was eager to see photographs of England that Heather had agreed to bring. These were passed around.

'Tell me about Yorkshire,' Astrid said, taking Heather to one side.

The Steinway piano brought Heather into a huddle with Astrid, arranging piano lessons for Lusikisiki. Astrid gave piano lessons to her neighbours children, for the pleasure of the company of children whom she adored. They knew she had no children of her own. She was kind enough to teach local children to play the piano. When her husband died, she went out to work until after her retirement.

Early in the afternoon before tea was served, Astrid, Nalini and Mandisa Matatiele, strolled into the garden for the pleasure of the floral fragrances released as the sun went down. When they reached the front gate they found a man untying a black refuse bag on the grass put out for Monday morning's collection. Two other bags stood open across the street, their contents strewn about over the neatly cut lawn. Astrid and Nalini rushed to the gate scolding the man in the manner they would have scolded misbehaving children.

The man stopped what he was doing to frown at them from under lowered eyebrows. Unperturbed he resumed rummaging through the bag, tossing things out on to the street with greater abandonment. The women were outraged. They opened the gate and began shooing him away but he would not budge. When he finished with the bag he turned it upside down and emptied the contents in a wide circle around him.

Not content with that he put his hands on his hips and shouted loudly, 'That's my pondokkie by the road when you come driving to this white street. I made it. With my two hands.' He offered the calloused palms of his hands for them to see. 'From cardboard and sacks and planks and tin sheets you people like to throw away. No one helped me. No one said, 'Here bhuti, I don't want this chair. Take it. You first must throw it away. You rather throw it away than give it to a person for nothing. Then I must come like a dog and take my pick from the rubbish dump. You people got so much things you don't even know when we stole something of yours. This street don't belong to you. I'll piss in this street if I feel like it.' He undid his belt – there was no zip on his trousers – and urinated in a circle by twirling round and round in the street.'

The women were scandalised. Astrid, Nalini and Mandisa covered their eyes and ran back into the house. Inside everyone asked, 'what's up?' But the women shook their heads. They were too embarrassed to describe the man's effrontery. Astrid, however, was undeterred. She bemoaned the habit men had of urinating in the streets in view of every policeman, nun, and street child. They exchanged stories of seeing men urinating on the motorway, in the city centre, in the suburbs.

'A man will turn his back to the street, avoiding the passing cars, and urinate facing the house!' complained Nalini.

'You remember that English girl who was teaching people how to use the ballot paper? She said she travelled with a group of men to the rural areas. When they arrived at a village, the men jumped out and they urinated against a tree, with her standing there!' They were careful not to say what racial groups the culprits were, unwilling to cause offence so early after the elections, and in their first mixed party since having the franchise.

Matatiele chastised them. 'I won't make no bones about it. 'Africans live without lavatories in their homes. They must go outside and queue up to urinate in one small latrine, and wash at a tap without any privacy. When you've been sleeping, and wake up with a full bladder, you can't keep it in and there are twenty people ahead of you in the queue, you don't have time to see if there are women admiring your backside!'

While the fire blazed outside Astrid invited everyone in for tea. The fire had to die down. The charcoal had to be red hot. Then they could arrange the meat on the grille. Astrid served real English tea, which she reserved for such occasions, 'not bush tea,' she remarked. She was counting the heads in the room.

When they were settled with a cup of tea in their hands the children were rounded up to put on an impromptu concert. They took the matter seriously and went into a huddle to decide what each would do. One of Smuts' children went cautiously to Astrid and whispered something in her ear. She in turn took a few minutes questioning the child then took a chain from around her neck and unlocked the Steinway piano. The Matatiele twins Mafeking and King Bisho recited nursery rhymes. Lusikisiki and the older children sang and imitated hip-hop dancers to their favourite music. Astrid kept the kettle on the boil to keep the tea going. She deplored their habit of serving hot milk with tea and grudgingly heated the milk when they persuaded her that tea came from India and they knew more about serving it than she did. Astrid did not have domestic help at home. It was safer that way. 'I know you'll think I'm prejudiced, but I can read, and South Africa is no place for a woman living on her own.'

They were embarrassed. Only Smuts took exception to her

remark. 'You can pull the wool over their eyes, but not mine. I've been out there. England is an island in chains. Whatever's happening here that you don't like, is also happening over there.'

Astrid related a romantic story about how she came to be living in South Africa, while Nalini diverted her attention with gin and tonic. Astrid appeared to have forgotten Nalini's earlier warning. She spoke freely and they half listened, half slept, through the tale of a holiday romance in Scarborough with a blonde sun-tanned youth from Grahamstown, a romance she wanted to prolong. 'I sailed out to South Africa when I was twenty-something, in nineteen fifty something, chasing the young man who romanced me in Scarborough. He chanced to take a day trip to buy Scarborough rock when we met. The small community of English people in Grahamstown were delighted with my Yorkshire accent, and my interest in the arts. I in turn was touched by their attempts to maintain their Englishness. At the time, it was politically correct to do so. They were descended from English families who settled in the early nineteenth century. The town grew around Rhodes University. My young man gave me a good time in the Cape. He took me around the small towns. Alice, Graaff Reinet, Kirkwood, Uitenhage, Cradock, Fort Beaufort were like English market towns. But when he took me to P.E. and showed me the promenade with seaside hotels overlooking the sea, the Campanile, and the monument to Elizabeth Donkin, I was reminded of Scarborough. It didn't take much persuasion for the company I worked for in Scarborough to transfer me.'

'I settled into my new life, spending my days off enjoying walks along the pavement, sitting in beachfront cafes, eating ice cream and staring at the sea, although I missed hiking across the moors and the dales, and the lakes in Cumbria.

We were married, and we set up home here. I sometimes went to Scarborough to visit my parents.'

Nalini drew Astrid into the kitchen, to brew more tea, to serve her guests, even to play the piano. Astrid, however, returned continually to talk about her past. She told Pragashini and Heather about the first time she saw Nalini. About when Anand was a little boy of two. She said, 'Nalini heard that the Blessed Virgin granted the prayers of any woman, whatever their religious affiliation, even Hindus and Muslims, provided when one prayed to her, one wore something blue, and prayed before her icon. Nalini did not dare bring an icon of the Blessed Virgin into her home so she wore a blue sari every morning and made her way to the Catholic Church to pray before a large icon of the Blessed Virgin. During those days, the church was safe from thieves and the doors were unlocked every morning at six and locked up at night at eight.'

'She kept up this practice throughout her pregnancies. After having several sons she finally prayed for a baby girl. I'll never forget the beautiful saris she wore. Kingfisher blue, dove grey, turquoise. It was wonderful to see her kneeling devoutly at the little side altar. I was drawn to her out of some form of attraction. The little boy played with a miniature car pushing it along the pews from row to row until he became bored and ran back to his mother wanting to go home. Here was a potential convert, I thought. Once I knew her I invited her to give Indian cookery lessons at the Catholic school as a kind of cultural exchange and I sat in on the class.'

Observing the two women, Ramgopal puzzled over their friendship. His wife received a third rate education in South Africa which ended when she was ready to learn the housekeeping duties that would prepare her for the life of a married woman. At that time few women of any race went beyond standard three in primary school. Those who passed Standard Six were allowed to teach without any formal training. His mother had several friends who were teachers but who never went beyond standard six. They were refined and cultured. Astrid on the other hand, was educated in England up to her 'O' levels and kept alive her interest in reading, music and the theatre.

When Astrid began talking about cross movement of people in and out of the separate areas it annoyed Smuts. 'What cross movement? I had to knock on doors up and down the street to ask the whites if they objected to my family moving in.'

'Why didn't you send Heather?' she asked.

'I did, but I don't want my kids to have a hard time when they play in the street.'

'You'd be surprised how resilient kids are.'

'Did anyone object?' Nalini asked.

'They were never in.'

'They had absolute power, the Nats' said Pravin. 'It was all force. No free will. If they could've forced a dog to dance, they would've done so.'

Listening to him, Pragashini wondered if he ever applied those ideas to her predicament.

During the evening Smuts slipped away into the garden to find Nolitando. The fragrance of honeysuckle climbing over the garage and around the fence exerted its exotic spell over him. On his approach Nolitando's young friends separated to make way for him. They knew of his interest in her. Now that he heard his mother tongue day and night, in casual talk, in hymns and prayers and readings from the Bible each time friends came to offer condolences in the house he could understand even the colloquialisms the students used.

Nolitando was shy in his presence. She considered him a rich man and related to him less easily than she would to a fellow student. Because he carried himself confidently and spoke with authority, it added to his otherness. He was anxious not to appear proud or distant.

'You know Noli, travelling outside South Africa gives you confidence,' he said. 'That's what living in England did for me. I'll never be humble, or even subservient to anyone. If I stayed here, perhaps I would be cautious, reluctant to speak my mind without looking over my shoulder. Like our grandparents used to be. I don't do it consciously. It's just – I don't know ... natural. I don't think about it.'

'Then how can a girl like me, refuse a man like you?'

'You should just refuse. Straight out. Refuse anyone. If you don't like them,' he said. 'Where the man comes from ... how rich he is ... has got nothing to do with it. It's about you and the man. Nothing else.'

'But to refuse someone like you would be' ...

'You keep saying refuse, refuse. You refusing me? Don't you like me? Just a bit?'

'It depends.'

He took hold of her hand. 'On what?' He twined his fingers between hers, like a teenaged boy, he was nervous when he was close to her. Her fingers were long and thin with a delicate look, her knuckles slightly darker than the rest of her fingers. He realised he had missed this experience in exile, that of falling in love with a young Xhosa girl. He could not tell what contributed to his feelings, if it was the atmosphere within the community of everyone knowing everyone else, the happiness from the election victory, the warm air, the relief of being at home, the security of the sounds of his mother tongue – things that England lacked, that gave romance to the place. He had not experienced this with Heather or Pragashini. He had never been shy or timorous with either of them.

'If you do that thing for me.'

'What thing?'

She moved away from him. 'It isn't my place to say.'

He pulled her back into the shadows. 'Let me kiss you then we can talk about other things.'

'Well, I suppose I can let you kiss me.'

He was suffused with warmth at her simplicity. He did not know how he would succeed in just kissing her. It was years since he was with a girl who was shy. She must be a virgin. He should just kiss her and leave it at that. It was wrong for him to be the one to take her virginity. She might expect something more, though, since she knew he was married, and a man could not stop with a kiss. The air was humid. Coming from England, he could no longer tolerate the heat, but then her skin felt cool to his touch. It was covered with a light film of moisture. Her lips were full and soft under his, making him forget his good intentions.

She put her hand between their lips, 'You know, you can only kiss me.' Yet she remained warm in his arms, resting her head on his shoulder, and he was at a loss. He thought it must have to do with Heather.

'I'll talk with my father in the morning. He'll know what I should do.'

She gave a slight giggle. 'Don't you know?'

He was taken aback. He was stimulated by the way she talked to him. It was new and exciting for someone his age to meet with someone who was fresh. 'What are you talking about?' he touched her neck with his lips.

'You truly don't know?' she teased him.

'I don't.'

'You know. You just want to challenge me to say it.'

'Is it my wife?'

'No.' She laughed softly.

'What then?'

'I feel shy to have to tell you.'

'I don't want to embarrass you. But if it's not my wife you're bothered about, then I don't know.'

'You won't laugh?'

'I'll promise you anything.'

She put her lips to his ear and whispered, 'You must go into the forest,' and then laughed softly into her cupped hands.

'What?'

'I can't be with a man who isn't - amadoda[30],' and she laughed continuously.

'I'm too old.'

'It makes you a man.'

'I don't need to prove I'm a man.'

'To me you're not a man.'

'I already have a wife and children. Doesn't that prove anything?'

'Not in our culture.'

'Look,' he held up his left hand with the little finger minus a joint, 'the clan accepts me as a man.'

'The elders in the clan are men. Your little finger is the man's test of manhood. The woman's test for a man is circumcision.'

He disentangled her arms from around his neck and stood to one side. It was the westerner's fear of initiation, the hygiene, the dangers, and the risk to himself, which surfaced. He perspired. She came up to him and touched his back. He turned and they embraced and kissed. There was so much he needed to experience. She seemed to fulfil everything he missed in exile. The gentleness, the respect for him, but above all, the shyness. All the qualities Heather and Pragashini lacked. So he said in a voice filled with emotion, 'For you I'll go into the forest.'

---

30 Amadoda is a man.

After they had eaten, Astrid slipped an Indian movie into the video machine. The room was instantly in total drunken uproar. No one understood Hindi very well, yet Astrid was confidently assuring everyone that she and Nalini, between them would make the whole movie clear. Both women were fans of the old actors Dilip Kumar and Rajesh Khanna. The viewing was hilarious. They pieced together the narrative and action with the help of badly translated sub-titles. What followed was a hotch potch of the two women explaining the story, the video machine put on pause, reversing to enable everyone to catch up as to what really happened, then the viewing resuming.

At every pause, Smuts raised objections to watching Indian movies in Africa. By now they were intoxicated and no one took offence. They laughed at his arguments. When someone said, 'Bollywood has a huge following in West Africa and in the Middle East,' it sent Smuts out of the room in disbelief, while they laughed drunkenly and called him back. Heather persuaded him not to spoil the party. He returned, sullen-faced. The braai continued into the small hours of the morning.

***

The Recluse: Pragashini's Journal

20.

I hovered in and out of a kind of mystical experience from the moment I first caught sight of him,. There was no space for reason. Now I look in the mirror. I don't recognise my face. It is illuminated. It has the look of ecstasy. An inner light glows behind my eyes. This is what they mean when they say the eyes are the windows to the soul. If there was a sensitive camera that could capture the aura around me, it would show up as light. My soul has met someone it recognises. This is spiritual recognition because I do not know him, my soul does.

Who in their right mind would not go in search of the soul's acquaintance, and once rekindled not let go? Who in their right mind would not attempt to understand such an experience? It is natural to search unashamedly in every face, to seek out opportunities to see him, even from a distance, to look at him and experience the exhilaration in my soul I enjoyed that first day.

***

21.

Racial past and rainbow future were precariously balanced at South Africa's universities. This culture fascinated Pragashini. Were she to stay on she needed to use a university library, and maintain contact with her tutors. With this in mind she visited universities in the locality.

Vista was one of numerous satellite campuses around the country originally intended for Africans. Matatiele told her it was rumoured Witwatersrand University was 'toyi-toyi-ing' with the idea of building a satellite campus in Soweto. 'Slegs for Africans,' Matatiele added. The phrase was only used when only whites were given access to a place. The implications for African students might have been revolutionary. But on hearing the rumour, the government proposed a counter plan: a university having campuses in black townships around the country.

In Port Elizabeth the Vista campus appeared incongruous because it was situated in the middle of a shantytown yet offered no student accommodation on or off campus. The building was in a modern architectural style, its unplastered exterior in fashionable face-brick.

Outside the gates Pragashini crossed the road walking away from the buildings until she was nearer the shantytown, its dusty arena, corrugated iron and cardboard, mangy dogs and goats. What could have been in the minds of the planners? She asked herself. Whose Vista did the name refer to: the shanty town dwellers looking at the university or the university viewing the shanty town? It was a mystery.

Inside the library she was able to count the books, there were so few. There were only two tables with half a dozen chairs. Students sat on the floor with books around them. The classrooms were furnished with long rows of wooden desks that were nailed to the floor. It would even be out of place in a modern class for little children. But she refused to be dissuaded from using the facilities there. Vista had opened its doors to all races to enrol.

The historically White University of Port Elizabeth was situated miles away from Vista in a prime location on the beachfront, where the golden sands and sea breeze of Humewood invited an early morning jog; where picnic sites and seaside promenades embellished the weekends. The university offered accommodation on campus.

At both universities, the lecturers were from all groups, perhaps recent additions were from the formerly disenfranchised. Both universities were new.

Some distance away from the city were another set of non-identical twins. Both were established before the separation of the universities, but in the consciousness of the people, Rhodes University was white and Fort Hare was non-white. Both used English as the medium.

It was difficult to choose. She met lecturers informally to discuss her options not knowing how she would pay for the use of their facilities without a job. If she rejected the idea of searching for the document in Bisho, and simply stayed on to wait for Nasaratt, she would still need to keep in contact with her tutors, and to use a university library and pay for it.

Part of her interest in the university culture was to gauge if White students were eager to study at the historically Black universities. She discovered Black students clamouring for admission to White universities while admission numbers were falling at Fort Hare, perhaps understandably. Fort Hare was situated at the end of a dusty road far from any major town. Sandy roads, hot winds and sand storms made the campus virtually inaccessible. The planners may have had in mind dumping the students near Alice and making it difficult for them to move about freely.

At the end of her visits to these places she applied for a few posts and was called to Bisho for an interview.

***

22.

Ramgopal was outraged when he heard that Pragashini had applied for a job in Bisho.

'Why d'you want to do a thing like that? Do you know that place? Do you know how to get there? Bisho isn't round the corner. It's past Uitenhage. Past Grahamstown. You've got to go miles and miles without anyone on the road. You'll be hijacked. Shot at! Read the papers. It's dangerous out that side. Car hijackings. Shooting. It's bad enough here. Work in PE. There are lots of jobs here. If there's any trouble, we're here to help you. You can't go out there!'

She was incensed listening to him yet attempted to remain cool. What did he mean, 'if there's trouble, we're here to help you?' They would first decide if it was in the family interest to help her. If she had trouble with Nasaratt, they would not lift a finger to help.

Roshni was watchful of Pragashini's eyes and grim face.

'The work I need to do, I can't do here,' Pragashini said.

'What work? University work? UPE's here. And Vista. You can go to Rhodes. What's in Bisho?'

'It's nearer to Fort Hare. There's a campus there.'

'Fort Hare? No one wants to go to Fort Hare. Not if they can go to UPE. Fort Hare is nothing compared to UPE.'

'It should be the other way around.'

'What d'you mean? You been to Fort Hare?'

'Actually, yes. It needs funding. Everyone should want to go there because Africa's leadership went there.'

'There was nowhere else to go.'

'Now we're spoilt for choice,' she said. 'I like that. I'd like to be able to choose. '

'That makes no sense to me,' Ramgopal said.

She let the matter rest. Ramgopal was disgruntled, perhaps anxious for his son to return and sort out the matter. It seemed to her Nasaratt had not contacted his parents. The Nasaratts rested uneasily, believing she had taken their words to heart and given up the idea of working in Bisho until she told them about the interview. After their initial shock, Ramgopal and Nalini muttered whenever they saw her, seeming to disown all interest in her. Roshni, however, offered to drive her to Bisho.

The night before the interview, they were seated around the supper table with Astrid when Ramgopal and Nalini registered their disapproval by eating their meal in silence. Roshni and Pravin were dismissive of the interview process. Pravin warned 'Never mind who interviews you, remember, they'll be White people, and they probably have never talked to an Indian woman. Trust me. Behave like a soft spoken, sweet, gentle lady. Like Astrid. Or they'll be hostile to you.'

'Look at her. She frightens me!' Roshni said.

'Ignore them,' Astrid advised. 'You speak up, Pragashini. You have to. Or you'll be feeding their stereotypes.'

'Of what?' Pragashini asked.

'Indian women!' said Astrid.

'And exiles. Coming home without having struggled,' said Roshni.

'I have stereotypes of them,' said Pragashini. 'When have I spoken to a White South African? Have you?'

'We've got Astrid!' said Roshni.

'Astrid's different. Keep politics out of it,' said Pravin.

'Don't be drawn,' said Astrid. 'They'll want to test you. There'll be trick questions. Be careful how you answer. I'm sure the people interviewing will be from the old Ciskei and Transkei. You have to be careful. They want to work with people who won't rock the boat. Don't even mention race. Remember anyone from a government department is from the past. The departments haven't been transformed yet. It's still early days.'

'Astrid, you sound experienced,' said Roshni.

Astrid ignored her remark. 'For the job interview say nothing about research or your theory. When you ask permission to use the university facilities, don't say anything about the job,' said Astrid.

'Who've you been interrogating, Astrid?' asked Roshni.

'Don't even hint at what you think about our universities,' said Astrid. 'If they try to bait you, just resist. If you take the bait you'll ruin your chances.'

'There's not a lot left over for her to talk about,' Roshni said. 'She won't give a good impression.'

'That's the way to do it. When it comes to exile, they'll think you want to import British ideas,' said Astrid.

'You want her to give the impression she's a blank slate, waiting to be written on? asked Roshni.

'Exactly,' said Astrid. 'My advice is don't say too much. Just ask questions. The universities can say 'yes' or 'no'. If they say no, stand up and walk out.'

'I like that,' said Roshni. 'Don't beg them. Let them go to hell. You've seen the inside of great universities. Universities don't belong to the guys at the top. It belongs to the hobo picking up papers thrown about by students. Those lecturers and professors, they're not even custodians. Academics think students are just passing through but even they're passing through. The way they controlled our universities, it's as if they owned it. That's wrong. Universities should belong to the people. We should have access to it. They've got computers, books, stuff we never see. We should all have access to it. We should be able to sit in the class even if we're not taking the exam. Why not? People as old as my mother and Astrid. The women dishing up their food.'

'Having all of you there will give them a headache,' Pragashini said. 'Anyhow, this is speculation. If they won't allow me to use their facilities, I'll just have to wait until I go back home. I won't take a job.'

'Go back? Where? To England?' Ramgopal pushed his chair back and stood up. 'It's bad enough you looking as far as Bisho for a job. What is this talk about going back? I thought you're home for good.'

'I'm going back to England,' Pragashini said.

'And Anand?'

She realised she had said too much.

***

23.

Two roads lead to Bisho. One white. One black,' said Roshni concealing a gun in the moulded pocket on the door, before she climbed into the driver's seat and secured the safety belt.

They were heading out of PE for Pragashini's interview. The risk of driving to Bisho, Pragashini shared with Roshni. Pragashini said nothing; amazed at how people separated themselves yet thankful for the gobbets of information the locals gave her when they travelled anywhere. It served as a fillip to her brain.

One road wound its way along the coast from Port Elizabeth's coast to East London linking up with Port Alfred, with a turn off to Bisho. This coastal road was quiet and scenic. But from the turn off to Bisho the road became a dust track narrow and isolated with little traffic to Bisho. People using this road might not intend going to Bisho.

Another road was rough and rocky and went through Peddie and Alice then on to King Williamstown and Bisho. Because there were no intercity trains, the road through Peddie and Alice was busy with taxis and minibuses and therefore susceptible to car hijackings. People without cars travelled long distances between towns and cities in taxis.

All motorists decided which road to take according to how safe they considered the roads to be. Black taxis and minibuses carrying African passengers used the black road needing access to Alice and Peddie. White motorists used the white road wishing to avoid the small towns and drive to East London. That is how the roads came to be named.

For women drivers both roads proved risky: the isolation of the white road, and the hijacking on the black road.

Roshni chose the black road through Alice. 'It's busier, therefore safer,' she said. She put her foot down hard on the accelerator and only slowed down when they entered King Williamstown. She averaged three hours without stopping. The condition of the road was worse than that of a minor road. For most of its length, it was just wide enough for single lane traffic.

Closer to Bisho the road was even narrower. When a car approached from the opposite direction they drove with the right wheels on the tarmac, the left in the dust. Except for a stretch of road approaching and exiting Grahamstown, there were no road markings. No cat's eyes. No road signs. No filling stations, drive in restaurants, or lay byes. The road was badly maintained, with potholes for most of its length except on either side of Grahamstown.

The countryside was dry on the approach to the former Ciskei. Pragashini counted three mountain passes on the road without protective barriers to prevent cars slipping over the edge. She scanned the road but found not one AA telephone box all along the route.

'Looking for a telephone box? If we have a flat tyre, if the radiator smokes, if we run out of petrol, if the fan belt broke, we'll have to rely on a cell phone and wait in the car for someone to drive from PE to rescue us, and risk being hijacked while we wait.'

At certain points on the road, the signal for the cell phone was cut off. Fences along the farms needed repairing. Goats, sheep and cattle roamed onto the road, hid behind the bushes and ran across the road when they had the inclination. For most of its length the road was deserted. Taxis loaded with passengers overtook them along the way. At an approach to a farm a tractor emerged from a gate forcing them to slow down. Then two or three cars tailed them and they had company until the tractor turned off the road at another gate.

King Williamstown was a dusty market town approximately a mile long retaining the look of a wild west town. Trading stores lined the street. They turned up a long avenue on an incline separating King Williamstown from Bisho.

'This is the Bisho Road,' said Roshni. 'You heard of the Bisho Massacre?'

Pragashini said nothing.

'Well, someone threw a bomb into the golf club killing and wounding White people,' Roshni said. 'The Bisho Massacre was alleged to be in retaliation. That's why papa's worried about you working here.'

'It's a bit late in the day for anyone to be worrying about me, don't you think?' said Pragashini.

'You still carrying a grudge about your wedding?'

'That's putting it mildly,' Pragashini said. Roshni was never entrusted with details of her marriage. The question of how far she could trust Roshni plagued her. This occasion for the two to be alone for any length of time was rare. 'I'm an adult now. I want to do something for the child who was Pragashini.'

'I don't like the sound of that.'

'You're not meant to.'

***

24.

Candy pink. The colour of buildings in the centre of Bisho. Was one of these buildings coated in candy pink like houses from Hansel and Gretel the former police building? What of the offices of the Public Service? Where was the proposed Legislature? Driving around the town they saw new houses built of face brick.

Having located the Legislature building and office block where the interview was to be Roshni waited in the car with the gun while Pragashini entered. Except for small numbers on the office doors, there were no marks to characterise one corridor from the next, or one office from another. There appeared to be a high level of punctuality and efficiency because there were no chairs or benches in the corridors for people to sit and wait for an appointment. There were no posters or notice boards on the walls to hint of any activity, social, political, or cultural. Pragashini had misgivings about the joy of working there.

One door stood ajar. When she tapped on the door and entered, a young White woman appeared at the counter. She wore a white blouse and navy blue skirt with a black velvet ribbon tied under the collar of her blouse. She politely asked Pragashini to wait outside and shut the door leaving her standing in the corridor. While she waited, a tall man came quietly into view from the distance and walked towards her unobtrusively in the shadowy corridor hugging the wall. She quickly turned to face the internal window that overlooked the entrance hall so that he would not brush up against her in the narrow space.

Yet as he approached and with her back to the corridor she felt her spirit surge the way it did on election day. She froze, afraid and unable to turn. He passed her. She turned. It was Mossel Klein. Her impulse was to run away. Her first panic stricken thought was, 'Oh God! What is he doing here? Don't let him interview me.'

She could not understand her reaction. Panic? At the sight of a stranger. She was not that romantic child who collected love tokens for her scrapbook. Why should she be afraid, when she had been longing to see him? Her reaction created a conflict in her. She persuaded herself his appearance was a coincidence. He might also be there for an interview. But if he was also being interviewed, would she be able to carry off Matatiele's instructions?

A few minutes passed before the receptionist opened the door and said, 'Come in.'

The room she entered was devoid of everything except a long table and chairs. Four men sat behind the table. Windows without blinds or curtains allowed the sun full access to every part of the room. The sun shone on their backs and onto the table. The four men half stood when she entered. To the people in the room the receptionist said, 'Pragashini Dev,' and left.

They invited her to sit but she was already of a mind not to work there. Mossel Klein opened a folder and began taking notes.

The man on her far left introduced his companions, then

himself. 'Dr Viljoen, Meneer Vermaak, Meneer Klein. I'm Van Staaden.' Mossel Klein sat on her far right.

Pragashini was conscious of her hands. Their initial questions she answered in single syllables. When Klein posed a question, she addressed her reply to one of the other men. When they spoke to her she could not raise her eyes to look at them. She reasoned her constraint was the result of years of silence she imposed on herself. She was conforming to the way the Astrid advised her to. But she did not want that. She engaged in discussion with them about the skills she could bring to the job while acknowledging to herself that she was damaging her prospects. Then she suspected they would have observed she was not looking at them. She struggled to overcome her uneasiness.

With an effort, she raised her head and focussed directly on Klein only to feel the satisfaction of hunger, when her eyes rested on his face. Then she observed that her eyes on his face affected him. The effect was visible. Now he seemed unable to move. She watched the blood drain from his face. She held his gaze for almost a full minute then she dragged her eyes away from his. As if a cold draught blew in from behind, he turned round to the window. The windows were shut. There was an air conditioner in the room. When he turned back to look at her she concentrated on her hands again.

Then she sensed a change in the room. Klein put his pen down. Now he appeared interested in the interview. Rather than put a question to her, he spoke to her. She sensed a deepening tone, a softening, in his voice. He sounded compassionate. She supposed he saw she was affected by his presence. Warmth exuded from him across the table towards her. She felt it. Nevertheless there was another sensation. It was unmistakable. Another part of him revelled in the power he had over her. She kept her head turned to one of the interviewers, yet could feel his eyes on her, willing her to look at him again. The softening in his voice was unmistakable. He changed from the man who was writing in his file at the beginning of the interview to one who was taking control of the interview.

The job was on screen editing. Although she was a Biologist, they considered 'O' level English adequate for their requirements. Klein made a slight joke about the fun of doing editorial work in nine languages. 'Members are free to stand up and speak in whatever language they feel like using on the day,' he said. 'We're all bilingual, or polyglots.' He spoke gently. She did not respond. She refused to look at him again.

'Will you have an editor for each language?' she asked.

'Yes, sure. For indigenous languages,' he said. Had he made up his mind that she should be offered the job? While his colleagues questioned her about how she would adapt to the new situation because she had been away for so long, he said, 'If your Afrikaans is poor – you may not have spoken Afrikaans since the Soweto uprising – do you know some Xhosa? You'll remember Afrikaans once you hear it spoken again.'

'I went to school in Natal,' she lied. 'I never learnt Afrikaans.'

'Then you can't know Xhosa!'

'Not a word. You know in Natal it's Zulu and I never learnt that either. No African languages, I'm afraid.'

Then, as if he recognised she was not doing herself justice in the interview because of her awkwardness in his presence, he seemed to want to help her. He outlined aspects of the job, the hours of work. One of his colleagues said, 'There'll be pressure on you to do well because you're from England.'

At one stage she was uncertain if the other interviewers were discouraging her from accepting the job or merely clarifying the situation. Her eyes travelled from the man on the far left, to each man, trying to establish what they were about, but stopping short of Klein.

These people were new to her. Perhaps they were suggesting she was unsuitable for the job. For one brief moment she was angry with Matatiele for telling her to apply for this post when she was neither a language specialist nor a computer technician. She cursed herself for agreeing. Then she focussed on Klein.

Now it was his turn to look away. He could not meet her eyes. She had power over him in the same way that he had power over her. She did not have time to think about the significance of this.

If she rejected the job it might imply she lacked confidence in her abilities – which she did. But Matatiele's confidence in her outweighed her own lack of confidence. She had to do this. The politics of oppression seemed still to be working here. If she took the job, and did badly it would reinforce their opinions and make it harder for those who followed. It would not help her either. Then they would feel their old policies of job reservation were justified. She was in an unacceptable position.

They were saying they had to maintain standards. Their manner was apologetic. She was not coming from their system of education. She lacked the background in African politics; she did not know the background to politics in the Eastern Cape. They patronized her. They told her she should be grateful either way, and that democracy does not affect the workplace. A job appointment is not a democratic process.

She recalled what Matatiele said about the compromise around the negotiation table that allowed the peaceful handover from apartheid to democracy. This was what it came to in real terms. At the same time she was thinking, 'If

I walk out of here I may not see him again. I won't remember what he looks like. I need to capture the colour of his eyes. I haven't looked at his face long enough to draw it from memory, his eyes and his lips. Yet my spirit knows his. When I look at him I feel I've known him all my life. How can I reveal this to him? To anyone? People will ridicule me. They'll think I've lost my mind.'

They had not stopped putting obstacles in her way. Their educational system is different from Britain. They would not know where to place her on the salary scale. Her qualifications would have to be assessed. Some institution did that, they said. Were they uncomfortable dealing with her because she was from England, she asked herself? It was more common for South Africans, especially academics, to work abroad than for people from abroad to work here. Sanctions and all that fanagalo. Did they sense something threatening in her? All graduates would have the same qualities of challenging authority, questioning and inquiring minds. But she had failed. She had not challenged them. Yet, even though Klein disconcerted her, something had made them wary of her. Did they suspect her?

Her inner voice urged if it's valid, say it. She wanted desperately to believe she was regaining her self-confidence. So she blurted out, 'I note all the disadvantages you've listed. Nevertheless, I want to persuade you to offer me the job. This isn't a challenging job. A child with 'O' levels could do it. I'm a postgraduate student. I'll soon have my doctorate. This job isn't my lifetime ambition. I'll be doing it as a sideline. Sort of moonlighting. What's more ... it's impossible for you to assess my knowledge and capability – anyone's for that matter – before I've actually done the work. That's what probation is for.' She looked at them in turn, including Klein then said, with a smile, 'I don't believe in prophetic judgement.'

They looked at each other and laughed. Then Klein, possibly to round up the interview, said, 'I was on a plane coming out from England and the exiles were singing a song about bringing back slavery.' He looked at her for a response. 'Do you know why they want to bring back slavery?'

This was the trick question Astrid warned about. Should I ignore him? Pretend he never said a word? Stand up and leave? Will it spoil my chances if I answer? Truthfully? Should I lie? Create a fantasy? Matatiele would tell me to keep my mouth shut. Should I lie? Say I've never heard it sung?

'You're from exile,' Klein added. 'You can hazard a guess. What did they mean?' he persisted with the question.

She blinked and swallowed. 'You might not like what I have to say.'

'You'll discover we love the truth.'

'When labour was free or cheap ... people were transported ... by the shipload to work ... in the States ... Britain ... wherever others didn't want to dirty their hands ... Now labour is well paid ... those same people ... their descendants ... can't find work ... It's black humour.'

While they glanced at each other and fumbled with their papers, Pragashini remembered Jairaj saying, 'Our people worked from childhood to death,' and Leela warning her 'don't joke about death, Pragashini'. The interviewers said, 'You'll have to attend induction and training to familiarise yourself with South African politics. This isn't England, you know. This country is multi-lingual and multi-racial.'

When she realised she had the job, the happier thought in her mind was that she would be working with Mossel Klein. She decided to call him MK. She did not know it had another meaning.

***

25.

Jacaranda City because of brilliant blue flowered trees that lined the streets is the tourist brochure's name for Pretoria which like Port Elizabeth is known by several names. The African majority call it Tshwane. On Monday 9 May 1994, in Cape Town, Nelson Mandela was elected President of South Africa. His inauguration was scheduled for Tuesday 10th May in the administrative capital, Pretoria.

The individual wishes of Pragashini, Smuts and Matatiele to attend the Inauguration, stemmed from an emotional desire to be there on the day. It was not their wish to be awestruck by the glitz, the glamour, and the lavish ceremony. Like millions of people around the world, Pragashini did not know Nelson Mandela personally. Millions took a stand against apartheid. Thousands marched from Scotland to Wembley to demand his release. Hundreds sold Anti Apartheid products and 'Free Nelson Mandela' badges. Scores of South Africans urged the alumni of Witwatersrand University to elect Mandela their Chancellor. People in Britain campaigned for streets and buildings to be named after him. They contributed to the Defence and Aid Fund; grasped every opportunity to speak in public about the horror of the apartheid regime; collected and distributed eyewitness reports and evidence to international media – their passion kept alive by the space-like image of Mandela secretly filmed when he was dispatched to Robben Island wearing his traditional clothes. Except for Winnie, none of these people saw him until his release. Pragashini, however, did none of these things. She remained true to her distaste for politics and in hiding from Nasaratt.

Her first sighting of Mandela was after his release from Robben Island, when he flew to London to meet Margaret Thatcher and stayed at a west end hotel. On separate occasions, Pragashini, Smuts and Heather, took gifts to Mandela's hotel. Pragashini bought him a Jacobs Lamb pelt from the north. Smuts and Heather bought him a tartan rug from the Scottish mills. They did not meet Mandela. He neither acknowledged nor thanked them. She excused the oversight. The gifts were left with the people controlling the media scrum outside. He may never have received them.

Three days before the ceremony, bound for Pretoria she flew from Port Elizabeth to East London a flight over the ocean and then overland to Johannesburg. In keeping with South African custom, Smuts, Heather, and Roshni saw her off at the airport. Smuts asked Pragashini if he should make plans for her to attend the various festivities surrounding the inauguration. Without this offer she would have been part of the crowd in the streets. At the time she appreciated his gesture. Later she regretted it. Reflecting on the violent events that followed the inauguration of the President, she wondered if they should have attended. It was in the Jacaranda City that she first heard the name Amina Khan.

Pretoria was in the Orange Free State, one of the four original provinces. Historically, Indians were only allowed to enter and transit through. If they did not leave within twenty-four hours, they would be arrested. It was difficult to reach Pretoria without contravening the twenty-four hour ban. This was her first visit. At the airport Matatiele's friend Duntsula, a shop steward in the trade union movement, met her and took her to his home in Mamelodi. After resting he showed her around the bird sanctuaries, and scientific institutes, places she chose to see. He introduced her to the sons and daughters of the leadership in exile who were now based around iGoli and Tshwane.

The potted history Matatiele gave fuelled her interest in the unions. The shop stewards were encouraging. The unions, they said, would become active in the Ciskei and Transkei now South Africa was independent. While conversing with them, she put out feelers about how she could discover who collaborated with the apartheid government. She mentioned that people were interested to know if an insider had betrayed Steve Biko to the police. They warned her that it was dangerous to be probing around sensitive matters. They advised her to leave the matter for the Truth and Reconciliation Committee. She accepted their advice.

The following day, however, alone with one of the shop stewards, he mentioned a woman named Amina Khan. She was not a collaborator, but worked undercover for the liberation movement, as a clerk in the Sanlam Building in Port Elizabeth where Special Branch had their offices. This woman assisted detainees by sending information to their families about their interrogation, torture, and death in detention. If anyone had information about collaborators during the early period, this woman would have it, if she was alive. No one knew where she was. She disappeared after Steve Biko's death.

Smuts ensured he was in Cape Town staying at the Town House when the elected representatives chose Mandela for President. Well before the elections he booked travel and accommodation in Pretoria anticipating that flights and hotel rooms would be booked up nearer the inauguration. When his parents protested at the costs, - prices were inflated with the arrival of international tourists and guests – Heather graciously withdrew from the venture. Smuts, however, was adamant. 'No way am I watching the inauguration on the box. I might as well have sat in front of the box in England' he said. He offset his costs by cleverly using contacts in England to clinch a commission from a small independent film company to video the ceremony. He also arranged to film an interview with the President for live transmission by satellite to some specialist digital channels in Asia. The interview would last a dozen minutes and was scheduled for a slot between the ceremony and the entertainment and banquet that was to follow. He was also equipped to record audio interviews for one of the minority radio stations in the north of England. In this way he gained access to exclusive media events.

Without Heather suspecting it, Smuts booked travel by air for four people and accommodation for five – his father and mother, Heather, himself and Nolitando. Nolitando was motoring to Pretoria with her family. When Heather withdrew giving the children as her excuse, she inadvertently played into Smuts' hands. He attempted no persuasion.

Matatiele, however, called him aside when he was in the midst of preparing his recording equipment. 'You're in the wrong, son,' he said simply, when it became apparent he was leaving Heather behind. Smuts was annoyed but booked the entire family into a guesthouse close to the Union Buildings where the ceremony was scheduled to take place. Because the children were now included, he cancelled the plane reservations, borrowed a Kombi, serviced it and prepared as if they were travelling to a desert with bottled water and sun creams: the Highveld is hot and dry compared with the temperate climate and sea breezes of the port. The family group motored to Pretoria, making the most of their new freedom to sit in roadside cafes and eat, drink tea, and use the rest rooms that were formerly out of bounds to them.

To save money, Matatiele took along his own boiled eggs and asked the roadside café to bring boiling water to heat the eggs. The staff refused, but the management relented when he stood up and danced slowly around the wooden tables singing 'Cho-cho-lo-za.'

Smuts arranged to meet Nolitando in Tshwane. With Heather present, his movements were restricted. If Heather mistrusted him, she might have considered his behaviour similar to that of an anxious cat when its young are out of sight. But she had no reason to mistrust him. For Smuts the reality of not having secured Nolitando's love was unsettling. Before he climbed into the driver's seat to begin the journey, he locked himself in the bathroom, with the cold-water tap running, and spent anxious moments on his cell phone plying Nolitando with questions. 'Was she definitely coming to Tshwane? What time would she set off? Where was her family staying? What time would she arrive in Tshwane? Would she stay in the room he reserved for her?' He insisted she telephone him as soon as their car entered Tshwane.

He travelled in a state of nervous tension, impatient with his children at every demand to stop on the motorway to eat or use the rest rooms. Yet he used these opportunities to telephone Nolitando. When their kombi arrived in Pretoria, he left Heather to stand with their luggage at the hotel's reception desk while he again went to the men's room to call Nolitando. 'Had they set off already? Who was delaying them?'

In their rooms at the guesthouse he left Heather to unpack and rushed downstairs to confirm the single room he had booked for Nolitando was vacant. Out in the guestroom grounds, he phoned her, telling her a room was ready for her. Then he took the kombi and drove out onto the highway to wait for the arrival of her family. Heather, unsuspecting, assumed he was preoccupied with planning to film the interview with the President.

***

26.

Smuts prepared a programme for a well-informed audience aware that the British government in the past, supported the old South African administration, while the British people supported the struggle of oppressed South Africans. As an introduction to the interview with the President, he filmed the Heads of State and members of the royal houses of Africa and Europe but he also wanted a flavour of the streets, the colour and the glitz he and his companions were confounded by .

The setting was uncomfortable. The President was from the village Qumbu a remote spot in rural Transkei in their part of South Africa. It was a village without running water and electricity for the majority of its inhabitants. Here in Pretoria, however, at the inauguration they found a lavish celebration staged to appease or impress the watching world.

Desirous of capturing the people's impressions, Smuts did a walkabout in the streets recording the crowd watching the ceremony on giant screens, asking, 'How do you feel at this moment when you see kings, queens, presidents, and their wives coming to our celebration of freedom? Do you feel uplifted?' Proud? Do you feel free?

'You want the gospel truth' they asked. 'Or a toothpaste ad?' They grinned and showed white teeth.

'The truth,' Smuts said, 'Just don't swear.'

The crowd responded: 'If a rich man comes by your house, you tell him 'make yourself by the house'. You sweep and dust but you can't buy leather armchairs. He's used to steak and chips. You're eating 'Ma and Pa'[31]. He drinks whisky and gin. You only got Ship Sherry. Rooibos. Fanta Orange.'

'They've got money for all this,' Smuts said.

'That money's for us. Not for overseas visitors. Not to spend in one day.'

'Our leaders go home and eat umngqusho[32] and they drink

---

31 Ma and Pa is the name for a stew of mealies and beans.

32 Umngqusho is a stew of samp and beans.

amasi[33].'

'It's showing off. Like a carnival. To make like we can do things like them.'

'We never struggle so we can have big parties. People sleeping in pondokkies[34] want houses. Hot water. Lights.'

'It's wasting good money. Giving rich people a good time. They got money to throw away.'

'I tell you, the people picking food with dirty hands from the dustbin they don't know apartheid is finished.'

But not everyone was critical about the celebration and its extravagance. The occasion, by gathering together all races was a renewal. Many were ecstatic about hosting an event of such magnitude. Nothing approaching the season of liberation had ever been witnessed on the streets of South Africa from the day of the elections until the inauguration. It was madness. The swings and turns of joy, grief, love, hate, sadness, exuberance and incredulity the liberated South Africans expressed now that victory was theirs, was best captured on film. Visitors, sympathisers, supporters, friends, neighbours from African countries, could not approach or touch the emotions South Africans gave vent to. They could only observe.

In the streets, the shops, hotels, colleges, schools, people were so many degrees above the quirky. Perhaps not a single tear of mourning was shed in that period. For weeks after the people asked: 'Did you see that hat? Do you know how long that red carpet was? From the Highveld to the Bushveld! They say if you put all those chairs next to each other it will go twice round Magaliesberg. You heard that? There was one blommetjie[35] for every day every prisoner

---

33 Amasi is naturally soured milk

34 A pondokkie is a shack.

35 A Blommetjie is a little flower.

spent on Robben Island. That's three hundred and sixty five days times so many years times so many prisoners and the leap years. And the people! Mense![36] There will never be another season like this. Talk about pomps and ceremonials. The dames'[37] dresses. Fantastic colours. The Generaals[38] and shiny medals. The wereld's[39] leaders. Even Fidel Castro came all the way. Pity about Che. Now he should be here. Jong![40] There was even halal[41] food and smoor[42] snoek[43] and boerewors and sosaties[44] and koeksusters[45] and samoosas all small and ladylike. We must mos[46] show the world we got our own food. The lights! The music!'

In Pretoria, Pragashini, Matatiele and Smuts, experienced the release from apartheid, the new South Africa, in a way they never sensed in the Eastern Cape.

For the interview the President wore the same black suit and red tie he wore for the inauguration with a fresh white flower and a clean white shirt. Smuts took a close up of the huge gold ring on his finger. After the interviews with the President ended the minders asked the recorders and technicians to leave.

---

36 Mense means people but it is also used as an interjection.

37 Dames is the Afrikaans word for ladies.

38 Generaals is the Afrikaans word for Generals.

39 Wereld means the world.

40 Jong is a youth, but is also used as an interjection.

41 Halal is meat that has been prayed over by a Muslim before being slaughtered.

42 Smoor is to fry

43 A type of fish that is smoked, salted or dried, found only around Cape Town.

44 Sosaties are curried meat kebabs

45 Koeksusters are a type of doughnut specific to South Africa, may be Dutch or Malay variety.

46 Mos is a South African expression that means 'actually'.

Matatiele had a confidential briefing with senior cadres of the movement. They said opponents of change planned to derail the election process and destabilize the country, in the same manner that the liberation movement made the country ungovernable. Having failed these forces were now targeting individuals by frustrating the aspirations of some and confusing others so they turned against the new government. If they succeeded the individuals might become informers or double agents. The incorruptible would be killed. The assassinations before the elections were the beginning of this plot. They then told him he was in danger and offered him a bodyguard.

The cadres said they would continue the underground activities conducted during apartheid. They advised Matatiele to locate a woman who would prove to be a reliable source of information. She knew who the collaborators were in the Eastern Cape. She had gone underground. She may have changed her name or left the country for her own protection. Once again, the name Amina Khan cropped up.

***

27.

On her return to the Eastern Cape Pragashini took up her post in Bisho. Behind the scenes she was given access to computers in the departments. She was to edit documents and files held on computers in government offices in Bisho that were then sent to the government printers for printing. Her job description included upgrading the programmes on computers in each building and installing the internet on a select few. Although familiar with programmes in use the question of how to access information locked in a document was a mystery. Her first step was to locate the computer on which a sensitive document might be hidden.

***

28.

The suberterfuge she became adept at practising while hiding from Nasaratt, was a valuable asset while she searched for the document. On Matatiele's advice Pragashini enrolled in a beginners Xhosa class. This gave credence to the lie that she did not know the language. She attended classes in Kwazakele and Zwelitsha. In one group she met a Zimbabwean who learnt Xhosa with ease while a Kenyan struggled. Not knowing the history of Africa to understand why this was so she heard the woman explain her language, Ndebele, was like Zulu, and that Zulus had migrated to Zimbabwe a century ago. The Kenyan had no links with South Africa that he knew of.

When it came to Afrikaans, Matatiele wanted her to pretend rejection of the language in line with the children's rejection of the language during the struggle. Pragashini was dissuaded from brushing up her language skills in a class. He advised her to use a language tape and to read if she needed to brush up, but never to confirm that she could speak, write, or understand the language. Because she was from England, everyone assumed she knew no Afrikaans. She never enlightened them.

It appeared to work. Colleagues' tongues were loosened while she worked quietly in their offices. She was party to intelligence that she would not have received had they known she understood Afrikaans well. But they also taught her to swear, to say 'I love you', and to know when she passed men loitering in the street if they were planning to rob her. Having learnt Xhosa before she went into exile, she soon picked up a basic understanding of the language, although she had difficulty making the clicks when she attempted to speak in the classroom.

To avoid detection her job ensured little interaction with civil servants. She felt secure with this arrangement because, if discovered, she did not expect Matatiele to come to her rescue. She worked quietly editing, scanning the computers for viruses and downloading updates to the programmes installed on each computer.

Given access to offices in several government departments she explored and wandered in and out of offices to do quick random searches on any number of computers. Matatiele was so convincing about the document being crucial to the new government, that she resolutely used lunch and coffee breaks and the long hours of late sittings of parliament, and department meetings, to steal into the offices of her colleagues and continue the search. He warned her never to disclose her real purpose to anyone, no matter how well she came to know them.

Then she found a room filled with discarded computers that were used for spare parts or waiting for repair. She found it daunting. If there were documents on those computers, how would she access them? None of them were up and running.

***

l

29.

Mellikhaya's funeral was scheduled for a Saturday to enable friends and family to travel from around the country to Port Elizabeth. On the Monday, Smuts accompanied his father to select a casket. He was dismayed when his father paid several thousand Rand for one. He estimated what his father could have done with that amount of money.

'It's money from Mellikhaya's burial policy,' Matatiele said, adding' 'Mellikhaya even took a burial policy for me and your mama.'

Smuts felt shame and guilt when he heard these words. With the death benefit from the trade union, his father needed no assistance from him.

At five on Thursday morning Smuts accompanied his father and uncle in a bakkie[47] to Fort Jackson, where they bought a 'beast', a goat, and two sheep. Family members living in the rural areas surrounding Fort Jackson gathered at a small farm where the men slaughtered the animals.

The carcasses were tied upside down from trees a little distance from the farmhouse and left to hang all day and night, while the blood collected in new buckets. After lunch, they worked quickly to remove the entrails. It was then the business of cutting the small animals into halves, and quarters, and the large beast into eighths and then smaller manageable chunks. They retained the heads, tails, and all the entrails. The chunks were placed in new black plastic bin liners, the bags loaded onto the back of the bakkie and by nightfall Smuts and his father were back in Port Elizabeth.

They arrived home to a house heavy with the odour of fermenting beer. In the back yard Smuts watched the women preparing Umqombothi[48] from maize and other ingredients, which had been left to ferment all week. It deepened his experience of a traditional ceremony.

Then the first hitch came when permission for the funeral service to be conducted in the church was withheld. The minister explained that vast numbers of mourners were expected. He advised them to hire a larger venue. Smuts

---

47 A Bakkie is a small van the rear open to the elements.

48 Umqombothi is African beer brewed at home.

admonished the minister for the refusal. Nevertheless they arranged to use a large amphitheatre.

Then there was another hitch. From the women in the family Heather heard that she should not attend the funeral. They said she should ask her husband for an explanation.

Smuts could offer none. He challenged his father about her exclusion. Matatiele also dismissed his son. 'Ask your elders,' he said.

Rebuffed and feeling like a distant relative in the family, he approached the elders for their explanation. Their reply was stark and unembellished. Mellikhaya died a violent death. It was the custom in such cases for women to keep away from the graveside. Puzzling over why his father could not have told him, Smuts relayed the information to Heather.

Mourners began arriving on Friday and had to be accommodated and fed. Neighbours, family, and friends assisted. Women began preparing vegetables for the funeral feast. All female friends and relatives of Mellikhaya, even the girl friends of his male and female friends had a duty to assist with the preparation of the vegetables. Heather was encouraged to peel vegetables.

***

30.

Amidst rumours that Madiba was driving through the Eastern Cape to his home in Qumbu and would pay his respects to the family, Mellikhaya's body was taken in the casket from the mortuary to the amphitheatre.

In the amphitheatre the Matatiele family sat on the stage with mourners packed in the arena. Smuts observed all the details with a critical eye, like an alien to his culture. He was appalled to observe the videoing of the funeral and could not contain himself from remarking on this to Heather. The reverend delivered a sermon. The President, dignitaries from political parties and organisations spoke briefly at this service. They sang hymns and the national anthem.

Smuts assuming it was because he was not initiated, decided he would speak at the funeral, initiated or not. He took the microphone from the last speaker. Beginning with a few words about Mellikhaya the child he knew before he left South Africa, he directed his speech against his father.

'uTata,' he said to his father, 'you are stubborn.' Then to the mourners he said, 'Tata said Mellikhaya would not be buried until he gave the word. We pleaded with Tata for Mellikhaya to be buried. He died long before we found his body. We wanted Mellikhaya to rest so we could celebrate our victory over apartheid. We wanted to feel the new democracy with a full heart. Tata shut his ears to our cries. Tata refused point blank. We Matatieles celebrated our victory and our democracy with heavy hearts. Our brother Mellikhaya died long ago. An enemy murdered our brother. Our enemies brought our brother's corpse to the Bisho March. If our brother was alive on that day, he would have marched to Bisho. Here is our brother lying, begging us to put him to rest with our ancestors. I call on Tata – uTata – respectfully – to explain to our ancestors – why he kept them waiting for our brother.'

Matatiele was angry. He stood up, thin and straight. He looked at Smuts for an inordinate length of time, offended by the public disrespect his son showed him on this sad day. When the assembly began to sing softly, he snatched the microphone from Smuts. 'You good people – you think I didn't ask Mellikhaya before I withheld him from the soil of our fathers? From the moment, they brought the news that Mellikhaya was found dead on the Bisho Road I had to resist. My mind is so clear. Can you not see the logic of it? Can you not sympathise with me? Can you try to understand why I had to resist the elders pressing me to bury my son quick quick so that my clan could speak to our ancestors without Mellikhaya's death crying in our hearts? I refused. It was clear to me. I told our ancestors spirits 'If Mellikhaya is buried as soon as his brother arrives from England, if his funeral is held while the apartheid government still rules South Africa, his young death will be in vain. Mellikhaya will be buried an oppressed man in an oppressed country. I spoke to Mellikhaya's spirit. I soothed him. I spoke to our ancestors. The spirits agreed to wait. Today, I tell you, South Africa is free! One hundred per cent free! We the African people have voted. We have won the elections. We have sworn in our President Madiba. Now I can truly say my son Mellikhaya is a free man. My son will be buried in a free country. My son will rest in a democratic country. Lala ngoxolo[49] Mellikhaya! Lala ngoxolo!'

The crowd stood up and chanted together, 'Lala ngoxolo Mellikhaya!'

Smuts was humbled by his father's argument, by the sense and logic of what he said. He sat thoughtfully in the row of bereaved members of his clan, examining his hands and his mutilated clan finger, asking himself, 'Who am I to mock, to challenge and disrespect this old man who has so much wisdom in spite of his immense deprivation?' Then, for the first time since his return from exile, he cried from his heart for his brother. He shed tears from the heart.

Then the men moved forward with Smuts to carry the casket to the waiting hearse. Hundreds of cars and busloads of people went in the funeral cortege to the graveyard. By the time the last car reached the grave patch and off-loaded its passengers, the body of his brother was already lowered in the casket and covered with soil and stones. There were no

49 Lala ngoxolo means rest in peace.

women present. The gravestone, made of grey marble, was erected when the earth was piled on to the coffin without waiting for the subsidence.

They returned to the ancestral home. They washed their hands in enamel bowls of water and metal baths that were left outside the house with soap and towels draped over the backs of chairs. Then they entered the house. There was a tent arranged with tables and chairs. The mourners filed into the tent sat down and were served food and drink. The politicians sat at the main table. Smuts was called and informed that his name was on the list to stand for the provincial government.

Except for his earlier chastisement of the reverend, Smuts made no comment on any of the proceedings. He did not wish to seem overly influenced by his exile in the west, or by his English wife, nor did he want to be accused of leaving his African culture behind. He also did not wish to position himself with Heather in criticism of his culture. He stopped wondering how this sophisticated funeral ceremony combined with their tradition. Later he was particularly attentive to the little groups of mourners, listening to their talk, wanting to hear their views on the funeral. Not one member of the clan remarked about the funeral ceremony.

***

31.

Late on Sunday afternoon the mourners began leaving for their homes. The funeral and its associated rituals of singing, slaughter, and ululating were over. Smuts took his uncle's car and drove to Humewood to walk on the beachfront.

Now he could free his mind. He could relish the musicality of his language; think in his mother tongue without translating into English before he spoke; anticipate the new parliament; and just breathe in and savour the joy of being on South African soil. His ear was now accustomed to hearing his mother tongue. When Heather plied him with questions about the burial rituals he had to adjust his brain to her words. He tolerated her inquisitiveness. It was natural for an English woman of the nineties to want to lap up all this cultural difference. He could patronise her.

No one would ever be able to tap into the levels of meaning this homecoming had for him. No one but an African would ever sense the spirituality that existed between one African and another. There was something from God in that connection between them. No other race on earth felt the bond with each other the way one African felt bonded to another. Perhaps because of their suffering and oppression. It was what God had blessed them with. This interconnectedness with each other and with the African continent. The interconnectedness that led him to believe there were never boundaries throughout the continent. He stopped, closed his eyes and prayed for peace on the continent and that all Africans would come to recognise their spiritual interconnectedness.

He approached the new pier that jutted half a mile into the sea. He noticed a couple in the distance. The enormity of the change in South Africa penetrated his soul. His own smallness in the face of the awesome transformation from apartheid to freedom struck him with the force of his father's hand against his face. He could not take in what had transpired here from the day he ran away to this day when he could stand here and look all around as far as the eye could see, and not glimpse a man in uniform. A triumph. He rubbed his hands vigorously against his arms.

He strolled a little closer to the pier. From where he stood he could see the sea lapping and crashing onto the rocks below. He wished he could have been there to see its construction. To know how far down into the ocean the pillars went. How much concrete did they use? Did they keep the sea out while they were building? How did they get the concrete to set with the sea all around?

The sea was the colour of green Verdi Gris, the harbour hidden from where he stood. He began to walk towards the town. All along the left were ice-cream parlours, steak houses, hotels, apartment blocks, and filling stations. He could never enter these places before today. Yet now he chose not to enter. On the pavement where he walked he admired pavement sellers from East, West, and North Africa. They were hawking beautiful hand crafted jewellery. Brown and black wood. Cream ivory. White bone. Green malachite. Chess pieces carved from wood and malachite. Yellow, red, orange, black, white, green, and blue beads made into necklaces and bracelets. Bottles filled with sand stained with orange, black, cream, and red to make patterns that did not change. Malachite boxes. Leather bags. Jesus sandals. Wood carved elephants, giraffes, heads, masks, shields, and wine goblets.

The certainty of the artistry made him tremble. This was never revealed in South Africa. Here Africans had been portrayed as uncultured, ignorant savages. The wealth of Africa was on display on these pavements. It showed the lie of the colonial past. From his years in exile, his friendship with other Africans, it was possible for him to look at the hawker and tell the Ethiopian from the Kenyan, the Zimbabwean from the Ghanaian. To the oppressor, all Africans look alike.

He strolled on. Two women sat on a bench, facing out to sea. One wore red, the other yellow. Their skins were ebony black. There were few people about because it was nearing five o'clock, and the sky was overcast with clouds. But the clouds were pale blue. He breathed deeply and caught the smell of salt in the air, the smell he had longed for when he was in landlocked countries and towns.

A man walked towards him. Before the man reached him, he stopped at a litterbin and rummaged around inside it. The bin was bright blue, matching the man's trousers. He pulled out a polystyrene box and ate someone's leftovers. Smuts did not feel touched, or repulsed by this action. He had seen it wherever he sojourned.

A car pulled up and parked alongside the pavement. The passengers and driver remained sitting in the car looking out to sea. They talked. They ate. The man in blue overalls tapped on the window of their car. He touched his stomach in a symbolic gesture. They wound down the window and offered the man a rolled up paper containing whatever they had been eating. They climbed out of their car and sat on the low wall. Then they strolled along the pavement like he was doing; to hear the sea. Smell the salt. See the waves crash and break. To be in awe of nature. To realise their smallness. Their belonging to it. The stretch of concrete pier imposed on nature. Planted palms from Natal waved pathetic dried up fronds in the breeze. Smuts noticed a senseless swimming pool built on the beach.

Three speedboats appeared from around the bend, made for the sea, and disappeared. Three surfers crossed the road to the beach. A rare blue car came under the attention of vagrants. They scrutinized the car from all angles. A third vagrant appeared with a jerry can of water and they proceeded to wash the car. Four children walked together, a Coloured boy of about five, another about seven, an African boy of ten, and a White boy about thirteen. They stopped a White man who was strolling along the pavement. They said something to the man. He appeared affronted, swore them loudly, and walked rapidly away.

Two speedboats stopped their engines and bopped up and down like corks in the bay. A yacht floated idly in the sea. There were no ships on the horizon. It began to drizzle. He got into the car, sat for a while, started the engine, and drove back to New Brighton.

***

32.

In England Pragashini was free to step out the door, walk anywhere, jump on buses and trains, only considering the fare, the timetable, and the fear of Nasaratt.

In South Africa, a country now deprived of an intercity rail network and modern buses running every three minutes, she was appalled to see the people in the grip of a taxi system apparently manned by rough youths and men, and controlled by gangsters, thugs and gun wielding ex-policemen. To walk alone was foolhardy for women and men.

Lacking a car, she had no option but to use taxis to move from place to place. The experience confirmed how apartheid changed the country. It seemed to her the political, social, and economic changes were no longer opposed by a racist white minority, but by an environment of black violence and crime, perpetrated indiscriminately on black and white people.

Travelling between cities it was common for a taxi to turn back when a rival taxi company blocked the motorway with taxis between Bisho and East London or Bisho and Port Elizabeth. Never before had she witnessed an army called out in full force with helicopters overhead, to quell taxi violence on the highway. The room she rented near her place of work brought the taxi violence closer.

The room was attached to a large house. The housekeeper was married to a retired policeman who used his savings to purchase a fleet of taxis. Every weekend taxi drivers turned up at the housekeeper's quarters with news of a disturbance. The taxi owner placed his gun in a little cardboard child's suitcase, then walked with his drivers to the taxi rank in the back streets and negotiated with his rivals. When they could not reach agreement about the routes each would use, each taxi company took the route they preferred and had a shoot out on the highway, cowboy style. For the first time she heard real live shooting. Living in England, she heard gunshots in films, perhaps the sound effects.

Nevertheless, having a room near the workplace gave her a respite from the Nasaratts. She felt restricted living with them. Never a sociable person in England, yet meeting old friends and returned exiles, she wished she could invite them round, but was not free to do so. Returned exiles were activists, and if not active, they were supporters of the liberation movement. They were accustomed to meetings and social occasions without racial barriers.

There had been high spots in South Africa where this mingling across racial barriers always took place. But it was by no means widespread. In the little towns and villages, - places that might not appear on the map, like Warmbads, Kirkwood, Naaupoort, Coega, - and in the racially created separate areas of Port Elizabeth, East London, Cape Town and Johannesburg, areas demarcated for a specific racial group – people organised within their racial groups. They went about their daily lives without interacting with other racial groups except perhaps in the flare up on the shop floor or in the religious communities they belonged to. Hindus, Christians, and Muslims had different political affiliations.

Throughout this period, she maintained contact with the

university in England and revised her research. The four universities in the province were amenable to her using their libraries, and facilities for her personal research. While travelling from Bisho to Port Elizabeth, it was convenient to stop and use the university library in Grahamstown. Her working week was spent in Bisho so she used the Fort Hare campus across the road, or the one in Alice. At weekends she used local universities in Port Elizabeth.

It seemed to her South Africa's university life was bleak compared with England where students were in possession of sufficient support to leave home, find digs, buy food, books, music, and music systems in addition to leaving college every weekend to joll around on other campuses. The whole purpose of going to university was to leave home and savour the freedom of doing one's own thing.

Here, a rich country by Third World standards, young people could not afford the luxury of leaving home. They attended doorstep universities. She did not know enough to appreciate how this came about. Matatiele assured her there had been a time when they could afford to leave home and study at Fort Hare.

***

33.

When she was in possession of a second hand car, Pragashini made the midday drive every Friday from Bisho to spend the weekend in Port Elizabeth. It was the worse time of day when there was little shade on the road. At five o'clock on Monday mornings, she drove alone to Bisho to be in time for work. It was cooler driving before the sun was up.

Over a period of weeks following their first meeting, she came into regular contact with Klein through her work.

These encounters were innocent, nevertheless, her feelings of happiness and pleasure being near him persisted. For the first time since her marriage, she was without the fear of men that Nasaratt engendered. She remembered her healthy interest in sex when she was a girl, and how her feelings for Smuts had been crushed before they could blossom. Although she hankered after that innocent love, she refused to have an affair with Smuts.

She sensed her feelings for Klein were reciprocated. From week to week there was nothing more than this awareness of his physical presence. She sensed when he entered a room. On looking round, there he was. She felt some extra sensory communication between them similar to when she woke in the night and sensed snow falling. When their hands touched, exchanging papers, handing coffee around, handling the telephone receiver, there was no romantic thrill. The connection between them was not physical, but spiritual.

These everyday chance intimacies that occur when people work closely over a project, were meaningless, except that she was experiencing the uncertainty, the hesitation, preceding the recognition of love. She could not be sure if she was in love with him, or if the spiritual connection between them was a mystical experience.

She imagined he chose to stand close to her when their working group chatted informally about something that carried over from a discussion, session or meeting. He had the habit of standing with his arms folded, a smile playing around his mouth, his eyes glinting with hidden knowledge of something, his whole being exuding much more than mere happiness. It might have been closer to arrogance, so confident was he compared with her. He was at ease. He gave out that aura of one who feels certain of his catch and was merely biding his time.

If he could not sit alongside her at a conference table, he sat across from her. But he rarely if ever spoke directly to her. She sensed him looking at her. When she looked up she would catch his eyes before he looked away. When she stopped writing and looked up she looked into his eyes and would turn his head to one end of the room.

She looked in the mirror to gauge if he would find her attractive. Still wearing neither makeup nor jewellery, and persistently shaving her head, she could only hope her connection with him did not depend on her appearance. And that it was not love.

One day she acknowledged she was too innocent for a man of his experience. She had no inkling of what would happen next. She did not know the strategy. She had never played this game of wait and see, yet she waited for him, in the same manner that she waited for a beautiful thought during her traumatic exile. Perhaps he would know her soul?

In South Africa when she was a girl, she knew Indian, Malay, Chinese, and Coloured youths, and one African, Smuts. Klein was the first white South African man she had ever been attracted to. She believed he would understand this. For an inexplicable reason, she trusted him.

When she looked at him she liked his hands. His fingers were nicotine stained, his hands large like a farmers. He looked strong and dependable. Sometimes she would forget the discussion and ask herself what did she possibly have in common with this man, except their South Africanness?

What could they possibly talk about outside these work meetings? Was he involved in the struggle? Could they discuss playback singers from Hindi movies? Did he know what that meant? Had he heard of Lataji or Ashaji? Kareena Kapoor? Hrithik Roshan? Would she be free to eat in his company using her fingers? Or would she have to hide the way she had been brought up to eat and make one more adaptation on top of all the adjustments and adaptations her race had already made since the days of the Raj? Worse still, was he one of those who could not stomach Indian food? Was love capable of resolving all this? If this was love.

Whatever her misgivings, the weeks were ecstatic. She noticed neither the days, nor the politics of her country. Now when she woke in the middle of the night, it was not to hear the crying child that haunted her, nor to dash to the window to see if it was snowing, but to find herself engaged in conversation with him. During the day she would be drawn to a place. Leaving her work, and following her instincts she would find him already there. He had the power to draw her to him.

When she observed this happening too many times for it to be coincidental, she tested her own power over him. She sat in her room one afternoon and called him to her. When she looked out the window, he was standing there, alongside a tree, looking up at her window. It made her less uncertain knowing she had the same ability to draw him to her. They were that close. She believed if he died, and she was on another continent, she would know.

***

Pragashini's Journal

34.

I choked every soft, feminine inclination while nourishing a life-long lifeless ambition to contribute to scientific knowledge. Where did it lead? To this weird recognition of a stranger. What is such recognition? Is this love? If it is love, whose love is it? Mine or my soul's? If it is my soul's, can it be a newborn love? Or the love of souls that new each other before my life began? Is this what falling in love at first sight really means? Is one soul recognising another, love at first sight? Is this how beauty came to love the beast?

***

35.

Hers was a blissful state of mind. Pragashini rushed eagerly to work to be near Klein. Later she felt guilty. A sense of dishonesty about living with the Nasaratts, possessed her. She had arrived at their home as their daughter-in-law overly sensitive to and fearful of how they would welcome her. If they knew or suspected the failure of her marriage, she expected them to reject her or receive her coolly.

The turnout at the airport when she arrived alarmed her. Their insistence that she first visit the oldest member of their family disconcerted her. As the days passed, and there was no hint, nor snide remark, she assumed they were unaware that she had run away from Nasaratt. After weeks of living with them, she felt reassured.

But in her mind she did not belong in Nasaratt's family. As a returning exile she should have returned to the Dev's. Yet she was inclined to blame them more than the Nasaratts.

The more they accepted her the more she regretted her dishonesty. She had never been in touch with them since leaving South Africa. They were ignorant of her life in exile. She lied to them about the reason for her shaved head, and that she had children in England. She even created stories about her children. When their curiosity was dissatisfied without photos she obliged with photos of children belonging to Fawzia, the woman who gave her refuge in England and whose scarf she wore every day.

There were times when she was tempted to confide in Roshni but invariably stopped herself. Telling Roshni would serve no purpose. She wanted to confront Nasaratt then leave their home. But her mind did not offer a method about how she should do it.

In conflict about deceiving the Nasaratts, she made efforts to adapt her style of living to the new South Africa. She maintained the habit of waking early, performing her puja, rituals, and meditation, and jogging. She worked on her thesis. She used the facilities in the various libraries. Still the adjustment was difficult.

***

36.

For every instance of terror, real or imagined; for every night in hiding; every dread; every humiliation; every insecurity; every death he, his father, his clan, had endured in South Africa and exiled from it, this moment assuaged it. This was the prize.

The sun warmed Smuts' back. Alcohol burned his throat – he was released from his promise never to drink while South Africa was in chains. He had not been engaged in the counting of votes in the days following the elections only with the security arrangements around the ballot boxes the night before. With all the celebrations over, and Mellikhaya buried, until the Legislature began, he had time to spend with his parents.

He was on the other side of town, a distance from New Brighton. He stood a few feet from his father as he sat in a low colonial armchair. Around him, short cut green grass undulated up to the Dutch styled house at his back. He was suffused with happiness just looking at his father. That this thin humble man survivor of the oppressive dehumanisation of his people, could finally come out of the township and experience entering a white suburb as a respectable visitor, to relax on a chair in a grandiose house, with a glass of ice cold Castle lager in his hand, just like the baas of the house would have done.

Smuts clapped his hands. The domestic helper materialised with a tray, a pipe and tobacco for his father. He realised he was going over the top with domestic help, but in other parts of Africa he had seen more. Heather and he decided to employ domestic help because it offered employment to people who had little or no education. They would pay a decent wage and educate the children of the domestic helper. When his father grumbled that he was not accustomed to being served, Smuts narrated an anecdote. 'When I was hiding in Zimbabwe,' he said, 'I saw with my own two eyes an African servant kneeling down and walking on his knees towards his African master sitting on the veranda. This is nothing compared with that.'

Earlier that morning he collected his father and mother from the township in his Black BMW. He misled them into thinking he was taking them for a drive to show off his new car. He had the four children in the car. He kept the front seat for his father. They drove into Grahamstown Road, into Main Street, up Cape Road over the flyovers, across Baakens Bridge, stopping for ice cream and cold drinks, but slowly driving in a roundabout way to the house, he and Heather had just moved into.

His parents were not even aware that Smuts could drive. Matatiele 'clicked' and 'clucked' at the beautiful houses on millionaires row. How clean the streets were. There were no children running about. Cars could be left parked outside the houses without the windows being smashed. 'Look at the shops. Right near the houses. So convenient'. They picked up fresh, hot bread and milk. They went over the motorway passed the sea and into Main Street in the city centre.

The end of apartheid was visible on the street. Wherever they looked they saw men and women sitting on the pavements. Apartheid would have chased them away. Tsotsis loitered on the street corners. Apartheid would have arrested them. Vagabonds stood at the traffic lights and pounced on cars waiting for the lights to change, with sponges and rags at the ready, washing car windscreens without invitation. Women weaved their way in and out of cars in a traffic jam balancing bowls of oranges on their heads, eager for a sale. In the car park, little urchins ran up to cars begging for bread or money. Where were they hiding all these years? They came from somewhere to take the country out of the hands of the whites before the elections, with such confidence that Smuts had no comment.

Smuts wished he had been here when the people marched against apartheid. When the Rivonia Trialists were released. When Bishop Tutu walked arm in arm with throngs of people to protest against apartheid. When Madiba emerged from captivity. Then all of this would not make his body reverberate like when an electric shock passed through him.

This was Madiba's achievement. It was also the liberation movement's. Never mind housing, running water, schools, electricity, and roads. This was the victory. Only one who had been here and experienced it from the wrong side of the colour bar could ever measure the difference between that past and this present.

In the shops, thin model-beautiful African girls now smiled sweetly at him behind the counters of Edgars, Woolworths, Clicks, the banks, speaking English, their fingers slim, nails polished, skin well cared for. African women now flaunted their bodies in orange, greens, reds, bright gaudy colours with matching headscarves or wide-brimmed nylon hats, where they formerly dressed in imitation of white women from Europe in skirt suit, umbrella and handbag. They no longer straightened their hair but wore beads, braids, cornrowing and hair extensions. Men wore embroidered shirts from Nigeria in bright colours. He could see he was in Africa.

Previously South Africa was like a state in Europe. But noticeably absent were the policemen in their grey uniforms with their wolfish Alsatian dogs. He had not seen or heard the siren of a police gorma[50] on any day or night of the week. It was glorious to be back to experience just that if nothing else.

They coasted over the motorway, and he finally drove into the white suburb and parked before a large house. Heather emerged from the front door, dressed like a Maqothi[51], her blonde hair hidden in a blue scarf, a towel around her waist, tucked into her German blue print dress, her feet bare. She came up to the car and opened the passenger door. She welcomed them clapping her hands like an African woman.

His parents were incredulous. They wanted to remove their shoes before entering the front door but Smuts would have none of that. He stooped and plucked a weed here, and deadheaded a rose there. He asked his father the name of a shrub and showed him how the sprinklers were hidden in the soil at the front of the house.

They listened to a train passing nearby, enjoying the view of all the houses neatly set back from the paved road, with trees giving shade, the pavement grassed over and neatly kept, and paving slabs for pedestrians to walk on in the shade and the sunshine.

He had to repeat several times that Heather was renting not buying the house. But they were convinced he had bought it but was too modest to admit it. He took them on a

---

50 A gorma is a colloquial name for the Black Maria or police vehicle used to transport prisoners.

51 Maqothi is the term used by family members for a woman who has married into that family.

tour of the house and grounds. His parents trailed behind them. He could feel his father's pride. They marvelled at the swimming pool and braai area, the size of the bedrooms, the built in cupboards. The housekeeper had a room that was as big as their house in New Brighton with her own shower. It was unbelievable. He told them Heather was considering buying the house if the landlord was amenable to the idea. She received a generous settlement from her grandmother when she married. Many whites were leaving the country. The house might come cheap. They laughed and told him he had done well to marry a rich woman.

While they were sitting out on the lawn, he asked his parents if they would live with him in the new house. The elderly couple were shocked. They considered him far above them. They were embarrassed. They were reluctant. They said they did not feel comfortable in such surroundings. They were afraid they might shame him when 'big people' came to visit him. Smuts and Heather would hear none of their excuses.

While they sat drinking in the sun, elders from the clan entered. Their message was for Smuts. 'If you go to the Legislature, when you stand up to speak, they will stamp their feet, so you can't be heard – because you are not a man.' The elders also wanted him to go into the forest.

***

37.

The Recluse - Pragashini's Journal

If she is falling in love, then it is uncanny that she should fall in love with him, and it is tragic that his soul is dead.

***

38.

The Sunday morning routine for Smuts was to wake his parents with mugs of coffee sweetened with condensed milk, and koeksusters. They had compromised. Instead of moving in with Smuts and Heather, they spent weekends with them. He drove to the shops with his children for freshly baked bread, milk, and the Sunday paper. The koeksusters were delivered on a plate to the front door. He gave the children their weekly allowance of chocolate, came home, and read the paper while his mother dressed for church.

Mandisa occasionally wore a uniform of maroon with a white collar and maroon beret that he noticed all the other women who attended her church wore. Sensitive to her feelings that he might be either criticising or ridiculing her, he never questioned her.

Heather on the other hand, went to the Catholic church dressed in jeans, shorts, flip flops, whatever the weather determined, her head uncovered, without prayer book or hymn book, with just enough money for the collection plate and the Southern Cross, the weekly Catholic newspaper. She drew the line at wearing a bathing costume to church – he never understood why. He observed everyone going into Heather's church was as casual about dress as she was. There was no such thing as wearing your Sunday best in Heather's church.

When the women were ready Smuts drove Heather to the Church she had on her list. She planned to visit every Catholic Church in the city. She went the rounds first to New Brighton, then intended to proceed to St Augustine's the cathedral, St James in Schauder Township, Our Lady of Perpetual Succour in Muhalla Asha, St Patrick's in North End, St Dominic's Priory on the hill. After dropping Heather he drove to his mother's church in New Brighton.

He attended the service and sat at the back of the church observing the people, listening to the preacher, joining in the hymns where he could. Sometimes his mother asked to be taken to an assembly hall where the congregation was much larger. He was soon bored and waited with his father outside the church. His mother's service lasted hours and he became tired and impatient with the preaching and singing that had no time constraints.

He also worried that his mother spent hours there with only a light breakfast. She had lunch at three or four in the afternoon. But he could see she looked forward to the service, and he could not begrudge her the time. The person he was angry with was the preacher. Yet he never questioned his father for not attending with his mother. He wanted to respect their different beliefs although he was no longer at ease with his mother's.

It was inevitable that Smuts finally made a habit of leaving his mother at her service. He came home, spent the morning with the children, collected Heather, had lunch and then in the afternoon he and his father collected his mother.

While they were driving home one Sunday afternoon Matatiele turned to the back seat where his wife was sitting and said, 'You remember Mandi, when he was small you told him about the boycotts? Turning to Smuts he added, 'I told you then your mama is a walking history book.'

Looking into the rear view mirror, Smuts saw his mother smile for the first time since his return. She seemed pleased by what his father had said and he detected admiration for her in his father's voice. When his father turned back and Smuts looked directly at him he saw tears in his eyes. His mother put her hand on his father's shoulder perhaps with understanding and reassurance. It was a rare occasion for Smuts to witness the relationship between them. 'I told you who led that first bus boycott. He was on Robben Island then. You remember?' she said.

'He remembers niks about his time with us. Back then he didn't even want to know,' Matatiele slapped Smuts on his shoulder. 'Like you forgot my commandments.'

'Sorry,' Smuts said.

'Now he's our premier,' she answered. 'From prisoner on Robben Island to premier of the province. Oom Ray.'

'No wonder Mandela lost patience!' said Smuts.

'Yes. It's a long time. For all of us,' she said.

Matatiele had allowed his wife space to think about Mellikhaya, to relive her memories of him, a mother's memories, memories he never shared. He observed she was now able to get through the day without her tears flowing.

He wanted to draw her away from thoughts about Mellikhaya to topics that stirred memories of when they were active. He prompted her to remind Smuts about the bus boycotts and the boycotts for a minimum wage called by SACTU. [52]

'We begged for a £1 a day,' Matatiele said. 'Imagine! Even when they paid us to work, we were slaves, getting slave wages,' he added.

'Yes, Tata. You know, in England they were singing 'bring back slavery, bring back slavery,' said Smuts.

'What? The British wants slaves again?'

'No. Black people were calling for slavery.'

'They mad? Or babbelaas?'

'There's logic in their madness,' Smuts said. 'They argue in those days when work was despised, when certain people lounged around, and others worked and got no pay or starvation wages, the Black man was always working, chained, made to work. Whipped if he stopped. These days, when workers earn five figure sums of money, the Black

52 SACTU is the South African Congress of Trade Unions.

man is never out of the dole queue. Now he begs for work, and they won't employ him.'

'I thought they really want slavery back.'

'They're being political.' He did not dare tell his father they were singing 'bring back slavery to the tune of 'Nkosi Sikelela iAfrika'. He would interpret it as an insult to the national anthem. He would never understand Black people doing that or their reasoning. And that he joined in. They all knew what they were coming home to – starvation wages to maids, nannies, gardeners, cleaners. It will change. But he was not ready to withstand the onslaught of his father's wrath.

'I remember them chanting 'Azikwelwa![53]' his mother interrupted them. 'I remember asking my Tata if they were going to do that dance we used to do called kwela. I remember it was iGoli's boycott. I remember we boycotted the buses for three months. We were very strong then.'

After Mellikhaya's funeral, Smuts was nominated to the provincial legislature. He prepared to swear the oath of allegiance and take up his seat in the Eastern Cape's parliament in Bisho. The Legislature and the various political parties were busy interviewing staff. During that time, there were no sittings of the house. Meetings were sporadic. For these meetings members of the provincial legislature were housed temporarily at Amatola Sun and other hotels in East London and King Williamstown until the houses in the ministerial complex were allocated. Members drove to Bisho from the surrounding cities and towns in the province to attend the meetings and returned to their various homes waiting for the formal opening of the Legislature. Smuts did the same. He lived in Port Elizabeth and drove to Bisho for a meeting or a short sitting of the

---

53 Azikwelwa means We Will Not Ride

house.

39.

A gift from the gods. That's how Smuts viewed the debate about where the capital of the Eastern Cape should be. It helped him organise his week around Heather and Nolitando. The problem of a clandestine relationship with Nolitando hidden from Heather for the time being, with his father's knowledge and connivance, was solved.

The debate centred round whether Port Elizabeth, Bisho or Umtata would be the capital. There was little in Bisho except a gambling casino in an elongated bungalow and a satellite campus of Fort Hare University. In its favour were the buildings that had been used for the Ciskei's parliament. It might take centuries for Bisho to grow to equal Port Elizabeth that had developed since the occupation by European explorers. Without the influx of settlers and manufacturing industries it might take longer. Umtata was slightly larger than Bisho.

While the debate raged, Smuts and Heather argued about where their children should attend school. Like any good parent Heather enquired about schools in Port Elizabeth and heard of good English language schools, Catholic, state and private. Like most people she took for granted Port Elizabeth would become the capital. Smuts assumed the infrastructure from the Ciskei government would be used by the new legislature so he wanted their children to attend school in Bisho.

'We shouldn't shunt them around,' Heather said. 'We've already taken them from their friends back home. Let them go to school in P.E. We can move them if Bisho or Umtata become the capital.'

Smuts had other ideas. 'Lover, you just don't understand.

Bisho and Umtata are black cities. iBhayi is a white city.'

'What d'you mean - black cities? White cities? Stop using those words. If you mean Africans then say so. PE's bigger than Bisho. There are more Africans here. Bisho's smaller than a village back home. You been drinking Umqombothi Smuts?'

'The capital's going to be Bisho. Wait and see. Start the kids off in Bisho so they'll get used to rural life. Come. Let's ask Mama. She'll explain it better than me.'

Mandisa was in the back yard reading a book on a sun lounge chair that Heather bought her.

'You've got to keep our history at the back of your mind, if you want to follow what people argue about today,' she said. 'It's too complicated if you don't know the history.'

'Just tell her about the Ciskei and Transkei,' said Smuts.

'I'm reading a good book. You tell her,' Mandisa said.

'Just tell her why Bisho will be the capital. She won't believe me.'

'It's about the Bisho Massacre. Before the elections some people wanted Ciskei and Transkei to remain independent states outside South Africa. Others said, we want Ciskei and Transkei back in South Africa! You could say it's like Pakistan returning to India. Or Africa going back to how it was before it was carved up.'

'Mama just stick with Bisho and the capital. Those places will never change,' said Smuts.

'You're right. Not in our lifetime,' said Mandisa.

'Why not?' asked Helen.

'Because something strange is happening out there.'

'Tell me,' said Heather.

'Some countries are uniting and growing bigger and stronger. Others are breaking up. Kashmir wants to break from India. Punjab, maybe Gujarat. Making India smaller and weaker. The people are blind, so blind, to this fact.'

Heather glanced at Smuts. They could both feel the despair in her voice. Smuts prompted, 'What about Bisho?'

'Well, Ciskei people didn't despair. Their dream was to be reunited with South Africa. You know, I'm surprised they didn't make Ciskei and Transkei two provinces. The way they're chopping up the new South Africa like colonisers.'

'Why did they make nine provinces?' Heather asked.

'So one province won't be too big,' Smuts said. 'We could have power struggles and all that.'

'They left Natal intact,' said Heather.

'I respect Buthelezi for that,' said Mandisa. 'Not chopping up Natal. I only wish they chose a better name. Natal is a memory from the colonials.'

'So are all the Capes!' Smuts said.

'But the name Kwa-Zulu is like apartheid and Bantustans,' Mandisa said. She pursed her mouth disapprovingly.

'What name would you like?' asked Heather.

'I'm trying to think of all the names from Zulu history. But no, it's for the people there to choose,' she replied.

'I like Gauteng!' said Smuts. 'It's got a nice strong sound.'

Without warning Heather said, 'Smuts, you've been very devious, distracting me with all this talk about capitals and schools. Does your mother know you were coming here for the funeral but you intended leaving me and the children at home? Now here you are taking up an important post. If I hadn't followed you, what would've happened to me and the children?'

'Smuts?' Mandisa sounded alarmed.

'I promised I'd come back for you,' said Smuts.

'Smuts?' Mandisa repeated. 'I can't believe what I've just heard'.

'No Smuts,' said Heather. 'I think you would've forgotten about us. We didn't figure in your plans.'

'That's not true. You're the mother of my children. I love

you Heather.'

Mandisa was troubled by what she heard. She continued the conversation about the capital as if there had been no interruption but she was distracted. 'Ciskei didn't want to be like Lesotho, a country inside South Africa. What they did gave them an advantage over Transkei when the time comes to decide the capital. They marched. They gathered and marched through King Williamstown up the Bisho Road into Bisho demanding to be reunited with South Africa. It was supposed to be a peaceful march but it turned into a terrifying day. I know some of the marchers. I talked to some women. If you know the Bisho Road, it's steep. Like the Hill in iBhayi. The police were at the top where King Williamstown becomes Bisho. The marchers couldn't see the police until they were on the top of the hill. They were marching and singing. When they reached the top suddenly the police stood up, took aim, and fired on them. People were running and screaming. Even women and children. The wounded trying to hide from the bullets. People were killed. That's the Bisho Massacre. They say they'll put a monument where it happened. Ask Smuts to show you.'

Heather knew that was when they found Mellikhaya. Still she asked, 'Is that the only reason? The Bisho Massacre?'

'You don't think that's a good reason?' Mandisa asked.

'What about Umtata?'

'People from Transkei didn't march. But Umtata is already a capital city. It will go down if the capital is Bisho or iBhayi.'

'So you think Bisho will be the capital?'

'People who don't know Ciskei and Transkei think iBhayi is the natural capital. Our grandparents are in Transkei and Ciskei. Our ancestors are buried there. Even Mandela comes from there. The leadership is from there. That's why apartheid removed people from iBhayi and put them back there. In iBhayi, Whites control the industries. English speaking mostly.'

'Is it wrong if I want the children to go to school in PE? They won't do well with other languages,' Heather said.

'That's for you to decide. People here prefer Afrikaans. If you go to Kimberley and Cape Town, you'll hear the people speak Afrikaans. It's a pity.'

'Why?' Heather asked. 'They have a right to speak their mother tongue.'

'Mother tongue? That's another debate Heather. Afrikaans is useful only in South Africa,' Mandisa said.

Then Smuts received a temporary schedule of sittings of the legislature. The members planned to sit from Monday morning to Friday lunchtime. 'What will we do in Bisho over the weekend? Gamble?' Heather asked.

'Lover, there's a beach in East London,' he suggested.

'Or you can come home at weekends,' she suggested.

But the memory that Smuts had not wanted her to accompany him to his brother's funeral remained with her. His assurances that he would have returned to England did not reassure her.

Heather never suspected that she facilitated Smuts affair with Nolitando. Their children began attending schools in Port Elizabeth. The twins attended a nursery school, while she began supply teaching. Smuts spent the week in Bisho, his weekends in Port Elizabeth. They kept this arrangement waiting for the capital to be declared.

***

40.

Nolitando shared Heather's antipathy to living in Bisho. Smuts was unprepared for her arguments. To him it was logical for Nolitando to move to Bisho if Heather remained in Port Elizabeth. He never anticipated her resistance. But Nolitando was adamant. She would never leave the city.

'Smuts, seriously, you expect me to leave a glamorous city to live where people go to sleep at five o'clock?'

He laughed at that. 'Don't let Bisho people hear you. They'll make muti out of you!'

'In my humble opinion, Bisho is okay for a travelling salesman. He can leave his wife at home, drive up here, have his sales talk, meet small time shopkeepers, gamble the night away in Amatola Sun, sleep, then travel on. But to live in a place a human being needs a life. Where's the life in Bisho? What's here? Movies? A park? A beach? Nightclubs? Theatre? Dance halls? Smuts, there isn't even a beer garden. There's nothing here but a gambling house full of people with no interest in jazz or talking. They sit like robots pushing coins into machines. No, Smuts, you can't be serious. There's life outside Bisho!'

'Bisho's got nothing going for it now. Apartheid's to blame. If Bisho is the capital investors will come here and think something needs to be done for this place. They'll pour money in. They'll build houses, shops, everything. When you wake up and want to buy a house, only millionaires will be buying in Bisho. You'll see.'

She laughed. 'Smuts look at Cape Town. Look at iGoli. Look at Durban. My hometown. Those places are alive. They're fast. Cars move fast. People move fast. There's noise. People. Cars. Machines. They talk like they don't have time to hang around. Nothing stops. The night is as busy as the day. Please. Don't ask me to live in Bisho. A capital must be like London or New York. Even Umtata won't make a good capital. Bring your wife to Bisho. I'm staying in iBhayi.'

'Listen Nolitando don't talk like that when there are MPs around. You'll be touching a raw nerve. People from Bisho and Umtata will cry if they hear you talk like that. They also want their city to be the capital.'

'What will I do there?' she grumbled.

'Wait till you see the Premier's House.'

Smuts was new to the government. Many of the members of the legislature had experience of sitting on local councils. They were active in political parties, and some were shop stewards in the trade unions. Since the debate about where to locate the capital of the province was still raging the ministerial housing complex was not fully occupied. The complex of one-floored houses was set behind a protected wall with tarred roads, swimming pool, green lawns, and security guards.

Adjacent to the ministerial complex was the Premier's residence. Smuts took Nolitando to a function in the Premier's house and showed her around the ministers' housing complex. She met young secretaries and civil servants who talked about creating a social life now they had to work there. She remained unimpressed. 'If they bypass my home town and make Bisho the capital, I've got a good mind to boycott this place.'

'Well, if you won't live here, you can forget about me going into the forest,' Smuts argued.

'You said I must never be forced. Let's wait and see.'

Before the function ended, however, the word was out: Bisho was the capital.

'If you live here with me, I'll go into the forest,' repeated Smuts.

Nolitando agreed.

Smuts approached his father with the news that he would undergo initiation. He was unwilling to explain why he changed his mind and Matatiele did not ask. He half convinced himself it was connected to standing for the provincial legislature. Even those willing to slip away from tradition would ridicule him if he was not initiated.

The older Matatiele clasped his son's hand firmly and said, 'My son, you'll see the size of the beast I'll slaughter when you come out of the forest.'

Smuts said, 'You honour me, Tata'. But he was afraid. He was afraid of the process of circumcision, using an unsterile blade, of surviving in the bush for weeks, eating leaves and other things, drinking water from a stream, that had not been filtered, or purified. But more than that he feared allowing himself to be influenced by the mystical elements of his culture, elements he had avoided for most of his life.

He told Heather. She was satisfied. But while he prepared to leave for the forest she was unprepared for her trial.

***

41.

Heather, who knew how to prepare for a test of academic skills had no means of revising for the test of her attitudes and prejudices. Not only had she agreed with the elders when they gave Smuts the benefit of their experience – 'go to the forest or you will be treated like a small boy in the Legislature,' she added her own arguments. 'It will deepen your father's happiness now you are home. It will lessen his grief for Mellikhaya. They haven't ordered you to do this. It's a request. You should comply.'

Then, following the knowledgeable manner in which she expressed her confidence that the Sangoma would use a clean knife, and the correct methods to sever the foreskin, that he knew which herbal leaves to encase her husband's member in until it had healed, - they tested her. She spoke with the authority of one who had been convinced by the clan. She believed she had persuaded Smuts.

In the run up to his departure for the forest she teased him about the impending trial and did not confine her teasing to when they were alone. In the company of family she took great pains to speak with a serious expression on her face, while alluding to the impending ceremony, making risqué jokes only the two of them understood.

Smuts took her humour in his stride. He pandered to her sexual fetishes one of which was to plait her red pubic hair. Her fetish for sexual innuendo was a game they indulged in when their children were with them on a journey or if they were playing board games. She never shared his trepidation as the day approached for him to leave for the forest. In fact, she was so keen to know what her role would be in the 'Uhluhluhlu' celebrations she questioned the women eagerly, willing to learn everything about their culture. She took out pen and ink and designed invitation cards. She was advised how to word the invitation. Someone working in an office photocopied the invitation on to yellow paper.

The women of the clan were delighted at the thought of celebrating the coming out from the forest of a man of Smuts' age. There was no prescribed age for initiation. Usually boys between the ages of twelve and twenty went for initiation, sometimes even younger boys. It had never been done before, that they knew of. They knew, though, of many boys who had run away during the mourning years and would be undergoing initiation late in life. There was a buzz in the house. Sometimes there was soft laughter that she could not comprehend nevertheless, she laughed with them so as not to feel excluded. The time was fast approaching when Smuts would leave for the forest. She was gratified he would give his clan a degree of happiness following their bereavement.

Before Heather's test, Smuts, to get his own back, informed her that women were also circumcised. Heather was well informed on female circumcision and infibulation, but ignorant about the societies that practised these rituals. She became very anxious for herself, but not for her daughter, knowing she would not have given permission.

Her anxiety was short lived. The women of the clan put her mind at ease. They did not practise female circumcision. Had she been required to undergo the rite, she might have failed. She was not put to that test.

Then Smuts came home one day and called her aside from the women in the kitchen, to their bedroom. He was agitated. She assumed, wrongly, that some aspect of the ceremony had made him decide to forgo initiation. He told her the elders wanted their eldest son Thamsanga to be circumcised with him.

Heather felt her stomach contract. She reached out to the dressing table to steady herself. He helped her to the bed. She sat down. This was the logical conclusion to Smuts being circumcised. Yet she had not thought that far ahead. If it was imperative for a man to be circumcised even at Smuts' age, then all her sons had to be circumcised. Why had she been so obtuse? She cried while the rapturous feeling she had of being part of the family ebbed away. She was no longer at ease. Now it was as if someone was tugging her child from her arms, threatening her child's safety. Clutching her arms as if she was actually holding a threatened child she begged Smuts to find a solution. 'I can't allow such a young boy to undergo surgery at the hands of a Sangoma. He's too young,' she said. 'Isn't there an age limit?'

'There isn't. They're afraid we may take him back to England and he'll come back like me, a grown man but not a man to them.'

'Something could go wrong,' she said. 'He could catch an infection. He could die in the bush. How will I know if he needs to be hospitalised? How will you contact a doctor? Where will you be in the forest? I have to know. No, I won't allow it.'

It was his turn to react. He was furious with her. 'Why were you so carefree when I had to submit to the Sangoma? You urged me to go along with my father's wishes! Why will I be safe with the Sangoma but not my son? If there's a risk, then I'm also at risk!' They argued through the night. She could produce no logical reason. Just her motherly instinct that the boy was different from his father, he was vulnerable, he would not survive the operation, he might die in the bush. He was not hardy. He had not survived torture and training in the underground movement.

From that moment Smuts viewed Heather in a different light. Soon the entire clan learnt that she refused to allow Thamsanqa to be circumcised. Then they changed towards her. Nevertheless, to appease her, Smuts appealed to his father who in turn spoke to the elders. A meeting of the clan took place. Smuts left for the forest without Thamsanqa. Heather breathed with relief while the women and elders of the clan murmured.

***

42.

Heather cried as if someone had died. Thamsanqa had left for the forest. The women of the clan and the elders scolded her for crying. They warned that excessive mournfulness would shower bad luck onto the clan. It foreshadowed something ominous. There were whispers that someone would become ill. They lit fires around the house to chase away the evil Thekwane.

Helen would not have agreed. Yet she had. While Smuts drove away the women called her to a meeting. They asked: 'Is it because you are a White woman that you stopped Thamsanqa going into the forest?'

That was their interpretation. She was a White woman. What could she say? Then Mandisa asked: 'Does it mean hamsanqa is not an African?'

What could she say to that? Where did she figure in what he was? She did not want him to undergo African rituals. Did that make his identity non-African? She withdrew her opposition.

Not usually one to show emotion, Heather was frustrated by her loss of power over her children. She remembered their fears about coming to South Africa, and the promises she made them, to Thamsanqa and the twins especially, when they left England. In her ignorance of Smut's culture, she promised them she would refuse permission for the mutilation of their fingers. She overlooked male initiation, another mutilation. Her children's fears were realised. Her promises to them were broken. Promises she believed she could fulfil the way she fulfilled their wishes to the tooth fairy when they wrapped a tooth in silver paper and tucked it under the pillow at night, and in the morning there was a silver coin, that she had put there. She had no power here. She had let them down. Her English ideas of her rights as a parent estranged her from her new family. She had changed her mind unwillingly. They had driven her into a corner in a way that challenged her thinking.

Now she was not concerned to bring the clan close to her. She was not motivated to help them understand her thinking. She isolated herself from them. She brought her children close to her, keeping them with her wherever she went. In her mind, she was already planning their return to England when Thamsanqa came out of the forest.

***

43.

Driving a four by four belonging to a friend Smuts took the

Stutterheim Road out of King Williamstown. It was a quiet country road without road markings except in places where there were warnings of animals. Here there was a different feel to driving in the countryside compared with rural England. Here it was dry. The bushes and the grass were green, but not England's emerald green. When he found himself driving on a road bordered by tall trees, he knew he was approaching the entrance to Sandile Forest where he arranged to meet the iNgcibi[54] who would perform the initiation rites. Because it would be foolish to enter the forest without a guide, he pulled off the road and waited.

The iNgcibi arrived in a minibus with ten young initiates and two acolytes. They clambered out of the taxi and stood with the driver on the road urinating, as was the habit when men travelled in the bush. When they turned to Smuts, he was astounded to find Thamsanqa in the group. Thammy appeared nothing short of terrified. The whites of his eyes were flushed pink with unshed tears. 'He is too young,' Smuts said without any discussion and ordered Thamsanqa back into the taxi. He instructed the driver to wait while he took the iNgcibi to one side. They had a respectful discussion, with Smuts repeating, 'He is too young, and I am too old.'

Then, to Smuts amazement, the iNgcibi produced a letter in Heather's handwriting, signed by her, giving permission for Thamsanqa to be initiated. He could not believe Heather agreed without some form of coercion. The iNgcibi explained that when Smuts left 'eQonce[55]' the women of the clan persuaded Heather. 'It was women's talk,' he said. He did not know what was said. She wrote the letter. That was all he knew.

---

54 iNgcibi is a Xhosa initiation doctor.

55 eQonce is King William's Town

Having Heather's agreement, the women called the young Thamsanga to them and explained that he would go into the forest with his father to learn the secrets of Xhosa manhood. They told him that after he experienced the period in the forest, living off fruit, hunting, surviving in hard conditions, he would be regarded as a man by the clan. Instead of feeling the challenge of the experience, Thamsanga became terrified for his thoughts went to his little finger and he feared that circumcision might include the mutilation of his finger as well as the scarring of his sexual organ.

The initiates clambered back into the taxi. Smuts, with the iNgcibi, the two acolytes, and his son went in the four by four. The iNgcibi gave directions with the taxi following them. They continued for a short distance then joined the road to Umtata that was in Transkei country. Just outside Umtata they turned off onto a little dirt track. They stayed on this track for twenty minutes before the iNgcibi showed them a spot where they should pull over. They jumped out and removed their belongings, placing it in the four by four. The taxi was sent back to East London to return in three weeks.

Smuts continued slowly over a bumpy road in the four by four with the young initiates trailing behind. When they were deep in the forest they stopped. The iNgcibi then instructed them to undress. They folded their clothes neatly into two piles. When they were naked, he took the brown Xhosa blanket and draped it around Smuts, under his right arm and knotted over his left shoulder. He did the same to Thamsanqa and each of the other initiates. He then instructed them to place their European clothes back in the car and to conceal the vehicle. They spent an hour cutting down branches of bush and scrub with knives he gave them, and covering the vehicle under this. When he was satisfied he led them away. He carried his belongings with him, wrapped in a bundle, with a long stick in his right hand. They had nothing.

They walked in single file along a path that was sometimes clear and sometimes came to an abrupt halt when they had to cut the grass to make a path. Smuts recognised that if anything were to happen to the iNgcibi – they would never make it back to their car. The man had an innate sense about where he was and where he was going without a compass.

When they were hot and tired and sweaty, he made them climb down, hand over foot, clawing into the sides of a short rock, until they stood on golden sand and looked across clear water into a shimmering waterfall. They followed him as he waded through the water towards the waterfall, although there were boulders in the water, which he chose not to walk on. They reached the waterfall and turned to look at where they had come from. Facing them was the grey rock they had just descended. The boys went to play in the water while Smuts and the iNgcibi sat down and rested. They brought neither food nor water with them.

They then walked along the river looking for a spot where they would set up a shelter for themselves. When the iNgcibi halted, the two acolytes marked off a large circle with their spears. The initiates were then instructed to clear within the circle by cutting the grass and shrubs. He then instructed them to build low shelters made of the grass they had just cut and the longest pieces of shrub they had trimmed. Some of the initiates knew each other. Those like Thamsanqa who were new to the others, began to lose their apprehensions through this combined effort to create a place for themselves that they would live in for the next few weeks.

While they rested the iNgcibi tied his knife to the stick he carried and waded into the water. He came out with three fish he had speared. They copied him, scaling, and gutting the fish, then washing each under the running waterfall. They collected pebbles and each sat patiently trying to start a fire. Their next task was to fish for that nights supper. The initiates were city boys. The acolytes showed them how to prepare a fishing spear from a branch and a spearhead. Although many of them were unsuccessful on the first day, they developed their skills as the week progressed, some being naturally better than others. On the first night, they were taught how to make a fire and by laying bare a wide stretch of sand around the circle they would inhabit, prevent a bush fire.

After their initiation, they would set fire to their rondavels but at the time, they did not know it. They were then taught how to cook the fish without cooking utensils.

That same night, however, Thamsanqa had nightmares. He woke up screaming saying he saw spirits walking in the bush looking for him.

'Don't talk nonsense,' Smuts said. 'They're going to make fun of you. There are no spirits here.'

'I saw them. They threw petals of blood on me.'

'Rubbish! This is not the bush of ghosts. Ask the iNgcibi. You think he'll bring us for initiation where there are spirits?'

Thamsanqa was embarrassed when the iNgcibi said, 'Weep not child, you can refuse to be a man until you're older.'

'Go home,' said Smuts. 'I'll phone your mother.'

But Thamsanqa was too embarrassed to leave the group.

In the second week they were taught how to roast meat over an open fire after some experience of hunting small animals. They caught snakes, rats; birds, lizards, frogs, and they raided birds' nests and beehives.

The iNgcibi did little in these activities. At night, though, he talked to them about the custom of initiation, how it was done in other tribes, why it was done, and why they should not be afraid. He also taught them about the plants that were poisonous, the berries they could eat, and the leaves that could be used as a dressing if they were ever wounded in the bush. One of the leaves he passed around the fireside he would use to dress their wounds when they were circumcised. They had an opportunity to ask questions of the iNgcibi. At home they wore jeans and trainers and were accustomed to the comfort of food cooked by women, warm beds, and hot running water. Therefore, out there the emotion that filled most of them was trepidation about the ceremony. They knew only that they would cover themselves with red and white ochre.

They lived like this for many days. The iNgcibi was strictly traditional. They were not allowed to leave the site, for fear of seeing or being seen by women. On the day before the actual initiation, they had to bathe in the cold river. The ceremony is secret by tradition. They were instructed never to speak about the ceremony. Smuts and Thamsanqa complied.

After many days they emerged, each to go in a different direction like the rays of the sun, to find a secret place to bury their own dried up foreskins. When they returned they gathered their belongings, sprinkled water all around the edge of their circle. They dismantled the huts, dragging everything into the centre and set fire to it.

Draped in their blankets they walked in single file back the way they had come, up the incline, to the four by four. The taxi was waiting for them when they came out of the forest. Smuts put his son in the taxi while he drove away.

Each initiate was given a name. Smuts did not disclose his name to anyone.

***

44.

In her bare feet Pragashini reached the French windows, then stepped out of the house of musty incense, brass ornaments, and brass replicas of deities, into the darkening garden of fresh frangipani, honeysuckle, and jasmine fragrances. She stood inhaling the fragrances.

It was early Sunday evening. She was dressed in a simple borrowed sari to attend the singing of Bhajans in the temple. But she was running late - the Nasaratt family had gone on ahead of her – and she decided not to go. The only person at home was Ernestina, waiting for the family to have supper so that she could wash the dishes before leaving.

Pragashini felt diminished by the fact that she was just one of millions of South Africans. Not in the leadership. Never imprisoned. Never tortured. Never speaking before the Truth and Reconciliation Committee. Yet she was one of millions who experienced apartheid. One of millions who were obliged to come to terms with apartheid and the past, each separately, each on their own. She walked along the path, which was not cobbled, but coarse brown sand. It was better to pray here away from distractions.

Then silently from around the darkening back of the house the family's large Alsatian dog appeared and stood looking quizzically up at her from the distance. She stopped, waiting to see if the dog would be hostile or friendly. When it seemed unsure of itself, she walked across to the front gate to check that it was shut. Then with her eye on the dog she turned to a path that took her into the large garden that ran on both sides of the house and led to the fruit orchard behind. The Alsatian dog cantered after her and having caught up with her matched its pace with hers. She sidestepped pools of light cast by the street lamps over the boundary wall, the bulbs of which were dulled by clouds of swarming muggies[56]. Tense and nervous, she fingered her prayer beads, she whispered prayers for the new leadership, prayers for peace, an end to violence, rest for departed family and friends. She prayed for everything and everyone but for herself. Chirruping crickets squeaked the responses to her prayers while her silent companion padded by her side, stopping when she stopped, walking wherever she walked. It was programmed to guard the house, and her, she supposed. Yet it was not her confidence in the dog that stifled prayers for herself. It was her fear that praying for what she needed would bring into consciousness her anxieties.

She and the dog reached the end of the flower garden and approached a small orchard of fruit trees, mangoes, lemons, oranges, apricots, and peaches. Without warning, the dog turned quickly and ran towards the boundary wall, then stood still. Pragashini also stopped. She stopped praying. The dog's fur detached itself from its body, rolling forward until it lay in furls around its collar. The hairs on its coat bristled. Its ears stood erect, alerted to someone crouching beyond the wall, waiting for the right moment to scale the wall, land cat-like on the damp earth, with knife, panga[57], gun, ready to carry out whatever barbaric possibilities the situation invited. She was afraid of the dog as much as of the unseen intruder. Then the dog let out a low guttural sound, like rumbling in its throat, warning her, and the intruder. It happened quickly.

In the stillness, she noticed the crickets had stopped chirping. Only the dog growled, waiting for the intruder to appear. Then she heard soft naked footfalls running. She could not distinguish how many. In her terror she could not

---

56 A muggie is a gnat.

57 A panga is a knife, wide, curved and long, used for cutting sugar cane.

discern in which direction the runners were going. She imagined a bent figure running between the cars, hidden by the low walls. All the while the dog crouched in that tensed, hostile pose. Long afterwards she sensed the dog relax. It's growling over. Then she breathed. The dog came over to her; stood against her legs it's curved tail brushing heavily against her as it turned to scan the dark behind them.

She looked down and talked to the dog in a hushed conspiratorial tone, praising it, conspiring with it to catch anyone else who dared enter the garden. She did it naturally out of habit. You do that when you leave behind an entire community of family and friends. You begin by talking to strangers seated next to you on a double-decker bus, in English tea-rooms sharing a table with a stranger, on the underground you take a chance with a young person or the elderly, with children whose parents have tired of playing with them, or a foreign looking face. People open up to you about their families, about themselves, you talk to dogs, cats, caged birds, pet tortoises, rabbits. You progress naturally, to conversing with yourself. You think elaborate extravagant thoughts, and then you blur the distinction between the two and lapse into uttering your thoughts believing you are still thinking. Which people say is the first sign of madness.

She and the dog continued their walk, she her prayers, making their way through the fruit orchard back to the house. Up ahead she heard a match, saw it flare, flame for a few seconds, then go out. Once again, the dog tensed. Then it loped away from her side, located someone coming towards them, and kept the person at bay. She approached tentatively. It seemed like a man draped in a blanket.

It was Smuts. He wore a long brown blanket decorated with a white pattern, and tied on one shoulder. In his left hand, he held a long stick. The dog looked at her and she put her hand out to Smuts. Warily, he put his hand in hers.

'Aren't you breaking some tradition?' she asked. 'I thought a man sent into the forest is forbidden to show himself to a woman.'

'You're supposed to greet me with bowing and hand clapping and ululation! Not intellectual nonsense, woman!' he said, adding, 'I've seen initiates wandering along the motorway between iMonti[58] and eQonce. They flout the rules. I haven't. There's another tradition. A man coming out of the forest must first show himself to the woman he loves. So here I am,' he said. 'Pragashini my love!'

'Honestly, dude, I might have believed you once upon a time. But I don't believe in fairy tales and magic, except'... She stopped herself from saying, magic folders.

'You're so silly. Here you have a whole Xhosa man coming to you straight from the forest, and you talk nonsense to him! I don't care what you believe. I'm not trying to persuade you. I'm here to obey the rules and the traditions.'

'Pity I can't ask you in. We could have a good romp in the bedroom. I'm alone at home, and already in their bad books.'

'I don't need a bedroom. Coming from the forest this Garden of Eden's fine for me,' he said. 'What's their problem?'

'This shaved head. It reminds them of naming ceremonies. I'm supposed to present them with a little baby. They keep asking me to grow my hair. People are talking, they say. They want to know what it means. They smell cigarette smoke on me. That's also not a good sign.'

'Well, I'm surprised you haven't given up yet. It's a filthy habit, and you a biologist and all.'

They were standing on the lawn near the house. She touched his arm and said, 'Best not let the housekeeper see

---

58 IMonti is East London

you. She'll tell them I had a male visitor.' They moved onto the path leading into the garden. Smuts gave her the cigarette he had lit and followed her down the path. When they stopped in the unlit part of the garden, he said simply, 'Don't send me away Prags.'

'I don't want to,' she said. 'I also want an experience to cherish. Being made love to by someone from my youth, my innocence. Someone who kept his love for me alive through the years of separation.'

Smuts was naked under his traditional blanket. Although they had known each other since they were at school, when they had opportunities to be together they held hands and kissed softly at the end of the Saturday morning classes his father taught in a hall on Perl road. They never went beyond soft kisses and gentle touching of each other's bodies. 'I love to feel your body against mine,' she said. When he held her, her body fitted gently and vulnerably into his arms. 'I used to love to stroke your hair. When will you grow it?' he asked.

She never confided anything to him about Nasaratt's treatment of her. Now he said, 'I only know that you hid from Nasaratt in England, yet you came to his home. I want to protect you, Pragashini, but I can't if you won't divorce Nasaratt.'

'You have no rights over me,' she said. 'Even if you were married to me. But you married someone else. I'll never forgive you for marrying Heather.'

'I can say the same thing. I'll never forgive you for marrying Nasaratt.'

'Forget it! It's too late for us. I'm an Indian female. Never mind betraying Heather, I can't betray myself. I'll never have an affair with you! You said the same thing.'

'You keep grudges, Pragashini,'

'We can leave it like this. With me, you have not violated your marriage vows. I'm tempted. Here you are, initiated into manhood. The first boy I loved and kissed. You've come to me, not to Heather.'

'Forget Heather. Heather lives for our children. Not for me.'

'Should I forget Nolitando?'

'Which gossip told you about Nolitando?'

'I didn't need a gossip. If Heather's eyes were open she would know. You gave all the signals at the inauguration. And I work in Bisho, you know.'

'Even so, I came to you, Prags.'

'This circumcision was not for me. Heather would not ask for it. Was it for Nolitando? If it was then go to her.'

'Nolitando is today's love. Heather was yesterday's love. You were yesterday's, you are today's and you'll be tomorrow's.'

'I'm not the child who loved you.'

'Just this once, Prags. For me – as much as for you. Then we'll have a memory for our old age. We can't turn back the clock. I will never leave Heather. Even if you're free.'

'You should've come looking for me. All those years ago. Now I don't need your protection. I don't need anyone. I've been blown about like a seed. I can't take root anywhere. The liberation movement would've helped you to find me. Instead you fell in love with Heather. I was waiting for you to kill Nasaratt. You left me to him.'

'Kill? Me? When you were indoctrinating me about Gandhi – ji? You should be grateful I accepted what you said to me. These hands can't kill. I failed that test in the forest. So did Thamsanqa. We didn't want to spear the fish. We couldn't knife the rats and cut them open. If I killed Nasaratt? What then? You'd still love me, Pragashini? Or remember Gandhiji when I touch you?'

She kissed him. She held him close. They stood together, lovers, touching and kissing each other, each knowing it was too late for them. He left her when she remained obstinate in her decision not to betray Heather. He had known all along, she would never do something dishonourable.

'I can't do this,' she said finally. 'Not to Heather. Now I know her. Not to Nolitando. Not to myself.'

***

45.

Heather shook off the shyness that accompanied her smile when she could not understand the women's humour, their jokes, their chatter. She failed to make small talk while they peeled vegetables in the kitchen. She was preoccupied. Her mind was concentrated on the manner of their departure for England.

When Thamsanga returned safely to her, she travelled with the Matatieles to their ancestral home in the Transkei, lulled into a tenuous sense of security. Her son was home from the forest. He appeared thin from the diet. His pale skin was still covered with red ochre. The signs were there that he was emotionally unprepared for the experience. But he had not died there. He had not been rushed to hospital. She was satisfied.

They held a celebration for father and son. Heather was herself initiated into the preparations for the celebration. She helped prepare the goat, succulent and flavoursome, in a rich gravy with fresh wholesome vegetables plucked by soft girls' hands in the early morning when still moist with dew. She accepted that her views and opinions counted for nothing. Only her agreement with the men would make her one of the clan. That would lead to her unhappiness. If there was a disagreement, she would be discounted. Hers was a small family unit in England. Smuts, adapting to English life, gave way reluctantly when they disagreed. Here she was outnumbered. She was diminished. Yet, she could not contemplate doing anything to place herself outside the family. She loved them too much. That was the reason she consented to Thamsanqa's initiation.

Mandisa was not fully recovered from the traditional rituals that accompanied Mellikhaya's death and burial. Her participation in the celebration of Smuts' belated initiation was low key and half-hearted. She did not prepare the goat or vegetables. Every now and then she was called to stir the pot a few times. She had grown thinner. Her sister, Shumi who was the tenth in the family, performed her duties.

On the day, Shumi led the procession of women who clustered near the rondavel where the circumcised Smuts and his son were sitting clothed each in his own traditional blanket. The women created a hullabaloo, dancing and singing, clapping and ululating, 'Uhluhluhlu!' to entice the men out of the rondavel to meet their mothers, aunts, sisters and other female members of the village. When Smuts and his son emerged the women led them in a slow dancing movement from the rondavel winding their way to the gathering of guests and family seated in the sunshine. The aunt Shumi, leading the women held a bottle of gin in each hand one bottle pointing from each breast, suggesting that the boy who drank milk from his mother's breast was now a man who could drink alcohol.

Like her mother in law, Heather had not recovered from the last week. With a heavy heart she joined the line of singing women, also holding two bottles of gin in her hands, one from each breast. She moved in an arrhythmic manner, her heart leadened. The heartfelt innocence with which she had entered her new family was gone. The number of young men who died from infections from initiation frightened her. She alertly observed Thamsanga for any sign of fever. She realised that the twins, Mafeking and King Bisho would also have their turn. The Xhosa did not initiate females, which meant Lusikisiki was safe. Heather had never stopped to consider the impact being a woman would mean to her rights as a mother over decisions affecting her children. The women noticed her unhappiness during the celebrations and they continued murmuring to each other, conscious that this ill feeling between them did not bode well for the clan.

***

46.

Following a frustrating period in which she went from one office to the next, searching, Pragashini decided to identify possible hiding places before proceeding further. So she concentrated on the computer allocated to her and systematically searched directories, subdirectories, folders, subfolders, and back up files. All revealed files that were easily accessed and no hidden files. Later she considered the documents might be hidden within system files. If this were true it suggested a high level of assistance to the creators of the documents because system files on computers were placed there either by the manufacturers or by those skilled in assembling computers. That type of assistance was consistent with what would be given to government agencies.

Here she met with some success. On her computer she discovered files hidden amongst the system files but these once again, were too easily accessed and proved to be of little significance. With this information, though she resumed searching from office to office, floor by floor, returning to the computers she had already checked, moving from one department to the next exercising caution, under the guise of loading and upgrading versions of computer programmes.

While searching she considered how she would approach the problem of passwords. The passwords could be written in any one of the languages in use, depending on which branch of the department held access to the secret documents. She could not imagine that the use of simple keywords would locate sensitive documents. Therefore, the passwords would also be complex.

While in her office, she heard the staff rushing up and down the corridors knocking on the doors, calling everyone out to the Chamber. The new members had been sworn in and some were making their maiden speeches. Smuts was one of the speakers listed for that day. She made her way to the parliament buildings to hear Smuts deliver his maiden speech. Heather was sitting in the visitors' gallery.

***

47.

Smuts called his speech his 'Letter to Africa.'

'Beloved,' Smuts began. His voice was loud as a praise poet. 'I loved you before I opened my eyes and saw the light in my mother's eyes, or the smile on my mother's face. I loved you when I crawled on your soil. I loved you when I put my barefoot down for your kiss. I loved you when I fell and you kissed my knees. I loved you when I ran and played on you. I loved you when you poured rain water on me. I loved you when you warmed me with wind and sun.

From your soil, my love, I am created. Eroded and fertile, desert and clay. In your waters I was baptised. Clear and salty, bloodied and spoilt. From your humble foods, Umbona and amasi, I ate and drank and grew. You nursed my uncertain childhood and steadied my tentative footsteps. You made a path for me to walk on.'

'Nothing will change my love for you. When you suffer

drought, I will still love you. When your rivers run dry, I will still love you. When fire and men destroy your trees, I will still love you. When locusts devour the crops you grow for me, I will still love you. When the sun dries up the water you give to me, I will still love you.'

'Beloved, I ask nothing in return for my love. Such is the nature of true love.'

'No other will steal my love from you. I belong to you. I will love you when I am dead and reunited with you. I want to sleep the eternal sleep in you and in no other.'

'But why my love, could you not sustain me into manhood? Why did I have to leave you and watch you, like a jealous lover, from a distance. From afar I coveted you. I longed for you with a simple lust.'

'But now I am home. Tell me you love me, more than I love you. Tell me your love for me is deeper than my love for you. And if it is so, if you love me, why have you stopped feeding me, my love? Why do your sons and daughters hurry us to our deaths with guns, when we are starving to death? When we are on the famished road? Tell me, my love, do you not love the elderly to come to you? If you do why do you call us, before our time is up? Why do you love the embrace of children and youths? Can you not bear to see them hunger and thirst?'

'Tell me, my love, answer me, what do you prefer, my love, and I will give it to you. Do you prefer to enrich your soil with the body and blood of your people? Or with ripe compost that other soils prefer? Tell me, my love and I will give it to you. Do you prefer me to plant seeds or bodies of the dead?'

'I lied, beloved, when I said I want nothing in return for my love. I want land, my love. I want land for burial. I want to bury guns. I want to bury tobacco. I want to bury coffee. I want to bury tea. Give it to me quickly, my love, give me the land to bury these things, and I will give back to you all the land you reserve for burying your sons and daughters.'

'I love you. I am yours. Forever. Smuts Matatiele.'

The assembly broke out into singing and Uhluhluhlulating when he finished. Members in the house came across the floor to clasp his hand in theirs. They had to be called to order to listen to other maiden speeches. Here and there, however, were frowns of disapproval.

***

PART FOUR

Outcast

48.

A gossip ferreting after rumours is like a squirrel rummaging in the soil for dormant flower bulbs. Gossip is never a preoccupation for scientists. Pragashini, therefore, did not anticipate the arrival of the gossip.

Residents in both neighbourhoods, Bisho and Muhalla Asha grew accustomed to seeing her twice a day, running with shaved head. She breathed hard, her eyes smarting and level with the ground at a runner's vanishing point that continually changed. She kept her eyes on the look out for would-be muggers, dogs, stray cats and stones. Cars were almost on top of her before she heard them. People waved, but she lost her rhythm if she waved back. Some called to her, but she did not have time to look around fearing she might lose her footing, what with the streets having stones at the ready for any volatile mob. It was her habit to fill up on water, warm up, jog around the block, then come in and take a shower early on a morning and after work. She did this in Port Elizabeth and Bisho. She always began running slowly, and then gained energy as she ran.

One evening while the Nasaratts were at home watching television, she showered after jogging, and entered the living room where they were gathered. There was a woman visitor. Nalini looked at Pragashini with raised eyebrows and said something in one of the dialects the polyglot family used. Pragashini's exile left her unfamiliar with these dialects. Not catching what Nalini said, she stood up as if she understood perfectly, and went into the kitchen.

Ernestina was still at work sitting in the kitchen with her folded arms on the worktop, head resting on her arms, dozing. She was waiting to be allowed to go to her quarters, which was a small bedroom and shower room built in the back yard. In many houses the housemaid's quarters were well decorated to the extent that newly married couples from the Indian and Coloured communities sometimes rented these as their first home when they could not afford to build a house.

Pragashini failed to persuade the Nasaratts to allow Ernestina to leave at five and arrive at seven thirty in the morning because they knew that her African friends kept their housekeepers on duty until their guests left. Some of her friends living in flats and townhouses, without quarters for staff, let the housekeeper sleep in the living room. When guests arrived unexpectedly, even late at night, the housekeeper woke, vacated the room and waited in the kitchen until the guests left. Even with separate quarters, when visitors arrived late at night, the housekeeper woke, prepared food, and slept after the kitchen was cleaned.

In the kitchen, Pragashini asked Ernestina to prepare tea and coffee then she returned to the living room.

The visitor turned to her. From the expression on Nalini's face, Pragashini realized she had misinterpreted her. The visitor was tall and sturdy. Her face displayed a permanent sulk. She wore a floral sari made of chiffon with the loose end over her left shoulder, brought around her back and forward under her right arm, tucked into her waist. While Pragashini hesitated not knowing whether to sit with them or leave, the visitor turned to Nalini and said,

'Nalini, tell this child who I am.'

Nalini sighed deeply, turned to Pragashini and said, 'Let me see. Ramgopal's sister, the one who moved to Jo'burg has two girls. One of them, I think it's the eldest girl, married a boy from Welkom, or was it Klipfontein? That boy's sister married a boy from Vereeniging. Or, was it Koffiefontein? That boy's mother has two brothers. One of her brothers married the sister of...' – here Nalini paused, then went on –

'Usha? Or Letchie? You remember her? She was a dancer or singer in your school days. This is her mother, auntie Ranghie. You don't know any of them so I don't know why I bothered explaining.'

Pragashini joined her hands and gave the traditional greeting. Judging from the circuitous description Nalini gave of her connection with the visitor, the Nasaratts seemed not too pleased to be related to her. They seemed embarrassed to have her in their home and she sensed the aunt had lost favour with them for whatever reason displeased them.

As was her habit, she conjectured. Some women, widowed or abandoned by their husbands, sold alcohol in their homes by the bottle or to men, who came to their homes, sat in their dining room and drank, then left. This was illegal, like the shebeens in African townships, but in the few Indian homes where this was done, it was very low keyed, and done discreetly. Occasionally White policemen came to drink in those Indian women's homes.

The visitor herself was unhappy with this description. She said, 'Agh no, Nalini. Why don't you tell her properly who I am?' Turning to Pragashini she said, 'I'm that poor woman from the council houses. What they call those houses, Nalini? Remind me.'

The visitor had come for a squabble. The family gathered in the lounge stiffened. Roshni compressed her lips. When Roshni had taken her round Muhalla Asha, the council houses were pointed out to her as the 'Smartie houses' because they were painted bright blue, pink, green, yellow, like houses are painted in India and the Middle East. There was nothing unattractive about the colours. She loved them. Here, however, the colours were despised. It was that old culprit colonialism, or apartheid, thought Pragashini, which made the colonised despise themselves and imitate the coloniser.

'You've got some chips on your shoulder, Ranghie,' said Nalini.

The visitor brushed both shoulders with some agitation, while the young members of the family giggled.

Pragashini empathised with the visitor. Every family has relatives who remain on the fringe of society, who never seem able to climb the ladder of success, for whatever reason. Nalini's outline of how the visitor was connected to them was meant to show she was distantly related. It was clear to her the visitor was an outsider, and the Nasaratt's were not doing much to put her at ease. She could also appreciate the Nasaratt's point of view. In a small community they would wish to protect their family name. She knew nothing more about the visitor to understand the situation. She also did not know that the visitor had already made the reason for her visit clear to them.

The family sat in genteel embarrassment while she hoped the housekeeper would come in with the coffee and ease the tension. But all they heard was the sound of cups and saucers rattling in the kitchen. After what seemed like a trial to see who would speak first, Nalini said, 'Auntie Ranghie's got a bone to pick with you.'

This piece of information was left for Pragashini to consider. Perhaps they expected an articulate rumbustious reply from a woman coming from England. Instead they had her. She never said much. She was aware of the customs here.

'She says you run up and down the street in front of her house.' Nalini stopped lost for words. Pragashini had no idea where this complaint was leading to but the visitor quickly stepped filled in the gap for Nalini.

'Morning, noon and night,' Ranghie added.

'You don't stop to greet Auntie,' Nalini said.

'She's playing White. Coming from London,' Ranghie said.

The found this remark humourous because Pragashini was the colour of cloves. Some fair skinned people who might have been classed as White during the time when the apartheid government was busy classifying people into racial groups would leave family and friends and begin a new life as a White person. Once someone was classified, playing White became unnecessary, but people still did it. Sometimes a child born into a family might ask to be re-classified. There were Africans and Indians who asked to be classified as Coloured. Malays were given the option to be Coloured or Indian, depending on where they wanted to live. One member of a family would ask to be classified Coloured and live in the area designated for Coloureds, the other would ask to be classified Indian and live with Indians.

Now, however, because Ernestina entered with the tray, no one said anything. She put the tray on the coffee table and looked at Nalini for instructions. Nalini said, 'Thank you Ernestina. I'll pour.'

'Can Ernestina go to bed?' Pragashini asked.

'If you wash the dishes,' Nalini said. 'Goodnight Ernestina.' Ernestina left the room. Nalini poured the coffee, put cup to saucer, added a teaspoon, handed it round to each one, passed the sugar bowl then placed the bowl back on the tray when it had done the rounds. All this was done in silence with each of them watching every move Nalini made, as if they were playing a quiz game where they were expected to name every item they saw. Then they stirred and sipped their coffee.

'If you heard what auntie said to us before you came in, the coffee might taste like vinegar,' said Roshni.

'How you like Bisho?' Ranghie asked, her question spoken as if she was saying, 'What's your problem?'

Roshni quickly said, 'Bisho looks like a lot of dolls houses.

The government offices are painted pink.'

'Like the Smartie houses?' Ranghie asked.

The Nasaratt's were embarrassed. But Roshni had not sidetracked the visitor.

'They treating you like a queen because you from London?' Ranghie asked. 'Don't get swollen headed. Your London accent is nothing,' she added. 'I don't know why everyone makes such a fuss over exiles. Tell them you from Mafeking. Then see who takes notice of you.'

It was a fair point. Pragashini sipped her coffee in silence finding it difficult not to laugh. Roshni intervened with a little laugh. 'She's not from London, auntie. She's from Yorkshire.'

'No! She's a London lady,' Ranghie said, moving her head from side to side. 'Big English lady. Full of airs and graces.'

Pragashini imagined herself in a romance. A handsome prince would come to her rescue, scoop her up with his left hand, place her on his horse, draw his blade and with one swipe cut off the visitor's head, then gallop away into the distance. But alas princes are very rarely handsome, and they certainly do not come to the rescue of damsels in distress.

'You make friends with any nice Indian girls?' Ranghie asked.

Pragashini felt the urge to put the visitor in her place but she took her cue from the others in the room. They were being well mannered. Actually they were shifting about restlessly waiting for the visitor to drop her bombshell. Roshni appeared to be the only one who refused to be stilled. 'Who are the nice girls, auntie?' Roshni asked. 'Tell us so we know who we should be friends with.'

'Nice girls don't smoke and drink,' Ranghie said.

Pragashini put her cup down tucking her nicotine stained fingers under her thighs.

'Pragashini doesn't smoke or drink,' Roshni said. It was

not that she was ignorant. She was lying. Roshni smoked with her and was partial to German beer.

'She'll get bad habits if she makes friends with bad girls,' Ranghie said.

'Pragashini isn't a small child. She's a married woman now. If she wants to smoke and drink, then no one can stop her. That's the best thing about being married!'

Pragashini sensed that Roshni was cutting close to the bone about what auntie Ranghie did in her spare time.

'She's your age,' Rangie said. 'She's a child.'

'She's a married woman, auntie. You can't talk to her like that.'

'She's your age.'

Pragashini became attentive, at the mention of her age. The Nasaratts, however, appeared exhausted with the length of the visit. But the visitor wasn't ready to leave or to deliver her complaint. 'What food you eating at work? You eating burgers and hot dogs? Why you not buying vegetarian food?'

'She takes a packed lunch,' Roshni said.

'Oh! She's highty tighty!' Ranghie said, moving her head like those ornaments in the back windows of English cars. 'London lady,' she added.

The Nasaratts sat with a mouth full of stones. For some reason Nalini was unwilling to put the visitor in her place. Finally, the reason for her animosity towards Pragashini emerged.

'I called you the other night,' Ranghie said and turning to the Nasaratts repeated, 'I called this child the other night. Not just once.' And to Pragashini, 'I called you over and over and over again,' Ranghie said, turning to Nalini. 'She heard me. She saw me.' And to Pragashini, 'You heard me. You saw me.' Then to the Nasaratts, 'She looked at me and ran away,' Ranghie said. 'Just like the children when they play in the street. If she says she didn't hear me, she's lying. I called her so many times. I could be having a heart attack.'

Pragashini stifled her laughter with a hand to her mouth. One of the memories that accompanied her throughout childhood was not answering to her name. Not from obstinacy, or disobedience, but from not recognising her name when it was called. When at school and the register was called there were times she did not answer. When running she rarely answered to her name. She could not remember when it first happened, this idiosyncrasy. Combined with the waking and not knowing who or where she was, the mystical waking to snow falling, the crying child, all troubled her. But she had no wish to mention this to the Nasaratts.

She remembered seeing the woman leaning over the railings on her balcony, calling to someone while she was out jogging. She distinctly heard someone calling 'Pragashini!' the name coming on the wind, repeatedly, but not registering as her name. It seemed to her this woman was calling someone else. She did not acknowledge her name even mentally the way you would when someone calls your name. She did not think about it. It happened the next evening and again on the third day. Because it seemed to be the woman's routine she paid less attention to it.

'What did you want her for?' Nalini asked.

'Bread from the shop.'

'You couldn't make roti?' Nalini asked.

'I finished the Ata flour.'

'You want to send her to the shop like she's a child?' asked Roshni.

'Listen Nalini don't get cross with me. It's your daughter-in-law misbehaving.'

This was the clue Pragashini should have picked up on. But she was afraid they might ask to see her hands and was again intent on hiding the tell tale signs of her smoking.

'More coffee anyone?' Nalini asked, holding the coffee pot. There followed a dumb refusal. The visitor was unwelcome.

'I came to tell you they're skinnering[59] about you, at your work,' Ranghie said. 'I take roti and samoosas to the café there. Sally makes halal food. I make vegetarian.'

Pragashini wondered what they were saying about her. She looked at Roshni, to see if she would ask, or if they already knew and were waiting for her to be told.

'The coffee still hot?' Ranghie asked. Nalini put the palm of her hand to the pot. Without a word she extended her left hand, received the cup and saucer, poured, and returned it to the visitor. Roshni handed the milk jug and the sugar bowl. The family waited.

'They're skinnering about you with some man in Bisho. What's his name?' the visitor asked, as if she or someone else in the room would provide the answer.

Pragashini stiffened, not knowing who she was referring to.

'Auntie must say who it is,' Roshni said. 'We don't know any gossips. Auntie is the first gossip to come here telling us about gossip,' Roshni said.

A suspicion came into Pragashini's mind. Had someone seen her with Matatiele? She spent much time with him. Lunch hours when he was in Bisho. She was with him in Bisho at the weekend when she reported her progress to him. Or Smuts?

'Remind me, what's his name?' The visitor rummaged about in her handbag. It's in my order book. Sally wrote it for me. She couldn't spell his name.' She pulled a rolled up soft exercise book from her bag. Wetting her middle finger, she leafed back and forth through its pages. 'He's got a funny name.' The family sat in embarrassed silence while she paged to the end and then paged from the back to the

---

59 Skinnering means gossiping.

front. When she found what she was looking for, she folded the book along the centre spine and sat back with a smile on her face. While looking at Pragashini, she said, 'Say his name. I can't say it properly. ' She stood up, came over and held the page for Pragashini to see. 'Everyone's skinnering about the two of you,' she said.

Pragashini could not move. Once again, she covered her mouth. If the name had been spoken, she might have thought that she had not heard correctly. But she saw the name in the notebook.

There was such stillness in the room she thought she may have imagined the woman speaking. Why would this woman possibly come to the Nasaratt's home, in this manner, with Mossel Klein's name written in a notebook, as if she were meeting him secretly, as if she was having an affair with him? She could understand if Smuts' had been seen in the garden that night. Even Matatiele whom she met openly. But not Mossel KLein. She never met him outside the workplace. She was speechless.

'Go on. Tell them. Is he a White man? Or Coloured? Or Malay? They say he's strange. Nobody knows anything about him. Who's his mother and father? What part of South Africa is he coming from? He's not a youngster, like you. They say he looks like a skelm and they don't know if he's married. He might be dangerous. You're a nice Indian girl, ma, married into a good family. These people don't behave like us. He's a skelm. You don't know what you'll be getting yourself into if you keep up this looseness.'

Pragashini could not think of what to say. She never had an assignation with Klein. She had not even been alone with him in the office. Was this about him or someone else? She wanted desperately to know why there was gossip about her in relation to him, but she was afraid she might arouse other suspicions if she asked. She let the question pass. She was not a talkative person. It was easy for her to say nothing.

Except for the few words Nalini and Roshni said earlier, no one in the room said anything. They were waiting for her to denounce the gossip, and defend herself. Nalini finished sipping her coffee in silence. Then she put out her hand to receive each empty cup on its saucer, stacked them neatly on the tray, stood up, bent down to lift the tray, walked out of the room to the kitchen. She did not return.

The remaining Nasaratts sat in silence. Then they stood up as a group, wished the gossip good night, and turned to leave the room with Pragashini the last one left in the room. Pragashini stood up quickly, while the Nasaratts bunched together in the doorway, anxious to escape.

'Did you attend my wedding?' Pragashini asked in a raised voice.

The Nasaratts turned to look at her, unsure whom she had spoken to.

'I did some catering,' Ranghie said, because Pragashini was looking at her. Everyone in the room waited to hear why Pragashini asked the question.

'I didn't hear you telling the family people were gossiping. Weren't they gossiping? The wedding guests? They must have been. About the Nasaratts and the Devs. They were marrying a schoolgirl to an old grandfather clock. Go home and gossip about that!' she said.

The Nasaratts pushed each other through the doorway in their haste. Pragashini said good night to the gossip, and left the room. The gossip let herself out. Pragashini went into the kitchen foolishly expecting to find the family there ready to explode into laughter at the strange visitor. There was no one there. Not even Roshni. She washed the dishes, then tiptoed up to her bedroom, wondering if she had overstepped the mark. The house was quiet. She was alone to reflect.

49.

The Recluse - Pragashini's Journal

Then there it was. Just the one line. A soft awakening. Giving nothing away. Suggesting change. I sensed mystery. Now I feel joy, happiness, fear, and trepidation reading that one line.

For years, I leafed through her journal like a disgruntled tutor checking a student's work, at times unsure if she knew I was reading her private journal, sometimes suspecting her of manipulating me if she did know.

It was a beautiful thought. Something beautiful is happening to me. Now it's on the page, it's out of my mind and my mind does not have monopoly over it.

What does she imagine is happening to her? God alone knows for I cannot search her mind, this dedicated follower of research. She is as secretive as the confessional.

With each reading of that line – something beautiful is happening to me – the word I habitually associate with her – 'laatlammetjie' – illuminates my soul. Radiating from that loving nickname 'laatlammetjie' are truths she hides from the outside world because they begged her to. Fellow exiles. Exile is not home, they said. Reveal all here and you divert attention from our struggle.

I am a recluse. I am floundering like a monk locked in his monastic cell wakes one morning to find the walls around him flattened. Can I cope with this freedom? I too am powerless. I fear the truth may be unbearable for a fragile mind.

***

50.

South Africa, like India and Pakistan, was no place for a woman, especially one needing protection from culture and tradition.

Without reassuring her that they had not taken the gossip seriously, without a light-hearted comment about the gossip the Nasaratts had turned in for the night, perhaps to hold a conclave in someone's bedroom. She expected Roshni to be waiting for her for a whispered meeting to make light of the incident. But Roshni was not there.

Pragashini was left to contemplate the meaning of it all in solitude, yet too perturbed to consider what she could do about it. She was stunned and unnerved by the confidence prompting the gossip's visit. Did people still gossip and interfere? Would she find a mob outside waiting to stone her? Recalling what she endured as a young bride, without a blemish touching the man and the families who retained their self-esteem, their status, without one word of chastisement levelled against them, she chastised herself for procrastinating about how to avenge herself.

To be accused in the presence of the entire family, without anyone coming to her defence was nothing compared with what she had survived. Then again why would they have any inclination to defend her from mere verbal attack when they must have considered her violation and judged it tolerable. She sat on the bed, reliving the gossips visit, seeing the room, the face of each person, going over what had been said, what she had said, still at a loss. What she had said seemed ineffectual against the gossip.

She was able to draw strength from the devotional meditation she performed at daybreak and sundown each day since her days in exile. But that night she had developed a headache and could neither meditate nor sleep. On impulse, she took a handful of flowers from her room and went quietly downstairs to the family prayer room. The door was locked. It never occurred to her they locked the prayer room at night.

In the morning, she was up early. The prayer room was still

locked. She left the house to go jogging. On her return the prayer room remained locked. The kitchen was vacant and there was no one in the dining room. The dishes had been washed. The plates stacked. The cooker switched off. The kitchen left as if they had not come down since last night. Ernestina was ironing in the utility room.

At lunch, everyone from the youngest to the oldest was out. In her innocence, she hoped they had gone mafia-style to sort out the gossip. At suppertime, they had eaten before the usual time. When she entered the dining room her greeting was met with silence. When she sat down, everyone stood up and left the table.

After supper, she went into the family room. All who were gathered there stood up and left. As the days passed, whenever she went into one of the communal rooms, the Nasaratts' dispersed. The family were avoiding her. She was an outcast. It distressed her. By the end of the week, she no longer went into the communal rooms but withdrew into her room. Ernestina began leaving a tray of food on the floor outside her bedroom door. She turned to Roshni but even she refused the opportunity for an explanation.

The Nasaratts were locking the prayer door at night, and during the day, unlocking it and locking themselves inside when they did their devotions. Now when she most needed to perform her daily puja she was excluded from the family prayer room.

She was aware that ostracising someone was commonly practised in previous generations of her family, perhaps also her community. It happened when a Hindu member of a family became Christian. That person was cast out of the house if a man, and shunned within the household if a woman who could not be evicted. It became difficult when a large extended family shared one house. A man could make his way in the world. A woman endured the isolation more keenly if she was confined to the home.

She knew of instances when an entire family were ostracised on becoming Christian, following the conversion of the head of the family. Whoever chose to remain Hindu within the newly converted Christian family, might isolate themselves, and perform all social duties apart from the Christian family. When a woman married to a Hindu converted to Christianity because her husband converted, she and he were ostracized. Later, if she were widowed, she would almost certainly return to her father's home, or the home of her eldest brother. If she were a young widow, there would be pressure on her to return to Hinduism and remarry. As long as she refused, yet remained within her father or brother's home she would be ostracised within the home and by society.

There was such an example in her family. Her mother's sister converted to Christianity with her husband. Pragashini and her brother were never allowed to visit their aunt and uncle. They were never told her married name or the name she adopted when she was baptized. Previously she had been known as aunt Karishma. After twenty years of marriage to a convert, her husband died and her aunt asked if she could live with Leela and Jairaj. Her parents expected her to revert to Hinduism on being widowed but she remained Christian. Jairaj, therefore, refused to take her into his home. When Pragashini's parents moved to Port Elizabeth to set up in business there, one of Karishma's sons bought a house for her so that she could be near her sister. Leela visited her sister every fortnight but Jairaj would not allow her to take their children with her.

Like her parents, Pragashini could not understand why Karishma remained Christian. She imagined that, being an Indian woman her aunt was obliged to obey her husband, which included converting to Christianity. To add to the puzzle, some of Karishma's children remained Christians, while others became Hindu on marriage to Hindus.

Although Leela was forbidden to take her children to see her sister she disobeyed Jairaj while the children were young. When she feared they might speak about Karishma she stopped taking them with her. Pragashini recalled that, to placate the Hindu Gods who were angered by her conversion, Karishma placed a saucer of milk in the yard of her Transvaal home for a snake that came and fed each day. Pragashini wondered if Karishma brought the snake with her to Port Elizabeth. Seeing the snake drinking milk from a saucer is all she remembered of her aunt.

Pragashini confined herself to her room, the Nasaratts persisted with their behaviour and Ernestina continued leaving food on a tray outside her bedroom door. When she returned home in the late afternoon the tray was already there. On Sunday when she came downstairs into the kitchen, someone pushed the door shut in her face when she appeared in the doorway.

Throughout this period, no one spoke to her. Her old school friend Roshni may have been in turmoil, perhaps torn between fear of her parents' wrath, respect for their age, and loyalty to her. Pragashini could only guess at this because Roshni avoided her eyes. Sometimes she caught Roshni looking at her furtively, her large eyes soft like a doe, moist and sympathetic, but apparently cowed into submission by the power of the collective. Roshni never created an opportunity for them to be alone together. Neither of them considered the real implications of the gossip, which would only be felt by Pragashini later. She resumed her lifestyle of silence and isolation waiting for someone to ask her for an explanation of the gossip.

In the manner of women, she made excuses for them. They were not to know how freely she moved about in exile. How

Asian women could travel unaccompanied, enter pubs, even cohabit outside marriage. The gossip may have brought the Nasaratt family into disrepute in the little Indian community. They might not have the strength to deal with gossip. Ramgopal was older than her father. He was closer to the generation of her grandparents. She should not react to their treatment of her in the way she could react to her own parent's treatment. Her upbringing was too strongly ingrained for her to disrespect her grandparents' generation, however much she disagreed with them.

There was, however, one instruction she disobeyed, notwithstanding their age. Ramgopal and Nalini repeatedly asked her to grow her hair. When their requests failed, they demanded she grow her hair. Respect for elders was not sufficient to make her comply, and her rebellious nature would never make her follow an order. Shaving her head had significance for her. At the first sign of stubble on her scalp, she shaved her head in the privacy of her room. They could do nothing about it. This may have added to their displeasure with her.

She came to terms with being ostracised. By the end of the week, Ernestina was the only person who had any form of contact with her. The atmosphere in the house was strained and unpleasant. She sat alone in various parts of the garden, reading her thesis, making corrections, adding footnotes. Ernestina came into the garden to hang the washing, brought her tea, and by her actions indicated that she disapproved of the family's treatment of her. Pragashini could not, however, leave the house until Nasaratt's return. She had to endure being ostracised.

Rather than waste energy on the gossip she asked herself repeatedly, 'Who is the source of this gossip? How and where did it originate? Who knows about my feelings? No one. I've not trusted anyone.' Each time she came up with only one name – Mossel Klein. She had never spoken to anyone about her strange experience on first seeing him, or of his effect on her. Who else could know? No one but he. Some men delight in the power they exercise over women. He seemed to be like that. She convinced herself he was the source.

***

51.

Golden light filtered from the sky and warmed the sand on the beaches, the rocks, and pavements, blessing the air. Here the sun was up before six. But she was barred from entering the family prayer room even while the rest of the family were asleep. Now she longed for her prayer room, for the simple arched window, for the northern sunlight shimmering through the jewelled glass, sunlight that was now for her more warming than the sun in South Africa. She created a little altar in her room.

Sympathetic friends and youthful members of the family urged her to move out of the Nasaratt home. They invited her to stay with them. Knowing they would be censured if they offered her a room in their homes, she did not make the mistake of accepting. Whoever helped her would be left in the turmoil she had created when she returned to England.

Her conflict with her in-laws was silent. They were old enough to be her grandparents. Their age, and the small community they lived in following the forced removal of Indians to Muhalla Asha, placed an added restriction on her after she had enjoyed a measured freedom in England. She understood her in-laws could not be seen to be condoning the behaviour of which the gossip accused her. But they never doubted the truth of it.

It was usual for the Nasaratt family to drive to the temple to sing Bhajans on a Sunday evening although the temple was within walking distance from their home. The older generation feared walking at night, even within the Indian township. She did not grasp the significance of Sunday in the Hindu ritual: on Fridays, Muslim men went to the mosque; Jews rested on Saturdays; practising Christians went to church on Sundays. She could only reason that the modern Hindu family living in South Africa could only come together on a Sunday. If they were living in an Islamic country, she supposed they would sing Bhajans on a Friday.

To keep the peace and demonstrate respect for her elders she made an agreement with herself to accompany them, like a dutiful daughter-in-law for as long as she was under their roof. She succeeded in keeping this up until the visit of the gossip when the Nasaratts began leaving for temple without her. At around seven in the evening she heard the car doors slam, the engines rev up, the cars crunch across the brick driveway, leaving her alone in the house. Not having been a regular temple goer in England she was unperturbed. However, having spent years away from family, she considered it unkind to exclude a returned exile from family gatherings. Her absence from the temple would be obvious. The temple goers looked forward to meeting visitors and knowing she was returned from exile they expected her to be there. She wanted to get the better of the gossips who would be attending temple.

One Sunday she locked herself in her bedroom and prepared for temple, determined to walk and make an entrance on her own. She deliberately protracted unlocking the door, so that the Nasaratts would not know of her intention. When Roshni knocked tentatively on the door to say they were leaving she kept still.

Hearing the cars drive off, she had second thoughts, as she

stood dressed in another borrowed sari. What purpose would it serve, her turning up at the temple? It would probably embarrass her more than the Nasaratts. She would be considered brass faced. Yet her non-appearance would be remarked upon by the community and the gossips. She forced herself to leave the house.

The streets of Muhalla Asha were dark and quiet but for the crickets chirping. She walked quickly. There were no pedestrians in the street. Here and there, people sat on the verandas in the dark. She approached the wide stone steps at the entrance to the temple, ascended, opened the door, and entered. In the vestibule, she stepped out of her sandals, and hovered at the back of the devotees. No one took particular notice of her. People sat on the floor on a large carpet. Near the front, a group sat on a dais playing an Indian accordion, a santoor, and the tabla. A man sat before a microphone leading the singing. A woman sat to his right with a microphone in her hand.

Glancing around at the sari clad women sitting on the floor, at the men, the icons of various gods and goddesses, flowers, and flames flickering in oil lamps, instead of feeling at one with the devotees, she was overcome by the pain of isolation. That same isolation of Paul's Himalayan Rose in exile from India now swamped her within this vibrant living community of Indians. She withdrew into herself, and realised she was an outsider. That same feeling she had in England was deeper now she was actually in the community where she belonged, where she should feel at home. She stood up and slipped away. Her one comfort was that if she was out of place here, so were the devotions she performed every morning and evening while she was in exile, under the light from her arched window.

52.

The Recluse - Pragashini's Journal:

She resumed wearing the Niqab. It is provocative because she appears like a Muslim woman in a Hindu household. Her gentle efforts to speak to them, even to Ernestina, have stopped. As if in another world, she floats around the house and garden, her silence and the Niqab drawing more attention than a scream.

***

53.

Her lustreless eyes, and the strain on her bleak looking face invited her colleagues concern. 'It's the heat. I've met so many new people. The pace of life is slower here,' she told them. Still convinced she was unaffected by the gossip's revelations, she persisted with her routine. She continued to wake early in the morning.

***

54.

The Recluse – Pragashini's Journal

In the middle of the night she clambered out of bed and sat at her desk. She selected a fountain pen she rarely used because the nib scratched, filled it with Black Quink, and composed a brief note.
She wrote with ease, as if communicating with a long lost friend. The note began in the middle of an idea, as if it continued from a previous one. 'Why don't you recognise me? Acknowledge me? Are you looking for a code? A sign? Have you become a coward? Afraid of public censure if discovered?' She ended her letter with fervent wishes for his good health. She blotted the ink, folded the paper, placed it in the brown envelope, and sealed it. Then she slipped on her running shoes, put the letter inside her tracksuit top, and jogged

to the government building, placed the letter in the internal mailbox, and jogged home. The letter was unsigned. Undated. The envelope required no postage stamp. It had neither post office stamp nor franking machine mark.

***

55.

Through the next week, in between computer searches, Pragashini went to her office and to section meetings. She fooled herself into believing there was no change in her, yet noted a change in Klein. He appeared tense and wary. He chaired his section's weekly meetings in a guarded manner. He trained staff and potential trade union members on the pillars of transformation he may have suspected any one of a hundred public servants, even colleagues. He sent the letter to his contact for analysis. She heard about it on the grapevine. In the meantime, he kept to himself. She had unnerved him.

***

56.

The Recluse - Pragashini's Journal

She has stopped eating. She is neither praying nor meditating. She wakes in the middle of the night and leaves the house, in her pyjamas. She wanders around the streets of Bisho and Muhalla Asha. I can't be sure she knows she is doing this. She may be sleepwalking. She may be searching for the crying child. I can't be sure.

There are drunken men sleeping in the doorways of shops shut up for the night; vagrants under trees on the roads leading out of Muhalla Asha and Bisho; under the darkness of the bridge; on the pavements. She is at risk. She has stopped looking at herself in the mirror again. If she did she might not recognise the face that looks back at her. She has a haunted look in her eyes, perhaps because she is not eating. She looks like someone possessed or deranged. I can do nothing for her. I hope I am not to blame for what happens to her.

***

57.

Ernestina called her out of her bedroom to hear Astrid and Nalini quarrelling. Astrid scolded. Nalini cried.

'I'm shocked at you,' said Astrid. 'You of all people. Someone else I could still understand. But you! Have you lost your memory? Have you forgotten when you were so desperate to conceive? Where were you running to every morning? To the temple? No! You were running to the Catholic church. You sneaked in to pray to the Virgin Mary! You Nalini! Not Pragashini. *You* should be locked out of the prayer room. You were more afraid you'd be caught and reported to Ramgopal. You never gave a thought to what Catholics thought about you coming into their church. Did you? How would you have felt if the nuns locked the church when they saw you coming? Wouldn't you have felt humiliated? Angry? After all, you were going there to pray. You didn't have a right to be there. Now you! You lock this girl, a Hindu girl, from your prayer room? I never imagined you could do such a thing. I'm ashamed of you! I can't call you my friend.'

'I never thought of it like that,' Nalini cried.

Later when Ernestina brought a tray of food to Pragashini's bedroom, she had more to report. 'Wait 'til you hear this, Pragashini!' she said, 'Astrid scolded the whole Nasaratt family in the family room. They were all standing there so

bang[60], you'd think they were in school, and Astrid was the headmistress. Astrid said, "Pragashini was a schoolgirl. Anand was old enough to be her father. The priest should have locked the temple door when all of you showed up."
'You know,' added Ernestina, 'They're crying crocodile tears. I think they're going to fast for a week! And then, guess what? Ramgopal tiptoed to the prayer room and unlocked the door.'

'I'll never venture near their prayer room again,' Pragashini said.

***

58.

The document was hidden in a folder on a junior office assistant's computer and not nesting within the system files. It was password protected. The computer would have been handed down when a new shipment arrived for senior personnel. She guessed if she opened it she might be discovered. Files usually showed the date last accessed. She would then have to leave Bisho.

Unwilling to arouse suspicion by spending time on a junior's computer, she returned to her office and waded through pages of rules and strictures governing confidentiality hoping to find a clue relating to the password.

***

59.

Heather regularly brought a parishioner home from church for Sunday lunch. After lunch, she the took the children for a drive before dropping the parishioner at home, leaving

---

60 Bang means to be afraid.

Smuts to spend time alone with his parents.

Smuts took them for drives in the areas surrounding Port Elizabeth. He loved the beachfront. If the wind was high, he left his mother wrapped in a blanket in the car, or on a bench on the promenade while he and his father walked to the end of the pier and talked. There was always some type of vessel in the harbour, or bobbing about in the water with any number of people standing and peering over the edge into the water below. Mandisa knew her son valued these sessions with his father and did not begrudge the time.

Smuts knew little of his father's views, and could not read the signs of his father's displeasure. He was more fearful of Matatiele, than of Heather or Nolitando. Alone with his father, Smuts broached the delicate subject of Nolitando's pregnancy. He was still to formulate an approach to Heather and Nolitando on the subject.

He was disconcerted when his father congratulated him. When he ventured on the topic of marriage and his father simply said, 'I don't ask to know your money affairs. You must calculate if you can afford two wives. For me life was a struggle. Or I would have done it,' Smuts was disappointed.

He suspected the women's movement would have an opinion about which favoured women more, polygamy or monogamy. Added to this it was strange to hear his father speak about himself in relation to another woman. He could not imagine his father in a polygamous relationship. He wondered how it would have affected his mother. He was surprised at how easy it was then to discuss a second wife with his father. Years of exile influenced his way of thinking. He expected objections from his father, and considerations about Heather, but none came. Nothing concerned his father, except that he should be able to maintain the two wives in comfort.

They discussed the feasibility of the two women living in

one house. It was then Smuts told his father Heather had bought the house. It was in her name. His father was displeased by this news. He could not understand how Smuts allowed her to do this. 'It makes you less of a man,' he said.

'Ikona,' Smuts said, imitating Matatiele's use of the word. 'Not these days.'

'Never mind,' his father said, 'she did it before you were initiated. If she acts like a man again - put your foot down.'

Smuts shook his head and smiled.

'So where will you place number two?' his father asked.

'Maybe I'll buy in Bisho, or eQonce – or iMonti - now I've taken a seat in iLegislature.'

'It's foolish to let a woman buy a house,' Matatiele said.

'In your time maybe,' Smuts said.

***

60.

Pragashini's Journal

I was sitting in a wicker armchair having draped a saffron cloth over my shoulders feeling tense and still having difficulty meditating. Since the gossip's visit and the locked prayer room, I performed the puja in my room. The curtains were drawn; the oil lamp and joss stick were burning. I breathed deeply to encourage the flow of prana; felt stillness in my body; achieved some cessation of though, yet could not meditate.

I stood up, walked around the room, drank a glass of water, and began again. My guru advised me never to miss a session of meditation. 'When you're stressed out is when you need to meditate,' he said. I remembered my beloved prayer room, chanted softly, whispered the chant, and chanted silently. Still I could not settle down.

So I concentrated on the flame in the oil lamp; steadied my gaze;

regulated my breathing; achieved a relative kind of peace. I began again with the mantra. Shut my eyes again; waited several minutes before I saw the explosion of light, that accompanies meditation; the colours moving through the spectrum, from white to amber, orange, red, mauve, blue; and these colours repeating. While contemplating the light, I was at ease. Prana pervaded the living cells and tissues in my body. Those potential cells. I felt calm and serene.

Suddenly I was stimulated to open my eyes. I had the strangest sensation of being outside my body. I seemed to be looking down at myself from the ceiling. I saw myself seated in the wicker armchair. I saw how I appeared to another person. I was observing myself. I was fully aware of myself. Fully aware that I was observing myself seated there below. I began thinking. What is happening to me? Can I move? Can I move my limbs? My head? No, I could not move yet I was fully conscious and wide-awake. Then I made a point of instructing my brain to move my body but my body did not respond. It sat there, apparently lifeless. I realised my body would only move once it was reunited with whatever part of me was out there looking at it sitting in the armchair. I asked myself 'is it my soul that has left my body or is it my sentient being that is out here?

The moment lengthened until I became anxious. I didn't know what I had to do to achieve unity, the return, my return to my body. It was my consciousness thinking. It was my consciousness looking at my body. My consciousness must return to my body. How did I leave my body? How do I return? My awareness was not in my body. How long can I remain outside? What will bring it back?

Now I was in torment. Have I died? If I died, why is my body sitting erect in the chair? What would happen if someone enters the room? What if someone touches my body? Will I fall over? Will I lose the chance to return to my body if someone finds me in this state?

Then as quickly and as suddenly as I found myself on the ceiling looking down at my body, I was myself, back inside my body. My awareness and my body were re-united. I did not know what achieved the return of my awareness to my body. But I felt utter relief.

Later that night, awake in bed I thought about my experience. I wondered if I could have left the room while I was outside my body? Could I have moved through the wall or door, or did I have to open the door? Could I have moved through the house? Could I have left the house? How long would it have taken me to go somewhere, and then return to my body? How long could I have remained out of my body? How long had I been in that state? I had not checked the clock. Was this a common experience for people who meditate? Did meditation bring this on? What did it mean? What was the experience called? How did I accomplish it? Was it an accomplishment?

If I had remained outside my body, would I have died? Was death voluntary? Did we acquiesce in our death? If I could bring my awareness back into my body, did it mean when one died one left the body voluntarily, or one could refuse to remain in one's body? Was this Nirvana?

Now I was afraid to meditate. Yet I needed to meditate because I was stressed out. I dreaded to think what would have occurred if someone had opened the door. But I must meditate. How will I meditate now? It's my only source of strength. Can I trust a Guru in Muhalla Asha to help me? Or will he betray me to the Nasaratts? I dare not meditate again.

***

61.

Pragashini's Journal

I found the following entry dating back to my childhood. It reminded me of the child I had been.

Yesterday I had a mind-blowing experience. I was sitting in my bedroom, minding my own business. The house was quiet. The windows open. A light breeze blew into the room. The soft nylon curtains billowed like friendly spirits. I thought I'd do a spot of meditating. Strictly non-religious. Meditation was all the rage. While sitting there, calm, breathing regularly, meditating on the correct way to spell Aftab or Aaftab, and if it meant I could have two chances with the different spelling, - I heard Leela – who claims to be my mother – scream. I imagined it, - Leela was out shopping at Greenacres. Nevertheless, I went out to look for her, in case she needed rescuing from an orang-utan. They love bananas, orang-utans. I often think she is – bananas I mean. A poor orang-utan might easily make a mistake. I had imagined it. Leela was not in the house.

Half an hour later, though, Leela – I like to call her by her first name in private – drove up in the car. She told me she was mugged in the supermarket car park miles away. She had screamed. At precisely the moment I heard her. I ask you. Was I floating out there while my body was sitting here meditating? Mind-boggling. And to think, I don't smoke daggha. When I told my friends – I wasn't even trying out a drag of daggha – a zoll[61] *as daggha rookers*[62] *like to call it – they reached for their saltcellars. Honestly! When I tell the truth, no one believes me.*

***

62.

After trying countless word and number combinations, Pragashini discovered the password. Suddenly the secret document displayed on the screen before her. She stared at it incredulously. It displayed the details of Special Branch headquarters in the Sanlam Building in Port Elizabeth

---

61 A Zoll is a hand rolled cigarette, but in SA it is a hand rolled joint of cannabis.

62 Daggha rookers are smokers of cannabis.

where people were interrogated and tortured. She read through the list of names before printing the document while praying the paper would not jam and that no one would enter the office. She hurriedly closed the file, exited the folder, and did a fast and safe cleanup that she hoped would erase evidence that the file had been accessed. She spent precious minutes striving to revert the access date back but failed.

Back in her office, she scrutinised the list to confirm what she had seen on first sight.

***

63.

A week after sending the first anonymous letter to Klein she wrote the second anonymous note. He asked the service officers to keep a watch on his pigeonhole. She spaced her letters a week apart. Each week she chose a different day and time, hung about until the service officers changed shifts then put a letter into his pigeonhole.

***

64.

Karishma, her mother's sister, preoccupied her on the drive to Port Elizabeth at midday on Fridays. When she was a child she searched for her aunt. People in the community had no wish to displease her father and refused to assist her. Now however, one of the locals took her to the house.

She assumed Karishma saw her when she was a baby when she could have no memory of her aunt. Her memories were of aunts who fed her rice mashed with potato from a curry, and the curry gravy, using their fingers, when she was a young child; aunts who cared for her hair, oiling it each week. Brushing and plaiting it at night. Aunts who knew she loved masala tea and brewed it whenever she visited. But Karishma never figured in her memories of family meals, weddings, birthdays, and naming ceremonies. She wondered why Karishma became a Christian when her husband converted? Why she remained a Christian when he died? What was the source of her strength? How she coped with being ostracized by family, friends, and the community at large.

She was taken to a townhouse with the signposts of South Africa's bloody violence. Thick wire with razor blades at spaced intervals along the wire was secured in large close spirals along the top of the boundary walls. Burglar bars in a pretty, curved design barred the windows. A tall metal door protected the front door. Without seeing it Pragashini knew that the back door was similarly secured. Entrance to the house was through an arched metal gate in the boundary wall.

Through the gate she saw a woman kneeling on a green plastic cushion on the lawn with a trowel in her hands, weeding a bed of roses alongside the lawn. She rattled the gate. The woman looked over her shoulder, stood up, and came over to her. Her shoulder length hair was brown. She was barefoot. She wore frayed blue denim shorts and a sleeveless white summer top. As she approached Pragashini saw a resemblance to her mother Leela. Karishma unlocked the gate and held out her arms to her.

'You found me,' her aunt said as she absorbed the warmth of hugs and kisses. Karishma led her round to the back garden to soak up the sun.

That was the first of many visits to Karishma. Over time, she revealed her fears, and offered little confidences that brought them close. It was easy for her to become infatuated with Karishma, who had shown independence of mind. She waited for the right moment to ask how Karishma could yearn to be close to her sister at one stage in her life, and then distance herself from that same sister.

***

65.

This bush is the closest thing to our human souls. Our souls have a past. Most of us don't remember the soul's past. We know only our present lives, the lives we are living. There are people who say they can foretell the future. Most of us don't believe them. Look at the flowers on this shrub,' Karishma said. 'This one's purple; this one's lilac; and this one's white. Three colours on one bush. Have you seen such a plant? No one has meddled with it. Crossing this with that. That's how it is. Naturally. We call it, yesterday, today, and tomorrow.'

That was Karishma's explanation to Pragashini. She led Pragashini back to where they were sitting and she continued.

Karishma rarely socialised. Pragashini therefore withheld information about the gossip's visit and the Nasaratt's subsequent behaviour. Instead she described her first meeting with Klein and of the happiness verging on ecstasy that suffused her; her conviction that she knew him; and how her certainty fell away from her, as if her soul deserted her, leaving her to admit she had never met him before. She described her ensuing confusion.

Karishma asked if she spent a great deal of time alone in England, which she admitted. Karishma gave no explanation leaving her to blame the experience on her isolation.

She also recounted the occasions when she experienced some form of telepathy with people. Karishma said this was natural. Bonds of love and family link people closely. She even confided the recurring dream she had since childhood.

She described how in her dream she was striving to place a glass object on a pinnacle. Each time she succeeded in balancing the object there, and was about to move away, the object fell and broke. Then she would hear a child crying. The crying child wakes her. She goes in search of the child but never finds it.

Karishma suggested something might have happened when she was a child. She said she would try to think back and remember if Leela had told her anything.

She grew close to Karishma, sharing many experiences with her. She described how she observed herself during meditation; how she failed to instruct her body to move; of being in a state of absolute immobility; that she was aware that some aspect of herself was separated from her body; that she was separated from herself.

Karishma listened without interrupting. That was when she took Pragashini's hand, and led her to the shrub in the garden.

'If you tell someone all the things you've told me, they'd be sympathetic. They'd say you're having a crisis of identity. You're confused about your identity perhaps having many identities. Even a split personality. That's because the spirit is dead in the west. Even God is dead for most westerners.'

'God is dead because of Darwin,' Pragashini said. 'Christians believed in creation for thousands of years. Then along came Darwin. He said every plant and animal evolved. There's no such thing as creation. From that day all Christians doubt and question everything to do with their religion.'

'Are you telling me the whole world of other believers never heard about this Darwin man?'

'Others don't have a creation story. If you believe God created everything and someone says this plant or animal evolved, it means living things were not created. To them it means there is no God.'

'I can't understand their reasoning.'

'It's simple. Other religions don't have a creation story so they can believe in God and in evolution.'

'Or they don't believe in God because they don't believe in the spirit. They think anyone who believes in the spirit is primitive. They love to believe in things. But they are obsessive. Whatever they're obsessed with they become fanatical about.'

'Perhaps. Once upon a time they wanted a sea route to India because they needed spices to preserve their food. After they invented fridges they lost interest in spices. Another time it was cheap labour when they didn't want to work with their hands. Then they placed a high value on gold. Then diamonds. Even coal, can you believe it? Today it's oil. Then it's money. Sex. Political power. We converted to obsessive desires. We've forgotten our own.'

Karishma seemed to have forgotten the purpose of Pragashini's visit. She led the way into the house. In the kitchen while Pragashini prepared tea she brought out home baked cake and crockery. Pragashini made tea the only way she knew how. She placed a tea bag in each cup, filled it with water from the tap, added milk from the fridge, opened the microwave, and put both cups in leaving them until the water had boiled.

'You've spoken to me for hours,' Karishma said while they had their tea. 'I'm the only one in our family you've met since returning home. Yet you haven't asked once about your parents. Don't you want to know where they are? Or how they are?'

'They died,' Pragashini said simply and putting her clenched fist to her heart said, 'in here.'

'They almost did die. Your whole family. All of us. Living here in Muhallah Asha. In the eighties. After you left. We had terrible rioting here. The sad thing is they weren't rioting against apartheid. They turned against us. Like they did in Durban. The grass roots set fire to our business area. Your father's shop was burnt to the ground. Not just his shop. All these Indians you see around you, living quiet lives most were in business. They stood and watched generations of hard work burnt to the ground. Your parents packed up and moved back to Durban. They're not safe there either. But they felt safety in numbers was better. There are more Indians in Natal than here. They were angry when I decided to stay on in PE.'

'Why did you stay on?'

Karishma refused to say. 'These people don't know our struggle, Pragashini,' Karishma said. 'The rioters marched up from the quarry to kill us. We still don't know why. The rioters – will they work the hours we work in our little shops? Will they make the sacrifices we make for our children's education? Did we arrive in this country with motorcars and money in the bank? We worked this land. We worked in the sugar cane fields. We worked the mines. Gold and diamonds. We laid the railways. We hawked flowers and fruit and vegetables. We were market gardeners. We worked in the hotels. Before we set up in business. That's how we came to have shops and cars and houses. But no one likes seeing what our hard labour earns us. The rioters. Did they work on the sugar cane fields? No they didn't. Did they work on the mines in Kimberley and the Rand? No they didn't. We were the first ones to work for this land. Our labour is in this land. What South Africa is today, it owes us.

They say we're not indigenous people. Other groups are. Before the indigenous people worked to develop this country, we did. Ask yourself Pragashini, what are we Indians doing here? There are millions of people here,

Africans, Coloureds, Europeans. Ask yourself, why did they have to bring us all the way from India to work on the sugar cane fields?'

'It isn't just one group, auntie.'

'I know. In Natal others burnt our shops.'

'I mean, it isn't just in this country that people resent those who put in hard hours and make sacrifices. It happens all over the world. In England the locals did the same thing to the Jews. Hundreds of years ago. They chased the Jews through the streets at night. They killed whoever they caught. The Jews fled from their homes. In York they ran through the streets into a small tower. They locked themselves inside, hoping the mob would not find them, or that someone would come and help them. The only people who came were the local mob. They started a fire around the tower. The Jews were terrified of coming out. They knew they would be butchered. They died inside. Some people say they killed each other inside the tower to prevent the local people killing them. The tower's still standing there. Evil never dies. It's all around. Everywhere. It slouches around looking for new bodies to control. Like jealousy and envy. That's why I pray, auntie. Because I hate my father. I hate Nasaratt. I pray that I don't do something evil to them.'

'And your mother?'

'I pity her. She is an Indian female, like you and me.'

***

66.

The dream in the present, the tree in the past.' That is what Pragashini thought when she asked Karishma about the mulberry tree that figured in her old journals. Her aunt told her that the mulberry tree grew in the backyard of a house in

Kimberley. Its trunk ancient, massive and gnarled provided handholds and footholds for any little girl to clamber into the tree, slide out onto its spreading branches, gorge herself on purple berries then hide amongst the leaves until the boys came out to play and pelt them from above until the yard was purple and blue with splattered berries.'

'The swing was made of two strands of thick brown rope flung over a sturdy branch, the ends of the rope threaded through holes in a thick flat piece of wood and knotted below the plank to keep it in place. Little girls were able to reach the seat of the swing by grasping the rope, running backwards, and jumping onto the seat as it swung forward. The movement filled them with elation. They were happy to play like this without concern for time.'

'One day you were swinging on the mulberry tree when your mother called to you but you refused to come to her. She punished you by not giving you supper and putting you to bed. Do you remember it?'

'Not at all.'

***

67.

The Recluse: Pragashini's Journal.

But I remembered the swing on the mulberry tree in the past. One day I was swinging on the mulberry tree when I saw a figure in the distance. It was a lady. The lady approached. She stopped a little way off, calling. I continued swinging. The lady was not calling me. As the lady drew nearer, I heard her clearly. The lady sounded very angry. I did not know the lady. The lady was not calling my name. The lady came closer and closer until she was at my side. The lady was furious. She said she had been calling and calling. Then she reached out and grabbed the rope. The swing twisted round and round. I fell off the swing. The lady took my hand and marched away with me to a man who appeared in the doorway. I did not recognise the man either. They put me to bed. I fell asleep crying, 'Mummy doesn't love me

***

68.

A soap bubble is the nearest thing to faith. It can not touch anything material. If it does, it simply pops. It is gone and can never be recreated. Faith is like that ... ethereal ... it should never be touched by reason. Heather said this to Smuts. Then she added, 'Don't belittle what I'm doing.'

It was the lunch hour. Smuts was in his office seated at the computer desk with his back to the room and to the interconnecting door between the two offices. He faced the wall.

During the lunch hour every member of staff locked their offices and escaped to the dining room where chefs prepared a range of hot and cold meals for them and for Members of Parliament in segregated dining rooms.

In his office was a wide director's desk running the length of a wall that had large windows. Facing the desk was a long wall with two doors, one at either end. The two doors opened on to the passage, the one to his left was always kept locked. To his right when he was seated at his desk was a small computer desk with computer, and printer attached.
To his left was a door connecting his office with that of his secretary. This door was usually left wide open. His secretary's office also had a door that led to the passage. She locked this door when she was out of the office.

While working at his computer, he heard a sound in his secretary's office. He glanced at his watch - it was just ten minutes into the lunch hour - she may have returned for something. He ignored the sound but it recurred. It was a dragging sound that repeated every few seconds. It puzzled him. He glanced over his shoulder. It stopped. He returned to his work. The dragging noise resumed. After glancing back several times, it occurred to him the general assistant who cleaned the office may have come in. She had a key and had the habit of sleeping during the lunch hour. She may have permission from his secretary to be in her office. He stood up and walked into the small office. There was no one there. Perplexed, he walked across to her outer door and tried the handle. It was locked. He returned to his desk. Whoever had been there must have left.

Immediately he sat at his computer again, he heard the noise. Without turning round he listened. It was a dragging, scraping noise coming from the smaller office into his. It approached quite close to him. When he turned round the noise stopped. Each time he turned to look at the computer screen the noise began again stopping at his back when he turned round. He thought there was something in the ceiling, perhaps a mouse, dragging something. He stood up and went to stand in the middle of the room. The sound and the movement came in a curve towards him then stopped. He looked up at the ceiling but the noise was definitely in the room. He went back to the computer and sat down and the sound began again from his secretary's room to where he sat.

He stood up and looked out the window. His office was on the second floor from the ground. There was no balcony on the second floor. He went to the outside door and opened it. He saw a workman he knew dressed in white overalls and maroon cap. The workman walked past his office, went through the glass doors and down the stairs. There was no one else about. Seeing the workman and realising no one was in the building he went to the other passage and looked up and down. He saw a woman unlocking her office door. Then he saw two men coming towards him from the right. The men nodded but he was too pre-occupied to acknowledge them. He went back to his office and concluded it was the workman. Perhaps he had been sanding or doing some scraping work. He may have been pulling cables across the ceiling.

This time he locked the outer door and sat down at the computer again. The sound, of someone dragging something began again. On impulse, he unlocked the door, left it wide open, and went to stand in the middle of the room. But the sound had stopped. He sat down again and the sound began again. He then stood up walked out the room, left the door wide open and stood with his back to the door in the passage to one side of the door. He heard the scraping, dragging movement approach the door, and pass out of the room and down the passage. He walked back into the office and sat down at his computer. The office was quiet.

He phoned Heather and described the occurrence to her. At the weekend she drove up from Port Elizabeth. They went to his office to examine the carpet. It was newly laid. But there was a white mark in the shape of an arc, on the carpet between the two offices that had not been there before. It seemed to be drawn in chalk. He had already called the cleaner and she went over the mark at length with the hoover but could not remove it.

Heather bought candles, lit them, and placed them on his desk. She walked around both offices sprinkling holy water in all the corners, around the doors and windows. She murmured prayers she knew by heart. Then she read from a prayer book, while he stood near the window feeling cold and troubled. She came up to him and sprinkled holy water on him. He laughed putting his hands up to shield his face. 'Get thee behind me Satan,' he joked. She pulled him close to her and said 'God protect you.' They stood holding each other in the office while the candle burned. She pleaded with him not to stay alone in the office when the building was empty.

That night they talked about what might have caused the strange happening. He asked friends who said the building was formerly the headquarters of the Ciskei police. Down in the basement there were police cells where prisoners were tortured. What he heard may have been something from that past. They conjectured about what had caused him to hear the sounds on that day at that time. Was the sound always there but he never heard it? Had something happened to make him hear sounds that are not real? Or did the thing that made the sound only come into his office that day? When did it come? At what time? Why did it come? Did it come with someone? The workman? The general assistant? The two strange men he saw? Who was in his office that morning?

He told Heather he remembered feeling cold all morning. He had told his secretary several times that he was feeling cold. She had turned up the heating and he had closed the windows and come to stand by the heater. He had gone down to a conference room for the caucus. The room was warm yet he wore his jacket. The caucus ended at lunchtime. Was it possible something accompanied him from the conference room to his office? He told Heather there was someone in the caucus who had an injured leg and who was hostile during the caucus. It was all strange. They could not understand it. He described the strange happening to his father who said, 'They've sent a spirit after you'.

***

69.

There's some similarity between the rituals of Hindus and Catholics,' Karishma said. 'When I first attended a Catholic service, I felt at home.'

'You're imagining things,' Pragashini said. Yet, fascinated by her aunt, she plied her with questions, the one uppermost in her mind being, 'Why did you remain a Christian after uncle died? He must have forced you to convert!'

Karishma appeared to be expecting the question. 'He did. He refused to marry if I didn't become Christian.'

'Wouldn't life be easier, if you were Hindu again?'

'Just because you have all these icons of fantastic looking gods,' Karishma said, 'the Europeans took one look and disregarded Hinduism. Primitive they called it. Pagans. But I ask you, look at the two religions, the Catholics and the Hindus. Not all Christians perform rituals. Some don't even have a church. Pragashini, don't we put our hands together in greeting? Who else does that? Jews? Muslims? Only Catholics. Where do you think that joining of hands comes from? What about oil lamps? Who lights oil lamps? Hindus do. Did you know there's an oil lamp burning day and night in our churches? Do the Jews burn lamps? I don't know. Then there's incense. It's such a Hindu thing. We also burn incense in our church. What about ashes on the forehead? Did you know they do that too? It's incredible.'

'They'll kick you out of the church auntie, if they hear you talking like this.'

'Christianity is a new religion. But think about it. We believe in three persons in one God. Hindus might say, Brahmah, Paramatma, and Bhagwan. There are your three Gods, Pragashini. Jews don't believe that. Resurrection of the soul. Where do Jews talk about the soul. They write about angels in the Bible, yes. Souls no. Hindus have atman. Resurrection of the soul is nearer to reincarnation than belief in one life. Jesus was born a Jew but Jesus taught totally new things to the early Christians. Jesus taught Christians not to circumcise. To eat meat that isn't kosher. Where does baptism come from? From the Jews? Never! Whose devotees are forever pouring water over their heads in the river? Aren't Hindus always in the river Ganges? Pouring water on their heads? That's why it was easy for me to become a Christian, Pragashini. The image of Christ's mother holding a baby, Indian motherhood, and Mother India. Joining hands. Lighting incense. Oil lamps. Promising that after death there is life. Blessing the bread and eating it like prasaad. I don't know why other people don't see this connection. You think they'll excommunicate me?'

'They will. To compare Hinduism with the Catholic religion! If you were living in the time of Galileo, they'd put you to death. Hinduism is pagan. Our religion is down there below the Jews, the Muslims, and the Christians. As far as religions goes, Hinduism is like the untouchables.'

They talked into the night. She told her aunt about her father's telephone calls to her. 'I punished my father by refusing to speak with him. When the phone rang, I lifted the receiver, heard his voice, and stood mute listening to his outpouring of remorse. He admitted forcing me into marriage was wrong. But I wanted a public admission, before the family, before the whole community, and all the wedding guests.'

Gradually Pragashini changed from implacable resentment to grudging leniency and understanding. She should forgive her father. She should forgive the elements embodied in Indian women that her mother contained, if for no other reason than that she might one day have to ask forgiveness for embodying Indianness in herself. Forgiveness was a new concept for her. Although the prospect of change in South Africa was a powerful enticement, as was the force behind the change, and the timing of her change and of her return, the need to learn to forgive should have brought her back. She had not learnt to forgive.

Watching Karishma move around her kitchen, she was homesick for her mother. Here was this aunt, a strong woman who could defy family and community, while her mother lacked the courage to defend her own daughter.

How could two people nurtured in the same family be so different? Was it that they had married men who differed in their outlook on life? Or were these two sisters simply different in their own right?

When she returned to the Nasaratts' home she no longer yearned to pray with them in the family prayer room.

***

70.

Bringing gifts to a party hosted by the secret police or our other enemies. The gift of people's names. Their hiding places. People the police may like as pen pals. Or to collaborate with on a writing project like an untrue confession. Some short of money who may like to work overtime as impimpis. Some little fish. Some sharks. So they can arrest. Torture. Maim. Kill. Maybe the gift is giving true or false evidence in court leading to a comrade's imprisonment. Strange deaths.'

That's what Matatiele said when he extended his hand for the document and Pragashini refused to hand it over.

'What is this document?' she demanded.

'I won't know till I see it.'

'What will you do with it?'

'I must see it first.'

'I won't give it to you. You must have some idea.'

'I'm guessing it's a list of names.'

'Guests at a wedding?'

That was when he mentioned guests bringing strange gifts.

Then she asked, 'If it's a list of names, what will you do to the people named?'

'If trusted people are on the list - get rid of them. There may be names on the list betraying us as we stand here. We need that list. We must have it. Give it to me.'

'How will you know there aren't errors on the list?'

'Hard luck!'

'What if it's names of your trusted people bringing gifts to you?'

'We'll be able to tell.'

'You think some are in line for seats in government?'

'Some. Not all. Then our democracy will be built on quicksand. Stop fooling around Pragashini.'

'If this is your list you'll be horrified,' she said attempting to prepare him for a shock.

'By a piece of paper? A piece of paper is niks. After all the violence I've seen, nothing can horrify me.'

She gave him the document and watched while he scanned each page. She watched him pause at the third page where Mellikhaya's name appeared, saw him look at her, then continue, while she waited for him to reach the end. He smiled.

'Mellikhaya's name is there,' she said.

'I see it,' he said. You know what you've found?'

'It's a list, like you said. Of collaborators names. You said to look for the SAP markings. It says 'Top Secret.'

'You think this is our document?' he asked. 'Don't you know what you've found, Pragashini?' he repeated. Then he began reading the names aloud, looking at her for a reaction, and finding none he paused and said, 'They're dead. Some of them. They've died violent or suspicious deaths. Look at these names. It goes right back to Chief

Luthuli[63].' Then he hugged her. 'This is an assassination list,' he said. 'This is priceless, this list.'

'I must go back,' she said.

'You can't go back. Someone else must find the collaborators.'

'When they discover the file has been hacked into, they'll give the collaborators list a new password. No one else knows which computers I've searched, which I still have to search. I didn't make a list. The computer was old, probably from the Ciskei police department. I know the computer. I've got the weekend to find the other list.'

'I'll go with you to Bisho,' he said.

***

71.

Late on Friday night Pragashini returned to Bisho with Matatiele. They parked the car on the Fort Hare campus and walked to the government buildings. The Legislature had a late sitting. Matatiele remained outside wandering around the exterior, staying in the shadows and keeping a watchful eye on the gate while she entered the building, and went upstairs. She closed the blinds and working by the light of the computer screen, searched the computer that held the assassination document.

It was past five in the morning when she came across a document with a coded file name. She foolishly entered the same password she had used to break into the assassin document: 'ashishin'. She did not strike lucky this time. The computer immediately began shutting down. She jumped

63 Chief Albert Luthuli former President General of the African National Congress was found dead on the train lines near his home on 21 July 1967. He was winner of the Nobel Peace Prize in 1961.

up, switched the computer off at the wall, unplugged it and sat waiting an interminable length of time.

Then she began again. Plug in. Switch on. Hard drive on. Wait while the computer loaded. While waiting she referred to the failed passwords, she had previously tried. She had found the correct one by chance. There was no time to go through the entire list again. She had looked up the word Assassin. It was derived from 'ashishin'. 'Ashishin' was not listed in the office dictionary. She came out of the programme she was in, logged on to the internet and did a search there. She found that the word 'ashishin' was the name given to people who used hashish and were paid assassins during a period in Middle Eastern history.

Knowing the link between the assassination list and its password, she used the internet to find the source of the word collaborator and found 'collaborare' from the Latin and 'collaborateur' from French. She was no linguist. Although the terminology in Biology is usually Latin, she had to take a chance. She looked up the Latin and French words. The Latin word was the labour and the French word was the labourer, sounding closer to collaborator, she thought. She was wary of typing in the wrong word in case the computer shut down again. She might not have a third chance. She opted for the French collaborateur. She was lucky. The list displayed on the screen. The collaborators with apartheid. She printed it, cleaned up the file, cleared the last access date, shut the computer down and left the building.

***

PART FIVE

The Welcome Lamp

72.

Her waking that morning to the sounds of strange knocking was not a signal for how the day would end. In the corridor outside her bedroom a little girl half the height of a broom was striving to sweep. Other little girls sat on the stairs, lazily dusting the banisters, and further along the passage, were more vigorous little sweepers. From somewhere downstairs she heard the high pitch of an electric hoover.

The air was saturated with a delicious concoction of braising garlic, green ginger and green chillies that could only mean they were preparing a cooked lunch. This alarmed her. Like most Indians in South Africa, her in laws ate a traditional Anglo-Indian lunch on Sundays consisting of an English roast followed by an Indian curry and English dessert. During the week they cooked for the evening meal because of the heat and because workers did not come home for lunch. If lunch was cooked during the week it was because visitors with a busy schedule of invitations were in the area from somewhere in South Africa, India, Canada, or Europe. Ernestina had not told her a visitor was expected. If they were expecting Nasaratt, she could not ask them, she was supposed to know.

She went downstairs. The kitchen door stood open. From the doorway she counted seven women, including Astrid, each woman engaged in some domestic chore. No one noticed her. They appeared hot and flustered. The air surrounding the hob was filled with steam rising up from stainless steel saucepans and there was an area of heat exuding from the oven as she passed. They must have been at work since dawn because all along the worktops stood an assortment of plastic, glass, enamel and stainless steel bowls filled with chopped vegetables, each protected from insects by cling film. They were preparing a mini banquet. She would have been asked to help, but for their estrangement.

She greeted Nalini, simply by putting her hands together and bowing her head, then Astrid, and finally the women in general, before doing the most obvious thing, which was to brew a cup of coffee. Only Astrid responded. Pragashini hoped to catch some remark about the visitor they were expecting. She loitered about in the kitchen moving from the fridge to the worktop to the place where the coffee mugs hung. In the cupboard with the coffee she found half bottles of port, brandy, and gin. The women continued their work and talk without dropping any hints.

If Nasaratt was coming, then Astrid and Nalini would be perturbed that she did not know. The fearful truth was that if they were expecting him, it meant he was in contact with them and may have heard the gossip. Even at this stage she had not planned what she would do to Nasaratt.

She finished her mug of coffee in the back yard. The search for the document left her stressed out. She went quietly to the kitchen sink, put the dirty dishes to one side, rinsed the sink, and filled it with hot water. She still hoped to overhear who was coming.

'Leave the dishes. The maid will do it,' Nalini said.

Pragashini continued to wash the dishes as if she had heard nothing. She was sensitive to their response to her. They raised eyebrows at her hair, and the absence of a single sari in her entire wardrobe. The women said nothing about the lunch guest. She sensed eyes furtively watching her, waiting for her to leave before the chatter and laughter would resume. She was out of place and impatient to leave but did not know under what pretext she could, especially since she felt she should do something to help them. She cleaned the bits of vegetables and rice that had been trapped in the sink strainer, put it in a plastic bag, and went out the back door to the bin.

She was escaping around the side of the house and into the front when Nalini called to her. She returned, embarrassed at trying to elude them while they became quiet when she re-entered the kitchen. These women could easily spend the entire day in the kitchen, protracting their activities with raucous jokes, stories she did not have a mind to listen to, cups of masala tea, and tots of brandy. If they left her alone in the kitchen she could prepare the meal in fifteen minutes using the microwave and complete a chapter while the rice simmered. All this braising and stirring and pot watching, was like making offerings to Durga.

They spoke in a circuitous way of times past when women joyously took up the task of concocting delicious meals for their husbands, delighting in cooking his favourite food, adding that extra bit of atcha[64] to stimulate the palate. Soon the talk was tinged with light sexual innuendoes, which led Nalini to ask if she had a special dish she wanted to cook. This was the hint she needed. They were expecting Nasaratt. She shook her head, not feeling inclined to speak to them at this stage of the game.

Since her arrival no one mentioned Nasaratt's name. They never talked about him in her presence, or stopped in mid sentence when she appeared. They took their cue from the moment she stepped off the plane. They saw her scan the group when she entered the terminal, and concluded she expected to see him there. But every one of them except she, knew he was in Johannesburg. Until that moment they believed he greeted her when she stepped off the plane in

---

64 Atcha is pickle, but is also used to insinuate something sexual, such as spicing up sexual activity.

Johannesburg. It was natural he should greet her at her first touch down after years in exile. When she made no mention of his meeting her, when she talked about how they would not put her on the connecting flight, and how she struggled with her luggage from seven in the morning until she caught the flight, they realised not only did he not meet her, she did not even know he was in Johannesburg. Their hearts went out collectively to her. They realised that something was seriously amiss.

Instead of embarrassing her, with hints and questions about him, they avoided his name like a taboo subject. At that time she warmed to their sensitivity to her.

Now, Nalini, perhaps observing her standing awkwardly in the kitchen, asked her to prepare something special for her husband. His favourite dish, she said. Pragashini reached for a purple onion, four tomatoes, and five beetroot bulbs from the pile of vegetables on the table. She had memorised something from Madhur Jaffrey. It might impress them since they only served cold beetroot in a salad. She never cooked for Nasaratt and had no idea what he ate. But while she chopped and stamped, Heather's advice about concocting something laced with Fly Agaric, made her smile secretively. If only... The women chatted around her and over her head as she sat by herself in one corner, picking through jeera seeds, thinking of how to cope with the several secrets she kept from them.

Suddenly Nalini shouted, 'But he hates beetroot!'

***

73.

Nasaratt looked down at a gun in his lap, gleaming each time the sun hit it. Early that morning, Smuts left home and drove across the city so that by seven in the morning, he was at Verwoerd Airport, waiting in the lounge to meet Nasaratt. He could never bypass an opportunity to sit in any lounge he would have been barred from during apartheid's days of glory. He ordered coffee and toast. When the first flight from Johannesburg landed, he went down to the arrival lounge.

'If your family don't necklace you at the airport they'll necklace you at home,' Smuts said. The two men laughed over the shared joke, - the floral Indian garland of African marigolds, the burning rubber tyre, and the item of jewellery. They exchanged the comrades' handshake then embraced warmly.

Nasaratt looking about the arrivals lounge, and seeing no one else there said, 'Thanks comrade,' adding, 'I really appreciate this. I dread those marigolds. They remind me of my wedding day.'

Smuts raised his eyebrows and said, 'Not a good memory then?'

Nasaratt smirked.

Smuts added, 'There's no escaping those necklaces, comrade. They're waiting for you at home.'

'At least I avoided the bandwagon,' said Nasaratt.

'I bet your women are cooking up a feast for you,' Smuts said.

'Pity it isn't Ramadan. I could easily fast,' said Nasaratt. 'Since I arrived I've been eating Kentucky for breakfast, lunch and supper.'

'My father tells me that used to be the old standby for underground meetings.' Smuts said. 'We must declare Kentucky our national dish.'

Nasaratt turned to the luggage conveyor belt while Smuts collected a trolley. He wheeled the trolley to Nasaratt then walked away to stand near the exit interested to observe who was being met but not wishing to draw attention to himself and Nasaratt. There were few people on the early morning flight. The luggage was quickly put on the conveyor belt. Smuts walked ahead of Nasaratt out to the car park. He unlocked the boot of the brand new black BMW and put the luggage in.

'Does it go with the job?' Nasaratt asked, running his hand over the roof of the car.

'What job? No jobs for exiles, comrade. The rumour here is we've had it good out there! It's from Heather,' he said. 'Anniversary present.'

'Not a lot of women can do that,' Nasaratt said.

'Forget women, think wives. She's my wife. Not a lot of wives can do that. That's why I'm selling up in England and bringing our cash over,' said Smuts.

'You're talking Rands and common sense, comrade.'

'We'll be millionaires.'

'If we all did that. Perhaps we should. Balance what the opposition are sending out with their kids.'

'Agh! Let them go, comrade,' Smuts said. 'They won't be missed.'

'So what are you up to?'

'I'm in the Legislature.' In the car he put his hand under the seat, withdrew something and placed it on Nasaratt's lap, then started the engine and drove off.

'You'll need one, comrade. I'm serious. Pick it up. Get the feel of it. Feel the weight of it,' Smuts said.

Nasaratt lifted the gun.

'Cold. Heavy', said Smuts.

'I've never used one,' Nasaratt said.

'Nor me. You may never need to, comrade. In the new South Africa, a gun is no tool for trigger-happy violence. It's this gun or your life. Ask anyone. Anyhow, it's not a present from me. My instructions were 'get him a gun.'

'Did you actually go out and buy this?'

'It's kosher. Registered with the cops.'

Nasaratt handed it back to him saying, 'And loaded.'

Smuts returned the gun to the cavity below the seat.

'When you're ready to buy, I'll go with you. Don't buy in iBhayi. Get one out of town. I went to eQonce. You could go to iMonti, or any one of the small dorps. Register with the cops out there. For your own safety. The last thing you want is for the local cops to know you have a gun. You'll be a prime target for armed robbery. Take shooting lessons. Buy a locking box. Get someone to make a hole in your bedroom wall. Lock the box there. Keep it locked away. But when you travel keep it in the car. Like I do. Everyone keeps a gun. You don't use it. Just point it.'

They drove in silence for some time, Smuts staying close to the beachfront. He caught the sea breeze through the open windows. He tasted salt on his lips. He brought the car up the motorway at Russell Road turned round and came off into Main Street. 'Our past was like a horror movie.' he said. 'From minute to minute we didn't know which monster was coming through the door. This in between time is the worst. Our future – we won't live to see. I want to strip naked, walk into the sea and just float there. Let the waves carry me wherever,' Smuts said. 'But we have jobs to do, comrade. We've come this far, there's no turning a blind eye now.'

Smuts reached forward and pressed the tape recorder on the dashboard. 'Listen to this,' he said. It was a tape recording of a police interview. There were three voices on the tape, with interference and other sounds. About ten minutes into the recording it stopped and the tape ran on crackling. Smuts reached forward and put the tape off. 'Whatever that's about won't come up before the TRC because we can't make out who's on that tape.' He ejected the tape and gave it to Nasaratt. 'That's all I could get to help you, comrade. Someone with know-how will be able to separate the voices.'

Nasaratt put the tape in his jacket pocket. 'Who had this?' he asked.

'I was just told to give it to you,' replied Smuts. 'We don't know who's on the tape.'

'That tape will have been transcribed,' Nasaratt said. 'Whoever had the tape also has the transcription. That document will say who's interviewing, who's being interviewed. I must get hold of it.'

'That's not my job,' said Smuts. 'Anyhow, they may only identify the voices as A, B, and C. No names. You remember this part of town?' he asked.

'Not much changed in old Main Street.'

'Few Indians know how to get about in African townships. I'll show you the way, comrade. You may need to know. Look for landmarks. Count how many times I turn left and right.' They entered New Brighton and drove down a wide main street busy with taxis. They passed a Community Hall on the opposite side of which people were disembarking from a taxi. 'The ghettos are still no go areas. Since the riots,' Smuts said. 'Our friends back home wanted to send flowers for Mellikhaya's funeral. The florist refused to deliver in New Brighton.'

'The funeral over?' asked Nasaratt.

'At long last,' Smuts replied, clucking his tongue with irritation. 'My old man had some notion in his head to delay the funeral, that I didn't understand,' replied Smuts. 'I went along with his wishes, to humour him. Now I can appreciate a parent feels more about the death of a son than brother can feel for brother. Anyhow, he gave a brilliant excuse for delaying the funeral.'

'What?' Nasaratt asked.

'He was waiting for the president to be sworn in. So, Mellikhaya could be buried in the new South Africa.

Brilliant old man!' They went deeper into the township. 'Look at this,' Smuts said 'Compare it with the Indian area when you get there,' he added.
Nasaratt said nothing.

'You don't want to argue, comrade? Imagine this place when it rains,' Smuts said. 'The dirt road becomes mud. Everyone walks in New Brighton.'

'No they don't walk,' said Nasaratt. 'They take taxis. People don't cycle any more. They don't walk. There are no buses. It's madness.'

'People can't afford cars,' said Smuts, 'but hundreds are coming off the production line right next door in Uitenhage.'

'Stop the bitterness, comrade. We'll build roads and houses,' Nasaratt said. 'We'll lay on electricity and running water,' he added.

'Then you'll come and live here?' Smuts asked, laughing. 'In New Brighton?'

Nasaratt laughed. 'You want a quarrel, comrade? Maybe I'll live here. Maybe not. I'm not afraid of living surrounded by Africans.'

'I won't live here,' said Smuts. 'I won't bring my kids to live here.'

'What's on your mind, com? You sounded odd when you were talking back there,' said Nasaratt. 'The way you talk about Indian and African areas, as if you're a visitor from overseas. You know the history. You know the tactics.'

'To come from England and go back to the township,' said Smuts, 'no fear. That's stepping backwards,' he added.

'You should hear yourself,' Nasaratt said.

'What do I care what I sound like. It's true. You and I can speak the truth to each other. I'll have to watch what I say to others,' Smuts said. 'Make no mistake. Heather wants to live here. We're fighting. I want to move to a White area, she wants to live in New Brighton!' He laughed. 'You know what they're like, the English. Their hearts bleed for the underdog. They want to suffer with us. But my father wants to see me uplifted. Not brought down to the ghetto. I'm his son from London. It doesn't matter that I'm penniless and my wife's rich. If I buy a house in New Brighton, it means I can't afford these white areas.'

'I suppose it's one way of destroying the separate areas,' said Nasaratt.

'Come on,' said Smuts, 'don't make as if the Indians aren't running away from the Indian areas to the white suburbs,' Smuts said.

They arrived at the Matatiele's home. They were deep in the township. Smuts parked the car on the narrow dust road. Even for him, it was always a humbling experience to see the township houses. This was a miniscule house, like an enlarged Wendy House, with two miniature windows, and bright blue painted door. In front of the house was a cabbage patch, just long enough for six green cabbages to sit proudly on the soil. Both men had to stoop to enter the front door.

The women came from the kitchen, wiping their hands on their aprons, to greet them. There was no denying that everyone in the house was delighted Nasaratt had come. Nasaratt came empty handed without flowers for Smuts' mother. Smuts recognised Nasaratt's lack of sensitivity to the needs of others and his mind turned to Pragashini.

Matatiele came from sunning himself at the back of the house to greet them. He was taller than both Smuts and Nasaratt. Smuts asked his father to show them round the footpaths, where the car could not go.

'My hat and my knobkierie,' Matatiele said. 'I can't go out without my two friends.'

On their return the women had prepared tea and cakes.

Nolitando entered carrying a tray with cups, saucers, teapot, sugar, and hot milk. There were coffee granules in a bowl and tea bags in another. Smuts took coffee; Matatiele and Nasaratt opted for tea. Smuts said something to the young woman in Xhosa and she looked down shyly. 'She belong to your clan?' Nasaratt asked, 'her head's shaved.'

'She's a neighbour's daughter,' Smuts said. 'Her brother was killed with Mellikhaya. That's why her head's shaved.' The young woman knelt on the carpet and made the tea and coffee there, pouring boiling water from the teapot, adding sugar and milk. She stirred each cup and handed each his tea and coffee.

'What about you?' Nasaratt asked.

Smuts removed his black beret revealing his shaved head.

'You won't catch me napping. I've become a stickler for culture, like a born again Christian,' he said.

'How does Heather fit into all this?' Nasaratt asked.

'She was willing to shave her head, but my elders refused. They said it's a Xhosa custom. It wouldn't be right for her to do it. People will ridicule us,' Smuts said. 'What would an English Hindu do - is there such a thing?'

'Didn't you see Sonia Gandhi walking round Rajeev's funeral pyre draped in a sari? Throwing his ashes into the river Ganges? I tell you she put a lot of these modern Indian girls to shame.'

'I'm talking South Africa, man. India could be on the moon, for all I care about it. It's of no interest to me,' Smuts said.

'That's your loss. It's like the Kennedy assassination. When you watch Sonia Gandhi draped in a white widow's sari, walking around the burning pyre of her dead husband, - its like seeing Jackie Kennedy in her pink Chanel suit, scrambling to the back of the car, pulling the roof back to shield her husband. Those are surreal images of our time,'

Nasaratt said. 'Women taking centre stage. Looking after their men. If you didn't see that, you've missed out.'

'So you won't laugh if Heather dresses up like an amaXhosa maqothi?' Smuts asked.

'Is she eager?' Nasaratt asked. 'What about you? Will you expect her to give up her ideas and beliefs? That's the issue.'

'She won't make a good maqothi if she wants to hang on to western ideas,' Smuts said.

When they had their tea, the men piled into Smuts car heading for Muhallah Asha.

***

74.

Golden brass. Rose petals, reds and whites; Mounds of red and yellow. Kumkum and turmeric. A rectangle of ice white naphthalene-like camphor, one corrugated brown nutmeg, a brass finger bowl filled with oil and a cotton wick fatly saturated in the oil. All jostling for a place on the welcome tray.

Since dawn that day Nalini had fidgeted with the tray, freshening the petals, touching this and that. Every few minutes she lifted the tray when she heard a car in the street, put it down when the engine faded away, did something, took it up in both hands, and stood breathing heavily, waiting. Now the tray sat for a minute on the little table facing the front door. Since this was not Pragashini's home, she was relieved that the custom of performing the welcome ceremony fell to Nalini. Nalini would welcome her son.

By early evening the family, friends and neighbours assembled in the small square foyer at the front door. Pragashini was dressed in a sari that someone had placed at the door of her bedroom and made to stand facing the front door. No one told her directly who was expected but from the feverish activity in the house from dawn that morning, and now her position at the door, there could be no doubt Nasaratt was returning home. She prayed for courage and guidance. What act of revenge could she quickly perform, and then escape?

Now Nalini hovered near the front door with a box of matches clutched in one hand, ready to light the welcome lamp. The small foyer and the doors leading into rooms off it buzzed with the laughter and chatter of family and friends. Pragashini was the only one ill at ease at suddenly being pulled back into the family and thrust forward to head the welcoming troupe.

Everyone heard the wheels of a car crackling over the brick paved forecourt and the motor running just by the front door as if the passenger would get out and the car drive off. Nalini became agitated and Pragashini's heart warmed to her mother in law, despite the treatment she received from her. She could hardly imagine what this mother must be feeling not having seen her son for – was it eight? Nine? Ten years? He may have nipped back on the underground during those years. She was not to know.

The high-pitched shrieks and shouts of the children playing all around the house; the engine idling, stopping; car doors slamming; the rush of cars, passing on the street; while inside the house everything was hushed. Pragashini glanced at Nalini's face. There was no mask. Tears ran freely down her cheeks. She did not dab at her eyes. Pragashini could not see what Nalini was doing because of the people packed into the small vestibule.

Nalini had not shut the matchbox. The matches fell on the floor. There was a unanimous long drawn out 'Oohhh!' They would be thinking this is not a good omen. There was no space to stoop and pick up the matches. Someone held another box in the air. Someone else fumbled with the matches, and finally lit the camphor and the cotton wick on the tray that was now held over their heads. Nalini had her eyes closed. She was praying, moving her lips. She lowered the tray and tried to place it in Pragashini's hands with a genuine smile.

Until that morning, Pragashini had not seen her face since the gossips visit. All she had was a glimpse of someone's back, rushing into this or that room, and the door shutting in her face. When she was offered the tray Pragashini shook her head and put her hands behind her back, refusing it. Nalini said, 'Please,' and Pragashini took the tray from her. Nalini gave her a little shove, because she was hesitant. Pragashini would be the first person Nasaratt greeted before stepping into the house.

The older woman stood with her hand on the door handle, ready to open it. Pragashini stood obediently where she was told to stand, feeling herself coerced into playing the role of an obedient woman, unable to break the hold that culture and family background had on her. She wondered if anyone had told Nasaratt that she was in South Africa. Smuts perhaps? The comrades at Shell House? He would have word of her arrival wherever he had spent the last few weeks.

The doorbell rang. The family looked at each other, smiling and giving the impression they didn't know who had arrived and was outside the front door. Nalini standing to Pragashini's right lowered the door handle, pulled the door open, and gave Pragashini another little shove forward.

Pragashini with her eyes closed obediently lifted the tray in both hands, with the little orange flame suspended in oil, amongst the rose petals, smoking camphor and Agarbatti sticks, and began the circular motion from the top to her right, down, to her left, up and once again. All around her she heard a soft drawn out sigh of dismay. She opened her eyes and let her eyes follow the movement of the tray. When she swung the tray up, she looked straight into the beaming face of Smuts, his thin moustache, and little goatee beard.

She inhaled on a laugh but did not stop the movement of the brass tray. Surely he deserved the welcome lamp. She completed a third circle, the blessing intended for Nasaratt, trying as best she could to suppress any signs of amusement, keeping her lips in as straight a line as possible. She sensed the consternation and disappointment behind her.

'Judas,' she whispered to him, adding in Xhosa, 'Hello, dude. How are you?'

He replied in Xhosa, 'Hello, Pragashini, we're fine. How are all of you?'

'All of us are well. Come inside,' she said making way for him to enter.

The family clustered behind her were murmuring. Nalini wiped her eyes with the end of her sari. The gathering retreated into the doorways leading off from the vestibule, making space for Smuts, yet still aghast. Smuts stepped round Pragashini and into the house. Behind him came Nasaratt. Pragashini looked up into his sunburnt face and saw his eyes open just slightly. It seems Smuts had said nothing to him.

All day she was stifled by a sense of being bound by in-laws, community, ritual, and now here was this man she hated. Their life together was a nightmare between her recurring dreams. What could she do? She raised her arms holding the tray above her head, to begin the circumlocution then she dropped the tray. It clattered to the floor. All the colours sprayed into the air, like Holi.

They screamed her name: 'Pragashini!' Nalini said, 'Oh God!' Pragashini moved aside so Nalini who was waiting to hold, kiss and bless, her son, could finally greet him after his exile, but Nasaratt put his arm out, drawing Pragashini to him. This was typical of men: playing the role of dutiful husband in the presence of family. His nearness repugnant to her. Tears welled into her eyes. Nasaratt's actions were for the benefit of the assembled family but also a warning to her. Everyone clapped and surged forward to embrace the two of them. She struggled to free herself. Suddenly Smuts put his body between them. Pragashini slapped Nasaratt hard in the face.

Although caught up in the moment, she wondered where the gossip and their ostracizing her were placed in this new situation. Had they told Nasaratt anything about what had transpired here? Was his homecoming meant to discipline her?

The gathering broke away from them. She was unable to look anyone in the face. But Nasaratt had his arm about her waist and his hand on her wrist, holding her close to him. At the time she did not see any other significance but that he was putting on a show for his family. His mother and all the knowing, observant eyes, looked at each other, unsure of what was happening. It seems she was no longer to be ostracized. Perhaps she would be allowed to join the family for their evening meal. At that stage she did not know.

She was angered by the pretence for the benefit of the onlookers and angered that the family pretended they had not ostracized her. She avoided their eyes and the tears in her eyes spilled onto her cheeks.

Indian men must surely be the worlds best at leading a double life. Even in ancient times they had courtesans and wives. In South Africa they had their mistresses and wives. Some even had two families and left their wealth to the children of the mistress.

Perhaps the Nasaratts imagined she had missed Nasaratt; that her tears of frustration were tears of joy. They were accustomed to the woman in an arranged marriage settling down and accepting her lot in life. It is impossible for the Indian man to imagine a married woman loving another man.

Now her heart raced with alarm. She was at a disadvantage. In its place was a feeling of uncertainty. She was trembling and afraid. She did not know what game Nasaratt would play in his parents' home. He had the upper hand. Her comrades might not be able to protect her now that she was back in this community. Back in England they did not want the scandal to bring disrepute on the liberation movement. Here the scandal could be absorbed. She remained a little hopeful. He might be misinterpreting her presence in his parents home.

Then Roshni placed a garland of African marigolds round her brother's neck, everyone exclaimed loudly, rapturously. While they assumed it was because they had not seen each other that Pragashini became emotional, only she and Nasaratt knew the true meaning of each other's actions. Pragashini could not predict what the next step would be.

They were crowded in the hall and spilling onto the paving outside, laughing and talking. She was still held in a vice like grip close to Nasaratt. She inhaled his aftershave a blend of stuff that brought back memories of her wedding night memories that nauseated and terrified her and she prayed to the goddess to guide her out of her situation.

The group backed into the house the way a crowd moves, taking Smuts with them. Smuts made an excuse. He had wrapped his father in the car for the drive. It was a common practice in South Africa. If you were going to the corner shop to buy a pint of milk you piled the car full of children and whoever else wanted to 'go for a drive'. The family would not allow Smuts' father to remain outside without coming into the house, not in the new South Africa. Matatiele was persuaded out of the car and coaxed to the front door.

Still held fast by Nasaratt, Pragashini reached for the garland around his neck lifted it and placed it over Matatiele's head. She whispered the Sesuto greeting she had learnt from a friend, 'Khena Ka Khotso,[65]' she said. Her first thought was 'here is my protector. Bhagvan shukriya.[66]'

They went into the lounge where Nasaratt sat like a visitor with Pragashini still held fast, his father Ramgopal, and brothers, Pravin, Saragan, and Ravindra, sat with and Smuts and his father, while they were served with little glasses of port and crisp newly fried samoosas. Nalini and Astrid were brought into the lounge to sit with the visitors.

Then Matatiele stood up, went over and said something to Nasaratt. He released Pragashini.

***

75.

Matatiele and Ramgopal knew each other from the period when sports enthusiasts in Port Elizabeth campaigned against South Africa's participation in the Olympic games. They belonged to the same group. Their meetings were about sport but the Olympic Games were on the agenda. Names were never publicised. Credit for the success of the campaign went to a handful of people in exile. They were relegated to the dust.

Through the campaign Matatiele had little time for Ramgopal, jealous because the latter was able to help fund their day-to-day expenses. Telegrams had to be sent to the Olympic Committee overseas. Their telegrams were long. Paper had to be bought to print leaflets and write letters to

65 Khena Ka Khotso means Enter in peace.

66 Bhagvan shukriya means Thank God.

the press. It was not a sharing of the costs. Members volunteered to pay. Matatiele was a graduate teacher who could not make ends meet. He was embarrassed to depend on others to support the campaign.

Ramgopal on the other hand, was a literate man, mostly self-taught but also a successful businessman who owned his own home. Not a lot of people did in those days. When he was a young man, Matatiele could not evaluate what was required for people from any community to oppose a government. He could not make the leap of consciousness to grasp that those without a university education may have been more politically acute than the graduates spouting western ideas and terminology irrelevant in South Africa. Activists like Ramgopal never heard the word Marxism; did not know what existentialism meant; socialism had no meaning for them; nor imperialism. But they felt it in their gut that everything around them was wrong in South Africa. Ramgopal was one of those who as it were put his money where his mouth was.

With education having a bad reputation, and looking at the size of Ramgopal's family, all living like an extended family, in one large house, Matatiele now realised the full worth of every penny Ramgopal donated for paper, telegrams, telephone calls, and postage stamps. But Matatiele's awareness that night came too late. Even before the inauguration Ramgopal and many like him, rejected the academic class. They despised doctors, lawyers, teachers, and dentists. Notwithstanding this, the two men exchanged the comrades' handshake and made small talk.

Matatiele did not have to be introduced to Ramgopal's family. He knew Ramgopal's wife, sons, and daughter. The whole family tended toward the Black Consciousness Movement while the ANC leadership ANC were on Robben Island and in exile or working underground, but he suspected this was not the only reason for the appeal of the BCM. Ramgopal's sons and daughter were school pupils during the student marches following Soweto, except for Anand who was ten years older than Pravin. The long gap between the eldest son and the second son was because Nalini helped in Ramgopal's business.

The person Matatiele did not know much about was the English woman, Astrid Roebuck. She intrigued him. Port Elizabeth was a place where most of the Whites were English speaking. He puzzled over how she befriended Ramgopal's family. Perhaps she was a music teacher. Perhaps she coaxed them in English. He was not sure. He recalled her conduct at the braai. Well mannered. Prim and proper. Correcting their English. No coarse language. He remembered she made a fuss about how tea should be served with Nalini reminding her tea did not grow in England.

The children from the street found an opportunity to run into the house clamouring for presents from London, embarrassing their parents but not Nasaratt. He came home empty handed. He brought nothing, not even for his mother. He blithely lied, saying there were too many presents for him to carry. The presents were coming by car with a comrade. The trusting children were satisfied. So was his loving mother who asked for nothing but the safe return of her son.

Like a true comrade in the struggle, Nasaratt declined the port still keeping the vows made by countless cadres and comrades not to drink alcohol. Smuts was reaching for a glass when Nasaratt asked if he broke his vow. Smuts left the glass and said, 'I'll keep you company comrade, for tonight. The struggle's over. I'm enjoying the fruits.' But the two men seized the samoosas eating them with such relish that everyone in the room looked amazed and astonished. Seeing the expressions on their faces each had a turn declaiming the stuff that masqueraded as samoosas in England. They cleaned the plate and more samoosas were brought in. The friend who prepared the samoosas – Selma - was called in to hear them sing her praises. Smuts said even he knew a samoosa from a duff one. Nasaratt said in England the samoosas were just 'onions and thick pastry'. Smuts added, 'Or thick pastry and peas,' Nasaratt said, 'Or potatoes and thick pastry. Or gristle and pastry.' They went on in this vein until Nasaratt glanced at Pragashini and said 'One thing I really regret. Pragashini left her parents' home before her mother taught her how to roll a decent samoosa, or I could have made a fortune out of her, supplying the Indian restaurants.' Everyone laughed.

Pragashini hated this deceit.

Smuts said, 'C'mon Prags, don't be so serious. Look at the funny side of life. Can you see yourself with a rolling pin in your hands chained to the kitchen table?'

Everyone laughed uproariously again. When they calmed down Pravin intervened. He said, 'Listen Pragashini, you're in South Africa now. We're all South Africans here, except you. Mind how you talk to your husband. No feminist is going to come to your assistance. In the olden days you'd be taken out and given to the first passing settler who had a fancy for Indian girls in see-through saris. You're lucky we'll just make you do the dishes tonight.' Everyone laughed again. South African wine was poured into their glasses. They were becoming light headed.

In the kitchen the women heated the food for the table. Pragashini had not known how to free herself from Nasaratt's grip without creating a scene by struggling. She needed to allay his suspicions while she thought of what her move should be. So she was grateful for Matatiele's intervention.'

Nasaratt had released her immediately. When she stood up

and said 'Excuse me,' the edge in her voice had an effect on the people in the room. The laughing and chattering was stilled. Perhaps remembering her slapping Nasaratt, they were perplexed. She left the room. When she returned she found a chair alongside Astrid.

Matatiele sat quietly observing Ramgopal, his sons, and Smuts. The newcomers talked about life in exile. The hosts talked about the changes in Port Elizabeth during their absence. Pragashini was silent. Smuts had a tension about him throughout the conversation. Something irritated him. He seemed ill at ease. He did not know his son well enough to understand what irked him, why he was no longer at ease. Nasaratt was either oblivious of this or he was prepared to let it ride.

Matatiele continually glanced in Smuts direction. He could not fathom what was going on. It was as if Smuts had pulled down a shutter between him and the rest of the gathering. He was not coming across openly. He had put up a front, or mask. He was not drinking, but the alcohol was taking effect on the others, so that the difference between him and the rest of the party grew more disparate.

'Did you drive pass South End?' Pravin asked. To Matatiele this young man seemed intent on arguing with his exiled brother.

'We toured South End.'

'So?' Pravin asked. 'You comrades still forgiving and forgetting? Even though they bulldozed the whole of South End?'

'Rudolf Street mosque is still standing,' Nasaratt said.

'They bulldozed all our schools. The temple. A church. A convent. Our community halls.'

'It'll never happen again,' Nasaratt said.

'You'll leave it like that? Indians in Indian areas. Coloureds in Coloured areas. Africans in African areas. Whites in

White areas?' Pravin asked.

'It's changing,' Nasaratt said.

'It changed long ago. People in white suburbs just didn't bother once they knew Mandela was coming out,' said Nalini.

'Be honest, Ma. We had to knock on doors and ask 'please sir do you mind if I buy the house next door?' said Ravindra.

'A dream for one. A nightmare for the other,' said Pravin.'

'Rubbish! Anyhow, the old people from South End are dead now. Today's kids have no idea what it was like living in South End. They won't want to move back,' said Ramgopal.

'South End's just one place. What about North End? Main Street shops? District Six? Sophiatown? That place they call Triompf?' said Pravin.

'What d'you want, Pravin?' asked Smuts. 'You want us to move the people back?'

'Don't force us back. Let those go back who want to. But force them out, those who took our homes and our land,' said Pravin.

'They won't move. They want to be close to the city centre. It's the same with District Six,' said Ramgopal.

Then Smuts turned to Nasaratt and said, 'Heather must see the Indian area, comrade. While it's Indian. Before others start moving in. It's mind boggling, when you compare it with our ghetto. I still don't understand. How do Indians get it right?'

The people in the room coughed and shifted about uncomfortably. Something was in the air. They anticipated yet wanted to avoid it. They had been relaxed. Now they became alert. They exchanged glances. Matatiele was dosing in an armchair. He had been drinking port. He roused himself.

'I must bring her in the daytime. Just to drive around. She

was dumb struck when she first came into Kwazakele and New Brighton. What's the other place?'

Someone said, 'Motherwell.'

Smuts continued. 'Comrade she couldn't believe it. There's nothing like it in England, is there?'

Everyone sat silently absorbing this. They appeared embarrassed but for whatever reason, unwilling to lose their cool and argue.

'Tata's never been inside an Indian home before now,' Smuts said. 'Can you believe it, comrade? It's worse now, than before we went into exile. I'm sure to him, its like going into a White home.' He turned to his father and said in Xhosa, 'Tata, do you want them to show you round their house? I'm sure they've got a swimming pool and servants' quarters. Like the whites.'

Matatiele raised well-manicured hands as if pushing the discussion away from him. He grimaced. He was perplexed at the change in his son. He and Smuts spent the whole day with Nasaratt. They showed him their hospitality, and finally delivered him safely to his parents. If Smuts disapproved of Nasaratt's treatment of Pragashini, why did he waste all day with him? Why treat him like a comrade? Smuts seemed another man. Maybe someone spiced his coffee in the kitchen with brandy or port. For sure something was loosening Smut's tongue.

Matatiele glanced at Nasaratt who smiled in his sly, unobtrusive way. He could see how the Nasaratt brothers bristled with restrained irritation. The brothers seemed to be waiting expectantly for Nasaratt to respond to the things Smuts was saying. Nasaratt, however, refused the bait. His eyes were on Smuts.

Ramgopal cut Pravin short when he began using offensive words. 'Don't use offensive words for any group.'

'Sorry,' Pravin mumbled. 'They built match box houses for

Indians too. The Indians just tore down the cardboard walls and put bricks in place.'

'You really think people voted in language groups? You think Mrs Roebuck here, didn't vote for the Nats?'

Everyone turned to look at Astrid.

'I'll never tell a soul how I voted,' Astrid said. 'That's my right. It's a secret ballot, after all. It isn't my responsibility to defend every English speaking person - here or wherever.'

'Spoken like a true Brit,' said Smuts. 'So why are you defending all Indians, Pravin? Because Indians have the money to pull down a house and rebuild it? It takes guts if you've been living in a squatter camp and suddenly you're given a council house. You wouldn't have the gall to pull it down. That's the difference. Indians are moneyed.'

Nasaratt turned to Matatiele 'Did you think you'd live to see the day?' he asked.

Matatiele shut his eyes and shook his head. He was reticent. He did not understand why his son was provoking these people. But his son knew more about them than he did. So he withdrew from the conversation.

Observing his unwillingness, Nalini turned to Matatiele. 'We've an aunt over ninety years old. She lived to vote. Others voted in the nursing homes. She came here to vote with all of us. She stood in the queue.'

'Election officers did go to people's homes,' Roshni said.

'She wanted to stand with the people, to be part of it all. It was a wonderful sight to see. Memorable. Was anyone that old where you voted?' Nalini asked Matatiele.

'We die young,' Matatiele said.

'So do we,' said Pravin. 'That's why our aunt's remarkable. We lost all the old people in our family when we moved here. Every Indian family suffered deaths. Year after year. One death after another. Go into the Indian area, its all young people there.'

'It's our superstition,' Nalini said. 'We believe when a community is uprooted, there'll be deaths in every family for seven years. It was proven here. A lot of karma will come back to haunt them one day.' Nalini put her hand to her throat as she spoke.

'Stop saying 'they,' Pravin said with irritation. 'Who are they? Your nameless 'they' didn't come to live in the ghettos with us, did they?'

'Didn't Trevor Huddleston?' asked Astrid. But no one agreed or disagreed with her.

'Did any Jew?' Pravin asked, almost rising to his feet with anger. 'Did any Jew remember Primo Levi's words? No, they fled Europe and were grateful to come here and keep a low profile while we were being hounded out of our homes, imprisoned, humiliated, and oppressed. I'm telling you I don't trust any White South African. They were happy to stay White, enjoy the fruits, and make the occasional protest.'

'What do you expect? The Jews suffered. They are Semitic people, just like the Arabs,' said Astrid.

'So?' Pravin shouted. 'That makes it even worse. 'They accuse people of being anti-Semitic, when Arabs are also Semitic people.'

There was silence again. Smuts picked up the thread about the Indian area again. He talked about the beautiful houses in the Indian area, the fine schools, the temple, the mosque, the community halls, and the number of cars parked in front of each house. Finally he asked, 'How do Indians manage it, comrade?' turning to Nasaratt.

Nasaratt smiled slyly. He said nothing. Perhaps he was content to be surrounded by his family. He may have been aware he and Pragashini were the focus of all their eyes, following the rumour that had come to their ears. Perhaps it was that he and Smuts were comrades. They could say anything to each other, without either one taking offence. His brother Pravin continued butting in. Pravin answered Smuts, 'Surely you know how that comes about. We live crammed in one house. Look at us. Father, mother, sons, daughters, daughters-in-law, sons-in-law, grandparents, grandchildren, even widowed aunts, and alcoholic uncles. We save on rent money.'

'That's no reason,' Smuts said. 'We also look after each other. Whether we're related or absolute strangers. Our homes are like free hotels. Anyone can come in and have a plate of food and a bed for the night. There must be another secret to your wealth.'

'Then it must be that we don't spend our money,' Pravin said. 'We're miserly,' adding, 'Maybe we don't eat so much. Meat. That's the thing. A lot of us are vegetarian.'

'Aha! And you save money on drink,' Smuts said. 'We Africans drink too much,' Smuts said, suddenly all good humoured on his part.

'I don't know about that, comrade,' Nasaratt said. 'You may not catch everyone of us here drinking in public, but I bet if you go upstairs now you'll find a bottle of dop[67] in every bedside cabinet, even my old lady's.'

'Prags, you're in South Africa,' Smuts said. 'Here we don't want you to drink or smoke in the presence of your elders. What you do in England is another matter.'

'It isn't a laughing matter,' Pravin said. 'Lots of people think like you, Smuts. That we have money we didn't work for. It can lead to trouble for us. Like in Uganda.'

There followed another silence. Then Ramgopal turned to Matatiele and said, 'Before the elections people marched up and down the streets pointing out which house they were going to claim after independence. It worried us. Do you

---

67 A dop is a shot of gin, whisky, etc.

remember when the rioters marched on the Indian area and torched all the Indian businesses in the northern areas?'

Matatiele said, 'It wasn't that long ago. We're still checking it out. No-one knows who put them up to it.'

'That's when your parents returned to Durban, Pragashini,' Ramgopal said. Pragashini nodded. She noted that no one asked when she was going to see her parents perhaps because they thought she had already gone there on the several trips she made around the country.

There followed another silence broken by the telephone ringing in the hall and the sound of children running to answer it. Ramgopal called out 'who is it?' and the children ran back to the lounge and stood grouped in the doorway looking subdued. 'No one,' one of them said. 'We asked. No one answered. They put the phone down.'

'You must've disconnected when you touched the receiver. It happens. Don't cry.' That was the beginning of the silent phone calls to the Nasaratt's home beginning the night Anand Nasaratt arrived home.

***

76.

Happy and ignorant of the strained atmosphere between Pragashini, the Nasaratts, and the Matatieles, the women of the family, their friends and neighbours appeared in the doorway, inviting everyone into the dining room.

In an African home, visitors are not asked if they will eat, the table is simply set with more places. Similarly, it was assumed Smuts and Matatiele would join them for the meal. The table was extended to make room for extra guests. They were placed around the table with Ramgopal at the head of the table, his sons Nasaratt to his right and Pravin to his left. Pragashini sat between Nasaratt and Matatiele. Roshni sat across from Pragashini between Pravin and Smuts. Saragan and Nargis sat on each end of the table with Astrid and Nalini together at the foot of the table. Ravindra gave his place at the table to Astrid. The table was covered with a blue cotton tablecloth that Pragashini bought from the da Gama factory shop in Bisho for Nalini. It was patterned with large yellow sunflowers. Two vases on the table held fresh orange and yellow African marigolds.

A blue bowl of water was passed around the table to encourage them to use their fingers to eat. Several of the men removed the cutlery set for them to the centre of the table. Someone recounted what the Mahatma is alleged to have said to Churchill about eating with a knife and fork. This seemed to put them at ease.

Roshni brought a bottle of red wine wrapped in a white linen serviette and poured into each glass saying it was from Wynberg. When all the glasses were filled, some preferred white wine, Ramgopal proposed a toast to the returned exiles. Then the food arrived in hammered copper bowls lined with stainless steel and in a variety of small porcelain and glass bowls. The vases were removed to make room for the dishes.

Roshni came to stand near Matatiele explaining what each dish contained. 'The first dish is a Biriyani. It isn't hot like curry. Rice and chicken are cooked in one pot, with buttermilk and butter and lots of Indian seeds like elachi, cloves, and cinnamon. Our Muslim friend Farieda prepared this for us. Our neighbours to the right prepared these yellow fish frikkadels. It's boiled stockfish mixed with turmeric and green chillies, and egg - shaped and then fried. It has a bit of a bite to it. Now these are frikkadels made of minced lamb with garlic, ginger, and green chillies. There's no egg in this. It's a bit hot if you bite on a chilli. This is dholl. We usually eat it with fish but other people eat every day. It's made of lentils and turmeric with chillies, onions, a little tomato, and what we call cudduseera that's our family's mix of seeds. This is Russim. Some people say Russo. We've been away from India for so long that we don't use the right words. Russo is a really spicy soup that isn't meant for eating with a spoon. We drink it. When we make a dry curry, we drink russim with it. Pour a little for him to taste,' she said. Saragan poured half a glass for Matatiele.

Roshni continued with her explanation of the food, encouraging Matatiele to try this and that. 'This is a dry curry,' she said. 'It's made of venison. There are no tomatoes in this curry. Just lots of garlic and ginger and masala. These prawns have been fried in butter with garlic. Just bite one and see if you like it. Here's mince curry made of lamb. We eat mince curry with roti, but you can have it with rice. These are our everyday curries. Chicken curry with green peas. Lamb curry with butter beans. We always put a vegetable with our meat curries. Now each of these vegetables is braised in oil. Green beans. Cabbage. Potatoes. Keera, - what's Keera in English?' Roshni asked looking around the table. She waited until Nalini said, 'Spinach,' then she continued solicitously guiding Matatiele in his selection of food. 'Pumpkin. There's dried red chillies and cudduseera with each vegetable. There's an egg with the green beans. This is – what shall I call it?' - she glanced around the table but no one came to her assistance this time. 'We call both this stuff Wurka.' She held a saucer in each hand. On one saucer was a round green mound. On the other was a round brown mound. 'The green one is made from mint,' she said, 'the brown is made from peanuts. The mint is ground with tamarind and chillies. We don't bother to grind the peanuts. We're lazy. We use peanut butter. That's cheating. But our neighbour made this. She didn't use peanut butter. The old people know how to make these things better than we do.

You should just take a teaspoonful and eat a pinch with a mouthful of food.' She passed the saucers to Smuts. She accepted a blue and white bowl from Saragan. 'This is Patcha chutney. It's made of raw tomatoes, onions, and green chillies. This is hot. You're supposed to eat this with Biriyani but you could also pour this over your dry curry. I think it may be too hot for you. I wouldn't try it, if I were you. These are homemade pickles. Lemon and mango. My mother made these pickles. She is the best pickle maker in our whole family.'

When Matatiele said, 'Enough! Let me try this first,' Roshni went to her place. Nalini had already heaped food into her plate.

***

77.

Smuts sitting across the table from Nasaratt and Pragashini, seeing them in their home environment, listening to Roshni explaining the food to his father, speculated about how they would deal with Pragashini and her exile type marriage, in the new South Africa and in this home of warm, welcoming people. Smuts did not know about the rumour that had reached the Nasaratt family concerning Pragashini.

To Roshni, who knew little about the circumstances of Pragashini's marriage, her sister in law's face appeared tranquil, as she looked down at her plate, yet attentive to the stillness around the table. While Roshni continued looking at her, she saw a little spasm touching Pragashini's face as if she were reliving some painful memory. Roshni blamed herself for the situation Pragashini was in but she lacked the skills and the support to do anything about it. Looking at Pragashini, she wished for many things. She wished she were not superstitious. She wished her brother was just a little bit in love with his wife. She wished her friend possessed that serenity that comes from knowing a man had once loved her - any man. She wished the miracle that was changing South Africa would achieve something deeper for her friend and her brother.

Roshni sensed that her brother and sister in law were each lacking in something. She did not know exactly what it was, some quality of spirit perhaps, which rendered each of them weak in character. Their weakness resulted in each shielding the other from something - again she did not know what it was. By shielding, deceiving, and hiding, they hurt each other in the process.

Astrid was intrigued by Pragashini and Nasaratt. She visualised Pragashini as a young girl, vulnerable, moving self-consciously from father's house to husband's, a virgin bride, naively expecting the chosen groom to fall in love with her, the way it is depicted in romantic fiction. When? She wanted to ask the girl. When did you expect him to fall in love with you, Pragashini? On your wedding night? Which man falls in love on his wedding night? Did you expect him to love you when he touched you in secret, intimate places, where no one had touched you before, - and you responded to his sexual passion? Dearest Pragashini, did you respond? Did he make love to you, or were you raped on your wedding night?

Who comforted you? When they came to inspect the sheets did your mother scold you or comfort you? Did you school your girl friends about the sexual act or was the subject taboo to them because they were virgins?

When love did not come with his sexual ejaculations, did you hope he would fall in love with you if you presented him with his first child? A son you thought would clinch that love. But when you delivered nothing, and he did not love you, what was left for you to hope for? Did you continue hoping that someday, something would make him love you? What could that something possibly be?

When did you first doubt that he would ever love you, Pragashini? Did you discover he had a lover? Did you suspect it? What made you give up hoping he would ever love you? Did you? Did you give up?

There were never answers to her questions. Nor would she ever utter these abuses to Pragashini when she wore her defeat so unashamedly for anyone with observant eyes to see. The answers were written in Pragashini's eyes, their inner light chilled.

Roshni still concerned about her friend, asked herself, how could she ask her friend the most searching question: Did you love him? The childish way girls idolise boys in the Indian community? If you do not love him now, did you love him then? Did you want him to love you? Do you still want his love? If you ever loved him, do you still love him, Pragashini?

Astrid glanced down the table at Roshni unaware that she too was speculating about Pragashini. Roshni was thinking about her mother and father. When your mother is deeply unhappy, you have scant time for teenage moods or rebellions. You grow up and hope her tragedy will not be yours. It was commonplace for girls to read romantic fiction which did not equip them for the realities of marriage to men they had never seen, perhaps seen from a distance, or in a photograph. Roshni hoped her parents did not intend to arrange a customary marriage for her.

Astrid and Nalini sat quietly at the table listening to the talk dominated by the men interspersed with the laughter and banter of the women replenishing the bowls from the kitchen. The women appeared serene as if their roots were watered by this simple scene of their men seated around a table eating food prepared by them. They were meant to be waiting on the men but their age and modern thinking allowed Roshni, an unmarried girl to sit at the same table with her father while guests were present.

At one stage Astrid, with a playful smile on her lips that only Nalini understood the true meaning of, asked for news about England. Her memory was hazy, she said. She could not keep alive the memory of her home. The visitors were too drunk the night of Astrid's braai to remember all she had said about her arrival in South Africa. Hearing her tell how she came out from England as a young woman, the exiles, especially Smuts, were reluctant to comment rudely about England, with her being an elderly woman. Had Heather been with them, they might have had fewer inhibitions. Perhaps because Astrid was Nalini's peer, the exiles were reticent. Smuts told her being in exile is like going on holiday. 'You want to see and do everything when you get there. After a bit you want to go home. The trouble is you're not on holiday. You can't go home.'

Nasaratt changed the subject by listing the many changes he saw on his drive through Port Elizabeth from the airport. Smuts asked Nasaratt if he noted how the apartheid government allowed Indians and Coloureds to work in the banks as tellers, but not Africans. Apartheid was a first class devil, they agreed.

The conversation lapsed. Then Smuts in passing mentioned that Nasaratt spent the day in New Brighton and Kwazakele. It sparked off outrage and consternation from the Nasaratt family, even from Astrid. Nalini chastised Smuts for taking her son into the township. He could have been killed. 'Townships are dangerous places,' she said. 'Especially for visitors. You take your life into your hands when you go into the township.'

'If Anand is attacked in Kwazakele it'll be because he can pass for a rich foreigner,' said Smuts.

When Astrid expressed concern for Heather's safety in Kwazakele Smuts said, 'I'm her security pass.' But Astrid's remarks aroused his hostility. He returned to his former mood. 'Why so much heat over one man for one day?' he asked. 'Africans are living in the township. We live dangerously from day to day. Democracy isn't going to change that.'

Nalini was shocked. 'You haven't heard about that poor student killed in Cape Town? She was with African friends.'

At that moment Matatiele chose to chastise his son. He spoke softly in Xhosa. He knew several around the table understood his mother's tongue, but he thought it better not to speak English. 'You picked this lesson to bring home from Europe?' he asked Smuts. 'Eat a man's food then pick a fight with him before the food reaches his stomach?

Smuts put his arm around Roshni. 'Are you offended, ntombi?'[68] And looking across the table at his father he said, in Xhosa, 'If we can't speak freely now, we may as well call apartheid back.'

'There's a time and a place for everything,' his father said.

'I'm in the home of Indians,' Smuts said, 'without the leadership present to discipline me. I might not get another chance. Let me speak my mind, please, Tata. Feel free to put me right. My friends don't mind.'

No one else spoke, although everyone around the table understood what Matatiele and Smuts said. The Nasaratts and their neighbours did not say a word in their various mother tongues, either. Smuts, however, assumed that no one but Pragashini and Nasaratt understood what was said.

---

68 Ntombi is a virgin of marriageable age.

He took this to mean permission granted to continue. 'Indians are too rich for their own good. Money comes to Indians like it comes to the Jews.'

'This is so racist!' Pravin looked again to his brother to alleviate the situation, who appeared to be sitting like a UN observer, not intending to butt in. Pravin said 'We're not moneylenders, like the Jews. There's no Indian bank I know of.'

'There must be Indian banks in India,' said Smuts. 'We just haven't heard of them. Apartheid wanted us to be ignorant about the outside world.' Smuts continued talking about everything he learnt once he left South Africa.

For Matatiele it was doubly annoying to listen to Smuts and to have to correct him. Smuts is a grown man, he thought. He would not have jumped into the car with the eagerness of a child if he had any inkling Smuts would embarrass these people. He is way off the mark. After all what does he know about iBhayi? Sweet all. And what do I know about Smuts the man? Niks. Matatiele coughed. Someone asked if he wanted water. He shook his head, cleared his throat, and spoke in English. He did his thinking in Xhosa. 'What d'you know, son, about before apartheid started shunting us around like a goods train?'

Smuts put his spoon and fork down.

'People met all over the place,' Matatiele said. 'Not just Africans. Coloureds and Indians went to church to plan a bazaar and talk. Yes Indians. Indians aren't just Muslim and Hindu. They went to choir practice, to sports meetings and talked. The change would affect them as well as us. You think they sat at home eating and drinking? Teachers, Coloureds teachers, Indian teachers, teaching in the two high schools in South End and Schauder, passed notes to each other through school children. I was a teacher, son. I know what teachers got up to. They talked to pupils during lessons. They sat marking exam papers in school halls, talking. They met us in secret. University students from Alice organised long before Black Consciousness. Indian doctors worked in iBhayi before there were Coloured doctors. Indian businessmen some literate, most only knew their mother tongue, without any education to speak of. They went to Tamil school and Madressa. No one taught them that apartheid was evil. The way the west had to be taught about apartheid. The way white South Africans had to learn about apartheid. Indians and Coloureds just knew.' He waited for a response from Smuts. Then continued.

'I'm wondering where you get your ideas from, son? Some big shot with degrees can't see how much more it takes for an uneducated person to oppose apartheid. I know. I was one of those big shots. We looked down on people who didn't have our advantage. We were unwilling to give the workers credit. We forgot we had book learning. Without books people can still think for themselves.' Again he paused, giving Smuts a chance to reply. None came.

'I went to meetings in people's homes in South End, in North End. In Schauder. Even when I was a child, I went with my father. I handwrote their letters because we didn't own typewriters. We sent letters and poems to papers in the outside world. Different people took turns signing letters to the Herald and the Evening Post. To protect the letter writers. Their wives dishing out leaflets outside the Alpha and Avalon bioscope. Coloureds and Indians I'm talking about. Hiding people chased by the police.'

'How can you know this?' Matatiele continued. 'You were overseas, sleeping warm, eating well. Coloureds and Indians in iBhayi don't even know. They're busy naming streets after people still alive who did nothing, because they don't know this history. I walk around the northern areas. I don't see one name from the fifties and sixties. Do you, Ramgopal?'

Throughout his speech everyone around the table sat frozen in their places, their eyes flicking from one face to the next, gauging the reactions, but seeing the same wide eyed look on each face. No one ate or drank. Now all heads turned to Ramgopal, all eyes focussed on him.

He appeared flushed. At first he too sat without responding. Then he spoke softly. 'Some left when South Africa became a republic. Some people found out we had a last chance to choose if we wanted to keep our British citizenship. A lot of people didn't know that. The government didn't publicise it. We all could have left, the way Kenyans and Ugandans went to Britain. But we weren't told. Those who stayed back, they're in the dust. Today it's all talk about Soweto. Robben Island. Who knows how South Africa was kicked out of the Olympic games? We played a part here in iBhayi. Who knows which Indian proposed to include Africans in a provincial football team here in iBhayi? Those forgotten, uneducated Indian businessmen were in that group. People only know the late comers.'

'You mean like Johnny come lately,' Smuts said, attempting to be flippant, remembering the Jimmy Cagney movie.

Still the group around the table left their food untouched.

'Eat up, everyone. The food's getting cold,' said Nalini. Her voice broke the spell. They looked down at their plates and began eating.

But Smuts was like a dog with a bone. He would not let up. 'I hear what you say, Tata, but do any of you Indians know what it feels like to be African?' Smuts asked.

Matatiele swore softly in Xhosa, 'In South Africa we license dogs, my son. You behave like the dog that's never been licensed. Only used to eating food from the gutter.' A silence followed his words. They stopped eating once more.

'You mean each race feels differently about itself?' Pravin

asked.

'I mean do you have feeling for the African continent?' Smuts asked. 'Or for India?'

Matatiele spoke in Xhosa. 'Even we don't get used to rudeness when we eat.'

'Is the truth rude?' Smuts asked his father. 'I can't explain it. I feel there's nothing between us. Nothing binding us together, Africans and Indians. Nothing like what binds me to another African man.'

'I feel bound to you, because we're South African,' Nasaratt said.

'I'm not talking to you, comrade. You're different. I'm talking to your family,' Smuts said, adding 'What binds me to another African has nothing to do with my country, or where I was born, or my language.'

'Is it racial, my friend?' Nasaratt asked.

'Not in the sense that would make me hate you just because you're not African,' Smuts said.

'There must be something to do with race.' Matatiele said.

'There's nothing you or anyone else can do or say to change it. There is just this bond I feel for another African. Comrade, I exclude you from this.' He looked across the table to Pragashini. 'You too, Pragashini.'

'Why exclude them?' Ramgopal asked.

'They're different,' Smuts said.

'I don't like hearing you say I'm different,' Pragashini said. 'I heard all that kind of talk when I was a kid at school. People making fun of Indians in my presence, then saying 'I don't mean you, you're different.'

'Is it because of history? Slavery. Racism. Apartheid?' Pravin asked.

Smuts shrugged. 'It has to do with the continent. African soil. The way we are brought up. I can't explain it. But it's there. I feel it.'

'You ran away from school,' Matatiele said. You're brought up English. How can you feel it?'

'Then it's even more remarkable. I feel it every time I meet an African. So it isn't something I learned.'

'I don't have that kind of feeling for every Indian I meet,' Ramgopal said. 'To be honest I don't like a lot of them.'

'You see? I'm not a racist. Even your father dislikes Indians,' said Smuts.

'You've never met an African you dislike?' Pravin asked. 'You like the sell-outs? The impimpis?'

'Even Popcru. And the Askaris,'[69] Smuts said. 'You'll never understand.'

'Where does that leave us?' asked Pravin.

Smuts shrugged. 'I think you must ask yourself, one, am I African? Two, am I Indian? Three, am I European? I'm a European because I married Heather. Because of Heather, I'm British. It doesn't end there. You have to ask yourself - do I honestly feel I belong to the whole of the African continent? Can I move through the continent and feel I am one of these people? Or do I only identify with South Africa? Is it family ties keeping me here? Do I have contact with African people? Do I have feeling for Africa and Africans? Do I socialise with African people? Do I have them in my homes? Like now? Friends. That I can quarrel with, and kiss and make up with. Or do I live my life in my little community of church, social life, and work? Who are my African friends? You make a fuss over Anand going to Kwazakele. Don't you know Pragashini has been into people's homes in Mamelodi, Dimbadza, New Brighton, Zwelitsha, Pedi, Mpofu, and you've not cared, but she doesn't have your fears. Anand wasn't fearing for his life. They belong in Africa. I know apartheid kept us apart. Now

---

69 An Askari is a soldier, or police officer.

is the time - sekunjalo - when you must change. In England they say seize the moment. Whatever will happen, will happen. If you're going to be killed in your bed, live until your killing. If someone is going to rape you, love until you are raped. Live your life freely. I was brought up African. I married an English woman. But I feel I am an African. Nothing will ever change that.'

There were tears in the women's eyes when he finished speaking. Smuts extended both his hands across the table to Pragashini and Nasaratt. Each placed a hand in his, and he gripped their hands tightly in his.

It was that moment Matatiele chose to say something in English that stunned everyone around the table, including the smiling women who came in from the kitchen to the dining room to begin clearing the table, and dusting the rice off the table cloth. It changed their mood from tearful emotion to terror.

***

78.

The women moved around the table like ghosts acting out a drama. Everyone else around the table sat transfixed. Their hands with a morsel of food suspended before their mouths, a tumbler of water held up as an offering to no one in particular, their eyes looking glazed at the air in front of them, the three exiles, Smuts, Pragashini and Nasaratt frozen with their arms across the table, their hands forming a triangular link. As if someone had cast a spell over them with the spirits moving around them in silence. Everyone had heard what was said.

Pragashini could not think. There she was again. Nothing coming into her mind, not even her beautiful thought, something beautiful is happening to me. Nothing. No emotion. No thought. No sensation of hot or cold. Just dull deadness. Later she wondered if this was what set in motion the tragedies of Astrid, Heather on the verge of suicide, Smuts wasting away.

That night when she was at prayer she would speak to her God. 'Bhagvan, why did he say that? What did he hope to achieve by saying that? Saying that didn't he place everyone in the room at risk? Why did he say that?' She would receive no answering thought from Bhagvan.

At that table she felt like the female skull in the laboratory; unable to formulate a thought; powerless to free her hand from Smuts. Feeling nothing. Not even dread. She sat there with the smile frozen on her lips, the warm emotion that engulfed her when she extended her slim hand into Smuts strong palm, dissipated, not even leaving cold in its place, just numbness. The first voice she heard was Ramgopal's. His softly spoken yet querulous, 'Who? Say the name,' dropped into the void.

No one else spoke. Not even Matatiele. Yet everyone waited for him to speak. Now they were straining forward to hear what he would say in answer to Ramgopal. The women who had cleared the table tiptoed in and stood one behind each chair as if they would prevent anyone from standing up and leaving the table until the question had been answered.

Each one in the room had the words in their heads, the accusation Matatiele had made, all except Pragashini. She had already dispersed the words out of her mind into the void. It was worse than anything Smuts had said all evening. She did not want to recall it. She did not want to hear it repeated.

Matatiele refused to answer Ramgopal's question. He left his accusation hanging in the air. Instead he repeated his first commandment: 'In a country where words can kill, if you value your life, you shut up.' Then he added. 'Tonight we talked too much.'

'Give the name!' Ramgopal repeated. 'You're not leaving until you say the name.'

Matatiele would not say any more. Pragashini hearing Matatiele's voice, and hearing his favourite expression - 'In a country where words can kill, you shut up' - from his own lips, with her hand still firmly gripped by Smuts, turned her body to look at her mentor.

He was looking at his own hands clasped on the table. This face she knew so well. The skin brown. The colour even across his face, without scars or blemishes. His head and face square. His cheeks angular. His mouth tightly set as if he was making a supreme effort to shut up. His eyes lightening with the onset of age. His hair beginning to grey. The voice she heard speaking wisely to her in exile, resonating with the timbre of a bass singer. Now she was trapped. Trapped in this house with people who ostracized her for her rumoured bad behaviour, her situation worsened because of what this man had said. She had feared the only danger to her was Nasaratt. Now it seemed there was an additional risk from someone else.

Matatiele half glimpsed Pragashini's movement towards him and turned his head slightly to look at her. He saw the look of strained terror on her face. He put out his left hand, reached over to take the hand that was in Smut's hand, loosened Smuts' grip, and pulled her hand free, across the table and holding her hand in his left hand, he placed his right hand over hers, holding her hands in both of his, in a reassuring gesture. He looked down at the table, at their intertwined hands. It should have reassured Pragashini. However, even this action was not well received by the Nasaratts.

Ramgopal looked down the table and saw Matatiele's action, disapproving of this show of intimacy between his daughter in law and this man. Ramgopal spoke again. 'I speak for my sons. For my wife. My sons must speak for their wives. It is not a Nasaratt!' He had been holding his glass half way to his mouth. He put it down with a thud and the water splashed onto his hand and the tablecloth.

Pragashini expected him to ask the Matatieles to leave, but that was all he said. With her hand in the warm hands of Matatiele, Pragashini half relaxed. She began to think about the rumour that brought the gossip to this house and caused her to be ostracized until today. This was the first meal she shared with the Nasaratts since the gossip arrived with her rumour. Tonight, here was Matatiele, her lifetime mentor, doing the same. Was this also gossip, rumour? Would he also bring havoc and devastation into this house if he comes out and says a name? The gossip also refused to say the name out loud. Only she saw it.

Pragashini looked at each face around the table. Certainly, there was no one that Matatiele's words could not apply to. It could be Nasaratt. Smuts? How could it be? They were exiles. Whatever they knew about South Africa was second hand. Worthless. Why would Matatiele say something about Smuts here? This was not the place. Could it be Astrid? Her background was clouded in mists. She was English. Only Nalini vouched for her. Her sister in law Roshni? Pravin or Saragan? The neighbours? Matatiele always boasted he knew everyone. Was it Ramgopal? His wife? Pragashini became afraid. She did not belong here. She made up her mind then she had to leave the house. Even without the act of revenge.

'If you won't tell us ...' Ramgopal began.

'It will out,' Matatiele said. 'When the time's right. The name is out there. In with a whole list. The guilty person knows. We're searching for that list. When we have our hands on it, we'll have all of them. Even the one who told the police Biko was on the road coming home.' Then he shut up.

Ramgopal made no response. They sat at the table having no interest in the meal.

In the uncomfortable silence Pragashini spoke. 'We need the great soul here with us. Gandhiji. To bridge the gap between Indians and Africans.' They sat and the women stood, contemplatively around the table when she said this.

Then Ramgopal asked, 'Well then, where's the pudding?'

As if released from another spell the women came to life, but listlessly. They left their places behind the chairs of those seated at the table, uncertainly. They moved into the kitchen looking back as if expecting to be recalled. They returned still in that soft, enchanted way, bringing back with them little glass bowls of carrot halva and boober. No one spoke.

Then as if nothing had transpired at the table, Roshni once again stood up and walked over to Matatiele, and went into laborious explanations of the dessert for his benefit. 'There is a family joke about boober,' Roshni said. 'It is a desert of lokshen, pasta thinner than vermicelli, fried in butter with elatchi and cinnamon sticks, to which milk is added then sweetened. It is reputed to act as an aphrodisiac. The men in the family become excitable when boober is on the menu.'

This allusion to an aphrodisiac failed to trigger alarm bells for Pragashini. She was caught up in the fear of the preceding moments. Roshni returned to her place. Then, as if he had not said anything to devastate the people in the room, Matatiele turned to Pragashini and asked her to tell the family something about her research. It was as if he personally released her from the spell. She shook her head unwilling to speak, afraid that the family would think she was in collaboration with Matatiele to sow the seeds of suspicion amongst them, in retaliation for their treatment of her. Fully aware of how she had been ostracized, Matatiele continued encouraging her until she said, 'It's unsuitable for the dinner table.'

Everyone sitting quietly at the table, was pre-occupied with the bombshell Matatiele had dropped on them, staring fixedly at some point in the room, not attentive to what she was saying. No one willing to participate in the conversation because they knew nothing about her field. Smuts half listened to Pragashini refusing to speak about her research. She refrained from saying she would present her theory at the Beijing Women's Conference, for fear of Nasaratt.

No one said a word. No one asked what her theory was.

'We also have an ancient mummy,' Matatiele said. 'We found it. Not far from here. The photo was in the Dispatch. The skin was still there covering the bone. Like an Egyptian mummy only there was no cloth. Just African herbs and medicine. Maybe the same medicine we use for initiation.'

'Is it Bhuqu?[70] We use Bhuqu in vinegar for all kinds of fever and aches and pains,' said Nalini. 'We learnt it from the Afrikaners. Like their Dutch remedies.' She began rattling the names, 'Haarlemenses. Rooi Leeuwentel. Lewens Essens. Jamaica Ginger. We used to buy them in the chemist shop. Now you can't get them anywhere.'

'The Afrikaners use it like that, with vinegar. You can't use vinegar for initiation. Maybe Bhuqu is one of the herbs,' said Matatiele. 'I'm not a herbalist. I know niks about African medicine.'

'Which university did they take the mummy to?'

'The Khoi-San refused to let them move the mummy from the burial place. I'm not sure what happened to it. I'll find out for you. The Khoi-San are protecting it. But you haven't told us your theory,' Matatiele said.

She avoided his question. She wanted to talk about CFC gases and the ozone layer to ask them what damage is done

70 Bhuqu a South African herb.

by the satellites moving around the earth day and night and burning up energy right up close to the ozone layer, but she could not do that. Nor could she talk with them about the moon causing the tides. Or the logic that reasons the more moons you place in the sky to orbit around the earth the more the oceans will be affected.'

'What's your research?' asked Nalini.

'Just things I think about,' said Pragashini.

'Well, so long as what your thinking doesn't get you into trouble,' said Nalini.

Is fear the reason no-one mentions these things? Pragashini wondered. Or money? There's big money in space research. Can a spaceship leave earth's atmosphere, without affecting the earth? In some manner? She thought the force needed for a satellite to break free of gravity might cause earth to shift slightly from its place in its orbit, or alter the tilt of its axis, just slightly, each time a satellite takes off. It might do so over time. It might be proven using maths and formulas, the same way in which the distance to the planets are measured.

'You've proposed a theory about what?' asked Astrid. 'Let's hear it,' said added

Pragashini smiled at Astrid. But she did not say a word about what she was thinking along the lines of Newton's laws of gravity. What goes up must come down. And hers: what goes down must come up.

'Aren't you going to explain?' asked Pravin.

She wanted to reach for a glass tumbler. Fill it with water and submerge the saltcellar into it. The water would spill onto the tablecloth. So simple. That's what happens in water. Harder to simulate an explosion. The same saltcellar dropped into the bowl of boober - the boober has to make room for the saltcellar. Now if you explode something deep in the earth the effects will be felt somewhere else. But she could not share her thoughts with all of them.

'I don't want to hear about your research,' said Smuts. 'Our government will lock you up. We have no women's rights in our constitution.'

'I know,' said Pragashini.

They were in a happier frame of mind. They went in good humour into the lounge while the table was cleared. The children were called in to sing and play musical instruments. Smuts asked if any of them knew the new national anthem. The children had been taught nKosi Sikelela at school as a prelude to the elections. Except for Pragashini and Nasaratt, the adults knew the tune, but not the words. One of Ramgopal's sons, Ravindra tuned his guitar, and with Ravindra strumming the tune, Smuts taught them the words verse by verse, with pronunciation. He asked if any of the children knew which other language was part of the anthem. They said Afrikaans, but he told them there was one verse in Sotho that the children did not believe.

Pragashini wished she could turn the clock back. She wished her ancestors had never left India. She wished she had not been born an Indian in Africa. She wished her father had never moved to Port Elizabeth and become indebted to the Nasaratts. She wished she had the freedom men have to come and go as they pleased. She had that freedom in England. She wished she was able to defend herself and protect her integrity. Everyone must wish that at some time, to turn the clock back. She wished at this moment that she had the wisdom then, which she thought she had now. She would not have made the terrible mistakes she made which she now had to face.

They were served coffee in the lounge. Matatiele asked permission to read aloud an extract from a book before he left. He had a slim paperback in his pocket. He held the book up with the front cover facing the room for all to see

Steve Biko's face. Then he read, "The great powers of the world may have done wonders in giving the world an industrial and military look, but the great gift still has to come from Africa – giving the world a more human face".

Pragashini believed Africa had given the world that gift but it was rejected.

They sipped their coffee in silence. Soon after Matatiele stood up and asked Smuts to take him home.

Pragashini asked herself where did her personal struggle fit in this huge struggle of Africa, and the diasporic Indians? Commitment to our struggle demands tenacity of spirit, she thought. The same tenacity people brought to the struggle carried over into unrelated aspects of their lives. She witnessed that tenaciousness that night Nasaratt returned to his parents' home. In Smuts' ideas about Africa and African humanism; Pravin in his defence of Indians; giving his sense of the tragedy of being Indian; Matatiele's commitment to broadcasting the names of apartheid's collaborators; Ramgopal revealed to her as a new person committed also to destroying apartheid with the means at his disposal.

While the Nasaratt sons drove Astrid home, she went to her bedroom. Since she no longer spent time with them, it seemed appropriate to leave the Nasaratt family some space to be alone with their son on his first night home. They were sitting in the living room waiting for their sons to return. She had done nothing constructive all day. Foremost in her mind was the gossip and her flight from the house. It was only now that she thought seriously about the implications of the gossip. Did the man who married her know of the gossip, or were the Nasaratts waiting up to tell him. She would read a chapter of her thesis before sleeping.

With these thoughts in her mind, she opened the door of the bedroom she had been allocated, but quickly stepped back out of the room in embarrassment, believing she had opened the wrong door. Yet something familiar about the room tempted her to open the door wider.

***

79.

The room was light with soft furnishings of cream and white, and heavy with fragrances. Across the bed was an antique satin quilt, embroidered and edged with Nottingham lace. It was draped over the bed to hang extravagantly over the sides and the foot, falling richly to the floor. The same creamy satin was stretched over the pillows puffed around the headboard. There were two Merino sheepskin rugs on either side of the double bed. A rich brocade curtain hung in sumptuous folds from the track behind a design of swags and tails. The room appeared fresh and clean. The windows and mirrors gleamed. The furniture exuded a hint of lavender wax. But the vase of fresh garden flowers overpowered the lavender with the twin fragrance of frangipani and roses.

Still puzzling over whose room this could be, she saw her satchel on the floor. Even then her first suspicion was that someone had been going through her papers. Then it slowly registered. This was the bedroom she used in their house. Everything, however, was changed. The rugs, the bedding, the Moygasel curtains.

Under apartheid, when couples married there were no hotels they could go to for their wedding night. It was customary for one bedroom in the house where they would make their home, or in one of the parents' homes to be sumptuously arranged, the furnishings and sometimes even the furniture, made by friends and family for the bridal couple. Suddenly she realised the horror of her situation.

In her naiveté she had completely overlooked their sleeping

arrangements. Not having lived with Nasaratt for years, she had never given it any consideration. The Nasaratts naturally expected her to share this room with the man who married her.

Her stomach churned. She was afraid to enter the room even to collect her satchel. She was overcome by nausea. She remembered. This was how the bridal suite was prepared on her wedding night. The Nasaratts remembered they spent only one night in the house as a married couple before leaving. They prepared this room for a bridal couple. Did Nasaratt know this? Was that why he put on that show of pretence when he came into the house? Did he expect a repetition of their wedding night? Did he believe being back in South Africa within the confines of an Indian community would give him control over her?

She did not realise the door was supporting her. When she let go of it, moving quickly to hurry down the corridor she collapsed onto the floor.

***

80.

When she opened her eyes Nasaratt stood by the bedside looking down at her. She was afraid. Who found her lying outside the bedroom? Who picked her up? Who put her on the bed? There was no one else there. Her abhorrence at the thought it might have been him brought nausea into her throat. She had no plan. No concept of how she would punish him. What action her revenge would take. No idea of what she would do. How she would escape from the house. What a fool. She had failed. Without even trying. She could not even imagine an act of violence against anyone, not even this man.

'This room is exactly how it was on our wedding night,' he

said. He glanced at the bedside table. She saw a gun. Then he sat on the edge of the bed. She sat up, moved off the bed and away from him. 'With your childish tricks you deprived me of my wedding night. Your little game put an end to that.'

She would not waste time and energy in argument with any one who did not figure in her life. Listening to him, she could not believe this same man violated her. What should she do? The gun was a temptation. Old Gandhiji. The great soul. He had crept slowly up on her and stole into her heart. She could have followed him if he were here with her. She would ask him what she should do. When he planned non-violence did he have women in mind? In a situation like hers? All her prayers to Saraswati were to help her pursue science, not revenge. What could she do? There were objects in the room she could throw at him.

'Why did you come here?' he asked.

He reached across the bed she imagined for the gun but he grabbed her cold hand, turned the palm up to reveal the scar matching his own. He brought her hand up to his mouth and kissed her palm, a prolonged kiss; with his eyes shut, inhaling what she knew was nicotine and chemicals that clung to her skin. He ran his scarred palm over the bristles on her head, and put his palm to her lips for her kiss.

Pragashini shrank in revulsion from him. She jerked her face away and pulled her hand out of his and wiped it on the bedding. It shocked her. This was his arrogance. He expected her to grow to accept his violation of her as part of married life. Was he taught that at his mother's knee?

She was never able to look at him without remembering the first time they were alone in this room, his eyes, deceptively soft, his outstretched hand, and the bloodied cut across his palm.

Now she was convinced honesty never pays. You have to

lie your way through all situations if you are to survive. That's why humans developed speech. The truth never sets you free. Heather's teachers lied to her. She turned away to avoid looking at him. Disgusting man. There is no knowing how an ignorant man will interpret a woman's looks. She reached for the vase of flowers – she knew Gandhiji would disapprove. But Gandhiji was concerned about the vote, and equality of Indians with Whites. He did not do anything for women's rights in the family. If Gandhiji had talked about women's rights in the family Jairaj would not have sold her to pay off his debts. Gandhiji would not want her to throw the vase at Nasaratt. She chose the next best thing and threw it into the mirror on the dressing table. The noise was horrendous in the sleeping house. She picked up an ornament and threw it at the window. The alarm sounded. She grasped anything that had weight and hurled it about the room. There were voices outside. Knocking on the door. She reached the door before Nasaratt could and pulled it open. Outside stood Ramgopal, Nalini, Pravin, Ravindra, Saragan, Roshni and Nargis.

'Ramgopal,' she said, This is what I think of your son. This marriage. Of all you Nasaratts! You are criminals. I came here to tell you to your face. I was a child. You were adults. None of you had the courage to stand up and say, 'this is wrong. You don't know what your son has done to me. You are all guilty of what he did to me!' she said and pushed through them to the bathroom.

She stood holding on to the washbasin, shaking, bathing her face, and trying to calm down. Then she heard another commotion. Loud voices in the house. Someone hammered on the bathroom door. When she opened two policemen from the station down the road stood there looking apologetic. The Nasaratt family were bunched behind them. The policemen explained that the family wanted her to leave their house. 'You should arrest them,' she said. 'They've committed a crime. Not me.'

'You can come to the station and lay a charge,' the policeman said. Then the policeman asked, 'Whose house is this?' Ramgopal stepped forward. 'Do you want her to be removed? It's late,' they added.

'I don't know what is going on here,' Ramgopal said. 'Son?' he turned to Nasaratt. 'This is my parents' home,' Nasaratt said. 'Take her away,' he said.

The policemen asked, 'Do you have a place to go, ma'am? It's late.'

She collected her suitcase and her satchel and asked the police to take her to Matatiele's home in New Brighton.

'Lady, you've got to be joking. There's no way we're going in a no-go area at this time of night! Even if the President calls us.'

Roshni elbowed her way through her family. 'I'm going with you, Pragashini. There's no way I'm staying in this house.'

Together they left the house with the police. A crowd had gathered outside the house. All the houses in the street were lit up. People stood in their pyjamas and dressing gowns, leaning over balconies, standing in the open front door, on the pavement as the police car drove away.

***

81.

Karishma woke to loud knocking on her door after midnight. It alarmed her. Men's' voices called her down to open the door. She looked down from an upstairs window and saw the police van. Then she was stunned to see Pragashini and Roshni huddled behind the policemen. She hurriedly prepared the brass plate and welcome lamp, the way Leela should have done for Pragashini. Then she opened the door.

Pragashini reflected on the aunts in her family, unmarried aunts, under sufferance of a brother and sister in law; or widowed, under sufferance of sons and daughters in law, or daughters and sons in law. Her new status would be worse because it would soon be known she left the man who married her. Asian men would forbid their wives to socialise with her. Karishma wondered what it foreshadowed, that anyone could do such a thing to a girl, a returning exile with no home.

In the morning wearing Karishma's white towelling dressing gown, Pragashini was taken to a neighbour who practised aromatherapy and massage.

A young White Afrikaner woman named Katerina, asked her to lie on a table covered with towels and to relax while she prepared a mixture of essential oils in response to a sequence of questions about her health and well being.

Katarina proceeded to wash Pragashini's feet, despite her loud protestations. It was this action of a young White Afrikaner woman that placed Pragashini on the first step towards forgiveness.

Then Katarina lowered the lights and massaged Pragashini in the darkened room for an hour. Karishma took her home to sleep through the day.

***

82.

Should I lie or tell the truth?' Pragashini asked herself. She had stepped out of the tangible African heat into the cool ice cream 'parlour', and chose a table near the plate glass window from where she could watch a motley band of musicians perform in the octagon where shopping aisles converged. The table was large and round, made of speckled blue Formica with cast iron legs. The cast iron chairs were thickly cushioned with powder blue wipe clean covers.

Outside the performers had a ghetto blaster, a pair of man-sized amplifiers, a couple of guitars complete with guitarists, a drummer, a drum kit, and a keyboard with player. Thin little girls, toddlers most of them, stood about moving their limbs awkwardly to the music while their parents doted on them. Disinterested passers by paused, watched for a few seconds, and then scurried away to do their Saturday shopping. The mall planners had not thought to name the aisles. It made arranging to meet someone a matter of how well one remembered the placement of shops. Saturday morning was the day people went to the banks and the cash machines, women put their handbags down, men their carrier bars, and soft footed thieves lifted the bags then snaked like computer images through thronging shoppers to safety.

She had been sitting a few minutes when a teenaged girl wearing a short skirt, company top, and white trainers, came over to her table, adopted a fashionable pose, and asked if she was ready to order. The girl was tall and coltish, and could quite easily have been a fashion model if the world had an eye for African beauty. Pragashini hesitated, her mind not on eating. In the café the blenders whirring and pumps spurting out liquid interrupted the voices shouting out orders and numbers. While she dithered, the girl stretched out her hand, displaying oval shaped plum painted fingernails.

The girl lifted the laminated menu from the table between thumb and forefinger, opened it and said, 'If you take our knicker-bocker-glory you get to taste all our flavours. Or... you can just take three, or four or five flavours. Small, medium, or large.' Still Pragashini hesitated. The girl added, 'D'you like chocolate ice cream? You won't go wrong with ours. It's got almonds, red cherries, and liqueur.' She spoke with the accent girls from fee-paying schools acquired. This was probably her Saturday job. It pleased Pragashini to see the girl's display of confidence that was not arrogant.

She looked into the girl's face and saw flawless dark brown skin, the shade of her own, wearing bright red lipstick. It was apparent the girl never indulged in anything on the menu. Pragashini smiled and said, 'Just Cappuccino, please.'

The girl drew herself up as if Pragashini had rejected an offer of friendship. Disapproval flickered over her face. She folded the menu card and balanced it between the sugar bowl and vase in the centre of the table. Perhaps she was wondering why anyone would come to an ice cream parlour if they wanted coffee.

In the time it took Pragashini to turn to the girl then to gaze back out the window, Klein walked into the shop and stepped up to her table. She closed her eyes inhaling his tobacco as he brushed past her, then looked up in fright and saw him standing at her table looking down at her, his face lined and haggard. An Alsatian dog was at his side. He moved his lips in an attempt at a smile, but he failed. It did not touch his eyes. She closed her eyes willing to shut out his image, feeling somewhere in her body acute pain. He remained standing there and she sat where she was for what seemed like hours. They said nothing to each other. She turned her face to look out the window again. She did not want to know if he was still standing there or if he had moved on. Part of her could not believe she had seen him. Part of her hoped it was one of the numerous mirages she was susceptible to; except here, there was no deceptive snow. Then the girl returned. Pragashini heard her clearing a space for the coffee, putting the cup down and asking, 'Anything else?'

She did nothing. She ignored the girl. She kept her head

turned towards the performers outside.

Then the girl said, 'Would sir like to sit?' Pragashini froze. She noticed the deference in the girl's tone that had not been present when the girl spoke to her. She heard a chair scraping on the tiled floor. Then the girl asked, 'Would sir like to order?' Pragashini did not hear him say anything. The girl walked away. Her coffee was on the table and she was caught up in the turmoil of how to behave in the situation. Klein's knees brushed hers under the table. There was a kind of immobility come over her that she could not overcome, that always came over her when he was close to her. With an effort she turned her head and moved her hands to place them around the huge Bistro cup. It was hot. Now her attention could focus on her hands and the dog that was now stretched out on the tiled floor with its face on its paws. It might appear she was snubbing him. It was, however, the only movement she could manage.

She had waited endless days, nights, weeks, to be with him, just to sit like this, to talk, to look at him, to understand what it was between them, what drew her to him, to know if he was also drawn to her, to know if she even liked him as a person. Now here he was and here she was behaving like a woman transfixed in stone.

What is the origin of such an experience? Was it because she coveted a pair of high-heeled shoes when she was a child that she now yearned for possession of this man? Seeds planted in the girl bear fruit in the woman. That was part of her thesis. Did that childish wish for high-heeled shoes nurture all her adult desires. Would she always desire what she should not have? What if that seed did create this obsession, should she heed the lessons of that precocious desire? She was then too young to walk in high-heeled shoes. Will the same prove true of this desire? The shoes at least were beautiful. A shocking red, to catch the beholder's eye,

eye-catching, but crafted to hold and please. The male object of her adult desire was handsome in her eyes, but singularly plain to others. He lacked the appeal of universally handsome men like Omar Sharif, Milind Sonam, and Clint Eastwood. This was the mystery. Something else drew her to him. She knew nothing about the man. Not even the simplest details to feed her imagination. Thinking about him she conjured fantasies about his being uprooted from his native soil. That would have been the bond between them. She wanted to know who he was. Who were the women who aroused his feelings of jealousy? Of protectiveness? Would she ever know? Would she ever arouse those feelings in him?

While she sat like a figure cast in stone, he said, without any preamble, 'Are you the one?'

His voice shocked her. It resonated through her. It was as if she had been sitting there imagining him seated across from her. Hearing him speak she jerked and spilt her coffee. She had not expected to hear his voice. She could no longer delude herself. It was his tobacco she inhaled. Her eyes found his face. His eyes. The eyes she yearned to look into. She could not look away. He looked terrible. Haggard. As if he had not slept, washed, shaved, eaten, or allowed a drink of water to pass his lips. His lips were dry and cracked.

She had waited for this moment. Every night in her bed she imagined this meeting. She rehearsed what she would say. How she would respond to his words. She practised how she would contend with his silence. She imagined their relief that the journey towards each other was over. She pictured bliss, emotion, passion, anticipating the reality. But this? Never this. Never this cold question. This accusation. Delivered as if in a court of law. He might just as well have asked – How do you plead? Nor could she ever have evoked her own dead feeling of being on the point of losing her mind. It was an utter miscalculation on her part.

She said nothing. She didn't know how she appeared to him; whether she seemed cold and heartless. Or afraid. Instead she asked herself, 'Should I lie or tell the truth?' There it was. Another question she never wanted to put down on paper. Either way she could not decide.

There was nothing, not a tremor, no hint, no softening, in his face, his eyes, nothing, no tenderness in his voice, to ease her choice. 'Does the way out of my conflict depend on who I am?' she asked herself. 'Where I am placed? Was I to lie on the stage where everyone else is acting a part, who would care? Were I a prisoner awaiting death, and I lied, would someone condemn me a second time? Is one expected to tell the truth when on the point of death?' Speculation did not help her because she was neither actor nor prisoner on the point of death. What should she do, while he waited for the answer to his question?

'Because I am female, does he have certain expectations of how I will reply based on his preconception of me, being female? Should I lie or tell the truth?' What does he want to hear? The lie or the truth? The night before she stood at her window, not her beloved arched window, but the cold square pane of glass in her aunt's home, and watched him standing below, pacing about in two minds. She had drawn him from his place of warmth to where she was. He could not have known she had left the Nasaratts' home. Yet there he was outside the room where she stood. She had that power over him. But did he know it? Now here he was, sitting across from her so close she could reach out and touch him. She wanted to reach out and touch his face. Rest her head on his shoulder. Weep. Feel his lips on hers. Make love to him. This man her spirit knew and loved.

However, the rules of the game did not allow that. A married Asian woman cannot within a small community reach out to a loved one belonging outside that community. That is one truth. She was able to recognise and deal with one truth.

The other truth was that he was not professing to love her, not asking if she loved him, but asking her the most rational question for the two of them, under the circumstances - was she the one? - when being cold and rational would not solve their problem. Was she the one writing anonymous letters to him?

Could she live with the truth? She had been living a lie for months. Pretending she was not the one. On the verge of forgetting that she was the one.

What it took him to come to her like this, she could never imagine. And he might never tell her. In romantic fiction this was where the lovers correct all past misconceptions. Where all mistakes and errors are excused. Where they kiss, hold hands, forgive all their enemies, and plan their future.

But true love is no romance. True lovers rarely end their lives happily ever after. In true love, love between souls, people die. They are killed. They commit suicide. They are separated, or one is banished. They die hoping to meet each other in the after life, never to be separated again.

'Were I to tell him the truth, it would sound like a ridiculous lie to him, a fabrication. But I am not a witness under oath. I could lie. If I am supposed to be innocent, I should at least play the part. Be affronted at being falsely accused. Should I do that now? If not, what should I do when there is nothing in his manner to help me explain why I did what I did? Should I confess that I am the guilty one? What should I do?'

After the initial shock when he spoke and she jerked her head up to look at him, she could not raise her eyes to look at his face again. 'To him I must surely betray the sullen, downcast look of a guilty person.'

While she weighed all this up, her eyes downcast she finally made an effort and raised her eyes slightly and noticed his hands, large and clumsy, touching the plain white tea cup which the waitress brought and whom she did not even hear coming. She stared stupidly at the table, the bowl, the Demerara sugar, and back to his cup, and she caught a glimpse of his hands trembling. Why does he tremble? Did he catch cold last night? Is he trembling for fear of the truth? Does he want to hear the truth? Or would the lie satisfy him? Would he be happier with the lie?

Everyone has his or her version of the truth. She wanted to be true to her truth. But it was supposed to come spontaneously from her, not to be forced out of her after been driven into a corner. Like this, in this noisy ice cream parlour, she could not help but draw on the countless lies she knew how to tell to save herself. But then she was afraid of his reaction to the lie, and even to the truth.

Late last night when she watched him from her window pacing about in the bitter cold air and she revelled in the fact that she had drawn him from his warm place by the fire to the cold ground below her window, she rejoiced in her power over him. Just now, when he came to sit across from her, she thought he had finally arrived at the truth. But his words proved he was not even close to realising it. He imagined he had come out of his own free will. So he asked this question. He had that confident belief that his question would receive an honest reply. 'Why?' she asked herself. 'Am I so simple? Doesn't it require intelligence to deceive? To dissemble? Can't he attribute the least bit of intelligence to me? How does he expect my confession to flow? With thoroughly female tears? Should I weep? Humiliate myself? Then suffer the remorse and guilt of the sinner. Another one of their Magdalena's?'

Is this love? Some people say that knowledge of the darker

side of a person is love. She had not even glimpsed his light side. How could this be love? If it is not love, is it obsessive madness? If she told him the truth and persuaded him that she was not lying, would he consider her mad?

If it is not love and it is not madness, if it is not the result of a weakness in childhood, is this a mystical experience? How did he come to strike fear into her heart the moment she first looked into his eyes? His eyes were pale, between hazel and green. She wanted to look at his face again and into his eyes. But she already suffered the desolation of her loss.

Poets see doppelgangers. Antagonists meet their match. Mystics see into another's soul. Theists see themselves in another's' eyes. Hers was most terrifying and simultaneously most uplifting. It was terrifying because it could drive her insane if her mind could not cope with the experience, and with the explanation were others to ridicule it. It was uplifting because it offered hope when she could not see the purpose of her existence, or the meaning of her life.

From the moment she considered this possibility she was lost. She plunged with natural born ease into unfathomed, mysterious depths for an explanation of what was happening to her. As blossoms burst from flower buds, stars shine from fading.

His look of desolation, his uncombed hair, gaunt features, the circles under his eyes – was she the cause of all this? Or was it set to coax her into a confession of guilt. Should she play into his hands? Should she fall trapped like a thrashing fish caught in the net he set for her? Was it a thing to rejoice over or to regret, her connection with this man? Were she to tell him it would be like a preposterous lie. She looked down at the tabletop visualising the mulberry tree with the swing in the garden of her childhood. She heard his chair scrape on the tiles. When she looked up he was gone.

That time they had reached a stalemate in their struggle. That was the nadir of all their meetings, a non-event, considering their first encounter, when she felt exhilarated, inspired even mystified, believing she had touched the essence of love. Now she wanted to die.

***

PART SIX

A Grain of Rice

83.

Unusually the metal security gate stood wide open. The front door was also wide open as if something large was to be moved in or out. Pragashini looked about for a sign of Astrid in the front garden before stepping into Astrid's house. Nalini was lying on the floor with her legs twisted under the weight of her body. A few feet away lay Astrid. She did not know which woman to attend to first. She suspected Nalini had a heart attack. But she went to Astrid to loosen the nylon stocking around her neck. Astrid was warm. Nalini was breathing and opened her eyes when Pragashini touched her.

She cleared Astrid's mouth and attempted to resuscitate her with one thought in her mind: things fall apart. She spent years in England, yet not once had she encountered a scene like this. After helping Nalini to the armchair she phoned the hospital and the police then returned to reviving Astrid.

Astrid still felt warm to the touch. It occurred to Pragashini the attacker might still be in the house. She ran outside calling for help. People from the neighbouring houses and the street rushed in. The attacker might even be mingling with them, she thought.

The police arrived but did not cordon off the house allowing people from the street to continue wandering in, looking around then wandering out. A doctor arrived and pronounced Astrid dead. He was trying to establish if Astrid had been sexually assaulted while Pragashini was anxious for the doctor to give Nalini a sedative.

Nalini was still collapsed in the armchair. Pragashini sat on the armrest cradling her shoulders. They were not alone. While the old woman began rambling about Astrid, her cat, the bathroom, the security gate, sewing basket, and other things. a third woman, uniformed, crouched at Nalini's knees straining to distinguish between her words and her dry rasping cough.

A variety of people milled around paying scant attention to the trio of women. Others stood gazing inquisitively around the room. Some looked desolate and disconsolate. Several policemen in slate grey uniforms commandeered the dining table and were taking statements. A photographer had gained entrance to the house and was snapping the room over the heads of the people clustered together, against the attempts of a couple of men who were pushing him towards the door.

Pragashini stroked Nalini's shoulders.

'She's nervous,' Nalini whispered. 'Windows opened one inch.'

'Why? What was she nervous about?' the kneeling police woman asked. 'She hiding from someone?'

'Always watching the skelms hanging about in the street. Peeping at the skelms from upstairs.'

'Was it a thief?'

'She folded the quilt on both beds,' Nalini began crying.

'Were you here with her?'

'Hush! Just let her talk,' whispered Pragashini not wanting to interrupt Nalini in case they lost information about who had been in the house when she arrived.

'That man sat at our table eating with us,' said Nalini

'Who? Was that the man? Did he know her?'

'I know her.'

'Did you see him? Were there more than one?' the police woman asked.'

'She mustn't see this room,' said Nalini. 'Put everything right before she wakes up.'

'Did you see a car?'

'No one slept in the spare bed since her hubby died.'

'The lady was married? Where's he?' asked the police woman.

'I told her don't have the braai. Someone will recognise you.'

'Who was she hiding from?' the police officer asked, and to Pragashini, 'Do you know?'

Pragashini shook her head.

'She was nervous. Afraid of a cat flap. Someone could put a thin child through to come into the house and unlock the door and let someone in.'

'There must have been a car.'

'The buzzer'... said Nalini.

'See if anything's on. Switch it off!' the officer ordered.

'He accused us. At our own table,' said Nalini.

'Who accused you? Was he the one who did this?'

'God knows how they got in,' said Nalini.

'Were there two people? Security gate's unlocked,' the police officer whispered to Pragashini. 'She may have let someone in.'

'She was very particular. Went through the whole house picking up tissues, hair, crumbs,' said Nalini.

'Upstairs the rooms are a mess.'

'One of us is a collaborator,' Nalini said. 'I gave her the sewing box. Look how the chair's broken.'

'Do you know who she's talking about,' the police officer asked Pragashini.

Pragashini shook her head. She wondered if Astrid was the collaborator.'

'He talked about a list,' said Nalini

'What list? Do you have it? Where is it?' The officer called across the room, 'Look for a list.'

'Did it rain? Is the cement wet? I told her don't unlock the gate. She lived alone, you know. Where's the cat? The grass is damp at six in the morning. It's a mystery. Next door's dog barks. Where's the cat? She never opened the windows. With burglar bars she was still afraid. It was too windy this morning. If the windows were open maybe someone heard. Look! cigarette stubs. Last night she phoned me when you left Pragashini. It was a game. Visitors hiding the ashtrays. She washed under running water. She never ate with friends who kept cats. Some people wash ashtrays with dishes. Pragashini you never smoked. She was too particular. Those ashtrays. She loves colours. You know people put cat food on the same plate for visitors? Ashtrays are see-through glass. I don't know what happened. Reds and greens. Air bubbles. I don't know what happened.'

'The saucers under the plants are full of water. What time did she water her plants?' asked the officer.

'I don't know what happened.

'Could someone have got in last night?' the policewoman asked.

'Pragashini are you a chain smoker?' she asked.

Pragashini did not answer.

'The last thing she'd do...puff up the cushions. Nothing out of place. It's a mess. She'd be so upset if she saw this room now.

'Did anyone come for bread?'

'The sandwiches are still in the kitchen,' said the officer.

'She used yesterday's loaf. One slice margarine. one slice peanut butter. Did the children come? Maybe they saw.'

'The knife's on the drainer,' said the policewoman.

'I told her never leave knives out. Don't waste money on sandwich bags. She said 'give the poor dignity. Is the bread there?'

'If we count the slices we can tell how many children came,' said the policewoman.

'Her piano. Yellow dust cloth? Scales for warming up. She

washed her hands.'

'The soapy water's still in the sink. Who would she open the gate to?' asked the officer.

'Always peeping. Even afraid of children She never unlocked the gate. Sandwich through the gate. It's windy today. Maybe she forgot the key in the door. Someone could put their hand through the security gate for the key.'

'She must have been sewing. The sewing basket was kicked over,' said the officer.

'She can only sew in good light. Waited for me to thread the needle. The basket by the armchair. Never ate before eight'.

'The tea stain has already dried on the carpet. Someone crushed the Melba toast. Two of everything, potatoes, carrots, onions, tomatoes. Frozen peas. All pap,' said the policewoman.

'The colours' ...

'The pan boiled dry. She was going to have a bowl of potato and carrot soup with a brown bread roll and a slice of melon,' said the officer.

'I phoned her. Did she hang the washing? Don't have a braai. Always look first ...she told me when someone came... Letters from all over the world. Maybe the postman came.'

'There's no mail downstairs.'

'The buzzer on the wash machine was sounding the end of the cycle when I came in,' said Pragashini not having registered anything said by either woman.

'It's brown bread for St Anthony.'

'There are Muslim pictures in her room?' the officer said, adding, 'Why?'

Nalini began crying again.

At that moment Pragashini made the connection between Astrid and Amina Khan. 'Presents from friends,' Pragashini said.

Nalini rambled on. In her rambling about Astrid, she included some words about the incident with the homeless person on the day of the braai. The policewoman stood up and left Pragashini with Nalini.

Then Nalini whispered, 'She wasn't from England. She's very fair. No one guessed. Astrid pretending. Special Branch. Pretending. Always pretending. In Sanlam Building. She's never English. Amina. Amina. Amina. If this house could talk. A Muslim lady. Only I knew. In this house. It's our secret. Don't tell Ramgopal. He doesn't even know. Don't tell anyone. I never even told Ramgopal. Don't tell the police. They're all skelms. The police. They're all skelms.'

Then Pragashini realized that Nalini may betray a confidence about Astrid. The officer returned and Pragashini said, 'Can't you see she's in shock?' Pragashini whispered. 'She's not making sense. Leave her alone.'

'The rooms upstairs are ransacked,' said the officer. 'Someone was searching for something. That list she was talking about. What's with the scraps of paper in the pedal bin?'

'I don't know,' said Pragashini. But before she could silence her, Nalini said, 'She cut things out of the papers.'

'She kept a scrapbook?' the officer called to a police man.

'Look for a scrapbook.' A policeman left the room.

***

84.

Nolitando's pregnancy presented only one problem for Smuts: Telling Heather. He would do the right thing by Nolitando. He would marry her. Buy her a house. Support her and their child. With this in mind he took her in his car, in the early evening, cruising the streets of eQonce and iMonti, sometimes driving to the surrounding areas admiring houses, asking for her opinion. Whichever house she liked he would buy and surprise her with the gift.

While he was packing a weekend bag, to spend with Heather and the children, Nolitando innocently inquired about the house in iBhayi. 'Who will have the house she's living in after you divorce?'

Her question alarmed him. He never mentioned divorce. Yet he ignored the issue and focussed on the house. 'It's hers,' he said. 'She bought it.'

'Is that why you're looking to buy in Bisho?'

'You want to live in the same house? Two women? One of you will be murdered!'

'You must put her out,' she said. 'Buy her a small flat or a townhouse.'

'That's not my style. Besides, I can't put her out of her own house. And I can afford to buy you a house.'

'Well, if she's moneyed you won't have to pay maintenance.'

'Moneyed or not, those are my children, not some other bastard's.'

'Do you want to test if this child is yours?' she asked.

'I might do, if you keep talking rubbish to me, woman!' She was annoying him.

'Okay. You wait 'til this child is born for your test. I'll wait 'til you're divorced before I marry you!'

'Divorce? What divorce? I don't have to divorce to marry under customary law.'

'I know,' she said.

'So?'

'That's why I'm waiting for you to divorce. I don't want to marry under customary law,' she said. 'I want to marry in court.'

'In court? What for? You're all for customary law. Tradition! Our ancestors! The courts are white man's things.'

'Not when it comes to customary marriage,' she said.

'You can't pick and choose – like sweets!'

'What d'you mean? I see it every day. People change bits of the law they don't like. Or they just scrap the whole law. I want to change those parts of customary law I don't like.'

He stood up and poured himself a gin and tonic. The struggle was over and he had begun drinking alcohol. 'You don't know what you're talking about. Our laws aren't written down so you can't change this or that. The elders keep the laws – up here – (he tapped his head) - in their heads.'

'So what if it's in their heads?' she said. 'I also have a head. I'll also be an elder one day.'

'Women don't become elders!'

'Still,' she said.

'Still what? If we don't respect customary laws, how the hell can we expect the whites to respect it? This is our country. Our customs are up there – high up. Not in the bush!'

'My child won't inherit if we marry in the bush,' she said. 'Her children will. That woman you married in England. That's why I want to marry in court. You think I'm a fool? From the bush? You've got a lot of learning to do, Smuts Matatiele.'

'You think so? You think all of us, millions of us, went to the law courts to get married? Stupid woman! Only the bourgeois marry in church and in court. You see photos in the Post and you think everyone does that? Those people are bourgeois. The grass roots marry by tradition. They go home to their villages. They slaughter a lamb or a goat. They sing to their ancestors. Are we going to send them all to court to marry again? Hey woman? You want our courts to be chock a block like apartheid's courts?'

'I don't care if the courts are chock a block. Customary law means a man can have as many wives as he can afford. The Law Courts means one man one wife. Law Courts children inherit. Customary law children sing and dance for their inheritance. You divorce that woman you married in London,' she said. 'I don't want her laughing behind my back at our marriage.'

He poured another gin and tonic. 'She won't laugh. She's not like that. Plus I plan to marry her by customary law on the same day I marry you. Both of you will be my wives by tradition.'

Nolitando screeched at the top of her voice. She took hold of a wooden carving and threw it at him. It hit him on the side of his head. The glass fell out of his hand. He held his head. 'What's up with you?'

She swore a string of abuses at him.

'If you don't want a traditional wedding, what the hell did I have to go to be circumcised for?' He was shouting at her.

'To make you a man, madoda[71]!' she screeched, and spat at his feet.

'Superstitious rubbish!'

'I believe in that superstitious rubbish!' she shouted.

'A man is a man without circumcision. I put myself at risk for you, bloody woman, and you look down on a traditional wedding!'

'You were a boy and you had children with that – that – umakhulu[72]! You were a man when you fathered my child!' she shouted.

'uThetha amasimba[73]!' He shouted and walked out of the room to the bathroom to wash his face.

She followed him to the bathroom. 'You show me divorce

---

71 Madoda means a man.

72 umakhulu is a grandmother

73 uThetha amasimba means you are talking shit.

papers then I'll marry! Or your child will be a bastard!' she said.

'What's a bastard? There's no such thing as bastard in customary law! You're confused woman. You're calling my child a bastard? Then have your bastard! I'm not divorcing.'

She screamed and cried. 'Because she's a white woman!'

'Because I can have two wives!'

'Because she's moneyed and I'm from the ghetto,' she cried.

'I can afford two wives. I can afford four wives if I want.'

She ran screaming out of the house. He went to the door and saw her running and screaming up the road to a neighbour's house. He kicked the door shut, went to the fridge, took six cans of beer, put on the telly and sat down. Late that night she hadn't returned. Without locking the door, he undressed and went to bed, as drunk as a palm wine drinkard. He was new to alcohol, and tired. He decided to get up early the next morning, drive to iBhayi and confess everything to Heather.

***

85.

Smuts woke at three in the morning with a full bladder and staggered sleepily into the bathroom. As he stood urinating, he screamed like a mad man. His pubic hair was completely shaved. He was as smooth skinned as a newborn baby. He began shivering involuntarily and could not control the shivering. At the same time he was wet with perspiration. He didn't wash his hands. Shaking and perspiring, he threw a blanket over his shoulders, found the car keys and his wallet, got into the car and sped out of the complex onto the road to iBhayi.

***

86.

Heather returned with Thamsanqa from the doctor to Smuts house in the Bisho complex. The women of the clan were already there. She sensed the women's displeasure. It did not bother her. She was more concerned that she let Thamsanqa down. To be in the clan's good favour was neither here nor there.

In Smuts house in the complex she found evidence of another woman. While coping with the hurt and anger a woman telephoned the house and asked for Smuts. On hearing Heather's voice the woman screamed at her to vacate the house.

Within minutes Nolitando was on the doorstep and pushed her way into the house behaving like the mistress of the house, which she was. She told Heather she was pregnant with Smuts' child. The women of the clan asked Nolitando to leave. This astonished Heather. She expected the women to shelter the other woman. She felt a measure of security as Smuts' wife.

***

87.

Arriving in iBhayi Smuts drove straight to the township where the Sangoma lived. In the back yard of the Sangoma's house was a tented enclosure. In one corner a fire burned. When he stepped out of the car the wise man made him drop the blanket. The blanket fell around his feet. He stood naked before the Sangoma.

The Sangoma motioned him to step away. Smuts stepped out of the blanket. Then the Sangoma took a piece of wood from the fire and beat the blanket in several places to set it on fire. The blanket was damp from his sweating during the two hours it took to speed from Bisho to iBhayi. The Sangoma sprinkled a liquid onto the blanket then it burned, slowly, like damp wood, and he had to continue sprinkling and beating it with the burning wood.

Only when the blanket was reduced to ashes did the wise man allow him to step into the tented enclosure. There was rush matting spread on the ground. While he sat naked on the rush matting, the Sangoma stood in the opening and made some loud incantations. He held a pouch in his hand.

When the Sangoma turned round he poured a potion over Smuts head. It ran down his face, his back, his chest. The Sangoma touched him lightly on his back and chest with a short whisk made of horsehair. He was still trembling violently from early that morning when he woke. With the touch of the whisk, he shook even more than before. The Sangoma threw a liquid over his private parts. He would have screamed if he had not undergone circumcision. Still he was shaking.

The Sangoma mixed a potion in a small calabash, heated it over the flames, and then gave it to him to drink. As hot as it was, it did nothing to warm him or to stop the involuntary tremors. The Sangoma then threw a blanket over his shoulders, tapped him lightly on his forehead, and he swooned backward. He remembered nothing else.

***

88.

Heather held her rosary in her pocket, her hand fingering the beads. They set off on the airport road then through some back streets leading her to believe they were heading for the short cut to Bisho or the coastal road to Port Elizabeth. Then she recognised the Umtata Road. She sat forward to speak to the driver. He stopped the car and blindfolded her. Can you believe that? In a free South Africa? Her children were in the second car. 'Cruel,' she said because they knew the children were terrified of their customs. Later, she would accuse them, after what was yet to happen.

In haste she had packed a holdall. Their suitcases were in Port Elizabeth. Without whispering farewell to anyone, she bundled her children into a car and sped to Port Elizabeth, picked up their passports and suitcases and drove to Verwoerd Airport. She sighed with relief when the plane took off. They landed in East London, and they remained in their seats for the flight to Johannesburg.

At some point the airhostess whispered in her ear and escorted them off the plane. If this had happened later, her heart would have leapt. The hope would still have been alive, buried in her depressed heart. She was told to bring her hand luggage and her children. God knows what she would have imagined. That her prayers had been answered. She would already be thanking God. Padre Pio. St Jude. St Anthony. The guardian angels. She would have been overjoyed. She would have cried. She would not see for tears. But it was not later. It was earlier. The tragedy would not have occurred if they had left her on the plane to return to England, or if she had remained in England.

She found two men waiting alongside two BMW cars. They simply said 'something happened'. They were to drive her back. They refused to tell her any more.

They travelled without stopping. Not to Bisho nor to Port Elizabeth. The driver drove at high speed along the narrow country roads, and she feared a lamb or goat or beast around every other bend in the road. The roads in those territories were not well maintained by the apartheid government. The fences were damaged with the result that animals wandered freely onto the road. Perhaps the driver was trying to discourage her from jumping out of the car. They were afraid of what she might do. 'Don't drive so fast,' she said, becoming angry. 'The children are in the other car.'

She had to guess which town they were passing, whenever the driver slowed down, or when she heard the bustle of a market place or taxi rank. By the time they arrived she reckoned they must certainly have passed through Tsolo, Umtata, Lusikisiki, and beyond that. From the colour of the sand on the hills in the distance – deep, dark red – like the colour on the skin of young men who have been into the forest for initiation - she could not tell where they were. Women never come near the initiation sites. Now her children and she were honorary guests of the clan they belonged to, made welcome, with smiles and jokes about the journey, as if they had not prevented her from leaving South Africa. But they had.

The village may have been three hours drive beyond Lusikisiki, she thought. We named our child after that place. Perhaps near the Wild Coast. It was hard to say. The driver drove in circles to confuse her. Smuts' ancestors were from the territories to the north and west of East London, what used to be Transkei and Ciskei during the regimes that included Matanzima and Oupa Gqoza. They taught her that history. From the time of her arrival she habitually travelled in and out of the two territories, to naming ceremonies, manhood celebrations, weddings, funerals, prayer meetings, and birthday parties. She grew to know the region well.

To be outmanoeuvred at East London. Caught napping. Stupid woman; tricked by men who outwitted apartheid.

'Burton Heather Smith,' they read. Her maiden name. Her mistake. An offshoot of her mother's assertiveness. It caught his eye, her father-in-law's. She guessed. What else could it be? Not her date of birth. Place of birth. Serial number.

Issuing office. Colour photo taken when she was expecting the twins. Blooming skin. Gleaming hair. None of that would interest him. Her name would. If the elders, standing in a thoughtful, polite circle around her feared what she would do when she left South Africa, here was the proof in writing that she would blow the whistle on them, disseminate it to the four corners of the earth. It meant she had not adopted the family name. Not even the name they graciously bestowed on her – Wethu – 'one of our family.'

'I could bluff my way out of it,' she thought. 'Say it was a mistake. Not mine. Theirs. The issuing office. If I could pretend to myself I was my mother. Stand taller than I am. Put on an air of hauteur. Look affronted. Assert my right to be called whatever I wished. Look down at them. But she could never be like her mother. Never pretend to be her. No. The answer was not written in the red sand coating her white trainers. Nor could she look down at any of them. They were all taller than her, and thinner, and quieter. All of them commanding respect *she* did not want to give them.

Naturally, her father-in-law did not look to her for an explanation. He would not bestow that honour and respect on her. All he read were those three words, Burton Heather Smith, the surest sign he could have asked for, that she would without a doubt, betray all of them. If there had flickered a minute spark of hope they wanted her there with them; that her life with them in that place of undulating hills and rondavels[74] was not over, the revelation of those three names snuffed it. It was all the proof the man needed that she rejected them, their struggle, their society, their culture, and every damn element that was part of South Africa, things she had once innocently embraced. She could not imagine what they would do now.

---

74 A rondavel is a round thatched dwelling.

It was her stupidity. Her arrogance. Forgetting that she married into a family of Africans who were diligently searching for signs that she was different from other Whites. She succumbed to a little burst of pride about her parents, her background, their wealth not measured in money. The wealth of learning, leisure, literature, and opportunity. That's what her name meant to her. Nothing to brag about. No achievements to be recorded by historians. They were not aristocracy. Not upper middle class. No horses, land, stately homes. No coat of arms. Except her name. It was a political statement. Her mother shoved the Burton before the Heather.

'A woman may have sixteen children from sixteen men,' her mother said. 'Is it too much to ask that each child carry that's woman's name? The man? He's a ship passing in the night. The woman is constant.' Keeping the names given to her on baptism was a simple human reaction to her sense of herself, her need to surround herself with a protective coat. She had recourse to nothing else. She did not intend them to know. Smuts was comfortable with it. However else she had changed, she had no wish to humiliate them. Even now.

She realised her stupidity. Immediately her father-in-law opened her passport. He asked for her passport with customary courtesy. She handed hers over in a way that was supposed to demonstrate her lack of interest in the proceedings. In fact, she was tense, edgy and uncertain of what was in store for her children and her. So she did as she was bid. She was unwilling to make a fuss.

She did not know why he opened it in the first place. It was not a departure point or border crossing. The fact that she handed it over was an indication of how different it was being here in South Africa. There was so much ease between people. She never experienced that anywhere else. Anywhere else she would have stamped and raged if someone took her passport. Being British. There she gave the little book to her father-in-law, whom she respected once, but not any more. He opened it. He just did it, perhaps involuntarily, for want of something to do, or to make it seem as if he were in control of the situation. Perhaps. Maybe even out of interest. He possibly never saw anything other than a domboek[75] in his life in that unspoilt village. It seemed like something unrehearsed in an unplanned situation.

She sensed they believed she betrayed them. She blushed. She looked at the ground and noticed the sand was a bright red, like brick, deeper than the colour of the streets in Cumbria. She put her hands to her cheeks and wiped them.

He was clearly unprepared for what he saw. He did not disguise his reaction. He looked shocked. He drew his head back as if what he saw was spitting out venom at him – such an innocent thing – this name in her passport. He glanced at her again, looked at the man next to him, passed the passport along, and the second man also appeared taken aback. The process was repeated until the hapless, thin, maroon thing which until that moment imbued her with so much courage and confidence, travelled without her all around the circle of men, until it came back to her father-in-law and he put it in a little pouch made of springbok skin hanging around his waist. Now it seems everything was justified. If they had any doubts that they were doing the right thing, this name was all they needed.

She felt nothing. No fear. No anger. Nothing. She was without feeling. But her body was strained. Her head ached. She wished she could die. Even knowing she did nothing wrong. It was not an offence. If it was an offence they had no rights over the matter. It was her right. She had no

75 Domboek is the colloquial word for the reference books Africans were made to carry under apartheid.

interest in sparing their feelings. They cared nothing about her. It was such a common practice for women to marry and keep their maiden name, or revert to their maiden name on divorce, that she never thought about the implications – in such a situation as this. They clearly did not know women could do this.

She had not planned it. It was not in her mind when she presented herself at the Consular office to apply for a new passport. The clerk's ashen face when he recognised her, impelled her to speak quickly, unguardedly, like a guilty person blurting out the truth, hoping that by the unrestricted flow of words, her mental stability would be proven beyond doubt. She did not want him to begin a conversation with her, to ask after her well-being or even to inquire if she ever wished to return to South Africa. Her photograph had been sprawled across the newspapers. She had appeared on national television. Who would not recognise her? People did not know what to say when they saw her, nor where to look after that first awful recognition.

So she maintained this unstoppable one sided conversation with the clerk, that anyone in their right mind would have recognised as the state of mind of someone unhinged. She told him her maiden name was the result of a feminist debate between her parents' that her mother won, that's how her mother's surname preceded her children's first names. Her brother was Burton John Smith. She should have shut up. She had always been such a quiet, studious person. Suddenly she had become a garrulous fool.

The poor clerk blinked just once. Perhaps he was not sure if he imagined seeing her there. Then he attempted to soften his glance, but could not even manage to do that. He just looked away from her with constrained tautness on his face. Each time he avoided looking at her she was impelled to say something more. She went on about how much her mother disliked double-barrelled surnames. The clerk looked past her with his eyes glazed. She thought if he blinks again the tears might spill over. She looked away to spare him, more than to shield her own lack of emotion. Tears do nothing for anyone.

She proceeded to complete the forms with her maiden name. If she had known she would be showing her passport to her father-in-law and the elders she might not have done it. They were not prepared for it. They had tricked her. She had been too trusting. Had she known they would confiscate her passport she might have given it to the pilot before leaving the plane. They were supposed to let her go. They had no further interest in her.

She wondered what her mother would have done. She was not ashamed to admit that she loved to hover in her mother's shadow, like a little mouse. It was a secure environment to grow up in. To be nurtured by an intelligent woman – and a man who nurtured intelligent women. Her parents believed anything could be achieved through reasoning and they taught her to trust herself and the trust she had in herself would encourage her own self-discipline. In a loving home, they said, there is never indiscipline. In a loving relationship there is never infidelity. They forgot to add – of equals. They took that for granted perhaps.

Only once in her life their reasoning clashed with hers. When they advised her to cohabit with Smuts rather than marry him under English law. They were worldly. They gave her anecdotes of friends who were bruised. He might be married back home, they said. You don't know his family. How right they were. But she brought them round to her way of feeling – it was not a matter for reasoning she said. Looking around that day in the village, she wondered where reasoning would get her. Until recently, she only had words of praise for how discussion and negotiations had unshackled their divided country. Not any more.

On marriage she became a member of Smuts' clan. Her married name placed her in that clan. It was romantic. Like marrying the laird of a highland castle. She had no qualms about relinquishing Burton Heather Smith for Smuts' clan name, and a tribal name his family sent by air mail to their London home, with beads, and clothes dyed in brilliant orange edged with black biased binding. Under the present circumstances, and in view of everything that happened since 1994, the year their lives changed, it would be foolish to disclose the clan name. They could see that she was ashamed of the clan name and the name they had given her – Wethu – one of our family, one of our tribe.

She was still wearing the clothes she was travelling in. Her luggage was in a rondavel on the edge of the sand clearing and she had no inclination to unpack. But she removed her trainers so that she could sit barefoot in the sun.

They told her she was free to wander about. The cars were driven away. The village children whispered to her the cars were driven into a rondavel that was cemented all over in the bush somewhere. The way stolen cars are hidden until the heat is off. The children were afraid to show her the way. What could she do if the car was hidden in a rondavel cemented over? Was she here with Smuts' knowledge, his agreement? Did he know about this abduction. Where had they placed her children? The village children were afraid to say. So she exercised caution.

***

89

A woman approached carrying a tray. With a little curtsy she knelt down on the rush mat and put the tray down. On the tray was a set of clothes, a pen, an exercise book and ball point refills. The pen was the sort you see displayed at Jan Smuts Airport along with giraffes, elephants, drums, and animal hide. It was carved from some indigenous wood, - perhaps Imbuia. The woman looked anxiously about before she reached out, put her hand over Heather's, squeezed her hand and said, 'Pumi'. Her eyes brimmed over with tears.

Heather drew herself up coldly. Everyone around her seemed prone to tears. She looked at the clothes on the tray.

The married woman's garb. Never again. She spat on it. She pushed it to one side. Pumi dabbed at her eyes with the corner of her wrap, scrambled to her feet and hurried away.

She took the pen in her hands. It had been sandpapered by hand, and varnished without being cleaned of dust and sawdust. When she ran her finger over the little bits of wood and sand, it felt like the protrusions on the shell of Echinoderms[76]. She preferred writing with ink from a bottle with a pen that has a refillable bladder. She collected pens. Her handbag was full of ink pens. Some of the elders knew this. Her father in law knew this. It meant this homemade ballpoint pen was the symbol of their ownership of the writing she was about to do for them.

They instructed her to make a written statement before she left South Africa. She refused to write under coercion. They would read it and censor it.

Her little protozoan under the microscope and Pragashini's potential cells were a lifetime away. When she was the heroine in the novels she read. When words fascinated her. When poetry had the power to enrapture her. When she experienced delight in fluctuating nature. Like Pragashini did. Right now what did she care for language? Or the life of a Protozoan? She could not bring herself to read a storybook

---

76 Echinoderm is a marine invertebrate such as the sea urchin.

to her children, let alone savour words created with precision for rhythm and sound and associative memories. What use would it be to her? She did not know the ending. Where she was at this moment could never be the end. So where would she begin?

The Matatiele's were not content to instruct her to write everything before they allowed her to leave. To add to her oppression they insisted on the truth. Whose truth? Theirs or hers?

To ask them would be to show she was contemplating writing as they prescribed. It would be considered disrespectful. Worse coming from her. Their truth was not hers. She knew that. They knew that. Yet, they expected their truth from her. Why speak about truth if there are several truths? Why don't they broadcast their truth in eleven languages and leave her with her truth and her language. She wouldn't even write about it. She would purge it from her mind.

That was not the half of it. She was the last person who should be narrating this. As much as she knew this, they also knew it. They shared that one truth. She was not the one who should be narrating this. Yet knowing this, they chose her. They elected her to tell whoever was interested, what happened after the exiles returned home to South Africa. She was not an exile. Yet they tasked her – they had a fondness for that word – 'task'. It was not asking, but assigning you a job, recognising it's onerous aspect, in this case writing about events your mind wanted to forget, and still laying down criteria.

Who would not feel oppressed? They, however, did not recognise this as oppression. They only recognised the oppression of apartheid.

They gave her free reign to tell it the way it happened. Free reign? Is there such a thing? How could she have free reign when they wanted the right to censor what she wrote? Why not just ask her to be fair to them? Why give her the task of writing what is true for them? They knew where she was coming from. The hold-alls and backpacks she gladly carried out from England, laden with paraphernalia, became baggage she will take back home with her, soul food she will take out and hold close to her wherever she goes. She came out with so much in the way of gifts for family she had never met. When she returns her luggage will be lighter her burden heavier.

In her heart she knew they set a trap for her. Born out of their combined, aged, wisdom. A trap even the elephant grass could not conceal. She saw the dangers marked, like cats eyes along mile after mile of pitch-black road ahead of her and when she looked back the darkness enveloped her.

She will fall into the trap. She knew she would. The way she tended to fall into traps. Eyes wide open. Ears shut to warnings. Like a blind woman playing blind woman's buff where there are no lights and blindness was immaterial.

Not everyone gathered in that rondavel that night, agreed to her being the narrator. There was unanimity that the story must be told to appease the press. But some did not raise their hands. She liked to think they were trying to protect her.

Smuts was not there. She needed his protection. There were dangers. It was dangerous where politics was involved, here as much as anywhere else in the world. Her father-in-law always warned, 'In a country where words can kill, its best to shut up.' Yet, he was one of those insisting that she put down the words that might kill her or who? The others who were against her were just mean-spirited and racist, although they would never acknowledge that. They hinted at political correctness in not so many words. She was not an Afrikaner. They may have had more feeling for her had she been one.

It was not politically correct for an English woman to tell this story to an English readership. To bring yet another pair of western eyes to Africa and beam the scene back to the west. Later Pragashini's aunt Karishma said the elders were having their revenge against Conrad. That aunt made connections between unrelated things. She said they were making her a female Conrad writing about the millennium's Heart of Darkness. Trust aunt Karishma to come up with that connection. She did not see the connection but it did not lessen her distaste for the task.

Had she been a reporter or journalist, it might have worked. But she lived with them. She was part of the experience. She was not an onlooker living in a luxury hotel, coming out to appear in front of television cameras with carefully groomed hair, pure white blouse, pashmini shawl carelessly thrown about her shoulders, and bombs exploding miles away. She slept in a rondavel. She ate umpokoqo[77] with her fingers. She got up at six in the morning to make tea and coffee for the elders, brewing each his or her preference, whether it was Five Roses, Rooibos[78], FG coffee. She wore the married woman's garb. In the eyes of the young African women who had a healthy distaste for the towel, the doek[79], and the German print, she appeared an utter fool and she knew it. How she loved being part of the family. Accepted by them. One of them.

Whatever she wrote had to be submitted to them, for their approval before she was allowed to proceed further. They might disagree with what she wrote, even how she wrote it, by virtue of her being the outsider in her African family.

---

77 Umpokoqo is mealie meal cooked and mixed with butter, eaten with amasi.

78 Rooibos is a bush tea that is red in colour.

79 The doek is a scarf worn around the head, usually plain black.

Like Smuts was the outsider in her English family for all those years he was in exile. That was why she suspected the majority selected her. They would have something to fall back on when the secrecy was broken. There were secrets there.

She did not have their permission in writing. Just the raised hands in a secret meeting by candlelight with no names mentioned, like the no-name brand on sale in their supermarkets. She could have refused. She could have bared her head, let down the pale hair they loved to plait. She could have walked away from this parliament of men and disappeared into the bush. They would have followed her. If they could stop her leaving the country they had the power to do anything. So she submitted. She played the part of a Maqothi[80]. Like a married woman she sat with eyes downcast like a sullen chattel, concentrating, trying her hardest not to miss a word they said. She was the most servile and humble woman this council of fathers must have seen.

By acquiescing to the meeting, by going when she was fetched from the kitchen, by sitting it out, by never demurring, whatever was said, she had wilfully placed one foot in front of the other, purposely, until she was an inch away from falling. She could have refused to attend. She could have protested loudly. She did not. It was a shrewd move on their part. By asking her to write this, they prevented her from going home and writing what she wished, if she had the mind to. She did not have the mind to do anything. She hardly knew where to begin. She did not know what to include and exclude. She suspected them. Her fears, self-censorship, the dilemma she was in, all indicated how much she had changed since her arrival. She

80 Maqothi is a married woman.

had no idea how her emotions would affect her.

So was it to be their story or hers? How would she determine that? Should she ask who suffered the most loss? She thought she did. But others thought they had. Who would be the judge of what is the truth?

Her view was western. They will think it is superior. The language will be wrong. The perspective will be distorted. It will disapprove of their point of view. The person who should have told this story was not there.

***

90.

Guilty and shamefaced the elders let her go. Pragashini had arrived. Her rescuer. When she neither wanted nor needed rescuing. Pragashini was also given a notebook. She was having none of it. She strolled about in shorts and tee shirt plucking leaves and flowers from the ground, and drawing them with a pencil. The eternal biologist. Did Pragashini believe, like she did, that the elders held the secret? Looking across the clearing at Pragashini, she was reminded of herself. Pragashini seemed also to be in her mother's shadow. Yet she never spoke about her mother.

When Pragashini appeared from the trees she walked across the clearing and looked down at the tray expecting tea. What amazed Heather was how relaxed and unperturbed she appeared. She had no fear. She buzzed with friendliness to everyone she met. Pragashini, always meticulously observant and analytical, delved in her bum bag and presented her passport. They did not ask for it. Then she joined her hands and gave a slight bow of the head.

They trusted her. She loved pretending she was a

traditional Indian woman. She should have been an actress. She chatted to the men, revealing a total lack of concern about Heather's plight. As if this was a normal everyday occurrence. Two women, one English one Indian confined to a village in the heart of nowhere, their passports confiscated. Pragashini even shared a bit of light hearted humour with the men, practising the isiXhosa phrases she had learnt to say – 'u de Klerk, uthetha amasimba' – and they roared with laughter each time she said it, substituting someone else's name for de Klerk's.

Then Pragashini sat cross-legged on the rush mat and taking Heather's hands in hers, she said, 'Heather,' and when she said the name, Heather remembered how they sat together in the lab in York. 'Remember the frost on the framework of deciduous trees in winter? Remember blossoms bursting from flower buds in spring? Those are your words, Heather, not mine,' she said.

Pragashini lied. They were her words. She loved nature. 'Do it, Heather,' she urged. 'Write it.' And Heather wrote. Feverishly. Frantically. Recalling everything. About life contained in a single cell. Her Protozoan. Containing all life's functions. But the elders when they read it tore the pages into little scraps and tossed them into the hot air.

Pragashini never gave up. She enticed Heather into the bush. She said, 'Come I'll show you something,' and they strolled into the bush, with one of the bodyguards following them like a chaperone, carelessly and embarrassed. They had not a hope in hell of getting far. Pragashini took her to a place where Cycads[81] – the rare plant – grew in the wild. They returned and she tried to sleep with Pragashini chanting softly – while she kept telling herself as she became drowsy, that Pragashini did not have a clue how to chant –

81 Cycad is a tall palm that grows in SA. Considered very rare and highly prized.

but she made a damned good effort. When Heather woke in the morning there was a drawing of a Coelacanth[82] - another rare form - on the mat beside her head.

***

91.

Smuts opened his eyes. He made out shapes of people sitting cross-legged on the ground all around him. He heard voices talking in low tones that sounded a great distance away, voices murmuring words in isiXhosa, incessantly repeating the same words, words about ancestors, praises and gratitude for bringing him home, his job, his home, his family.

The room was filled with smoke. His eyes were stinging. His throat was dry. His lips cracked. He could not swallow his spittle. He identified no one in the room. He saw a thin hand stretching out towards him, thin as a child's, then quickly pulling away. He heard someone saying no one should touch him. He heard his father saying, 'The iNgcibi who initiated you has come.' He fell asleep.

Each time he dozed and woke he heard the same voice droning on and what sounded like his father's voice saying the same words, 'He's sitting outside waiting to help you. He travelled a long distance. He refused food and drink to give you strength. We'll take you home. I'll tell uHeather you're ill. She doesn't know where you are.' It was as if each time he opened his eyes, he was waking at the same moment in time. That was all he knew.

***

82 A Coelacanth is a fossil fish that was thought to be extinct, but was discovered alive off the coast of East London.

92.

Like a grain of rice dropped into the outstretched hand of a victim of famine. Perfect. Polished. Without additive colour or flavouring. Yet having the potential for change. Ready formed, the idea appeared in Pragashini's mind. A seed that has pushed leaf buds through the soil. Like a monkey not knowing what to do with it, she marvelled at it, and at the human spirit. 'Something beautiful is happening to me.'

She turned it over the way the starving and the fasting save the last grain for another day, because she was utterly starved of imagination and had no inkling when her next thought would be served. But also because she did not know what was happening to her. She cradled it with a sense of wonder. Were she in possession of a pearl she could not have prized it more than this single thought. It belonged in Lillian Too's wealth jar. Something beautiful is happening to me.

She had stepped out of the temperate Eastern Cape sun into the house that now belonged to Heather and Smuts, their new home in a former white suburb. The room was heavy with smoke but she detected a hint of Rooipoortjie[83], a form of daggha[84] in the air. She tensed, alert, her impulse to step back out and run from the house.

The smell of light daggha released a memory of a classroom and a wall of windows overlooking the quarry below the school, where skollies[85] lay prostrate on their bellies inhaling daggha fumes from a hollow dug in the ground while they, the school children looked on as if they were gawping at sweets in a shop window.

In the room, she also inhaled a puzzling mix of other

---

83 Rooipoortjie is a good quality form of daggha

84 Daggha is the term used in SA for marijuana or cannabis.

85 A skollie is a Coloured petty thief.

South African herbs. There was Buchu[86], and something medicinal that grew along the beach she could not identify, even with her knowledge of Biology.

She found it difficult to breathe. The smoke hid something sinister taking place in the gloom, she was sure. The South African herbs disturbed memories of fevered illness, pain, and death. She tasted the bitterness of Lewens Essence[87], Rooi Leeuwentel, Haarlemenses, Jamaica Ginger, and Bors Druppels as if they were administered to her now. Yet she saw nothing distinct in the room.

Overhead a slow whirring drew her eyes upwards to the ceiling where she made out a colonial fan, the kind she saw in government hostels and hotels in Zambia and Zimbabwe. It was suspended in a smoke free pocket above the room, its flat brown and maize coloured paddles playing with the air and lethargically wafting smoke to the four corners. The fan made little difference. The smoke was too dense.

Then behind her she heard a muffled sound. Turning she stumbled over cushions and toys on the floor towards Heather huddled in an armchair with her knees pulled up to her chin. The picture she presented was so unlike her that Pragashini shivered involuntarily. She dreaded what she would discover in the house. All it needed was for Heather to suck her thumb and the image of a forlorn child would be complete. The way the armchair was pushed into the far corner of the room almost facing the wall, gave the impression its occupant was of no consequence to the people there.

She flung herself onto Heather, her arms outstretched

---

86 Buchu is an indigenous herb used by the Khoi San. In the home, it is infused with vinegar and applied to the abdomen.

87 Lewens Essens, Rooi Leeuwentel, Haarlemenses, Jamaica Ginger, Bors Druppels fall under the category of Old Dutch Remedies used in SA.

attempting to enfold her, to sooth and comfort her. Heather's posture and unkempt appearance shocked her. Her blonde hair was matted with perspiration. She feared whatever precipitated Heather's look of terror. Close up Heather was more pallid than ever. She could not tan. She recalled how they placed their arms alongside each other on the Formica lab table and Pragashini would say, 'I should compare you to a Pascali rose,' after Heather gained her trust.

But Heather was distressed to see her. Now Heather mistrusted her. Previously it had been the other way round. Heather visibly shrunk away, shoving her away as if Pragashini might harm her. Pragashini put out a hand, tentatively. She touched Heather's hand and brought it to her own head, running Heather's hand across her head. It had no effect. Heather jerked her hand away. She would not tolerate Pragashini even sitting on the arm of her chair.

Pragashini withdrew. Between them leaving the bush and this moment something had transpired. Better leave her and find the rest of the family. Heather muttered incoherently. Pragashini trembled. This was enough to frighten the strongest. She moved back into the centre of the room waving the smoke with her hands to the source of subdued male voices in another part of the large room. When she was close enough to the far corner of the room and could make out the people there, she gasped at what she saw and clapped a hand over her mouth stifling a cry.

***

93.

Smuts lay naked on grass matting spread over the red-carpeted floor, his pubic hair shaved. African men of the clan including Matatiele sat cross-legged on the floor around

Smuts' sweating body. A Sangoma[88] in full ceremonial dress of furred headdress, a skirt of animal pelts, beads and braids across his chest, a white blanket over one shoulder, and fur leggings around his calves, sat near Smuts head flicking his whisk over Smuts wet body and damp face.

With her hands cupped over her mouth, choking with smoke and the horror of what she had seen, she retreated from the sight of Smuts lying helplessly naked on the floor.

She knew what it meant in South Africa when someone's pubic hair was shaved, man, or woman. This was no bikini line depilatory job. The shaved hair would be used in a preparation to perform powerful witchcraft against the person whose hair was used. In the potion they might add fingernails from the victim, menstrual blood, and hair from the hairbrush. That was the reason she found Heather's habit of biting her nails unnerving. Whoever shaved Smuts' pubic hair would have taken it to a traditional doctor and he would have concocted some evil potion to be used against Smuts. But how was it done? Had Smuts been drunk? All committed comrades in the struggle abhorred alcohol. Did he begin drinking now the struggle was over?

This witchcraft was the evil the struggling oppressed in South Africa never brought to the world's attention. Believers in the power of witchcraft feared it. It was widely used. They could not root it out. It was the sore festering beneath the bloody tear-filled foundation of the infant democracy. People on all fronts were afraid to legislate against it. Smuts? He could not be overpowered by this evil practice. Smuts laughed at tradition. He dismissed witchcraft as rubbish. How could Smuts succumb to this evil?

Cautiously she retreated, afraid to distract the group of

---

88 A Sangoma is someone who practices traditional medicine. There are categories of traditional doctors.

men, feeling with her feet for marbles and Lego on the floor, back to where Heather crouched. This must be the reason Heather was in this state. Heather, a Catholic would be appalled by this. Without taking her eyes off the tableau at the far end of the room, putting out a hand feeling for something to sit on and finding a chair, she gripped the seat and sank down. She stayed there until her eyes grew accustomed to the gloom.

Now she could make out other men. They stood around the walls of the room, aimlessly, like full-length photographs blown up to fit the walls. She counted two Coloureds, three Indians, four were Africans not of the clan. Near the door leading into the rest of the house, she saw an Imam from the local mosque, a Brahmin Pujari[89], a Buddhist in saffron robes, an African minister of the cloth, a Black Rabbi.

None of the men standing around the room said anything to each other or to her. She knew them all. They knew her. They knew her story. They were shocked by her appearance, as Heather's shocked her. She could tell. The way they glanced furtively at her and quickly away when she looked straight at them. But none of them could think of a way to reach out to her.

Guilt. That's what they suffered. They never expected to see her again. And now? They were waiting for something to happen. For Smuts to wake from his stupor? Or to die? She did not know how long she remained in shock, just sitting dazed on the chair, hating them for their power, and their impotence when they were appealed to for help.

It was too much. Without realising it tears streamed down her cheeks. As if Astrid's violent death was not enough to break the heart of any liberated South African now here were Smuts and Heather. The thought of Astrid made her

---

89 A Pujari is a Hindu priest. A Brahmin Pujari is a high caste priest.

sob aloud. It was still so vivid. Defenceless woman. When she was able to control her trembling and sobbing, what in the name of Bhagvan[90] could she say? That it was Astrid's karma? Forever keeping sandwiches at the ready for urchins and beggars. Would that alleviate their collective anguish? Could she dare challenge those who castigated South Africa's violence? Would saying it happens all over the world balance the equation from the euphoria of the election victory to this tragedy? Her anger was tempered with anguish for she had no answers. She only knew Astrid, in her meticulous way, would have preferred to say 'It's my kismet, Pragashini, not my karma'.

That was the clue no one picked up on. Until it was too late. At the time she was blind. All of them were. They were fixated on the danger facing them, the free and fair elections, the fragile new nation, the whole world observing them, the enemy right there in their midst, masquerading as a comrade, yet unknown to them, that they overlooked Astrid's vulnerability; a dignified lady playing her part to perfection. Beyond these three she could not bring herself to think. Oh Bhagvan.

Here she was back in South Africa, sitting in this house of death, stealing furtive glances at Heather, demented, dishevelled Heather, her face the nearest to crazed she had ever seen both in and out of exile; Heather's glazed blue eyes over-bright, without a trace of the joy that should bubble at source; Heather nervously watchful for another opportunity to steal away to take her own life. That message, of Heather's attempted suicide, brought her breaking the speed limit to get here.

She felt trapped. For the third time in her life she felt utter and absolute desolation. For the second time in her life no

---

90 Bhagvan is an Indian word meaning God.

matter whom she appealed to, no one would help her. They would stand around the room like today, powerful and powerless. Her tears flowed without her being conscious of it.

This was the most devastating development. She wanted to stand up, go to the windows, and draw the blinds. Hide the room from prying eyes. The outside world would jump on this tragedy, seize it and broadcast it to the four corners as yet another heart of darkness, with necklacing, that picture flashed across the world of Winnie, the match poised above the matchbox, black on black violence. It is self-hatred. Hatred of the image of oneself one sees in another. She was utterly helpless as she had been before. She could do nothing.

***

94.

Then, at that moment, in helpless despair, it came to her, another beautiful thought. Throughout her years in exile, whenever despair gripped hold of her, when she sunk to the lowest level, when the sun hid itself in the sky, and life was joyless, her spirit made a little offering to rouse her.

During her exile in England, the England of labour, strikes, rivers of blood speeches, the Thatcher years, skinheads, vigilantes, and quangos, her spirit lay dormant like a cattle tick living in suspended animation, for a life time, waiting, for the off-chance that a warm blooded mammal might amble by. Like a cattle tick waiting, she waited for her first thought. Her mind was barren.

It was like living in a corrupted form of no man's land. Instead of sprouting, germinating, branching, flowering, and bearing fruit, your mind is utterly bereft of thought.

Nothing, not even your dreams, dared tiptoe into your waking consciousness. In the no man's land of the mind you cannot decide. You cannot choose. You cannot speculate about anything abstract. Your mind moves in circles around whichever object your eyes light on, never moving forward, nor finding a solution. You are not in the conscious or unconscious world.

Then, as if from the divine goddess herself, 'Durga[91] shukriya[92]' she was offered a thought. It allowed her to gather the remnants of her confidence around her, the way another female of her species might catch a slipping towel, or one of her race might salvage the end of a badly draped sari, if there can ever be such a thing. The observation marked a silk shift in her awareness, soft and light, yet enough to suffuse her with warmth in a cold country.

Each time a fresh thought came she associated it with a fragrance and filed it away. The first thought: 'something beautiful is happening to me', was like the natural fragrance of rain on the soil in the north of England. Soil mixed with leaf fall and conkers.

Her next thought 'Snow is the most beautiful dishonesty', was like biting into fresh sliced lemons. The thought she was afraid to write down because Nasaratt was reading her journal.

Another thought felt like crushing thyme underfoot. One was like smelling fresh green coriander on one's hands. Or grinding mint on a stone with a stone. Even then, each thought was a lifeline, vague and imprecise, when her life was not worth living. When nothing could be worse than it was then. Yet, look at today.

The dining chair she sat on was made of South African

---

91 Durga is the name of one of the Hindu Goddesses.

92 Shukriya means thank you.

yellow wood. She touched its roughness and the lines of the carpenter's chisel where she held onto the chair. It was half a dozen steps to the sliding doors leading to freshly cut green grass, blue skies, and frangipani air. She was tempted to make a dash for it, to escape the tragedy enacted in the room. She had lived through her own private tragedy. She could not bear another. Especially if it touched Smuts. Beloved Smuts.

But groups of rainbow nation men stood about in the room and on the grass, down spirited men, speaking in lowered voices, smoking, pacing about, waiting. They inhibited her. She knew how united they could be in their power against her and Heather. Two women.

Were she to run away, what about Heather, collapsed into an armchair, staring wildly about the room like a trapped animal that has experienced pain and is terrified of the people around it. She could not leave Heather here. Heather, even in her deranged terror, would never leave Smuts, she believed.

Then hearing Heather biting her fingernails even though she was in this broken state she still felt that old irritation from when they worked together in the laboratory in York. She half listened to Heather and to Smuts, beloved Smuts, half hearing him muttering insanities in an unnameable fever, oblivious of loved ones around him, prayed over by every religion's pundit, his sanity and his soul ebbing away.

In the choking atmosphere of encroaching death, Rooipoortjie, Buchu, smoke, heat, and sheep's fat, Pragashini watched for the arrival of a doctor to put Heather out of her misery and to treat Smuts. She had phoned the doctor. Heather needed sleep. Nothing else could be done for her. Smuts might need an anti-biotic.

But no doctor materialised in the smoke filled room. Men from outside stepped into the room, and men in the room stepped out on to the grass. Each time a new face appeared she whispered a first name, almost to refresh her memory, she knew them all, and beckoned them to her. She wanted desperately to take Heather to her car. Drive her away.

None of the men felt inclined to speak to her. Each man turned, looked at her, closed his eyes, and shook his head. As if the situation was a hopeless case. They indicated several things: their refusal to interfere; their concern for the two women's plight; a mute indication that she should not interfere; and their desperation just looking at her.

Once again her spirit attempted to elevate her, out of the tragedy enacted in the heat of the Eastern Cape. Her spirit offered a thought as solace. 'Women are born, not to fall in love, not to bear children, not to equal men, not to attempt the impossible, not to enrich themselves, not to make a discovery, but to die the most beautiful death possible.'

However, this time in South Africa, land of free and fair elections, when her spirit offered the thought she checked herself. 'This is hardly the place, Pragashini. Not this room. It isn't even the time to think elevating thoughts.' Yet she hungered for the reminders of the joy of homecoming, reunions with family and friends, the sun, the salt air, sea sand, the elections, the inauguration, the sense of being unbound, released, free. 'Cadres and comrades bahut[93] bahut shukriya'. South Africa is free. Apartheid is dead. She craved beautiful thoughts. She repeated the phrase to herself, like another one of the inscrutable mantras that kept her mind from disintegrating in England. She couldn't say it out loud. Who else could it help in this room? Heather? Smuts? Both crazed and fevered. They were unhearing. She needed to stay hopeful. Only Bhagvan knows what will happen to Heather if she walked away from this house and

93 Bahut means very man, or very much.

left her here. Even if she stayed here she might doze off and leave Heather vulnerable. She could hardly expect to keep watch over her throughout the night.

She could not appreciate the blue sky streaked with purple paling into pink, but she understood why a doctor might be reluctant to come. With a Sangoma present and all attention and concern focussed on Smuts, Heather's state of mind was of no concern to anyone else in the room, not even to Matatiele. They would have little faith in the power of a conventional doctor when a Sangoma was at hand.

They must be the only two women in the house. If there were other women they would be waiting upon these men, hand and foot, as they say. Cups of tea and coffee would be coming, and going back empty for washing up in the kitchen. There would be the activity of crockery and cutlery swirling about in the sink, chopping, stamping, and sizzling sounds coming from the kitchen. The aroma of cooking food would mingle with the sleep inducing concoction in the room. But today the house was still except for the sombre male voices, deeply resonant, intoning heartfelt supplications that were as old as the earth.

She had no idea where the women of the family were. When she walked into the house none of the elders said a word to her. She did not know what had happened to Smuts. Only the Sangoma had no doubts. He continued to perform the ritual for someone who was bewitched. She had witnessed the ritual before.

Even then she could not comprehend Heather's state of collapse. Heather did not believe in the power of witchcraft. She would expect Smuts to recover from whatever he was suffering from if a doctor treated him. Could something else have triggered Heather's state of mind? Something the men of the clan might keep from her? Or, was she fearful Smuts might die without a doctor? But what? Smuts was bewitched.

Heather deranged. Astrid murdered. Mellikhaya killed. Was the connection Matatele? Why was he unscathed?

Sometimes Heather made a soft sound that unnerved her. She was not crying, wailing, sobbing, or moaning. The sound was strange, reminding her of an animal caught in a trap that does not cry out in pain, a frightened animal waiting for some nightmare only it has access to, to end.

The house they were in had glass windows from ceiling to floor on two walls, every window protected by metal burglar bars; carpeted floors, fancy light fittings, and the droning electric fan in the ceiling. Something in the room, perhaps the smell of the herbs set off her longing for her prayer room, her beloved arched window, space to meditate, her mystical waking to snowfall. But Heather continually brought her back to the South African room; biting her nails, once leaping across the room to reach Smuts, struggling with the elders, grabbing Pragashini's hands, attempting to claw at the face of anyone who came near her.

Fortunately Heather's nails were bitten to the quick, that habit of hers, so she could not do any harm. Just once, she succeeded in bringing Heather close, but not to relax. Heather struggled free. Pragashini could think of nothing that would lull her to sleep. How could she, in her world of Indian apartheid, lull this English woman coming from a background of nursery rhymes, fairy tales, Christmas carols and lullabies?

More to comfort herself, than the other woman, she began rocking and humming in a soft voice, the only song she knew from memory, 'Om Jai Jagdish', from her daily devotions, the way they sang it in the movie. It attracted irritated murmurs from the clansmen seated on the floor.

'What are these women doing here? Our women are long gone. Women don't belong here. Pragashini! Take that woman to her room!' they scolded but no one stepped forward to help her. Pragashini clucked her tongue loudly at them. How did it come to this?

***

95.

Grotesque a shadow fell over the glass sliding doors blocking the streetlight. It was cast by a group of men who stepped together hesitantly into the room, hovering in the entrance until they were accustomed to the gloom, then moving like a dark cloud of locusts to the spot where Smuts lay sweating on the floor. Long after Pragashini despaired, the medical doctor arrived.

Now she hoped he was angry. She wanted him to pounce on the elders squatting on the floor around Smuts. But the elders sensed the threat and spontaneously rose in a body and whirled round on the intruders like Dervish dancers; Matatiele grabbing his knobkierie; the Sangoma his fly switch; all of them threatening to sjambok[94] the intruders. They knew a medical doctor, perhaps two were in amongst the group.

The elders shouted at the top of their voices, demanding to know who sent for them. They swore. They ordered them to get out. 'Hey wena![95] Who sent for you? Get out of here! Hamba![96] Hamba! We don't want White man's medicine here!' The elders of the clan remonstrated loudly and aggressively pushing and shoving them back, not wanting any interruption to their life saving vigil.

The group of interlopers were forced back defensively, and

---

94 A sjambok is a whip made of rhino or hippo hide.

95 Wena is a Xhosa word meaning 'you'.

96 Hamba is a Xhosa word meaning 'Go away' used discourteously. Perhaps equivalent to 'Voetsak' in Afrikaans.

in their retreat, they espied the two women crouched in the corner. She recognised the doctor who had been at school with her. He was one of the youths she had begged to help her before her marriage. Now he was an active member of the local branch of the liberation movement. For that reason, on sighting the Sangoma he knew he could not stay. There would be hell to pay if he offended the traditional doctor.

She stood up and slipped her hands under Heather's armpits, expecting one of the newcomers to help her guide Heather to the car. Another uproar exploded into the room, vented by the elders who had resettled themselves around Smuts but with a watchful eye on the intruders. Matatiele shouted, 'Hey Pragashini! Why you want to smuggle her away? This is her house. Not ours. She paid for it with British pounds not Kruger's Rands and nonsense. You can't take her away from this house! Where must she go? Hey Pragashini? The British Embassy? To skinner about us. Tell them we're savages? No fear! She's staying put. If anyone leaves this house, it will be us. We've also got houses to go to.'

'She can't sleep here,' Pragashini said.

'You want a bedroom?' Matatiele asked. 'This house has got bedrooms like Holiday Inn. Go on! Take your pick, Pragashini.'

Given this roundabout go ahead, the doctor's companions sprang into action like an emergency medical team carrying Heather to a bedroom further down the passage, lifting her on to the bed, holding her down while the doctor touched her forehead and pulse, and examined her tongue. He shone a torch into her eyes, opened his bag, removed a syringe and gave Heather an injection without a by your leave, all while she struggled and four men held her hands and feet. The group were out of the house in minutes. They appeared to have grasped the situation.

Heather's eyelids drooped, her body slumped, and she became drowsy. As Heather relaxed, she appeared to recognise Pragashini and moved her hand to touch hers. Pragashini took her hand. When Heather slept she slid off the bed and tiptoed to the door then glanced back at her.

What would happen to Heather if she left her here? If Smuts died? There was no saying what would happen. She remembered an exile dying in England and the family in Africa blaming his English wife for his death. The other side of the coin was if anything happened to an English wife, the African family back home were suspected of using African medicine on the wife. There was no way out of the grip that witchcraft had on the people.

Her mind preoccupied she went quietly back to the room where Smuts lay. The door was wide open. She hovered in the doorway without drawing attention to herself, and silently scrutinised each of the shapes in traditional clothes, presiding over Smuts, each elder, the Sangoma, even Matatiele, her life long mentor, came within the scope of her accusation.

Were they hiding guilt? Responsibility for what ailed Smuts? What pushed Heather over the edge? Even if she discovered the truth, what could she do? She could hardly call the police to arrest someone for practising witchcraft. There was no law against it. When the Parliament of Traditional Leaders sat, traditional medicine was on the agenda in a positive manner. There was little talk of witchcraft and muti. If Smuts died, some doctor would provide a death certificate with the cause of death being fever, or pneumonia. In the same manner that some Aids deaths were recorded to avoid losing the insurance benefits. Feeling powerless and treacherous towards Matatiele, the only friend who had stood by her, she turned away from them.

Matatiele saw her leaving the room. He raised himself from the floor, crossed the room, and followed her in his bare feet. Just as the bedroom door was shutting behind her, he put out his hand to stop it. She looked back in alarm he had come so quietly up behind her.

***

96.

Matatiele stood with his thin brown hand on the door. Pragashini, the clove brown young woman with her shaved head turned back to stare accusingly at him. He seemed hurt. He blamed her for failing to understand his desperation over his surviving son and the power of the elders over him. She blamed him for whatever had happened to Heather, although she had no conception of what had transpired before her arrival, except that Heather had attempted suicide. The sight of Smuts and the Sangoma condemned him in her eyes. Although the eyes of the two friends were lustreless, his were bloodshot from the smoke in the room and weary, the expression on his face hardened and angry.

He was a man she trusted with her life. He was educated. He spoke high Xhosa, not the stuff spoken by the tsotsis or the man in the street. His Xhosa was so good whenever trained salaried translators were busy in court translating from English to Xhosa or the other way round for African defendants, and he was in the public gallery, he would stand up and object strongly if their interpretation was loose or off the mark. The magistrate would ask him to translate, and after he had done so, the public gallery would erupt in applause, and the mollified translators would ask if they should retire.

Now he said, 'What you know, I know, Pragashini. Nothing. Niks.[97] Smuts drove from Bisho straight to the Sangoma. The Sangoma sent for us. We sat three days and three nights with him. The way you see him, that's how we found him. He said niks to anyone. We brought him home. We don't know what they did to him. Or who did it.'

She stared into his face without blinking.

'You think the Sangoma can't help, so you want me to chase him away and call the doctor?' he asked.

She still thought of him as 'Sir' from the days when he came in to their school in Muhalla Asha from New Brighton to teach Xhosa.[98]

He looked at her but he was not seeing her. His mind was on Smuts and his illness. 'This is African sickness. It needs African medicine.'

She did not like arguing with him over his customs and tradition, but he knew that she loved Smuts, as he did, so she dared to disagree with him. 'I know Smuts. He would want a doctor.'

'You think Smuts doesn't believe in African medicine? You think it can't have power over him if he doesn't believe in it? You think he isn't bewitched?' he asked her.

She nodded. 'This illness is from when he was in the forest. Or something from Bisho.'

Although he was angry, he kept his voice even. His years of experience as a teacher gave him that ability to throw his voice to the end of the classroom. He did that now, so the elders in the other room would certainly have heard him. 'Rubbish! My Ingcibi[99] initiated Smuts. Mellikhaya.[100] All

---

97 Niks is an Afrikaans word meaning nothing.

98 Xhosa is an African language spoken largely by people in the Cape.

99 An Ingcibi is a Xhosa doctor who performs the circumcision during the initiation of young males.

the
men in my clan. None of us got infected. You think only western medicine is clean? Smuts was A1 when he came out of the forest. I ask you, if Smuts doesn't believe in African medicine why in Satan's name did he go to the Sangoma? Hey wena? Tell me! I never took him. I never forced him to go for initiation!'

She rudely turned her back on him and walked into the room. She did not care to listen to him. Talk about Sangomas and African medicine was irrelevant. What did it matter what Smuts believed? They must recall the doctor. That was all she wanted. When she turned her back on him, he also stepped into the bedroom and shut the door.

***

97.

With the bedroom door shut and Heather on the bed, Matatiele spoke in a lowered voice. 'See here, Pragashini, I'm the one to blame. Call me stupid. Old fool. Ignorant. Whatever names you want. Through my own arrogance, I made a deadly enemy for myself. This what you see – Smuts' life flowing out of him, Mellikhaya dead and buried, - all this is my enemy warning me. I never called Smuts home.'

She looked towards the bed to see if Heather had stirred. She was heavily drugged. Then she turned back 'What have you done, Sir?'

He shrugged. She knew he would not confide in her. It was foolish of her to even imagine he would. She had learnt her mistrust of people from him. Yet she persisted. She repeated, 'What have you done, Sir?' and waited, with her

100 Mellikhaya is an African name. It means 'the one who looks after the home'.

face showing expectation and attentiveness. 'If you know who your enemy is, why don't you do something? Tell someone? Maybe someone could help you.'

He stood staring into her face for some time thinking that he knew almost everything there was to know about her. She might have been his daughter-in-law if it wasn't for culture, tradition, racism and apartheid. The more people who knew, or who were suspected of knowing, the wider the evil would spread. She had endured enough. He could not put her at risk. Not openly. 'If I knew my enemy I'd kill him. He's lucky I don't know. My bad luck. It could be anyone. I think it's a comrade turned enemy. It could be someone in my family. In your family. I saw the way Ramgopal looked at me at the table that night. And that man who married you – Nasaratt - he knows I helped control him. Maybe he suspects something about you and Smuts. And this' – he looked at Heather on the bed and Pragashini saw an emotion she was afraid to name pass like a shadow across his face – 'this English woman. She had good reason.' He wanted to say, 'Even you, Pragashini' but that would wound her too much. She had been wounded by so many, he could not add to her hurt. He trusted no one, now. Not even her. She who planned revenge against Nasaratt, had reason to take revenge against Smuts.

She instinctively sensed he withheld an accusation against her. She appreciated that he had not included her in his list of enemies. Now she was back home she appeared to have lost her calmness. She was provocative. She was easily angered. She blurted out the first thing that came into her mind. Perhaps she felt safe, knowing he was near her. She did not need to say, 'I don't do witchcraft. The Nasaratts don't do witchcraft. None of them do. The man who married me doesn't believe in God or the devil, never mind African medicine. And Heather's a Catholic, for God's sake.' He knew it all. He did not need her to tell him or to remind him.

'I know what you're thinking,' he said. 'You think only Africans go to the Sangoma for witchcraft? Why don't you go for a drive around iBhayi's[101] townships on Sunday afternoon? Or go to Ciskei[102] or Transkei[103] on Sundays. Ask someone to point out the Sangoma's houses. In fact, you don't need to ask anybody. You can't miss it. You'll be lucky if you can find a space to park. Whites flock to the Sangoma on Sundays. After they've gone to church and taken communion. Before they go gambling at Amatola Sun[104] and Fish River[105].'

She was not getting anywhere. He would not re-call the doctor. She was at a loss. She believed if Smuts drove from Bisho, then the culprit was there, in Bisho. Her thoughts turned to Nolitando. 'What about Nolitando? Have you asked her what she knows about this?'

Now he was growing exasperated with her. 'You're thinking like an outsider, like a scientist doing an experiment, cut off from the people you know, looking at the problem as if there are no humans involved. Nolitando is getting married to Smuts. She's pregnant. Why in Satan's name must she bewitch him?'

She did not even attempt to answer his question. Her mind had already snatched at the answer to the riddle that had been puzzling her since she stepped into the house. 'So

---

101 IBhayi is the name given by Africans to Port Elizabeth. It means 'the Bay'.

102 Ciskei is a former Bantustan under apartheid.

103 Transkei is a former Bantustan under apartheid.

104 Amatola Sun is a gambling casino in Bisho

105 Fish River is the colloquial way of referring to the Fish River Sun gambling casino near the Fish River.

that's why Heather's – half crazy,' she said.

He saw her glance at Heather on the bed and look accusingly at him. He was shocked at her conclusion. He looked contemptuously at Heather and said, 'It's Smuts who's dying, Pragashini. Not this English woman. She's not bewitched.'

They were quiet for a considerable length of time, frozen looking at Heather. When she moved it was to ask her original question. 'What did you do to make such a powerful enemy? Tell me, Sir.'

He shrugged. He dearly wanted to talk about this with someone. He was afraid for his wife. For months he withheld this from her, while it burned like an ulcer inside him. He suspected every person he met. He locked his wife in their home and cautioned her not to leave for her safety. There was no one else he could confide in. Now he said, 'I forgot to keep my commandments. I opened my mouth like I was babbelaas in the shebeen.'

She remembered how he taught them other things superfluous to their language lessons. 'That's the first thing you taught all of us, Sir. Keep silent when you're with strangers and known enemies,' she said.

Of course he knew that. Of all of them, she had the best motives to learn her lessons well. Her family betrayed her. He shrugged again. 'I was with comrades, Pragashini. I relaxed.'

She feared he would turn and walk out the room. With each question she asked she knew he was becoming increasingly uneasy. 'Why would a comrade become your enemy, Sir?'

He knew what she was eventually going to ask. She was young. She still imagined he would forget himself and actually tell her. 'I thought I could trust a comrade.'

Then she came back to his teaching. 'You taught us never

to trust anyone, Sir. Even a comrade,' she said.

She was too young to know even the experienced have moments of weakness. It was so difficult to look out for enemies day and night. 'I dropped my guard. The elections were waving to me round the corner. How can you feel how it was here? You were in exile.'

Still she coaxed him. She would not give up. She was smiling at him, inviting him to be honest with her. 'So then tell me, Sir. What was it like? I can't imagine what you could say to make a comrade your enemy.'

He had all his wits about him. He was no fool. The few hints he had dropped were all she would get out of him. 'You think I'll tell anyone? Ever? I'll take it to the grave with me, Pragashini.'

She tried again, forgetting she was dealing with a man she had a great deal still to learn from. '*I* have questions I'll never dare ask out loud. Who knows, perhaps your question is the same as mine,' she said.

He smiled, recognising the ploy she was using to get him to talk. When the smile wore away his face looked drawn and anguished. She could not be sure it was his anxiety over Smuts or this problem of the comrade turned enemy. She looked at him with a stricken expression on her face. Now she needed a beautiful thought but none came to her assistance. 'Sir, how could you ask a sensitive question when you know what you taught us? All of us have questions we dare not say out loud. Even now we are free. You should have left it for the TRC.[106]'

He relaxed. She realised the futility of trying to make him talk. She had given up. She would stop her soft interrogation. 'The TRC will throw the bones at our enemies. Not at our comrades. We've got enemies

---

106 TRC is the Truth and Reconciliation Commission.

pretending they're comrades at all levels. They're the danger to us, Pragashini.'

She accepted she had lost. She could not persuade him to share his secret with her. She wondered what he would do. 'Will you do anything, Sir?'

He put his hands to his face and drew them over his head, like an Indian in prayer. 'I must do something. I brought this on them. First Mellikhaya. Now Smuts. I'm to blame,' he said. 'None of this would've happened.'

She saw once again a chance to persuade him to call the doctor. 'Does it matter who did this to Smuts? The main thing is to cure him. He might never tell us if we don't call a doctor, Sir,' she said.

He was not listening. 'Smuts should've stayed in England. You too. This woman and her children.' His face looked as if he had spread white ash over it. He looked helpless. 'You keep forgetting why you came back. You didn't come back to vote. You would be in England still, if I didn't call you back. You didn't even want to come back. I told Smuts not to bring his wife and kids. Someone tricked him.'

She put out a hand and touched his arm. She felt his body slacken as if he needed someone to lean on but she could not provide that support. She lacked his strength of mind and character. He was slightly taller than her. She put her arms around his waist and held him close. 'Smuts won't die. I'd feel it if Smuts were dying,' she said. She prayed silently that he would recall the doctor.

The expression on his face was anguished but she could not see it. He knew if she ever found out what had been done here, she might kill him, however much she took him to be her father. 'I've broken my commandments,' he said.

She did not know what to say to that.

'Next time you do your devotions,' he said, 'put in a word for Smuts,' and he left the room.

Something about the way he referred to Heather made her anxious for the English woman. It might be unwise to leave Heather and go home. She lay beside Heather on the bed suddenly becoming anxious about Heather's children.

Matatiele did not refer to them as his grandchildren. Perhaps in his anxiety over Smuts he distanced himself from them. Of course, they must be with the women of the family. If Smuts were to die, would Heather want to remain in South Africa with her African in-laws? Would the Matatiele family want to keep their grandchildren here? She had no answers.

***

98.

While in a fitful sleep that night alongside Heather, with Smuts in delirium, watched over by his clan, Pragashini heard a child crying. She slid out of bed, and walked through the house searching room after room, and into the room where the elders and the Sangoma were keeping a vigil over Smuts. The men looked with consternation at her, recognising that she was sleepwalking.

Matatiele stood up. He went in his bare feet quietly up to her, gently turned her around, and guided her back to the room where Heather slept without waking either woman.

***

99.

Pragashini's Journal

When I was a little girl asleep in my bed, I frequently woke to the tormenting sounds of a little child crying in the night somewhere in the house. I was too young to soothe the crying child, yet being inquisitive, a quality that would develop and motivate my research,

I would sit up in bed, rub my eyes, tiptoe from my room, push at my parents' bedroom door, listen, glance around the room, even look under the bed, pad through the moonlit house, listen at the door of each room, expecting to find the crying child in every room I approached, and hearing only the cricket in the kitchen chirping loudly in the stillness.

I had no reason to doubt a child was crying somewhere in the house. I only heard the crying child at night and each time I repeated my search of the house, never giving up, never relinquishing the search, always expecting to find the child before the crying stopped. My searches never brought any satisfaction. I never found the crying child.

The crying child tormented me with its crying throughout my childhood and into adolescence. The crying child accompanied me to England and stayed with me into young adulthood until I realised no one else heard the crying child. It is hard for a child, to comprehend that only she hears the crying child. It was even harder to understand what that signified. I asked myself who is the child crying in my sleep?

***

100.

In Heather's house that night, Pragashini's search for the crying child was again fruitless.

***

101.

Sunlight in the room was harsh. Heather's eyes felt dry and stony. Her head throbbed. She could not move her lips to speak. Her tongue swollen, her mouth parched, her throat rasped when she swallowed. She could not part her lips to ask for water. She saw a model plane hanging from the ceiling. Thamsanqa's bedroom. He assembled that plane. There was his poster of Brenda Fassie, the voice he discovered when he arrived in South Africa. Looking for him, she twisted her head and saw his computer in an alcove behind the door. Switched off. He never switched it off. He downloaded a screensaver of a lion that roared. He was in love with Africa. The bedroom door was shut, another sign of his absence. The room was too quiet. Something was wrong. Had someone died? His music played even while he slept overcome by the heat of the day and the night. Where was he?

There was someone in the room. She turned in alarm towards the window. Pragashini stood there. Her back to the room. Straight. Her head shaved. Why was she in Thamsanqa's bedroom? What was she doing here looking out on the garden backing their new home? Their new beginning. The new South Africa. This same Pragashini Smuts was calling for in his fever, professing from some part of his fevered mind, his love for her. Smuts? Loving Pragashini? What more was she to discover about him?

She continued staring at Pragashini's back, waiting for the image to fade from the room. Something happened. She could not remember what. Without recalling anything tears seeped into her eyes. She could not understand why she cried, but something she could not cope with was there waiting to come into her consciousness. She could not cope with it, on top of all the things she had to adapt to coming to South Africa. She was lost. Smuts never prepared her for this. He was too engrossed in the struggle to think about a woman adapting to another country, a new culture, language, dress, even food. She tried. God knows she tried. 'I failed,' she accused herself. 'I failed this last test. What was it? I passed the others with various levels of mediocrity. The final test I failed. What was it?'

Almost as if to test her presence Heather moved her lips in a hoarse whisper, 'Pragashini?'

Pragashini whirled round. She barely heard the croaking voice. She crossed the small space from window to bed, poured a glass of water, and lifted Heather, holding her around the shoulders, putting the glass to her lips, kissing her head. Heather parted her lips, the water spilling out of her mouth, down her chin and neck, and on to her clothes.

The drug administered by the doctor left her mouth dry. Pragashini could not gauge if Heather was still hostile to her. Before she could turn to place the glass on the bedside table, Heather gripped her wrist splashing the water onto Pragashini's hand and the bedding. Supposing her to be frantic about Smuts, Pragashini said, 'His fever's lower. He isn't awake.'

Heather shook the arm she still gripped and whispered, 'My children?' She turned her head to the door saw the aeroplane and computer and closed her eyes tightly. It appeared to Pragashini, Heather was imagining the answer.

'Who could I ask? The men were fretting over Smuts, all day long. The women ... they're not around. Heather what happened?'

Heather struggled onto one elbow and sat forward on the pillows and whispered, 'My children.'

'Don't worry about them. The women must have them.' Heather seemed to be still in a delirium.

Heather swung her legs off the bed and in trying to jump up collapsed on the floor. This did not deter her. She crawled under the bed and came out clutching her shoes. Pragashini stared blankly at her. This must be the effect of the drug. Suddenly Heather was pleading, softly while she struggled with her shoes. 'Don't tell them I'm awake, Pragashini. Please don't tell anyone, please, I beg of you. Take me away from here, Pragashini. I beg you.'

'Heather, what are you afraid of? No one here will hurt you. You know these people. They're family. You're delirious.'

She recalled all the events of the day before. She regretted failing to take Heather out of the house when she arrived. Should she go along with that feeling she had yesterday that Heather was at risk? Should she tell Matatiele that Heather was awake? She was torn between the two. Then Heather knelt where she was on the floor, put her hands together, and began praying, silently.

Pragashini moved around the bed and helped Heather to her feet. She did not know what had happened, but was moved by the sight of her in this state. Heather was unconcerned about Smuts and his illness. Something else had pushed her over the edge. Still half convinced she opened the glass sliding doors, slowly, and supporting Heather guided her out of the house.

Outside the house was quiet. The air was fresh. The back garden was deserted. The front lawn was wet with dew. The gates were shut. Through the gates, she could see her car parked alongside the pavement. They walked on the grass avoiding the gravel driveway. They opened one gate and slipped through, she feeling uneasy about the action she was taking, suspecting she had chosen the wrong person to side with, already regretting she had not waited to hear Smuts account of what happened to him.

She intended taking Heather to Karishma but Heather asked to be taken to the beachfront. Afraid for Heather, because she had attempted suicide, she nevertheless drove the car to the beach and they sat together in the parked car watching the waves. Heather said nothing. She watched Heather's face, and seeing tears on her cheeks, she was afraid to say anything that might add to her trauma. Heather should speak only when she was ready. They had been sitting in the car for almost an hour when Pragashini observed that Heather had fallen asleep. She started the engine.

***

102.

Pragashini made the long drive from the beachfront in Humewood to Karishma's home in Muhalla Asha. Having put Heather to bed, she received a telephone call from Bisho. Its urgency prompted her to rouse Heather, wrap her up in the car, and drive straight to Bisho. She took the road through Alice and arrived there within three hours.

She feared another murder.

The grounds of the housing complex swarmed with police searching the garages. A policeman stood at the entrance to Smuts' house. He assured all visitors and inquisitive onlookers that the investigation was under control. When she stepped across the threshold, she saw a policeman interviewing a young girl in a room that opened at the end of the short corridor.

***

103

It was like visiting a Catholic funeral house hearing the combined voices responding to a voice leading the rosary. Pragashini opened the door of a room and encountered women kneeling together in prayer and tears as if someone had died. Had Smuts died while they were travelling? On the table was a cross of gold, surrounded by flames from night lights. On seeing Heather their voices trailed away, the group spontaneously struggled to their feet, and milled around her, holding, touching, and kissing her, steering her through the crowd to an armchair. Heather sat down, and from somewhere in the room her children appeared and clambered over her.

Pragashini could not obtain a coherent account of what had happened. The only consistent words she heard were: No one remembers anything. No one saw anything. She was puzzled to find the children in Bisho, when Heather and Smuts had been in P.E. But then it seemed the reasonable thing to do, with Smuts being ill, to remove the children, yet they could have been taken to Matatiele's home in New Brighton.

***

104.

For Heather the sight of her children prompted the memory of another failed test for her. Who could pass? Which mother? Which father? She had the head start on Smuts. He had yet to overcome the witchcraft, then hear and withstand the news. How would he come through that? What did they expect from her now, these Matatieles? What would Thamsanqa expect, her eldest initiated son?

That she should carry on as if nothing happened here? They could not expect that. Not the women, if the men did. That would be madness, for them to expect that. It would be madness if she were able to do that. She would be declared mad. No, she must leave.

Her dream of seeing him free in South Africa was fulfilled. He is free. She witnessed that. Her dream of living with him and contributing to his people, of seeing her children rooted here, was a fantasy. It was over. You cannot do it. Remove children from one soil and transplant them to another. They will not take root. Like seeds. Some might. The mutants. The majority will be stunted. Not reach their full potential.

Not flower, produce fruits and seeds. They will die. That was Pragashini's theory of evolution. Heather's spirit was heavy. It would engulf her if she remained in this house.

***

105.

Watching Heather, Pragashini noted how unmoved she appeared by the warmth of the women's greetings, even the touch of her children. Women clustered around Heather. One woman stroked her hand, another her back. But there was no warmth in her cheeks. She looked ashen. She stared vacantly into space without seeing. There was no means of comforting her, of communicating with her, of reaching her. Heather was only physically there with them. She concluded Heather had already accepted the worst. She was already in mourning she believed for Smuts. Only Heather's eyes swollen with tears spoke of her earlier emotion.

They resumed their prayers and Pragashini knelt with them. She who visited mosques with Fawzia and Feroza; fasted with them during Ramadan, broke the fast at sunset, and celebrated Eid with them. She attended multi faith services held in Christian churches in England through the struggle years where the Jewish Rabbi, Hindu Pujari, Muslim Imam, Buddhist Monk and Christian priests and pastors each led prayers in their own languages and rituals praying together for South Africa and the release of Mandela. She who made a daily pilgrimage to her beloved prayer room – locked out of the Hindu family prayer room.

And Heather, who believed in one God, who would not enter a mosque or temple, who believed in forgiveness, - now called upon to forgive – but forgive who?

Then the women of the clan, praying the rosary, reading psalms from the Bible, on their knees, humbling themselves before an unseen God, - leaving the bewitched Smuts in the hands of their men and the Sangoma. They prayed together.

When the prayers were over she was anxious to ask Heather if she wished to return to Port Elizabeth but Heather's mood remained unchanged. Heather could not be told to snap out of it. Smuts' argument that these things happen all over the world would not bring comfort to Heather. Whatever was in Heather's mind was now a closed book. Nothing she said could penetrate the protective layers Heather had enclosed herself in. Discussion would be too cruel.

***

106.

Heather beckoned to Pragashini to come close then whispered in her ear, while looking fearfully around the room at the other women, 'Take us away, Pragashini. Help me. I'm afraid. Watch over my children.'

All the words she could use to persuade Heather to wait, jostled for space. 'Smuts is ill,' she wanted to say. 'He needs you. Smuts doesn't believe in the power of witchcraft. I know him. He knows nothing about witchcraft. He left home when he was so young. I know Smuts. He's a good man. I don't know what has happened here, but Smuts isn't responsible. I know his father. I've known his father all my life – he is a good man. I trust him with my life.' Unfortunately, looking at Heather, at the pain visible in her face, at her spiritual absence from what was taking place around her, she compressed her lips. It would have little effect on Heather. What about prayer?

***

107.

Prayers ended. Mandisa with a slight movement of her head motioned to Pragashini. In a subdued voice she explained.

'We were in iBhayi,' said Mandisa. 'All of us. With Heather. The next thing we knew all these cars arrived – eight, nine, ten – blocking the road. The drivers jumped out, running into the house. We thought the cops were chasing them – like in the old days. We thought something happened. Shooting. An accident. People were sitting in the cars. There was no chance to see who were in the cars. The drivers chased us women through the back door. They locked the door. They herded us like cattle into the yard, round the front and out the front gate. Shooing us, shooing us further and further away – like cattle – away from the house until we stood on the opposite pavement a long way from the house. We had no idea what was happening. We couldn't see the people in the cars. We were puzzled and worried. But I suspected.'

'While we women stood in a group far from the house all the cars drove in through the gate, up to the front door, round to the back yard. When all the cars were inside, they locked the gate. We stood outside like we had no home. We could see men climbing out of the cars and standing around to form a wall. They were carrying someone but we couldn't see who. The men went into the house singing. Quiet, low singing. Because they were so many, we could hear them. I knew. In my heart I knew it must be Smuts they carried.

When they were inside the house, they drew the curtains. They locked the front door. Someone came out to tell us women of the clan we must sleep far from the house. So we did. We slept with neighbours. Some of us didn't sleep at all. We watched the house all night.'

'It's a good thing we didn't sleep, some of us. At four in the morning a car left the house. It was five thirty when the car returned. All the elders were washed and dressed in traditional clothes. A bakkie followed the car. On the back of the bakkie was a young live calf. The elders slaughtered the calf in the back garden and the blood of the beast was sprinkled all around the ground surrounding the house, on the doors and all around the fence that protected the house up to the gates and the road.'

'Pragashini, you will think we Africans are evil. You will think our customs are primitive. I tell you Pragashini, you're not a Christian, you don't know this. The same sprinkling of blood on the doors is there in the Bible. So the Angel knew which house to protect. So don't look down on us, Pragashini.'

'Our men lit small fires and placed them under each window, at the front and back door. They formed a ring right round the house. They sang hymns, they prayed, they changed places, they praised our ancestors. All the time the sun was rising. Sometimes they stopped. They stood silently there. They stoked the fires. Twelve o'clock time other men from our clan arrived adding to their numbers. They continued in the afternoon until it was night and into the next day.'

'There was a stink from the house. The fans in the house, the smoke, the burning wood, nothing lifted the smell. There was evil there. The stink was in the street and in the houses. Our elders huddled together outside the sick room. They talked with the iNgcibi who circumcised Smuts and the Sangoma that Smuts went to visit. I know this because my husband phoned me.'

Mandisa said, 'I took all these signs to mean someone in my family was bewitched. Women in my clan spotted Smuts' car on the grass near the house. Heather was with us. They chased her with us. You should have seen how troublesome she was. She got it in her head Smuts was ill from initiation. We all knew she didn't want Thamsanqa circumcised. You can imagine, what she will do if I told her my fears about witchcraft. I said nothing.'

'You should have heard Heather speak to us. Like we were all children to her. She told us Smuts is infected from initiation. She panicked for Thamsanqa. The more we were quiet, the more she panicked. No one was worried about Thamsanqa. We worried about Smuts. You should have seen how she behaved. She just stood up and said she's taking Thamsanqa to the doctor. She took all her children with her. Like we will do something to them. uHeather? Heather showed us her true colours. She comes back with Thamsanqa. Smiling. Not worried about Smuts. The doctor said Thamsanqa was fine.'

'So I decided. Before she suspects what's happening in the house with Smuts, all us women must go to Transkei. To our ancestral home. Heather? We were halfway there. Then Heather becomes fidgety. She asked to get off at the complex in Bisho. She doesn't want to go with us. So we break our journey at Bisho to drop her off at Smuts' house. uHeather? We saw Heather's true colours.'

'And the police? Do they suspect someone here bewitched Smuts? Or killed Astrid?' Pragashini asked.

'Heather didn't tell you?'

'Look at her. She's broken. She's not talking.'

'Her child is stolen.' Mandisa said.

'Oh my God.' So that pushed Heather over the edge. Not Smuts fevered illness.

Then Mandisa put out her arms and brought Pragashini close. 'I know everything,' she whispered, 'about you and Smuts. You are my daughter; one of our family. Do what you think is best for us.'

***

108.

Heather half-listened to Mandisa. She showed no interest in correcting her or in giving her account of events. She was concerned only for her children even in her emotional state. She whispered to Pragashini, 'I must leave South Africa. We don't belong here.'

Pragashini did not ask 'which child is missing?' There were many children in the house. She had not observed how many ran to Heather when she arrived. Perhaps what Mandisa said was too frightening to register with her. Or she was pre-occupied with Smuts. 'Don't leave Smuts. He loves you, Heather,' was all she managed to say.

Heather laughed a bitter croaking laugh that brought on a spelling of choking. She would never tell Pragashini that Smuts cried for her in his delirium.

***

109.

At three in the morning, Pragashini stole out of the house with Heather and the children all in their pyjamas. In the house the women were singing, a low, soft song. They did not say goodbye. After tucking them into the back seat of her car, and adjusting their safety belts, she moved out of the grounds quietly with the car lights switched off. She headed for the filling station, checked oil, water and air pressure then made for the Stutterheim Road.

The idea she could not shake off was if she were now in England, Heather would be moving heaven and earth to help her. Just as Heather knew England, she knew South

Africa. This thought impelled her to do what her conscience prompted her to do, although her inner sense warned her not to. She left South Africa from Ciskei heading for Transkei, and then Lesotho, driving through villages untouched by modernism and technology, beautiful, serene villages, round rondavels, clear waters, villages at peace and in harmony with nature.

***

PART SEVEN

The Condemned House

110.

England.

Coney Street in the centre of York, early in the day, its narrow street pedestrianised while permitted vans and cars off-loaded people and goods forced Pragashini to weave her way with urgency to the post office on Lendal. With a growing sense that someone was following her she darted across the road, and leapt up the steps leading to an American style coffee bar. On the top step she whirled round to confront her stalker but identified no one.

Transfixed in blue jeans and black leather blazer - only her eyes, - like a frightened rabbit's - showing above the blue and green niqab covering her head and face. She scanned the street, still uneasy, yet failed to pin point a suspect face. The crowd herded by some instinct moved in one direction towards the post office. She shivered. Then accepting the futility of standing there, she turned, pushed at the door and was enveloped in the aroma of freshly ground coffee.

Uppermost in her mind was the need to safeguard the papers she carried with her. Eyeing the coffee addicts in the bar she judged from their dress they were not from the student community and felt safer. They looked like people from the surrounding villages in town for the day, wearing shapeless parkas of green, beige, or grey. If they were students desperate for money they might be tempted by the price someone would pay for the papers she had with her.

When she asked hesitantly for a cup of coffee three girls who had been observing her nervous behaviour, promptly began fidgeting with the coffee machine. They now spoke to her over their collective shoulders. The machine was playing up. They were trying to fill it with milk or coffee or some E-numbered concoction, they confessed. Hot chocolate? It's faster. 'Cappuccino,' she said. No sugar. They told her abstractedly, to choose a table. Sit down. One of them would bring the coffee over. Their agitation added to her unease.

She turned away half-heartedly, hovering in the middle of the room, watching the door and the street through the plate glass windows, doubtful the girls would remember to bring her coffee over, and reluctant to sit. Some of the tables had screens around them, the upper half of transparent plastic, or steamed-up glass, the lower half of MDF[107]. She flopped down in a leather club chair at one of these tables.

She had been on the point of posting the assortment of papers and notebooks without sorting them. Reading it made her nervous at home and timid in a public place. Yet the comfort of strangers around her might give her the necessary courage. The stalker might even grow tired of waiting. That would give her time to make a dash for the post office. She could see out through the doors and windows without being seen so she rummaged about in her shoulder bag and placed a hardcover notebook with typed and handwritten papers on the uncovered round coffee table. Documents belonging to South Africa.

After wiping her sleeve over the laminated cover of the notebook she flipped it open. Immediately you write something on the page you are released from its terrors. You may be terrified to read what you have written, but committing it to paper frees your mind for whatever else has the gall to venture in. Psychology's Catch 22. Cathartic catharsis. You either keep it in your mind where it becomes an obsession, or you release it on to paper, and make room for what Bhagvan knows is coming next.

She read the entries she had made when a child in South

---

107 MDF is medium density fibreboard.

Africa:

"Life is beautiful."

"My days are filled with dreams of becoming a scientist; my nights with dreams of the boy I love."

"Love is a strawberry bon-bon".

"I love falling in love. I love being in love."

"I found a way to combine my two loves. I'll go systematically through the alphabet and fall in love with a name. The boy is an added bonus."

"English will have to do – even with its impoverished alphabet. Tragically I don't know the Tamil alphabet - reputed to have three hundred letters."

"On Mondays I fall in love. On Fridays I fall out of love. Then I have the whole weekend to look forward to the dawning of my day of love."

"Smuts turned up on a Monday when I reached the letter 'S'. There was no boy with a name beginning with 'Q'. I might not have any luck with 'X' either. Will have to check Xhosa and Muslim boys."

"Smuts slipped me a Xhosa textbook sealed with sellotape. Sandwiched between the pages was a love letter."

"Now I have his photo and a lock of his African hair in my scrapbook."

"Smuts is another one of my admirers fascinated with my hair – a South African thing. Like skin colour."

"He asked me when I'll cut it. Showing off my knowledge of Biology, I said, 'When it reaches my coccyx.' He pretended he knew what that was. To put himself on a par with me he said, 'It's almost time for me to go into the forest for circumcision.' I didn't bat an eye."

"I am a storyteller. That's a euphemism. I lie. With a straight face and a crossed heart."

"I lie out of the goodness of my heart. To entertain my friends, living in South Africa, in violent times, where the news is censored to the extent the newspaper is often blank

newsprint except for the title and the days date."

Reading the entries, she could not recognise the child she had once been. Flicking the pages the writing suddenly stopped. One, two, three, four. Blank. Pages that for months lay blank between William Morris covers. Months in which she stared at the blank page, terrified of discovery if she were to put pen to paper, afraid of the consequences once she did, if the notebook were discovered. There would be no rejoicing in heaven or hell over what she had recorded.

The waitress arrived softly and stood there carefully balancing a gigantic navy blue cup and saucer in mid air until Pragashini sensing her presence, looked up and cleared a space on the table. She extended her hands and shaped them around the hot cup, inhaling the coffee, with her eyes closed and a smile on her lips. If Heather were here, she would name this cup from some nonsense nursery rhyme that she probably made up herself, and Pragashini would be none the wiser. Then again, Heather was changed. The last thing she wanted was to be reminded of childhood.

'I didn't spill it,' a voice said.

She glanced up again, surprised. The waitress had not left. She was a young Asian girl, black hair cut short and streaked with red, in her early teens wearing an apron over a short skirt, her legs covered in thick pink, and white striped stockings.

'How you doing?' the girl added.

She raised her eyebrows. Her eyes darted in the direction of the girl's face and back to the cup. She moved her head in a kind of nod.

'People are gob-stopped seeing me working here. In Coney Street, I mean. It's like a no go area for us. To work in, I mean,' the girl said. 'They're happy enough to pocket our money.' She spoke with a Yorkshire accent. 'Aren't you surprised to see me? I was born round here. I gave up begging me mum and dad to move to Leeds or Bradford. They just would not give up on this place. I still don't understand why, knowing their history. Mum and dad's. Mum always said 'York will change, beTi[108]. Don't give up on it. To become Yorkshire you need true grit!'

Pragashini saw the girl looking at her almost as if to gauge her reaction to what she had just said, but she gave no sign of softening and refused to engage in conversation, so the girl stepped back from the table. 'Can I at least ask you why you're wearing that scarf? You're not Muslim!'

Pragashini put her hands up to the blue-green scarf. It was soft with the feel of angora but made of cotton. Her face was covered by one end of the scarf. She tucked the ends into the collar of her top. The waitress did not look Muslim either, she thought, and was reminded of Amina Khan.

'If you're not Muslim then you're just wearing that scarf to hide your face. And it's so o-ld. It spoils your outfit.'

'I'd know you anywhere from that scarf,' the girl said.

Pragashini gave her a meaningful look.

'Is it just me you won't speak to, or is it still that vow of silence?' The girl sighed in frustration when Pragashini continued to ignore her. 'Haven't you changed? Just a little? Like grow up?' After a pause she added, 'Oh! Well, there's no reason why you should remember me. I didn't do anything heroic.'

'Goodbye,' Pragashini said.

The girl jumped. 'She talks!'

Pragashini sighed. 'It's bad enough some loony tune is waiting outside to stalk me, on top of that I have to bump into the Spanish Inquisition,' she said. 'Listen kid, I'm in no mood for chit chat!'

'Kid? You calling me kid? You don't remember me? I knew

---

108 beTi means daughter

you when you were fourteen.'

'And you were being potty trained?'

'I was there. I watched them shave your head.'

'Don't push your luck, kiddo!'

'I was there! I swear to God Almighty. I saw it. I even saw who gave you that scarf.'

Pragashini looked at her momentarily, then said, 'Make my day.'

'A Clint Eastwood fan! He's too old for you. You were in a Victorian House with three floors, an attic, and a basement. It's still standing, y'know. A bit run down but it's still there.'

'Nice try, kid. There's just one problem! Victorian houses are two a penny. And our folks have a weakness for giving rooms to every betel leaf chewer from the subcontinent. Do you know an Asian who hasn't done time crammed into a Victorian house?'

The girl tut-tutted. 'So cynical. For one so young!' Then she put a hand out to touch Pragashini's scarf. Pragashini pulled back.

'O-oh! Touchy!'

'You work here? Or loitering with intent?'

The girl took a cloth tucked into her waistband and began vigorously wiping down the adjoining table.

'Give me a break!' she whispered. 'Not a lot of our people come in here. Look at those posers. Forever chatting to hunks that lounge around the place looking cool. If I'm lucky the next person I get to chat to will be an Asian Father Christmas!'

'Just don't get into trouble for my sake!'

'I won't! Don't I remind you of someone?' she was speaking softly.

'Yeah! Mr Bean.'

'You remember me! I was the one always spilling things. Knocking over cups and vases and things.'

'You a glutton for punishment, then? How many cups you broke here?'

'How else can I meet up with lads?'

'Do I look laddish?'

'I need to see your face to answer that.'

'You'd make a good interrogator!'

'Thanks! Anyhow, It's good to see you haven't forgotten me mum.'

Pragashini didn't look up. 'She the Lady Mayor?'

'Don't be daft! York hasn't changed that much! You're supposed to ask who's me mum!'

'Remind me.'

Now the girl just stood there, looking at Pragashini.

'I haven't got all day, kiddo.'

'Me too! I've got work to do. See you at the movies,' she sang out.

'People like you get strangled.'

'I'll tell me mum I saw you,' she said and walked off.

'Ok', Pragashini called after her. 'I'm sorry. I'm stressed out. Some weirdo's following me.'

'Whatever!'

The girl returned, and wiped the leather club chairs around the table. 'That's me mum's scarf you're wearing.'

Pragashini looked up at her. 'How's that? I'm not a charity.'

'From that day when you were fourteen. You scared the living daylights out of us. I still have nightmares about that day. I dream of you standing at the top of the stairs in your gym. Looking like'...

'Trick or treat?' Pragashini asked.

'I never went up there after that day. It gives me cold shivers standing here just thinking about it.'

'So which one was your mum?'

'Fawzia.'

'Who does that make you?'

'Hajira.'

'Nice try!'

Hajira reached out and pulled the scarf off Pragashini's head revealing her shaved head and face devoid of make up. 'Pragashini!' she said, holding the scarf to her mouth, her eyes filling with tears. She cried uncontrollably and struggled to find a place to sit.

Pragashini jumped up and snatched her scarf. When she covered her head and face she eyed the girl steadily. 'Look I'm sorry! So many people heard the story about me, you could be one of them.' But the girl could not stop crying.

'Stop crying. I don't look that awful, do I? You really Hajira? Look at you! Your dad lets you dress like that? A husband will soon get you out of that kit, my girl!'

'What you doing in this God forsaken place? People think you went back to South Africa.'

'Don't talk about South Africa to me.'

'That day - I didn't understand what was happening.'

'And you do now?'

'You've no idea how it affected all of us. We still talk about it when we get together.'

'Talk is nothing. Talk is cheap. I'm not the first one. I won't be the last. Has anyone done anything about it? When all of you 'get together'?'

'What can we do? You still hiding from him?'

'Nasaratt?' She shrugged. 'That snake? Naah! He's hiding from me, more like it!'

'You divorce him?'

'Naah! He wasn't worth the time or the money! I just let it go. Anyhow you don't divorce in that kind of marriage. You have it annulled. I was underage, remember?'

'Is he the one following you?'

'I don't think so. After that day he scarpered. I caught him in South Africa. I gave him such a beating. I broke his nose. I clawed out one of his eyes. He's blind in one eye now. I chopped off his finger. Naah! He'll never follow me. He's scared of me. You should have seen him shivering when he saw me. It must be some other mad man. Maybe I've got a secret admirer, who knows?'

'Pragashini! You're still such a liar! I don't know when to believe you. Is someone really following you? Be careful. What if it's him? It might be him.'

'I'll give him a clean uppercut! I'm not fourteen anymore. I know where to hurt a man! Between the legs. Remember that! And I'm not a liar, I'm a story teller. Sounds better.'

'Shouldn't you go back to South Africa? You'll be safer there.'

'Wake up! I went there. Wild horses won't drive me back!'

'They're talking about elections.'

'Honestly! Don't you kids read? The elections are over. We're Indians, kid. It's South Africa for the Africans now. Maybe Coloureds. Maybe Afrikaners. Indigenous, or something. A South African Idi Amin is waiting for Mandela to die so he can kick all of us out.'

'Pragashini, you don't believe that! I know you. Did you see your family?'

'They're dead and buried. Years ago! I told you.'

Hajira put her hands to her mouth. 'Don't say that! At least go and see your mum!'

'Your mum is my mum. I don't need no spare. I'll never forget your mum. She helped me survive. I sleep with this scarf. In my hand. Under my pillow. Around my neck. I'll wear it till I die. Amen!'

'Don't talk about death, Pragashini. Come stay with us. You're in danger if someone's following you.'

'Naah! I'm a survivor, kid. I can take a walk in the night alone. Look after yourself. Next time I'll visit when you're at home.'

'What about that teacher in South Africa? You said he was your friend.'

'You mean Matatiele? Useless. Teachers are useless. What did he ever do to help me? Nothing! He's just a long distance talker! All talk and no action.'

'Did you see him in South Africa?'

'Naah! I was too busy. Meeting my lovers. One in every college. That's what you must aim for. That's the best reason to go to college.'

'Why should someone follow you?'

Pragashini shrugged. 'Who knows? My thesis? Too radical. Plus I don't take bull from any Tom, Dick or Harry. Those days are in the past. People don't like that. They want us rubbing our hands together, hands out for a handout!'

'They won't try to' ...

'Kill me? Naah! Worse!'

'What's worse?' ...

'Than killing? I'm not telling you, kid. One nightmare's enough for you!'

'Don't make jokes, please.'

'Listen kiddo, I'm cracking jokes so you can sleep at night. I won't wish my life onto you. You're too sweet and innocent.'

Hajira was summoned back to the counter. Pragashini called out, 'Don't forget – say your prayers!' then she sat down.

She would never forget Fawzia repeating the same mantra: 'Things will change. York will change. Britain will change. South Africa will change. The world will change. There won't be any borders. People will come and go. We'll be one nation. No rape. Murder. Guns. Wars. No world powers.'

Some people are all hope. Fawzia praying five times a day. Others despaired, like her, trusting no one. Who has time to wait for change? People lived and died lifetimes waiting for change in South Africa. The elections were over. People were still dying. Who is to say how many will die? There's a limit to how long you can wait for things to change. Who says change is always good? Good for some perhaps.

She pushed the cup and saucer to the far edge of the table and retrieved the journal. She dipped into the book again then suddenly slammed the book shut, putting both hands to her heart to feel it racing, shocked at the sight of the words scrawled on the page. After a minute or two she reached for the cup brimful of coffee, sipped, put it down, put her palms to her eyes, then when calm she pushed the hot cup and saucer back to the edge of the table.

She reopened the journal and turned the pages, with some degree of trepidation, foolishly hoping to see nothing but blank pages again, hoping it was a projection of her imagination, like a mirage or some such thing. But there it was again, a single line on one page. She took a deep breath and cautiously turned the page and drew back in horror. The next page was filled with writing, line upon line, from the top of the page to the bottom, the one sentence. Down to the end of the page. And the next page. Page after page. As if an unenlightened teacher had imposed hundreds of lines as punishment. Was this her handwriting? Scribbled in the dark in bed? In her sleep? She continued paging through her journal. Yes. There it was. Her secrets. And South Africa's.

She shut the journal and shoved it into the envelope. This journal must never be read. Not in her lifetime. Nor the other papers. South Africa's damnation. Neither must they be destroyed. She would donate all of it to some organisation; have it put away for safekeeping, for a hundred years, for another generation to read, in the cold light of day. She was addressing the envelope when Hajira stopped at her table.

'You ok, Pragashini? You look'...

'Like I've seen a doppelganger? As bad as back then?'

Hajira shook her head. 'Honestly! You're not serious.'

'I need a favour, Hajira. It means leaving the shop. I'll give you a handsome tip.'

'Don't be daft! I'm due a ciggie break,' Hajira said. 'Don't panic! I just hang around outside with the chimneys.'

'I'm the last one to talk. I need a chimney sweep. I need this taking to the post office.'

'No problem. Slide it onto the tray so they don't see it.' Hajira put the tray on the table and lifted the crockery. Pragashini put the journal into the jiffy bag, sealed it, then slid the jiffy bag onto the tray and put a twenty-pound note on it. Hajira covered the jiffy bag with the crockery. 'What's in it?' she asked.

'Your nightmare,' said Pragashini. While Hajira arranged to leave the shop she finished her coffee.

Half an hour later she looked around the coffee bar for Hajira. An hour later she went up to the counter to ask after her. The girls looked at each other blankly, apparently not recognising the name Hajira. They gave the excuse that they worked part time. The permanent staff would know. Pragashini walked round to the post office. Hajira was not there. She hurried home, bolted the doors and windows, and took refuge in her prayer room, waiting for the phone to ring.

***

111.

Pragashini huddled in her prayer room while it darkened. The telephone never rang. Instead, someone came hammering on the door, urging her to follow him. She unbolted the door and walked through the darkened streets of York to a condemned house.

She entered and stood poised in the doorway of an unfamiliar room scanning the faces of the people sitting on the floor in the gloom, each face uplifted, placid, in anticipation of some pleasure – expecting perhaps to tap into her repository of dreadful secrets.

Gandhiji was right. Truth is obstinate. The deeper you bury it the more it struggles to come up for air. Like the survival of the fittest, truth survives whatever the odds. Even at this ungodly hour, on the cusp between unholy Saturday and God forsaken Sunday, when it was hard to be certain about anything and a fatal time for anyone to be out, truth comes up for a breather. In the distance the wailing of high-pitched sirens signalled some unfortunate person's distress.

She shivered, not from the cold - she was acclimatised to frost, snow, and biting north winds, - but fearful of this meeting and its repercussions. She tucked one hand inside her overcoat, pulled the lapel tightly around her neck, and kept her hand there as if shielding herself from harm. Draped around her head and neck was the blue-green pashmini belonging to Fawzia.

Without the messenger telling her, she was afraid of what this meeting was about. He simply said 'Hajira' and she followed him fearing the girl was in danger. Awesome how a chance meeting can set in motion a series of events, the way an ovum fertilized by the sperm begins it's programmed division of cells.

As if a summons after midnight was not in itself chilling, when the soft-spoken messenger whose face she knew escorted her to this derelict house she trembled with hope that it would end happily. She felt heartened when she sensed, not anger, but disappointment, in the way the upturned faces, arranged in an ellipsis around the long room, avoided her eyes. They sat on the floor, women, men, youths, each face illumined by soft light from candles and paraffin lamps placed at arms length from their feet, with their bodies in shadow, so that they appeared like beautiful spirits floating in the gloom. And yes, to her they seemed utterly disappointed in her, she with her head covered in a blue green cowl, and her collar drawn up to her chin. No one smiled at her. They were all metamorphosed.

She, however, instigated this change in them. She was to blame for acting impetuously, from the heart. Brushing aside the consequences, she had stepped out of the circle of allies, to Heather's side when she should have stood shoulder to shoulder with them, her comrades. Why did she do it? After all what did she know of Heather's heart and soul?

Could she have done otherwise? Their concern was for the common good. Hers was just a natural human impulse. She thought only of Heather and her sanity. They would have too, if their loyalty to South Africa had wavered just one iota. While Heather, poor Heather, through no fault of her own would never come near to imagining what it meant to belong to this gathering of outsiders, or to be part of a liberation struggle, however much she might support them and campaign with them. Heather would never know what it meant to lose the trust of this gathering.

To these comrades and allies her decision to help Heather was a simple act of betrayal however much she did it out of anxiety for Heather. For this gathering, it was wrong. Now the sense that she let them down accounted for the mistrust she read in their eyes, mistrust they could ill afford, since they, even she, had few people they could trust in the European part of the global village. Every one of them was an exile or born to exiles from Asia or Africa.

In the flickering light she did not see Hajira, but she identified a man just from his hat, before she glimpsed the dark side of his face. Matatiele was here from South Africa. She was astonished and hurt. He dared not come in the days, the months, the years, when she needed his help, when he could not risk leaving South Africa and still hope to return to his wife and family. Now here he was. For what reason, she wondered?

His hat was deep grey felt with a wide black silk ribbon around it. It added to his rakish air. From force of habit, even though she was unsure of her reception, she threaded her way between the people on the floor to stand alongside him, waiting for him to notice her shoes and to look up at her. He was still the gentleman tall and thin and meticulous about his clothes. He remained her mentor in and out of exile, until the incidents that precipitated this summons: her secreting Heather first from the house in Port Elizabeth where Smuts lay in a fever, and then to the border.

It was his habit to greet her with a grin, a wink as if she had his tacit approval. They would exchange the comrade's handshake as if she were his comrade, while he laughed until his slight frame shook, because both knew she had not participated in the children's struggle in their homeland. Now while she stood there looking down at him, he held his back like a ramrod, seeming not merely a stranger to her but a hostile one, refusing to acknowledge her. His knobkierie lay below his knees with a hand gripping each end. He was poised to strike.

Even he had reached the point of no return with her. She wondered if his summons compelled her to this house or if he too had answered someone's command.

Pragashini could bear the loss of all their combined trust, but not this man's. Without him she was like a bat without its radar. She had no one to guide her. Her parents and family ceased being a part of her life years before. She trusted him. The politics of her country was too complex for a girl barely out of college and from exile to understand. Without his guidance she would land in the same mess she was in now, for that was exactly how she made her error of judgement. She acted precipitously without asking for his advice, knowing he would have stopped her. Yet even now she was glad she did what she did. She had to help Heather. She would do it again. Anyone would but those protecting South Africa's good name and reputation. Resigned to Matatiele's refusal to look at her, she sank cross-legged onto the floor, turning her head to steal a glance at his profile. There was no light at his feet. They were both engulfed in shadow.

***

112.

In the companionable quiet in the shadowy room, with each person engrossed in their private world, someone struck a match and the sound amplified in the silence. Across the space from where Pragashini sat a white hand reached out to touch the burning match to a candlewick that in its turn glowed red like an ember before the flame took hold.

For a second the two flames stood alongside each other, the candle flame tiny and struggling, the flame on the match grotesque and racing along the match to the fingertips of the hand that with several rough shakes killed the flame. Now the candle flame illuminated the pale gaunt face of Heather, her straw-coloured hair shining like a halo around her floating face.

Heather pushed the candle in its holder away from her feet keeping her gaze down, avoiding the eyes of the estranged couple sitting across from her. Then she entwined her fingers loosely as if she were praying, and fixed her eyes on her hands. This was where she wanted her father-in-law. Where she could watch the play of light on his face.

Without the threat to Pragashini he might never have left South Africa. She rejoiced. There is a God. He has heard my prayers. Here her father-in-law was unprotected. He had been drawn out of his hunting ground to where *he* was now the fish out of water, and she was in her element. Having him here was not enough for her. She wanted more.

When she and Smuts left England for South Africa before the elections, the exiles teased her playfully, every step of the way, from Heathrow to Jan Smuts to Verwoerd airport – for jotting down every little thing she saw. For everything was new. They delighted in her need to capture the name of every sun struck colour, every grotesque insect sound, every fruity fragrance she inhaled and stinking odour she turned her nose up at. She overflowed with passion for their country and its people, her husband's people, people he told her so much about, that sanctions, apartheids immorality act, and his political involvement, prevented her from visiting.

Now? After that time in South Africa, what had she become? Had she actually become anything? Even becoming is a process. Even death is a process. Even a stone can be acted on by wind and rain by erosion from its surface. She had become nothing. Therefore, she was less than a stone.

How simple and logical science can be. She carried a stone inside her. The dead weight of an unloving thing, heavy and cold, unmoving, like a child that died, dead in the womb, its mother alive, still waiting, breathing, living the days and weeks to deliver the dead child. This, however, was worse. She was a dead thing carrying a stone. She carried with her that burden.

113.

Heather was here. Even Heather refused to smile across the little space. Even Heather could not bring herself to give a little nod of reassurance. Even Heather rejected her. More like an apparition of Heather, though. Why? What was in her mind? Still, Heather she could forgive. She had to. She would even persuade this gathering to forgive her for whatever she might yet do, for there was no telling. Heather was capable of anything. Of everyone in this room, Heather was of this place, yet irreversibly changed. Perhaps if she disclosed everything to them, no holds barred as they say, she might redeem herself in their eyes, regain their trust, make a case for Heather, even if it meant betraying her own private dilemmas, her love for both Smuts and Klein, and her secrets.

But she was jumping the gun. She should wait to hear why they called her here. Still it rankled that even Heather had not greeted her. What did Heather's presence here mean? Did the Matatieles want their grandchildren to return home to South Africa? Heather would never allow that. Not now. Or were they attempting to reconcile her with Smuts? They would not succeed without Smuts. Was he here? Pragashini closed her eyes, attempting to let go of her troublesome thoughts breathing deeply, silently repeating her personal mantra. The stillness of meditation flowed through her.

***

114.

A buzz beginning near one of the doors swept like a swarm of bees across the room. Pragashini opened her eyes in time to see a man dressed in a long black coat, and sporting a black beret, like a Frenchman, walk in, pausing to greet individuals, stooping down to people, who clasped his hands, smiled, and watched his progress to the far end of the room with pleasure on their faces. Behind him, a handsome Alsatian dog padded, pausing when he paused, moving when he moved. The man greeted them in the glut of salutations they usually bandied about: 'Molo... Namaste... Salaam ... How's it? ... Before he turned, crossed his feet, and deposited himself elegantly in a cross-legged position on the floor.

She felt the chill of recognition, unlike that joyous first meeting. Someone placed a candle in front of the man and the flame lit up his face, his devilish eyes, and quirky smile. She cursed fate. Mossel Klein. In England. If she was afraid before, she was now petrified. Now she had no ally in the room. Her heart, already cold with her reception, filled with dread. He had not stopped to greet Matatiele. Was that good or bad? She had no way of knowing.

Her resolve to be truthful in her testimony was shaken. Her intuition warned that the other two men, she could not see in this room, Smuts and Nasaratt, might not be far away. The three men would do whatever the struggle demanded. They were obsessed with freedom, the rights of man. They stopped short of the rights of women. She looked about the room to see who stood at the doors should she need to escape. Smuts and Nasaratt might be lurking somewhere in the shadows of this dark house.

A house considered too dangerous for human habitation was placed on the council's list for demolition. The homeless, those on the run from immigration, the law, or from themselves, unable to afford the going rent for safe houses and desperate for a roof over their heads, were not in short supply. They were unperturbed by risks, from fire, leaking gas, explosion, the roof caving in, rats, disease or drug users. What more was there to risk when they risked their lives for democracy? Landlords turned blind eyes. If discovered the risk takers would simply be labelled squatters and bailiffs would happily evict them.

The house was dark. Flames threw grotesque shadows onto the walls. Little flames flickering in the darkness united them in conspiracy. This meeting was clandestine. She did not know what was on the agenda.

Klein began speaking, enticing them with a beguiling tone of voice and bewitching movements of his hands, introducing himself as a man of the people, an emissary from the struggle, sent here to do a job for his country. When prompted, he refused to give his name or the names of whoever sent him. 'Guess what?' he said, 'I won't even tell you my dog's name.' He turned and stroked the dog's head.

The Alsatian dog lay couchant at his back. 'No names,' he said, and the gathering smiled, and shifted about. 'No Names' was a brand name in South Africa. Then he reminded them about a series of fires that destroyed an ashram in Kwa Zulu Natal, an art gallery in Alice, a language centre at Rhodes University and part of a church at an undisclosed location. Four places that had little connection with each other.

To Pragashini it appeared some of the gathering did not know about the fires. It caused whispers. Heads came together. Hands were raised to mouths to conceal the movement of lips for those who could lip read.

'The ashram went up like a haystack,' said Klein. 'The art gallery – what can a person say? Canvas, paint, hardboard, wood, frames – ashes to ashes, dust to dust, what happens to a man, happens to his work. The third fire had itself a feast. Give a fire wall-to-wall books, what can a person expect? The language centre went up like bonfire night. The last fire was in some church somewhere. That fire made mince meat of family records. Baptisms, weddings, funerals. Jong! I tell you!

Fires don't discriminate!' He grinned, looking around at them.

There was not even a snigger. The gathering pursed their lips. They disapproved. Yet he was speaking as if he was from the grassroots, using their expressions. Pragashini understood their unease, their discomfort. Books were always at risk from the match, especially if the ideas were unacceptable to whoever held the matchbox. However, Klein's remark was too close to their experience. Even in exile, they experienced discrimination. Yet, it was memories of discrimination at home they were reminded of, where matches and matchboxes were at the ready during their various struggles.

'Sure,' Klein said. 'Stained glass windows, icons of this and that God, holy saints, canvas, wood carvings, paper, brick, wood etcetera, etcetera - everything damaged. Stuff like silk,' he continued, 'and waxed cloth - destroyed. Then there was stuff taken out of cases, waiting to be catalogued, papers sitting on tables waiting to be scanned. All went up in smoke.'

She knew the ashram. A simple structure. No show of riches. A world apart from the art gallery that housed both naïve and modern art that was in turn culturally distant from the language centre preserving the heritage of a minority group and possibly a majestic church situated in a country now freed from colonial ties. When the fires were reported in the press she waited with foreboding, while, fire fighters controlled and eventually extinguished the several blazes, while staff, students, clergy, and the public rescued artefacts from the flames. She waited for news that one of the fires had given up its secrets. Hers were buried at the Ashram. Nothing further was reported in the press. Months passed. The danger seemed past until Hajira disappeared with the documents she was to post.

Klein elaborated on how the fire fighters damped the fires. How the powers nosed around to see what sparked the fires while librarians and custodians checked scorched items, listed missing stuff. 'By a stroke of luck,' he said, 'people at the four places began working together to restore things. They compared notes. At each fire they found things they never knew they had.' He looked around the gathering to observe the impression his news had on his listeners. 'In the sand around the ashram there was a stone box, like soapstone - buried there. Lucky for us sand don't burn, what you say? The papers were safe.'

'There were a journal, a thesis, audiotapes, and typed transcripts of the tapes. At the heritage centre were transcripts, evidence given to some investigation. The museum of art and culture also had documents about some inquiry. We don't know what they found at the church. Y'all know churches obey their own laws. Churches don't cooperate with the laws of the land. Churches love secrets. This church was no exception.'

'Everyone thought them fires were sparked by drunken students,' he continued. 'Or it was overworked clerks, or watchmen watching football, or janitors sleeping on the job with girlfriends. They were wrong. Them fires wasn't provoked by carelessness. One fire all by it's lonesome, a person can call 'accidental'. But I ask you, four fires in four places and each place hiding documents about something we all don't know nowt about? And its got to do with our country? That's fishy. On top of all that when fires happen like this' - he snapped his fingers, 'one on top of the other, it's sabotage.'

She dreaded what was to come. Instead of burning her documents, the fires exposed them. Without the fires her documents written over the years, would have remained hidden from public scrutiny, and she would be spared this inquisition - what else could it become? Her journals she remembered with chilling fear. Reading it was unnerving. She could only hazard a guess about what secrets the other documents held. Heather's at the church perhaps? Mellikhaya? Mandisa's unwritten history of the struggle on tape. A plea - let my people go. At the language museum - Matatiele's unspoken question. At the university? She glanced across at Heather to see what effect the news had on her, but she sat poker faced studying her hands.

'You accusing her of starting the fires?' They pointed to Pragashini.

Klein craned his neck to look down the row of people. Then he stood up. The Alsatian dog followed suit. With the candle in his hand, he strutted between the two bulbous rows of people to where Pragashini and Matatiele sat while the Alsatian dog followed outside the perimeter of the group. Standing before Matatiele, he looked at Pragashini, sidestepped so that he was in front of her, then crouched down holding the candle up so that it he could peer into her face. She was gripped by that same paralysis that overcame her whenever he was near.

He whispered, 'Are you the one?'

She loved his voice. She once believed she loved him. But she had no respect for him. He was unprincipled, unscrupulous, protecting his name and reputation while making her the victim of gossip. It was the second time he posed that question. It plagued her the last time she saw him. He was not worth her consideration He could not measure up to the values she brought to her friendships. She ignored him.

***

115.

Klein stood up turned abruptly on his heel and walked back to his place in the candlelit room. 'If y'all came here to find out who sparked them fires y'all won't get no answers from me. Go ask the cops. That's their job. This is not about who started them fires. That's not why I'm here for.'

'Then I'm out of here,' someone said. Others agreed. There was some activity with people preparing to leave.

'Hang on!' he shouted, standing up to confront them. 'Don't y'all want to know why I called you here?'

They hung about, picking up their belongings, talking to each other, while he explained that the same names kept 'popping up' in the documents. When they pressed him to say if Pragashini's name was there, he reminded them, 'We said no names, remember?' They began leaving the room.

Until Matatiele's voice brought them to order. 'Cut the crap! Get to the point!' The movement and the chattering stopped. In the silence all eyes turned straight ahead as if he had reprimanded a class of students. Pragashini sat upright. Then Matatiele added – 'Comrade!' in a much quieter tone, as a kind of concession to Klein.

There was an explosion of laughter that sounded to her as if they were jeering Klein. He was no comrade. Unlike the exiles who absconded from their homelands each with their country's equivalent of a packet of biltong[109] and a tin of zambuck[110], Klein was like an overseas student who jetted from home with leather suitcases and stocked up on winter woollies from Jaeger. The room settled down.

'What you want from Pragashini?' asked Matatiele. What

---

109 Biltong is a thin strip of sun-dried meat, beef, venison, ostrich or other game. Unique to SA. First made by Afrikaners.

110 Zambuck is an ointment sold in a small green tin.

about the other one? What's she here for?' With an inclination of his head Matatiele indicated Heather. Klein looked down the line to where Heather sat. 'You ask her. She's *your* family,' he said.

Matatiele ignored his advice. 'How come you bring women here at this time of night?'

'They've got nowt to fear from us,' Klein said.

'You think if the law walked in here they'll take off their shoes and make namaas with us?'

Pragashini recognised Fawzia's voice. Fawzia was standing, and beside her Hajira was tugging at her coat urging her to sit down. Although they were doing nothing wrong, the threat of a police raid unsettled Pragashini. It reminded her of the South African police, how powerless she had been, and the varying roles they played towards different ethnic groups. 'Am I on trial for my country, I wonder?' she wanted to ask, but held her tongue.

'No disrespect intended, ma'am,' said Klein, 'your friend's got nothing to fear if she tells us the truth.'

'She can lie if she feels like it!' Matatiele said, 'You can do niks to her. Our laws don't apply here.'

'She must come home,' Klein said. 'Those people won't let us read the documents. She must answer to the people. Tell us how she got them. Why she took them out. We need the truth. No secrets. No hidden agendas.'

'There's an old Chinese saying, 'truth defends itself. Lies need armies. Whatever's in those documents don't need the likes of you to protect it, if it's the truth,' said Matatiele.'

'Let her tell the truth, then, so the people can judge her.'

'If it's the truth you're after,' said Matatiele, 'why not go around the room and each one tell some truths. You begin,' he said to Klein. 'Tell them who you are.'

'I've got strict orders - no names,' said Klein.

'Governments don't spend money on little girls diaries.

You won't make head or tail of her thesis. Tell the truth. Then you might get the truth from her.'

'There's one document we'll give our eye teeth for.'

'Enkosi[111]. What's in the document?'

Klein turned to the dog and ruffled its collar.

'Let's play a guessing game, comrade. You nod if I guess right. Is it to do with corruption?' Matatiele asked. 'Or the gravy train? Is it proof some hotshot politician authorised government money to spend on his girlfriend's birthday party? Does it show how someone used the Public Service code to arrange BMW's for managers who don't rock the boat in his department? Is it the inside story on how civil servants are promoted? How they calculate annual increments? Is it evidence that the gravy train exists?'

Klein neither agreed nor disagreed. He played with the dog. Matatiele pleaded, 'Just give me one more chance. Is this document a list of names? Comrades working with the secret police? Comrades in bed with apartheid?'

The gathering turned furiously on Matatiele. They pulled him to his feet. The elders scrambled to their feet using their sticks to beat the attackers. Above the din Matatiele shouted, 'If you want a list of names. Give us your name. All of you know my name,' Matatiele continued. 'I'm Matatiele. If you don't know her name, she's Pragashini,' he said, turning to look at her. It was the first time he looked at her since she came in and sat beside him. His glance was too quick for her to gauge any change in his mood towards her. He continued, 'So stop effing about. Eff no names. Say your name, then speak. That's how we conduct meetings.'

'Let him go,' shouted Klein.

They released Matatiele. After dusting off his clothes and straightening his collar and tie, he refused to sit. He stood

---

111 Enkosi means Thank you.

tall and angry in the condemned house.

'No disrespect, Sir,' said Klein. 'To get back to the point of this meeting, the documents were kept off the inventories on purpose, Sir, and the fires were meant to destroy the documents.'

'That's obvious. So?'

'Don't you want to know how come these documents are not listed on the inventories?' asked Klein. 'When they belong to us? Who hid them in those places? If they're not listed, no one knows they're there. Anyone can take them out of South Africa and no one will miss them. Okay, it is a list of names. Collaborators with apartheid. We want those names. We caught that young girl' – he pointed to Hajira – 'Too late. She posted a big packet. She won't tell us who she posted it to. We've been keeping an eye on Pragashini. That's how come we think she's the one.'

***

116.

Heather observed the brief interchange between her father-in-law and Pragashini. The events of the past weeks left her feeling detached from her surroundings with a barrier between them and her as if she were back in the laboratory observing a newly discovered life form under the microscope. It hurt her to see them avoid meeting her eyes.

What had she done? Nothing unlawful, nothing criminal, or immoral. Yet, the way they shunned her, anyone would think *she* was the miscreant. They once accepted her into their family, now her father-in-law sat like a paramount chief protecting Pragashini, when he should be caring and supporting her. It might be a clever ploy on his part, for he was shrewd, this show of shielding Pragashini. It drew attention from his involvement in the affair. She did not trust him.

Would he have come to Europe if Pragashini were not under suspicion? Like hell, no. Pragashini was the bait to bring him here. The ties that bound both Matatiele men to the girl were strong, something she only came to understand when Smuts cried out in delirium for her. The old man knew about them. That made him forget his duty to her, his daughter-in-law. He was careless of her state of mind. In his anxiety for Pragashini, he forgot the crisis was hers, more than anyone else's. It was her heart, wrenched from her body, cut up like a dissected specimen to expose bloody ventricles and auricles. It was her loss. She wanted to hear him speak openly and honestly about what he knew, although in her heart she believed she already knew.

To confound matters, his strategy was working. The party faithful, friends, the hoi polloi from the street poking their heads through the windows and the doors, all warmed to his sincerity and his status in the whole affair. It was after all his family crisis too. Her loss was his. His son married her. She traipsed like a simpleton into their maelstrom and eagerly accepted and adopted their habits in her effort to adapt to Africa. Now they disowned her.

Still in shock from the events of the past weeks, she felt stunned by their rejection of her. She had to make a last ditch effort to rescue herself from the edge. Her mother came to mind. Her mother's indefatigable energy, her mother taking on causes that were not her own. Sanctions against some far off country; freedom for remote political prisoners; letters of support to the imprisoned; money to destitute wives and children; all causes that Heather grew up to accept as part and parcel of life in the free world; now surely it should give her the edge on all of them in the room.

They were experts in campaigning for their own causes. Which of them had made a plea for someone unconnected to them, someone on the other side of their world? That was why they shunned her. They could not empathise with her. They only saw the problem she created with her westerner's lack of understanding of their worldview.

Looking at her, they would not know that there was a remnant of fight still in her. She knew she resembled a wraith. Nevertheless, her spirit stirred the minute she heard her father-in-law speak. There was a doggerel the Catholic nuns made them chant each morning in assembly – Veritas vos Liberabit - the truth will set us free. It was imperative that she hears the truth – or lose her mind. They would not sleep at night until the truth was out. She would do nothing to them. There would be no prosecution, no retaliation, nothing, no revenge. After all, it was their customs. Their beliefs. Their evil they had to come to grips with. Who was she to cast the first stone? God knows her church had its turn of terror and killing. All she wanted was to hear the truth of what happened. Then she would let them and their people go.

***

117.

Klein invited them to question Pragashini. They jumped to the fray, shouting questions at her, from all sides of the room: about her place of birth, her parents, her loyalties, citizenship, if she were a spy, the documents, why she left South Africa, had she renounced citizenship, if she wanted to destroy their democracy. She listened without answering. Her silence aggravated them. They disliked non-cooperation. It hinted of Gandhi whom they mistook for a pacifist because they misunderstood him. They murmured. When they exhausted their questions, Klein again asked 'Are you the one?' and she was unsure if he was referring to his old question, or to the secret documents.

Then Matatiele raised his voice. 'I've known her since she was so high,' he said. 'A little piccanin[112],' he used his hand to indicate how small she was... 'She used to have strange dreams. It made her strange. Like someone whose got second sight. Born with the helm[113]. She's a child of two worlds.' He told them about her recurring dream. 'That's how come she got mixed up with,' his voice faltered. He made a dismissive gesture in Heather's direction, unable or unwilling to say her name. The expression on his face said it all.

Pragashini thought perhaps he concluded that Heather coming into their family brought about this crisis. 'Prags hasn't got a bad bone in her body. She's always on the lookout to help somebody. One night she was in one of your big cities. She sees a man in a wheelchair looking lonely, turning the wheels on his chair, in the dark, waiting to cross the road. You know what she did? She pushed him across the street. The cars would have knocked him over. He was going to some supermarket. She pushed him all the way in the dark, up and down dark narrow streets. You know an Asian woman will do that? At night. Anywhere in the world, never mind in this country? Coming from South Africa as well. For a White man! Look at her. She's no traitor to South Africa. She's an African. She has the soul of Africa in her. She isn't claiming to be African. I'm telling you she is

112 A piccanin is a small child.

113 The helm is the amniotic membrane that sometimes clings to the newborn infants face. In English the caul.

African. Ubuntu[114]. She is one of us.'

It made her feel a surge of gratitude. He had forgiven her. She made as if to rise believing she could leave with his consent. But he placed a hand on her shoulder and restrained her. It was his family's crisis. But others were dabbling in the affair, elders, and tearful women, hot under the collar young people, and the raging street because it was now a question of their national importance. The documents would embarrass the nation.

'Can't she speak for herself?' asked Klein.

In reply, Matatiele glanced quickly at Pragashini for her permission. Then he put his hands up to her face and tipped the hood off her head onto her shoulders. He snatched a candle and held it up to her face. 'Look at her,' he said. 'She looks unnaturally plain and unadorned for an Indian girlie, what you say?' he said. 'No lipstick. Kohl. Earrings. Nose ring. Bangles. Gold. Silver. She's not even sporting a red dot, never mind a wedding ring. Take a good look at her head. Where's her black hair. I knew her when she had long, long hair. It's shaved like she's a released prisoner from Pollsmoor. You know the place. Where South Africa loves to imprison Black women. You look shocked! Is this a shock to you? It can't be. Some of you know her,' he said, 'but which of you know why her head is shaved? Why she refuses to speak to us who failed her? Hands up who knows!' Then he swung the candle away from Pragashini and pushed it in Heather's face. 'Do you know, madam? Will you tell them what's your name?'

With all eyes on her, Heather shrank into the darkness. They waited. She had no answers. She could think of

---

114 uBuntu is the shortened form of uMuntu nGumuntu nGamuntu. It means I am a person through other people. My humanity if tied to yours. I owe my being to the people around me.

nothing but the manner in which he addressed her, her father in law. Referring to her as 'madam'. It held all the connotations connected with apartheid and white supremacy. It showed such hatred of her. His hatred of her. She did not deserve that. She hated him for that.

***

118.

Pragashini was vigilant, her intuition never diminishing that Matatiele expected someone to walk through the door.

In a light mood Matatiele said, 'Comrade No-Name, to me you sound like a man who's in love with the sound of his own voice. If you're so keen to get this girlie to talk, why don't you sing us your little song? Don't be backward in coming forward. You want honesty from Pragashini? Set a good example. Tell all of them who the bladdy hell you are!'

'With respect Sir, you know more than these others. I'm a man without a name.' said Klein.

'How about that name on your ID comrade? Share it with us.'

'You know full well that name don't mean a thing, Sir!'

'Well then, we must say totsiens[115] to you and you can say totsiens to those documents you want to get your hands on.'

He extended his hand to Pragashini and pulled her to her feet. In a body the members of his clan stood up. They moved in a group towards the door while the gathering began singing, softly, the way the workers sing when they protest on the shop floor. Klein left his place, came up behind Matatiele and touched his shoulder. Instinctively, the old man swung round with his knobkierie raised to strike a blow.

---

115 Totsiens means goodbye.

Klein pulled back, raising both hands to shield his face. The dog, leapt from where it was, into the air and plunged its teeth into Matatiele's wrist. His knobkierie clattered to the floor while he struggled with the dog and the clan members clawed and beat the dog from all sides. It was only the touch of Klein's hands on the dog's jaws, his soft words while prizing its jaws apart that persuaded the dog to relinquish its grip. Pacified, the dog stood by his side its fur smelling of heat.

Klein said, 'Relax,' to the Matatiele clan. 'Come. Sit.' The clan looked questioningly at Matatiele. When he gave a slight nod, all of them turned and with Pragashini in their midst, went back to where they had been sitting.

Something in the looks the clan exchanged made her suspect they had not intended leaving at that moment; someone they expected was running late. Who were they expecting? Smuts? Was he cured? Heather might be soothed were Smuts to come. It might speak for his innocence. Then again, would it? It might, were he to refuse to return to South Africa with his father and remain with her.

Or were they waiting for Nasaratt? They could not hope to trap him. He was elusive. Would the list of names draw someone here? What could they do here? Without knowing what they could do she wished there was some way for Nasaratt to be caught by this crowd, to feel powerless, to be imprisoned here in England. But there were drawbacks to his imprisonment.

They sat down as before. The only difference now was that the Alsatian dog patrolled the room, padding behind their backs, stopping every now and then to be patted by its master who began telling the gathering about himself.

'Hey, who knows, the next person to come through that door may be our collaborator, looking for that document. What you say, while we wait, I give you my spiel. I'm called

Mossel Klein,' he said. 'Called, not baptised or anything,' he added. 'Y'all know exiles give themselves place names to protect families back home. So saying, Mossel Klein isn't my name. Even so, I'm an exile with a twist. I can't remember my name. It's buried somewhere in my memory. If someone was to hypnotise me it were sure to come to the surface. For the present it's lost. You see, I was indoctrinated to forget my name. I was indoctrinated in my own country. South Africa! What a country to belong to! Mense![116]'

She could sense the interest in the room. She suspected Matatiele knew what was coming next. Listening to Klein, she warmed to his voice. She fell under his spell. It seemed he also had the sympathy of the gathering.

'Even my indoctrination was twisted,' Klein said, 'like that old sixpence in the one and only English rhyme my oupa knew. You see mine was an indoctrination of love. My own oupa and ouma indoctrinated me. South Africa! Hêre![117] How evil can a country make it's people?'

His voice was hypnotic. She was free to watch him, to look at his face played on by the flickering candle flame. She listened, wondering how much of what he said was true.

'Exiles have a bad habit,' he went on, 'we look for names when we run away from home. We adopt place names when we chuck ours away.' Then he laughed. 'We're heroes outside South Africa. A false name gives us mystery. It's really so we can confuse Special Branch. Y'all know Special Branch is also in exile. The donders![118] They're like diplomats. They're immune from prosecution. They're state terrorists. Your flea market terrorist has no privileges. State

---

116 Mense means people. It is used as an interjection.

117 Hêre means God. It is used as an interjection. It's pronounced 'hear-re' spelt with a cap on the first 'e'.

118 Donder means thunder but is used as an expletive.

terrorists can come and go, burgle, raid, plant bombs, kill or maim, no questions asked. For South African exiles there's no safe houses.'

Pragashini shivered again. Klein would certainly be courting trouble if someone here was an informer.

'So I also used place names. Y'all know Mossel Bay and Klein Karroo. Relax! My family isn't from there. If I hear a man's name, I can tell if the poor 'rooker'[119] is an escapee or a tourist. 'Mossel Klein' has a nice ring to it, don't you think? Some people would know the connection and be thrown off the track. My oupa gave me that name. Back then when I was a barefoot boy, a kaalvoet[120] klonkie[121] as we say running around on a plaas[122]; going to a plaas school; learning stuff by heart; sukkeling[123] to read and write, how I struggled; at ten going to boarding school. Then one day they came to fetch me, my oupa and ouma in their bakkie[124]. They pulled me out of school and took me to their plaas. After that I never saw my ma and pa.'

'Then my own oupa and ouma told me my name is Mossel Klein. They played a game with me pretending to be startled whenever I said my regte naam[125]. Even while the old couple was persuading me 'Mossel Klein is your real name', I repeated my own name, the name they knew me by. When they said I was making a mistake; when they said I was

---

119 A rooker is someone who smokes daggha.

120 Kaalvoet means barefoot

121 Klonkie used to mean a Coloured youth, but is used for any youth.

122 A plaas is a farm.

123 Sukkeling means struggling.

124 A bakkie is a truck that is uncovered at the back.

125 Regte naam means correct name.

deurmekaar[126] when they asked me to tell them why they would lie to me; when they said that they weren't mistaken; they knew who I was; even then, I remembered my real name and rejected the name Mossel Klein. A stupid made up name. Hey, mense! South Africa was a snaakse[127] place.'

'Sometimes they lost patience with me. They wanted me to promise I would forget my real name. I couldn't believe that anyone forgets his name. I thought I could never forget my name. They refused to call me by my real name, but I promised myself I would never forget it. I could never. How could I? It would mean forgetting my ma and pa. I wrote my name down in books, on scraps of paper, on the walls, behind the door in the lavatory. They found my name and painted over it, tore it up, washed it away. They gave their bible to the church. It contained our family tree in beautiful writing on the front pages. They bought a new bible and wrote the name 'Mossel Klein' on the family page.'

'I was a child. I was scared something would happen to me if I forgot my name. My bedtime prayer was my name repeated every night and every morning on the way to plaas school. I said my name like I was saying the times tables.'

'It weren't easy. There were times when I gave myself a headache sukkeling hard to remember. I was scared the old couple would have me in their power if I forgot. Sometimes I was scared of them for wanting me to be Mossel Klein. They never told me why I must forget my name. Maybe they were scared I might let it slip, since I was still a child.'

'I lost the struggle. I became deurmekaar. I began to doubt myself. I had no reason to mistrust my oupa and ouma. They loved me. They took care of me: she sang to me; she told me stories; she held my hand at night when I was

---

126 Deurmekaar means to be confused.

127 Snaakse means strange.

scared; he taught me how to fish and hunt with a real rifle. They gave me Bogart's mother as a pup.' He put his arm around the dog's neck. 'Later when I remembered my real name, I was overcome with doubt that it was my name, and had to stop and ask if I weren't making a mistake.'

'It grew worse as I grew older. Their indoctrination was that good. I didn't know it was indoctrination until I grew older.'

'Then I knew it was coming from love. As I grew older, so did they. In the end, they became deurmekaar. They turned to me to remind them of little things they had forgotten. They forgot where they put things. They forgot to do things. They forgot where they were. They forgot the way home to the plaas. Finally, they forgot who I was. They could not remember me. The name Mossel Klein didn't ring a bell. They didn't know a Mossel Klein. They'd forgotten my real name. I'm one of those children who grew up never understanding what was happening in my country. So you see - I am a man without a name. I take my hat off to South Africa.'

'Crawling out, from a control freak country like South Africa, would give anyone a kick if they can get away with changing identities. The loss of my name, my parents, my identity, affected me. I learned a name has no value. I place no value on a name. A name is no guarantee of identity. I have no past, no present, no future.' When he finished, he said, 'Fluit, fluit, my stories uit.[128]'

The gathering sat in silence when Klein finished. Then the room hummed with their voices. Pragashini could see their fascination with Klein from the vitality on their faces. They were sympathetic to him. She believed she now understood her connection with him. She did not answer to her name. She did not recognise her name when it was called.

---

128 Fluit, fluit, my stories uit, means my story is over.

119.

Matatiele was like a hunter who has cornered his prey, wounded it, watches it bleeding and vulnerable, bides his time waiting to move in for the kill. He was ruthless.

'You left out one little 'stukkie' of information,' said Matatiele.

'Feel free,' said Klein.

'What did you find out about your ma and pa?' asked Matatiele.

'Niks,' Klein said with a shrug.

'You're telling me you've been jolling[129] overseas with freedom of information buzzing in the air all around you, and you haven't found out if your ma and pa are part of our struggle? Or maybe you found out they worked for apartheid and you washed your hands of them?'

'I know niks about them. I still don't know their names.'

'Shame! Not even what happened to them?'

'Not even if they're dead or alive,' Klein made a helpless gesture with his hands. 'Y'all think they're on your list of collaborators? Why don't y'all tell me?' he asked. 'Who's to say you weren't a collaborator, Sir?'

'You didn't find anything about your ma?'

'I told you. Niks.'

'Pity. Your ma could have told you who is a collaborator and who isn't. She could vouch for me. You should have asked her. Shame, it's too late now. She knew all the names on the list. If you knew her you could have asked her.'

'You knew both of them? Are they dead or alive?'

'Too bad they're both dead now. That's why it's hard to say for sure whose side you're on. Knowing what I know about them.'

---

129 To joll means to play around, to have fun.

'If their name's on that list, or mine, y'all must show it to me. I've got people who can vouch for me.'

'You didn't come to that braai. Pity I didn't know who she was then.'

'What braai?'

You weren't there. Even if you were, you wouldn't recognise her. After the elections. We went to Newton Park or Walmer. An English lady.'

'There were hundreds of braais.'

'She was playing piano at her braai. Astrid Roebuck.'

'I've heard about her. That woman's no ma of mine. She's from England. My ma and pa were South Africans.'

'That's what she told everybody. She wanted people to think she was a sweet old English lady. She acted so well. She was no English lady. She was Muslim. One of us. She had to hide from Special Branch when your pa disappeared.'

'Who says she's my ma?'

'Take my word for it.'

'What was she hiding for? They say she was harmless.'

'She was a good actor. She even got her voice right. She acted so well, you were all taken in. Like all of us. Even me. You didn't recognise anything about her? Your own mother? Well you say you never saw her. You were a small piccanin when your pa disappeared. Your ma was no Catholic.'

'Was my pa also in the struggle? I didn't know whose side they were on.'

'I suppose you can call it a struggle. One person can't struggle. There's got to be someone to struggle against.'

'You mean he was not in the struggle? How did he die?'

'I don't know. He was not one of us. He was one of them. He worked for Special Branch. You know how your ma died. In the struggle we called your ma Amina. In those days people married across the colour bar. You can be proud of her. She took risks. Because she was married to your pa, she got herself a job right in the heart of Special Branch. In Sanlam's Building, she was listening on the switchboard, opening their letters, typing letters for them, and passing information to us. That's how we got to know their methods inside that building.'

He turned to Pragashini. 'The only one who knew Amina's secret was your mother-in-law, Pragashini. Nalini kept her secret. I didn't recognise Amina that night we had dinner with the Nasaratts. Remember? I warned everyone the collaborator was sitting with us at the table. Ramgopal didn't like what I said. If I had recognised Amina Khan, I wouldn't have said that. She knew who was a collaborator, who wasn't. The comrades told me after she was murdered. Not even Ramgopal knew the truth.'

***

120.

In that stillness, in the hush that descended on the room, were undertones of uneasiness and suspicions that made it difficult to determine which of the two men it favoured. Pragashini was horrified that Klein was told in a cold, callous manner that it was his mother who was brutally murdered. She glanced furtively at Matatiele. Having witnessed his cold treatment of Heather, now his harsh revelation to Klein, he seemed a stranger to her.

Was this what apartheid did to people? Did it do this to him? She turned her gaze to Klein. He was staring fixedly at the ground showing no interest in his surroundings. He was not the same man who came jauntily into the room earlier that night, his manner flippant, even arrogant. Now he sat rigidly with one arm slung around the neck of the Alsatian dog his gaze focussed on the candle flame as if he were meditating, his thoughts somewhere else. The longer he remained motionless the more she looked around the room for someone to go to him. No one moved.

Then she rose from her place and treaded her way between the lighted candles to where he sat. She stooped over him, took his hand, felt its coldness, and asked, 'Are you okay?'

He was startled to see her. She repeated the question. Not knowing what else to say to him she squatted on her haunches, her face level with his, while he continued staring into her face as if looking right through her. 'I'm sorry,' she said. He opened his eyes wide, uncomprehendingly. She added, 'For everything. Your mother's death. The way he told you. And everything else.' He removed his arm from around the Alsatian dog and clasped both her hands in his without saying anything. 'I'm the one,' she confessed, knowing he would understand she was the one who wrote the anonymous letters to him, but unwilling to explain about the gossip and how the Nasaratt family ostracized her. 'I know,' he said. 'If I didn't know, why would I come and ask you? I've felt you calling me.' He kissed the palm of one hand and then her scarred palm.

***

121.

Matatiele called the meeting to order. 'Mossel Klein,' he called. 'I've got Pragashini's documents. What you say, we do a swap?'

'No, we want to take her home with us,' the gathering was laughing now. 'Maybe we'll even take her to a Sangoma. She can tell him about her dreams,' they said. 'Maybe someone came to her in a dream and told her what to do. Like that princess.' They laughed, narrating to Fawzia and Hajira and others the legend about the young African girl[130] who dreamt that if the Xhosa slaughtered all their cattle, then the dead souls of soldiers would reincarnate and defeat the European colonisers. While Klein sat with Pragashini the people chanted, 'Tell us your dreams, Pragashini,' the rule about no names finally discarded.

Listening to Klein's story and observing the effect on him of Matatiele's revelation about Amina Khan, Pragashini had forgotten about Heather. Suddenly Heather stood up and raised a strident voice above the babble.

'You're wasting your time! Pragashini won't tell you a thing. I worked in the same lab. I sat next to her, eight hours a day, Monday to Friday. She never talked to me. She never told me a thing. Not even what she was researching. If you ask me, she won't speak about the weather even in confession. That's how good a spy she is. She knows how to keep secrets. You may have to hold a gun to her head to get a whisper out of her.'

Matatiele turned to Pragashini. She appeared about to cry. He remembered her when she was a child at school with long hair, when she had used forbidden vibrant red lipsticks. When his son had loved her and she returned his love. She was lost to Smuts because of Smuts infidelities. If Smuts had the strength of will that she had they would be together in a free South Africa.

'Why must Pragashini trust you, madam?' He shouted up at Heather who stood in the room, having lost her momentum, overcome by the attention focussed on her. 'Why should any of us trust you? *You* don't trust us do you, madam? Isn't Pragashini the one who helped you? Why are you biting her hand?'

'I'll tell you why. Because I'm not the one under suspicion

---

130 The Xhosa maiden was Nongqawuse.

here. You and she are, ' said Heather.

'You should be under suspicion, madam,' said Matatiele. 'You've got more reason to bring papers out of South Africa, than she has, madam. She could've told you about Smuts, but she wanted to spare your heart.'

'There he goes again', Heather said, 'addressing me as if I'm a White South African woman, spoilt by maids doing housework for me. I hate him calling me madam. Tell him to stop. What did I ever do to him? I only hold him accountable for his son's infidelity. He is accountable. He could have stopped his son. Is it because he suffered under Whites that he refuses to accept me? Should I blame apartheid? I don't think so. I shouldn't have to blame apartheid for how he behaves towards me. I'm sure in his heart he wishes he could lay his hands on me, but he dare not,' and turning to Matatiele, Heather said, 'I dare you!'

For the first time since coming to the condemned house, Pragashini felt impelled to intervene. She stood up and Klein rose with her. 'Heather,' she said, 'I hear what you say. I feel for you. I know what's troubling you. I promise you, you're mistaken about me.'

'Am I?'

'This inquiry about missing documents is nothing,' Pragashini said. 'There were other inquiries. About smaller issues. Money misappropriated. Cases of wine stolen. Vehicles misused. Workers sleeping on the job. Ghost workers drawing salaries. Nothing like what happened to you. People collected the evidence on tapes. They transcribed the hearings. They handed it out to all and sundry to read. When each inquiry dispersed they left papers lying around the place. All I did was bundle my papers and leave the country. What I couldn't carry, I burnt. On the face of it, this inquiry is about a minor crisis. It's a question of betrayal. All of you came here believing I have sensitive documents about South Africa. What are documents compared with people? This woman, Heather, tell them Heather. What's more important? Her tragedy? Or your documents? She wants to question us here, where British people marched on South Africa's behalf. That's her right. She feels safer in England. I don't blame her. Aren't women at risk in South Africa? All women? All races. Young, old, and even children.' Then turning to Heather, she said, 'I ask you, what can I possibly know about your tragedy? I know who collaborated with South Africa. I know who apartheid assassinated. I know who apartheid plans to assassinate. But I don't know anything else. So don't accuse me, Heather. Don't put me on trial for my country. Don't speak to me as if I've betrayed you. If it were not for me you'd still be in South Africa with your children. I betrayed my lifetime comrades to help you. You're in shock. You're in mourning. You've been betrayed. By Smuts, not by me. But I forgive you.' She sat down. Klein put his arm around her shoulder. She shrugged off his arm.

Heather did a slow hand clap. 'I'm in my country,' she said. 'You're right. In my country I'm protected. In your country, women are nothing. Children are victims. Old people are victims. The vulnerable are victims. You South Africans, you do nothing about it. You don't even talk about it. Tell me what you do to your victims! I want to hear with these ears, how your doctors kill little children. How they cut them. What they do with the blood.'

'That's sick talk,' said Matatiele. 'There are millions of people in our country. Millions of people didn't kidnap one child. Millions of people are not guilty of what you're accusing us. We're making changes,' said Matatiele. 'South Africa can't change overnight. It's a question of power. We have people who still believe in the power of witchcraft and muti. There are people who think they are superior because they don't believe in witchcraft. But they believe in the power of tradition and customs. Look at what happened to Pragashini. We can't promise it will never happen again. People who know Pragashini know why she shaved her head. We know why she wears the veil pretending to be Muslim, why she refuses to speak to those of us who didn't help her. Our government and the trade unions promised to make changes to our Constitution. They're busy working on a clause for women. Divorce. Maintenance. Traditional Marriage. Marriage Age. Lobola. Rape. Wages. Everything women want will be in that clause.'

'You didn't mention muti!' Heather shouted. 'That evil thing. Will the constitution ban muti? Using hair and nails and blood to terrify your enemies until they waste away and die. Like Smuts, a healthy man, wasting away. Dying from fear. What about bewitching your enemies when you can't fight man to man, fair and square?'

'Mellikhaya was killed. Apartheid did that. Smuts is ill. My clan never did such a thing. My grandchild is missing. My clan would never do such a thing.'

'What about using innocent children's body parts for making muti? Never mind your sons. Never mind your grandchild. It's *my* child. What about *my* child? What do you know about that? What about using *my* child to cure *your* child?'

The words were hardly out of her mouth when Matatiele threw himself across the room at her, onto the burning candles.

***

122.

In the condemned house, even members of the clan pulled Matatiele away from Heather. She had not shielded herself.

When they stood facing each other again Heather expecting an answer, Matatiele affronted by the accusation, Pragashini could not choose between the two. It would be so simple for Matatiele to reassure Heather, the way he reassured her. What was wrong that he could not feel for her? Heather lost momentum. She might become hysterical just listening to what he had to say. Whatever his motive his actions were dismissive of her and all she said. His reaching out to Heather across the darkened space had been violent. Now he behaved as if she had not spoken. Heather had peeled layers of herself exposing her vulnerability. Matatiele's response frightened Pragashini. At that moment had she wanted to speak, she would have choked.

'You ask him Pragashini! He won't tell me. I must know if they're implicated. My child is missing. Presumed dead. His body not found. My husband is bewitched. Calling your name Pragashini. His mistress is pregnant. Did they know he had a mistress? Did she steal my child? What did these Matatiele's do to my child? What happened when the women left my home? Who proposed that my son be used? What reasons did they give? Who made the decision? Was it you old man who gave the order for my son to be abducted? Who said when he should be killed? Pragashini can you blame me for trying to escape with my children before anything happened to them? I'm angry with you, Pragashini because you never told me you knew Smuts. I'll forgive you, if you ask. But I'm asking him – this Matatiele – to tell me – did he and the elders of his clan steal my child?' she asked.

In her heart Pragashini whispered, 'Shukriya Bhagvan, that we can't read each other's minds. I don't want to know what is in Heather's mind. Or Matatiele's. How terrifying if we could just look at someone and read their minds. Think of what the state would do if it could read our minds. That is the only barrier science has not crossed. Science broke the sound barrier. Men can travel faster than the speed of light. Men overcame the force of gravity and explored space. The mind, however, remains our one safeguard.

Science may overpower the mind with hallucinatory drugs, or use hypnotism to tap into it, but the frontier of each mind cannot be invaded at will at any moment of the day or night. It was something to be grateful for, to preserve one's integrity, that one could keep one's thoughts secret.

My thoughts that the Matatiele's would do anything to save Smuts now that Mellikhaya is dead, was not a beautiful thought. My thoughts that the families of exiles love us more than they can ever love our children because they do not know them, was not a beautiful thought. The beautiful ones are not yet born.

'Ja, madam, you hate our witchcraft,' Matatiele shouted. 'but you're not against hypnosis. White mans hocus-pocus!'

It seemed to her Heather craved details about her child and about Smuts. Above all else she wanted to hear Matatiele's account, his confession. So it seemed did the gathering. But Matatiele had made his mind up. 'The more you give, the more they want,' he said to Pragashini. He stood up, and with a hand extended pulled her from the floor and manoeuvred her towards the door. He struggled to control his agitation.

The assembly murmured. Someone began singing a song from the protest marches. Others joined in. They began a slow hypnotic handclap. Pragashini hesitated. She whispered, 'Do it,' she said. 'Tell them everything. I'll even let them hypnotise me. Where's the harm? It will give her peace of mind.'

'Don't throw it away, everything I taught you!' he said.

'It may help.'

'Didn't you say that before? It might help you. Hypnosis brings memories. You don't understand your experience.

Will they be satisfied? No! People are greedy when it comes to listening in on someone else's troubles. They're never satisfied. They won't stop questioning you until you've told them more than they need to know.'

'Look at her,' she said, with a movement of her head she looked at Heather.

'She wants them to put a gun to your head!' he said. 'She won't stop there. It'll be my head next.'

'You blame her? Look at her. She needs someone to pull her back from the edge.'

'You owe her niks.'

'Don't you wonder what's going on in her head? Where's your heart? Because Mellikhaya is dead, Smuts is ill, and' ... She could not bear to think about his final tragedy. His tactics were now at odds with the person she knew. Yet his hostility and antagonism to Klein and Heather she might never comprehend.

'She's not worrying a damn about you, that's for sure,' he said. 'You'll get no justice here. Not even sympathy. I've seen these kangaroo courts. I trust no one. I suspect Klein might hand the documents to his minders, whoever they are. They will sweep the names under the carpet, never mind all this talk of transparency. Another imported word for their democracy. I want to publish the document. The Dispatch might do it. Where Biko worked.'

'Kangaroo courts. Rough justice. It's one and the same.'

'You don't mind the devil hearing what you say under hypnosis?'

'They can make what they want of it,' she said. 'I've given up on our country. I'm never going back. Rape is one thing. It's worldwide. Murder too. But muti? Children used to make muti. And not a single law to stop it, or punish it. People from the top to the bottom fear it. I give up.'

'So soon? You're not a fool. Only fools think our struggle's over. The struggle goes on. But not here. Our struggle belongs at home.'

'But she belongs here. She's your family. Look at her. It's her child missing. Was her child used for muti? She believes that. She believes all of you are involved. That's why she's here. She wants you to own up.'

'Ikona! She's here because she thinks Smuts will come over. She wants him here where she can control him.'

She shrugged. 'She's forgotten Smuts. She won't cry if Smuts dies. She's grieving for her child. Look at her,' she said. 'Where's your heart? Remember what you felt when Mellikhaya died? You buried your son. She has no child to bury. I *had* to bring her away. I'll do it again. I know it looked like I believed you were guilty of witchcraft when I took her away. I never believed it. Forgive me. I've forgiven her. Whatever she may still do.'

'I've come, haven't I? You're forgiven.'

'I never thought it would come to this.'

'Don't worry. I've got the list. It arrived. I'll get your documents back.'

'I meant it when I said, I know who killed Mellikhaya. I also know why,' she said.

He placed his hand on her head and held it there as if he were saying a prayer over her and blessing her. Then he called the meeting to order. 'Mossel Klein,' he shouted, 'your pride is one sided. Unbalanced. On one side, Amina Khan worked for the struggle. On the other side your pa worked against us. What he did against us – your ma's work balanced. Your pa worked for Special Branch. She even dared to marry into the Special Branch family. Amina told us all his sins. Until we made him disappear one night.' Matatiele snapped his fingers. 'Into thin air. Just like he made our people vanish. Like my son, Mellikhaya vanished one day and reappeared hundreds of miles away – dead.

Now all you good people, you've been asking Pragashini all these questions. I've this question for you, if she's not your traitor who is?'

While he waited for an answer, smiling and enjoying the fact that he had turned the tables on them, Heather rushed towards him and put a gun to his head. 'I asked you nicely,' she said.

People screamed and ran about in the room.

***

123.

This was the same woman who crooned to her Protozoan, who sang nursery rhymes to her children, read poetry to them, and now held a gun to their grandfather's head, determined to get the response she wanted from him.

Pragashini may have been the only person in the room who was not taken off guard by Heather's actions. She would not be shocked if Heather pulled the trigger. She had witnessed the change in Heather. She watched Heather prod and push Matatiele to the spot where Klein stood, while everyone else cowered in the room. Heather was visibly agitated, shouting at him, ordering him to stand with his feet apart, to face the wall, pushing at him, the way children do when they want to initiate a response from someone unwilling to fight. 'Tell me everything,' Heather ordered, 'every single step of the way from the minute you knew Smuts was having an affair.'

Even with the gun held to his head Matatiele refused to take instructions from Heather. He stood with his eyes shut, his shoulders straightened his back stiff. It was impossible to guess what emotions he felt, but he had prepared his body for the force of a gunshot.

From where she stood Pragashini coaxed her, approaching

them between the lighted candles until they stood together the three of them. 'Heather,' Pragashini said. Her voice, its husky, emotional tone, affected Heather immediately. Heather moved her eyes fleetingly to Pragashini's face. 'You have three children, Heather,' she said. 'Shall I remind you about them. Thamsanqa. A handsome young man. Initiated. A Xhosa amadoda. Anticipating a lifetime of learning about South Africa. Lusikisiki. A beauty. Her name roots her in South Africa. Mafeking also named to belong to South Africa. Who is torn in half. He has lost his identical twin. They need your love, Heather. Three children will have three views on the shooting of their grandfather. Thammy will stand by you because he is a man and your eldest. Mafeking may love you for anything you do to revenge his brother. Lusikisiki may hate you. Then what about you, Heather. You have work to do. Your research. You can expose this witchcraft and muti and the work of Abathandazis[131] until South Africans are disgusted and stamp it out.'

'I can't move forward, Pragashini,' Heather said, 'until I hear from these Matatieles, a true account of what happened. Can't you understand that? When I found out about Smuts and that woman, I needed time for myself, so I sent the children out to play. It was too much for me to deal with. I wanted to sleep and wake to a new day. When it grew dark the children came running in to say they could not find King Bisho.'

'Heather, don't you feel their innocence. They're innocent, these Matatiele's,' Pragashini answered. 'They're also hurting and grieving. For Mellikhaya. For King Bisho. Perhaps for Smuts. It's terrible that you can believe someone you love could do such evil to any child. These people love you.

---

131 Abanthandazi is a spirit medium.

When they should hate all White people. I'll tell you what I think happened. People, who have never seen identical twins, are fascinated and fearful of them. The crisis when Smuts became ill took everyone's attention. That was the opportunity for someone to snatch Kings. Perhaps someone like a Jack Roller[132] came by sent by a bad Inyanga[133] or a bad Iqira[134]. There are good ones, Heather. All African medicine isn't evil. How can it be? What do you think African people did when they became ill? Before colonisation? Do you think they sat and waited, they died waiting, because a prophet said 'One day big White men will come with White medicine? Use your head, Heather. African people had their own medicines to cure disease before White people came here.'

Heather shut her eyes and shook her head. 'You're playing games with my mind,' she said.

Pragashini praised Bhagwan. If she had told Heather she believed South Africans understandably love the exiles more than they could possibly love the children born in exile it would feed into her fears that the Matatiele's were implicated. That they could kill an exile's child to save an exile. That was certainly no beautiful thought.'

'Stop playing games with my mind,' Heather repeated. 'Those who remained in South Africa throughout the struggle said those who had gone into exile changed since leaving. I never left. My coming to South Africa was new. It was fresh. It was an arrival. Theirs were homecomings. Yearned-for returns from exile. They should have left me out of it. I was the outsider. I have failed. I failed before even beginning. God knows how I failed. My child. Lying dead

---

132 Jack Rollers are gangs who drive by in cars, abduct girls and rape them.

133 Inyanga is a herbalist who makes muti

134 Iqira is a witchdoctor with psychic powers.

somewhere in South Africa. Unburied. In unblessed soil.'

***

124.

Two shadowy figures entered the gloomy room, hesitantly. They paused seemingly until their eyes were accustomed to the gloom, then they peered round the variously lighted room. Perhaps blinded by their tears, or under a compulsion greater than fear for their own safety, perhaps impelled by their own need, they ignored the woman with the gun, and went rushing to where Pragashini stood and sank at her feet, holding her ankles, crying out her name, crying loudly, uncontrollably, and begging her forgiveness. It was unexpected. Heather faltered.

Pragashini jumped back as if she was burning. Prostrate at her feet were her parents, Jairaj and Leela Dev. She had erased them from her memory and heart. They did not exist to her. They died years ago. She never anticipated seeing them here in England. It horrified her to see them humbling themselves at her feet, weeping, and asking her forgiveness. This was something she never imagined nor even desired.

Overcome with emotion, she shouted, 'Don't touch me! Get them away from me! Don't let them near me!'

Not knowing who Jairaj and Leela were, the gathering shouted, 'Remember what we said. Whoever comes through that door is the collaborator!' With that, a group of people came over to where Jairaj and Leela were huddled on the floor, manhandled them, and brought them to the centre of the room. Everything in the room was chaotic. Heather still held the gun to Matatiele's head. No one had used the opportunity to disarm her. Jairaj and Leela were surrounded by a group of youths. Matatiele was speaking to Pragashini with Klein hovering nearby.

125.

In the diversion caused by the arrival of the Devs, Smuts entered. Without a word of greeting to anyone, he went up to Heather with his hand extended for the gun. Just for one moment Heather appeared to reflect, but then she backed away from him with the gun still directed at Matatiele said, 'Don't play games with me, you bastard. Speak! Speak! Or so help me God I'll shoot this father of yours.'

Smuts stood close to his father while focussing on Heather. He began telling her what she already knew. 'I was working in Bisho for the Legislature, Heather. They allocated me a house and car, an office equipped with a telephone, a desk, and a computer literate secretary, who was female, multi-lingual, and African. What more could I want, Heather? In England I was running around doing low paid jobs. You were the bread winner. Yet you refused to bring our children to live in Bisho. You made it easier for me to have an affair.'

'I trusted you,' she hissed at him.

'Forgive me. Blame exile for my affair with Nolitando. I missed out on my youth in South Africa. I intended solving the problem to the satisfaction of both of you. I was fearful about telling you about Nolitando. I put off telling you for as long as I could. I wanted to be fair to you and to her. I was in Bisho preparing to drive to iBhayi early the next morning to tell you about Nolitando and what I planned. She asked what I would do with the house when we are divorced. I didn't know what to say. She misunderstood. I was not divorcing you. I never intended divorcing you. I told Nolitando the house belongs to you, Heather. Only then I anticipated the problem. I'll never divorce you. I love you. But I also love Nolitando. I cannot abandon an African woman. She is also the mother of my child. Don't ask me to do that. I wanted a traditional marriage with you. It was supposed to be my gift to you. I thought it would lessen your fears and insecurity about my second marriage. It would give you that extra status in the community if I married you under customary law as well as English law. Some people believe the traditional marriage holds more value,' he said.

Heather wept unashamedly while Smuts gave this account of himself. He was thin and haggard, his skin yellow as if he was jaundiced. If Heather warmed to the sincerity in his voice, or his appeal to their love, to the years they spent together, she gave no indication except for the tears on her face that may have symbolised her sorrow for the combined loss of trust, love and child. She never moved to reach out and touch him. She never once moved her eyes from the elder to the younger Matatiele. She may not even have been following the twists and turns in the explanation he laid before her like the clothes she folded and placed in the suitcase of the missing child who had not been found.

Smuts only heard the news that King Bisho had been kidnapped when his fever broke. Now he waited for Heather's forgiveness. She was a Catholic. A sinner who repents is forgiven. She believed that.

***

126.

In a bitter voice Heather said, 'Smuts, I know you too well. Your confession is made to ease your guilt and your shame. Not to ease my pain. Even in confessing your guilt, you blame me. You feel more shame in my presence than in your father's. If I were a priest in the confessional, I would not give you pardon and absolution for your sins. I would send you away unforgiven. Because you have confessed to me, I am your priest. I can tell you, you are unforgiven, Smuts Matatiele. For as long as I live, you will remain unforgiven in my heart. In place of forgiveness for you, my heart is filled with failure. I failed my children. There is only room in my heart for my lost child. There's no space for you or your clan. I can't bear my loss. I will never hold my lost child in my arms and weep. I will never bury my child. Or water his dead roots.'

Pragashini could not stand by, witnessing the desolation and grief on both their faces. She moved to take Smuts' hand and join it with Heather's, but the gun was still a threat in Heather's hand. Heather drew away from his hand with a look of disgust on her face. 'Heather,' Pragashini intervened, and the change in Heather was immediate, just hearing Pragashini say her name calmed her. 'Smuts has feelings of loss. Kings is his son as much as yours. You share this loss. It brings you together.'

'No, Pragashini,' Heather said, 'My feelings of loss are different from his. I will give my life for my child. He took my child's life to save his. He is alive because my child is dead. My child is dead so he could live.'

Smuts drew in his breath, he groaned, and bent forward shielding himself as if she had struck him. Holding on to someone for support he walked away.

'Smuts!' Heather shouted after him, 'Don't run away! I was not waiting to hear your love story. I want to hear what happened to my son. Tell this father of yours to tell me what happened to Kings!'

'Heather,' he looked back at her but spoke hoarsely, 'you stand there and tell me to my face, you think my family...' Smuts could not say the words.

'Say it, Smuts! What are you afraid of? You weren't afraid to carry on with a woman. You weren't afraid for everyone in Bisho to know. You weren't afraid to get her pregnant. You weren't afraid of your father knowing you were cheating on me. I'll say it. You coward! Your family – you Matatieles

– you slaughtered my innocent child. The way you slaughter goats and sheep. And sprinkle blood to protect you. It is no coincidence while you were lying bewitched and dying my son was stolen. If you were delirious then ask your elders what they did. Did you Matatieles use my child to make medicine to cure *your* son?'

'Heather, don't say such a devilish thing. You're a devil for even thinking it,' Smuts said. 'It's despicable! I don't know you, Heather. Men have affairs. Men have children outside marriage. Men beat up their wives. Men kill. Men rape. But you're accusing us of killing one of our own children for muti? Muti is evil. What you're suggesting is evil. We're not evil. The Matatieles' are not evil! I am cured because of that Sangoma and the prayers of my clan.'

'You heard my son,' said Matatiele, with Heather's gun still pointing at his head. 'He is innocent. We are all innocent. I am not afraid to kill to protect one of my clan. But I draw the line at killing my own. The day you grow to understand that, - you need to grow - then you will become 'Wethu' one of our family. Member of our clan. Until that day the Matatieles disown you. We take back our name. You can stick with your Burton Heather Smith.' He spat the words out. Then he spat at her feet.

Heather could not win. Pragashini watched her expression alter from defeat to hardness, and immediately feared the change. She looked at the gun and saw the moment Heather pulled the trigger. She lunged at Heather as the gun went off. Smuts threw himself at his father and brought him to the ground. They struggled on the floor all four of them, Pragashini, Smuts, Heather, and Matatiele. In the struggle that followed the gun went off a second time.

***

127.

No one knew who was injured. Smuts wrestled the gun from Heather. Matatiele was shot and bleeding. People rushed to his assistance. Pragashini said, 'You survived South Africa's violence. You can't die here. You'll live.' He was carried to a car and taken to the hospital. Smuts accompanied him.

To appease Heather the gathering proposed offering a large sum of money to persuade someone to come forward with information about King Bisho. The proposal was seconded. They went around the room obtaining donations.

Pragashini had no idea if Heather was to be charged with shooting Matatiele. She walked towards the exit with her. 'Heather, if you believe I've wronged you, then I must ask you to forgive me,' she said. That was all. Explanations would come later when Heather had grieved. Heather looked at her friend and said, 'I'm changed, Pragashini.'

'I know you are. But your children need the Heather who loved the Protozoan. Bring her back. I want to see her in the lab. I want to explain my theory of evolution to her.'

'I don't know where she is. You left it too late,' she said and left. The sun was rising as Heather left the condemned house.

The gathering discussed what they had come there for.

Pragashini said, 'I went to work in the public service in Bisho for one reason only. To search computers for a document with the names of people who collaborated with apartheid. I wanted to see Anand Nasaratt's name on the list. The administrators were suspicious of me. They made life very difficult for me in Bisho. Notwithstanding this, I found the document and others. However, the crisis over Smuts and the missing child, and my wish to help Heather meant I left South Africa in a hurry and had to take the documents out of South Africa when I left. Hajira posted those documents and my documents to Matatiele. He deposited my journals and other papers in the Ashram in Natal. I asked him to distribute the other documents at the art gallery and the language centre. Heather placed her documents with the church.'

'While I searched the computers, I found an assassination document from the old administration, listing names of potential assassination victims, and people already assassinated. I also found other documents that I gave Hajira to post. The documents show that money was used to pay for expenses that had nothing to do with running the departments. Other documents show how people were promoted if they were afraid to challenge the misappropriation of money. I found documents showing how the Public Service Act was used to put people on the gravy train and how ghost workers could operate within the system. A whistle blower prepared a document showing how people at the top of a department could terrorise those working under them into committing acts of fraud and harassment with impunity.'

'In our province, the Eastern Cape, we must put in place checks and balances, to regulate the most senior civil servants, even our Permanent Secretaries, even our elected representatives, in the Councils, and Legislatures, our Mayors and Speakers, to curb them. Or they will be out of control they'll become dictators each in their department. We must put an end to the gravy train. We must put an end to ghost workers. We must put an end to dictators even in our Legislature. We must also protect whistle blowers. So that if a civil servant sees something wrong, they may report it, if not to the dictator who is running the department, then to someone else.' Pragashini sat down.

'Pragashini was followed when she left South Africa' said

Klein. 'People desperately want that list of collaborators. They want to force the document from her. I didn't come here to question her. I want to make the documents public.'

'One night I was at the dinner table with the Nasaratts, Matatiele, Smuts, and Amina Khan, whom we knew as Astrid Roebuck,' Pragashini said. 'Matatiele told us that someone in that room was a collaborator with apartheid. I became afraid. Then when Astrid was killed, we all supposed the collaborator recognised her and knew she was Amina. We supposed Amina typed the lists. The collaborator eating with us was afraid she knew who he was. We expected Matatiele to be killed next. Then I realised our mistake when Mossel Klein told his story. He said he never saw his mother or father from the time he was taken out of primary school. That was a long time ago. When Klein was taken out of school, he said his father and mother disappeared. The lists I found were recent. Drawn up after Amina Khan went into hiding. The names of collaborators and assassination victims are from the nineties, not the early days.'

'I want Matatiele to hand over these documents at a press conference in South Africa. The collaborators' names must be printed in the press,' she said.

Then one of the Matatiele elders shouted in a loud voice, 'Sekunjalo!' Immediately two men entered with Anand Nasaratt.

***

128.

Anand Nasaratt entered the condemned house with a man on either side of him, each gripping his arms. His hands were bound. Ramgopal and Nalini and their sons Pravin, Saragan, and Ravindra followed Nasaratt.

'Nasaratt is here straight from South Africa,' said an elder

Matatiele. 'He didn't come willingly. We forced him here. He isn't here to answer for what he's has done in South Africa. He's from the struggle. The liberation movement disciplines its cadres. It has a code of conduct for cadres. But we brought Nasaratt here for what he has done against Pragashini. He isn't alone. All these men, his father Ramgopal, his brothers Pravin, Saragan, Ravindra, Pragashini's father Jairaj, her mother Leela, her brothers aren't here. Come Pragashini. Now is your time. Sekunjalo. Take hold of it by the neck. Like a chicken. Squeeze the life out of them.'

Pragashini hesitated. Here was another opportunity to confront her lifelong fear of this man and to satisfy her urge for vengeance against all these men - and women - because women are complicit in the crimes against Indian girls. When she had the opportunity that night to do something in the bridal suite, she could do nothing significant, she could not raise her hand to strike him, with or without a weapon. Non-violence, although she had not listened to Jairaj's words, was ingrained in her. Now she was satisfied. She knew Matatiele had come to England to help her. What should she do? She wondered if her parents recognised, could even conceptualise, the harm Nasaratt had subjected her to. They had not seen her since her wedding day.

She came forward, removing the niqab as she did. Jairaj and Leela saw her for the first time with her shaved head. Pragashini stopped near them and stood tall. 'Jairaj and Leela – she loved calling them on their first names – it showed her utter disrespect for them - I cursed you on my wedding day,' she said. 'I cursed you each time this man violated me. In my heart, you died every night of my life since my wedding day. I've had to look to others to mother and father me. I pity you. I pity your ignorance. I pity the narrow confines of your mind. I pity your fear of community. I pity the way you cling to tradition. I pity the way you worship your sons. I pity your contempt for your daughters. I don't want to harm you. I have nothing more to say to you.'

Then she turned to the Nasaratts.

'Ramgopal, I learnt that you were part of the struggle in the early days. I respect you for that. But you allowed Jairaj's debt to your son, to be used against me. Your sons, and Jairaj's sons, are no different from Jack Rollers who drive around abducting girls and raping them. What these sons of yours do is worse than Jack Rollers. They chase their own sisters and force them back to be raped by men under the name of marriage. I am a biologist. My message to Indian men and women is this - only have sons. Don't wait until an Indian girl is born so you can kill her spirit. Kill the egg that will become an Indian girl. Then you won't have murder and suicide and rape on your hands. Then you may sleep peacefully at night.'

'Pragashini, Pragashini, please hear me,' cried Jairaj.

She ignored him.

'Pragashini, when I gave Nasaratt permission to marry you, it was not permission to violate you. I am here in England to be punished under your laws. Charge Nasaratt. Charge me. Charge your mother. Call the police. Let our community see the wrong we've done. I want to go to prison for your suffering. If you don't charge me I'll kill myself. Pragashini! Pragashini!' he broke down, sobbing bitterly.

'You are dead to me,' Pragashini said. 'I don't listen to the dead. I pray for them.'

While the gathering squabbled over whether Nasaratt should be charged in South Africa or England, she knew that to charge Nasaratt meant charging her parents because they had permitted her marriage when she was underage. She could not move forward with this action. But Jairaj had threatened suicide if she did not charge him and she could not live with his death on her conscience. Seeing all of them together, her need for revenge was dissipated. It would be a lesson for South Africa if he were charged there. The liberation movement could discipline him for his other offences. It was good enough for her, sending Nasaratt back to South Africa to allow the people to deal with him.

However, before she could tell them her decision, Jairaj said, 'We have something to tell you, Pragashini. Anand was attacked the other night. By a mob.'

Whatever the words Pragashini was about to say - died on her lips. She was speechless and horrified. That was not what she wished for him. Gradually it dawned on her she need never fear him again.

***

129.

During Pragashini's daily visits to Matatiele in hospital she confided in him. 'I know the significance of the list of collaborators,' she said.

'You're a good pupil,' he replied.

She held his hand. 'I'm not. What now?'

'I won't hide it. Those days of secrets are gone.'

'Why did you want the list, if you weren't going to hide it?'

'I wasn't sure about Mellikhaya. My comrades told me, but I thought maybe they lied. They only told me after I asked my question. They hated me for my question. It went straight to my heart like an arrow of God. From then I turned my back on uThixo.'

'Did you warn Mellikhaya?'

'No. I never saw him again.'

'And Smuts? Did you tell him?'

'Never.'

'You'll tell him now?'

'I told you. No more secrets in South Africa. Smuts, and everyone have a right to know.'

'I still don't understand.'

'I used you, Prags. I'm sorry. That's why I'm here. To help you. To make you face Nasaratt. To bring your parents to ask forgiveness. Ramgopal and Nalini also.'

'That needs time. Maybe one day. That list - how can you be sure those aren't collaborators names?'

'Because Amina's name is on that list. She was no collaborator.'

'Why did they assassinate Mellikhaya if he collaborated with them?'

'Maybe he served his purpose. If the secret police didn't kill him, the comrades would have.'

'You think he was killed by one of us?'

'You never understood politics, Pragashini.'

'Tell me what would make him collaborate?'

'I think when Smuts disappeared he became afraid. He was a small boy. If they could make Smuts disappear into thin air, they could do anything. He used to sit for hours on the doorstep waiting for Smuts to come home. He missed Smuts. He worried what would happen to all of us if he disappeared.'

'What did you do when they told you he's a collaborator?'

'They just said they suspected. There was no proof. They told me to warn him they were on to him. We asked him. He didn't deny it. We disowned him. We threw him out of the house. For Mandi and me, he died that night. When they found him ice cold on the Bisho March, I knew he stopped collaborating. Our tears, Mandi and mine, were because we kicked him out. Poor Mellikhaya.'

'How will you bear the shame?'

'We'll have to bear it. Only Mellikhaya was a collaborator. I am not. Smuts. Mandi. The leadership knows that. We'll survive.'

'I still have my doubts. Why was his name on the assassination list? If he was a collaborator?'

'He changed his mind. Once we found out. Maybe he changed his mind when we knew for sure Smuts was alive. Maybe he refused to work for them after that. I don't know. He never came back to us. So we can't be sure.'

'You never told me your question, Sir.'

'I never will, Pragashini.'

'Mine was simple: its about betrayal. Who betrayed Steve Biko?'

He reached out and put his hand over her mouth.

***

PART EIGHT

The Theory of Evolution On the Origin of Women[135]

135 © Agnes Sam 1984

The Origin of Women

130.

Beijing.

In Beijing Pragashini prepared to address the 4th World Conference on Women. Ten weeks before the session she was to address, she sent a 2000 word written statement outlining her theory on women to the Division for the Advancement of Women. The Division forwarded her written statement to the Commission on the Status of Women. The Commission distributed her statement to the delegates. Pragashini asked permission to make a three-minute statement. The Division requested twenty-two copies of her two-paged statement that they distributed to the Commission's Bureau. She complied with all the formalities.

She invited Heather to travel with her to Beijing. Heather refused then relented. At the appointed time Pragashini's approached the podium to make her three minute statement.

'Delegates,' she said, 'the world will never address the status of women in the new millennium without understanding the origins of women. Understanding the origins of women is essential for an understanding of the roots of women's oppression. I am proposing a theory on the origins of women that will make clear the reasons for our oppression by men.

My theory stems from the research I conducted. There is much interest in human evolution following the work of Darwin, the discovery of DNA and the human genome. Prior to this evolution was interested in the evolution of Homo Sapiens how the species came to walk upright, the development of the hands as an implement for holding tools, the development of the brain, speech, problem solving, writing, reading, basically how our intelligence developed. Archaeologists still search to find the first human. When we study evolution, we look at ancient skeletons of life forms that were not yet fully human dating back millions of years.'

'Men put forward theories of how humans evolved from those pre-humans to the way we are today. They find bones in Africa, in Europe, in China. Some of our ancestors did not stand upright, some of them had small braincases. Some of them had huge eyebrows that hung over their eyes. Some had receding chins. They put all these discoveries together and charted our progress from prehistoric times to the present day.'

'The first thing that brought me to my theory,' Pragashini continued, 'was something we all know, but because we consider ourselves human and not animal we do not relate it to it's meaning.'

'In the animal kingdom when any female animal goes on heat, the males become aware the female is on heat and cluster around her. In humans, however, the male has no way of knowing when the female is fertile. The human female, herself, does not know when she is fertile. No one has taken any notice of this fact.

Another fact is the human female only produces one egg a month. In other animals evolution would have done everything possible for that single egg to be fertilized. Survival of the fittest cannot allow the egg to go unfertilised. Were the human female producing a dozen eggs each month, it would not matter.

The human male, on the other hand, produces thousands of sperm, every day, every night, sperms that are mostly lost because they may be released when the female does not have an egg waiting to be fertilised. That fact is significant, but it too is ignored.'

'Then there's the matter of sexually transmitted diseases. In the animal kingdom animals do not bath. Yet they are not prone to sexually transmitted diseases. That raises the question why humans are susceptible to sexually transmitted diseases? In nature there is no protective device such as a condom.'

'Finally there are the x and y chromosome, you may have heard of. When the sperm fertilizes the egg, the x and y-chromosomes determine whether the child will be male or female. There is something else about these two chromosomes that I will refer to later.

'These facts led me to formulate a theory.'

'I am proposing a theory that the male and female of the human species do not share a common ancestor. Women were descended from one ancestor. Men from another. At some period, they came together. That accounts for the biological differences between us. But I also have a theory about the kind of research that does not consider the earth.'

'My theory is that women, are not descended from the ancestor that gave rise to the men who presently inhabit the planet with us. Our male counterpart is dead. Our male counterpart did not rape us. Our male counterpart was not violent. The man who lives today through violent methods exterminated our male counterpart. Women have an origin that is separate and distinct from the origin of men. At some stage in our prehistory, the male who is presently living destroyed the male of our species.

My theory on the separate origin of women is based on the following: Consider the following questions:

One, why is there no signal to the man when an egg is released from the ovary of a woman? In all higher animals, the male receives a signal from the female of their species i.e. when the female is on heat. I am proposing that men receive no indicator so that a woman's fertility is safeguarded from men. Because the man cannot sense the woman's fertility, his chances of impregnating her are lessened. Is the present man not intended to impregnate the present woman? If it is so, why is it so? A woman produces one egg, once a month that is fertile for a few days. The man produces thousands of sperms, daily.

'Two, why are humans susceptible to sexually transmitted diseases? In the animal kingdom, there are no sexually transmitted diseases. What does this mean? Does it mean that sex between the male of our species is not intended to take place with the female of our species?

'Three, during Meiosis,[136] which is cell division, each chromosome finds its homologue. A homologue is a chromosome that is descended from the same antecedent. The pair of homologous chromosomes line up along their entire length. All homologous chromosomes pair up and line up along their entire length. Even where a chromosome has been damaged or distorted it strives to line up with its counterpart. However, if we look at the X and Y chromosome we see a unique behaviour. Instead of the X and Y chromosome aligning side by side lengthwise, they align themselves end to end. What does this mean? It means the X and Y chromosome are not homologous. If they are not homologous chromosomes, it means they are descended from different antecedents.

'Four, the evolution of Homo sapiens has been studied as if women and men evolved as a single unit, at the same rate, in unison, in parallel lines, congruently, and continuously, and in the same direction. Why? Why do we study the evolution of women with the evolution of men as if women and men are identical?

---

136 Meiosis is cell division

'My conclusions, are that the behaviour of the X and Y chromosome during Meiosis suggests that the X and Y chromosome are not homologous chromosomes. What are homologous chromosomes? Homologous chromosomes share the same genetic material. If the X and Y chromosomes are not homologous chromosomes it means they do not share the same genetic material. What does it mean if the X and Y chromosomes do not share the same genetic material? If the X and Y chromosome do not share the same genetic material it means they do not arise from the same antecedents. This means that the X chromosome has descended from one ancestor and the Y chromosome has descended from another.

'The suggestion that the Y chromosome has lost a part is invalid as far as pairing during Meiosis is concerned. The rest of the Y chromosome should meet up with the rest of the X chromosome if they are homologous. In all other chromosomes, whatever the changes that have occurred, the pair of chromosomes still attempt to match up all along the length.'

'Simply put this means the female and the male of Homo sapiens have different ancestors. I am proposing a new theory of evolution that the female of the species Homo Sapiens is descended from one ancestor and the male of the species from another.

131.

The women delegates received Pragashini's theory enthusiastically. From Beijing Pragashini visited India and places associated with Mahatma Gandhi. On her return to South Africa, she took leave of her aunt Karishma, returned to England where she presented her thesis and received her doctorate. She remained living in England with the families who hid her during her early days there. Having spent her life disguised as a Muslim woman, and under their protection, Pragashini was naturally drawn to the religion and considered converting to Islam. After much consideration, however, she felt her Hindu devotions had sustained her during her struggle years and she remained a devotee.

***

132.

Matatiele returned to his wife Mandisa in the Eastern Cape.

Nolitando gave birth to a son. Both were taken into the Matatiele family. The child was raised as their grandchild.

Smuts resigned his position in the Legislature and went to live in England with Heather and their children.

Heather treated him like a lodger in the house. She hovered in between states of despair over the loss of her child, and inability to forgive Smuts. She could not rid herself of the suspicion that Smuts, Nolitando and the Matatiele clan were implicated in her child's disappearance, because neither the missing child nor the kidnapper were found.

Leela was reconciled with her sister Karishma who travelled around the country lecturing on the similarities between Hindu and Catholic rituals.

Pragashini returned to England to live in the Victorian house in York. She waited for Jairaj and Leela to return to South Africa before applying for the annulment of her marriage. She was a frequent visitor to Fawzia and Hajira. Once at their home to mark the anniversary of South

Africa's independence Fawzia said she was in touch with Smuts and Heather and they were both expected. Smuts arrived alone, however.

He noted the visible changes in Pragashini. She had grown her hair. She wore lipstick and makeup, and a vibrant blue Chalwa Kamees. Smuts did not make his presence known, but stood listening to her entertaining Fawzia's guests with the reasons why she had proposed the theory on women. She talked about her trip to Beijing. She seemed more like the girl he had known before both their marriages. When he entered the room she asked after Heather. Smuts was reticent and would only say that she was progressing. He had much news from South Africa.

There was some information about who had abducted King Bisho. It was not hopeful and he did not wish Heather to dwell on it. He would tell her at some future date what the police had discovered.

Nolitando had confessed to shaving him and to visiting an Iqira. His illness, he said, was due to Nolitando.

Amina Khan's murder was attributed to an opportunist criminal and became another statistic in South Africa's roll call of violence against women. Her murderer was never found.

***

133.

Snow lay thick upon the ground. The sky was saturated with dulled vapour. Each day at dawn, the sun put in a weak appearance. For weeks even its impotent glimmer from behind grey-misted skies was denied light-starved eyes. Here and there Pragashini discerned figures, misshapen in bulky clothing ploughing leadenly through the deep snow. Occasionally, a car rolled cautiously along the main road, its headlamps glowing feebly in the drab light. Winter had set in, in the north of England.

She sprayed the front and rear windows of the car, started the engine using the choke, then left the engine running while she scraped snow and ice off the windows with wet gloved hands. Then she drove the car to the local shop. Inside she stepped onto wet muddy floors and picked up bagels, creamed cottage cheese, salmon, and semi-skimmed milk. She chatted to the girl behind the counter, gave two five-pound notes in error, confused by the colour of the notes, apologised, left the shop and clambered back into the car, flinging the brown paper bag onto the front passenger seat. She lifted her eyes to see into the rear view mirror, released the hand brake, looked in front of her, and froze as the door of the little paper shop opened, Klein emerged.

He hesitated in the doorway. She caught an expression of bleakness in his face as he stared at the dead scene before him. He wore neither hat nor gloves, uncommon for that time of year. But he did wear a muffler which itself was not common in the north of England. It was tucked into a heavy Harris tweed jacket. She watched him as he stepped down into the snow then turned and walked away from where she sat in the car. All the while she stared at him. He adopted the same plodding movements and forward thrust of the body used by people moving through the snow. She inserted the key, with her eyes on him. He walked up the street and stood on the little traffic island at the junction, waiting for an opportunity to cross. She drove the car slowly up the street and gave him the signal to cross the road. He nodded curtly and walked away from her. She sounded the horn. He looked back, bent forward and recognised her in the car. She pulled over and they spoke.

'You went to Beijing, I hear,' he said.

'I presented my very own theory of evolution. You staying

on?'

'That depends,' he said. 'You?'

'I belong here.'

'I don't agree.'

'You wouldn't. South Africa doesn't nurture women. Much like India.'

'Then I may see you around.'

'I wouldn't bank on that. I'm not looking forward to it.'

'I'm sorry to hear that.'

'You won't ask why?'

'Will you tell me?'

'Yes. You need to know. To me you're a coward. You're certainly not a gentleman. With the power you have, you've kept it for yourself. In the animal world you'd be compared with a jellyfish. You have the staying power of a jellyfish on a window pane.'

'If you say so.'

He leaned into the car as if to kiss her. But she put her foot on the accelerator and drove away. She smiled, believing she had achieved the soft vengeance of a freedom fighter.

***

PART NINE

The Soul's Question

The Recluse - Pragashini's Journal

134.

The Soul's Question: I am a recluse. I lived a hidden life. I wasted years agonising over whether it is in the Divine plan for me to assist Pragashini. Was I meant to stand on the sidelines and observe like a spectator at a game, feeling the highs and lows of whatever was happening to her? While I endured conflict about my role, I watched for signs she was relenting. If she succumbed, gave in, gave up, let go. If her private actions were devoid of struggle, if she released emotion, I would be free of my obsession.

There was, however, no feeling. None that I saw. Sensitivity to others was scarce. At least that was the face I saw her turn to everyone. Even tears of unhappiness or frustration might have sufficed. I might have been less anxious about her future. I also prayed. While I did not know the Gods she prayed to or for what, I prayed she would experience some degree of tenderness. For anyone. That someone would show tenderness to her. It is uncanny how her life replicated mine.

My soul asked: Who could I have been in a previous life? What a poser. Is that why I am chained to fate? What other explanation is there for this seeming powerlessness to plan the events in my life? If I am living someone else's life, will all the elements from that previous life repeat itself in my life? When does the life that is being lived, the life that I am living, assert its independence, from the life already lived? Whose life am I living? Is my life merely the repetition of someone else's? I don't have the answers.

Buddhists believe the Dalai Lama is a reincarnation. Christians believe in life of the spirit after death. If the spirit does not die, why should it begin? The whole world should ask the soul's question: who could I have been in a previous life?

I know who I was in a previous life.

END